To George –

with appreciation

Setting the Record Straight

The music and careers of recording artists from the 1950s and early 1960s … in their own words

Anthony P. Musso

Bloomington, IN Milton Keynes, UK

authorHouse®

AuthorHouse™
1663 Liberty Drive, Suite 200
Bloomington, IN 47403
www.authorhouse.com
Phone: 1-800-839-8640

AuthorHouse™ UK Ltd.
500 Avebury Boulevard
Central Milton Keynes, MK9 2BE
www.authorhouse.co.uk
Phone: 08001974150

First published by AuthorHouse 2/5/2007

ISBN: 978-1-4259-5986-9 (sc)

Printed in the United States of America
Bloomington, Indiana

This book is printed on acid-free paper.

This book is dedicated to the memory of my friend Peter Mancinelli, whose encouragement and support during the interview process of this project motivated me to focus on the objectives and quality that I committed to preserve with respect for the artists featured within these pages.

Table Of Contents

Acknowledgments

It is with a deep sense of gratitude that I acknowledge the professional courtesy extended to me by the following promoters, radio personalities, and others who assisted me in gaining access to the fifty recording artists interviewed in this book. It is through their effort that the music of the 1950s and early 1960s continues to be heard today. I encourage all readers to visit their respective Web sites listed below and to patronize the high-quality shows that they produce and/or broadcast. My ever-grateful thanks and appreciation also goes out to the artists featured within the pages of this book, for their willingness to share their time and special memories from their careers in music. As pioneers of a style of music that helped to define a decade, they serve as the guiding influence of the countless recording artists of generations to follow.

Jon "Bowzer" Bauman, Jon Bauman Productions—*http://www.bowzerparty.com*

Tony Butala, Bob Crosby, and Tracy Rogers, Vocal Group Hall of Fame— *http://www.vghf.org*

Joe Cavanna

Nicky Ciaramella

Jimmy Jay, Rewind Radio—*http://www.rewindshow.com*

Paul Mennett, *Cruisin' New England Magazine*—*http://www.cruisinnewengland.com*

Mickey B. and Donna, LCR Productions, Inc.—*http://www.mickeyb.com*

Harvey Robbins, Harvey Robbins' Productions—*http://www.harveyrobbins.net*

Paul and Lori Russo, Cool Scoops Ice Cream Parlor, North Wildwood, NJ— *http://www.coolscoops.com*

Norman Wasserman, Friend Entertainment Ltd.— *http://www.friendentertainment.com*

Foreword

Having grown up in the East New York section of Brooklyn during the 1950s and 1960s, I gained a deep appreciation for the music that first emanated on street corners, a few select radio stations, and, in my case, the St. Michael's Friday Night Dance. It was a time that pre-dated the club scene or discos, was pre-British Invasion, and was one that boasted a period of adventurous and groundbreaking music. Clearly, the music of the period has served to inspire and influence generations that followed.

It was a time when the latest recordings of the Moonglows, Flamingos, and the Coasters, along with solo artists such as Jimmy Clanton, Brenda Lee, and Frankie Ford, streamed from small transistor radios and created an identity for teenagers around the world.

Many, including the very producers, promoters, record label executives, artists, and entrepreneurs that developed, recorded, and released the new style of music that captivated a restless younger audience in the 1950s, readily admit that they initially considered it a fad, one that would certainly fade away after a brief period of time. That style, never considered to be one with a lasting attraction, continues to serve as the roots of an industry itself that continues to prosper more than fifty years after it began.

It started in a most simplistic and rudimentary way, in some cases with a group of youngsters vocalizing on a street corner in an inner-city environment, entertaining at community centers or school talent shows, or simply touting their harmonies on a subway platform where the acoustics seemed to resonate off the tiled walls around them. Many of the male participants cited an increased ability to attract girls as a motivating factor for getting involved in it, even though realizing the ultimate harmony was always the primary reward.

The evolution of vocal-group harmony was a product of urban living. Many of the earliest and most successful groups were pre-teens plucked from street corners by older and savvy industry people who ended up managing them. In many cases, those same people procured the music and writing talents that the youngsters created. Let's face it: for a thirteen-year-old used to singing for free on the street, hearing their voices coming from the speaker of a radio was beyond comprehension. Unfortunately for many of them, so were the royalty checks and appearance fees.

The music clearly had a vast background to play off of. For the most part, rhythm and blues greatly influenced the innovative sound. But then, so did classic recordings of big band singers, country artists such as Hank Williams, and even to some extent operatic and classical music styles. If America truly was a melting pot of nationalities and traditions during that period, then the roots of rock-and-roll, soul, rhythm and blues, and even today's rap music are clearly a melting pot of every style of music available for teenagers and producers to weave into their defined and unique sound.

While a vast number of the later groups of the era credit artists such as the Flamingos and the Moonglows as having influenced their sound, earlier groups such as Lee Andrews and the Hearts listened to the melodies of a then-popular Nat "King" Cole.

Solo artists began to emerge and develop individualistic and trademark attributes, many times originating from a high school or neighborhood rock-and-roll band. As more and more teenagers with aspirations of making a stab at the music industry began to pick up instruments, primarily a guitar, piano, sax, or set of drums, the stage was set for new, self-contained outfits that amplified an unorthodox and somewhat foreign sound to parents that were used to listening to the more soothing sounds of Frank Sinatra, Tommy Dorsey, and Vic Damone.

When a then-Cleveland, Ohio disc jockey came to dub the new style "rock-and-roll," community officials decried the sound as barbaric and irreverent. Many of the new breed of entertainers, while performing to sold-out and wildly enthusiastic teenage audiences around the country, were condemned for performing what was deemed a rebellious, vulgar, and raunchy sound. In some cases, local authorities banned the sound as well as its multi-talent package shows from their communities.

And while vocal-group harmonies created a smooth, symphonic sound that came to be known as doo-wop, solo artists honed a blend of musical styles that defined an energetic and bold sound that was purely dedicated to its teenage audience, giving them the identity that they so wanted and so eagerly seized.

Having a passion for history as well as music, I found it increasingly disturbing to identify a significant number of misrepresented, conflicting, and/or inaccurate biographical accounts of the recording artists of the 1950s and 1960s when reviewing different sources. Given the significant impact that these artists and their music have had on American and worldwide society and culture, it seemed absurd that their origins and life experiences were skewed in history. I can only assume and truly believe that a number of inaccuracies documented in countless works is unintentional, and more than likely the result of second-hand accounts and hearsay.

That being the case, it became quiet apparent early on that the only way to discover and present a true and factual representation of these artists' music and careers from the very beginning was to limit interviews and accounts to those of founding, original members in the case of vocal groups, and direct conversations with the solo artists themselves. I never assumed the project would be an easy one to accomplish. Given the fact that I set out to represent a diverse cross section of artists that began their careers during the 1950s and 1960s in an attempt to accurately portray the period itself, the artists' impact on music, and the struggles and determination each endured in pursuit of their chosen career path, the project would require many logistic challenges. It meant a cooperative effort with concert promoters and with family and friends of retired artists, and a willingness on the part of the artists themselves to participate.

That said, I feel truly blessed for having had the opportunity to meet and speak with the artists featured within these pages, many of whose music I had the distinct pleasure of listening and dancing to during my own teenage years. I found the stories of their early influences, entry into the music industry, and subsequent career experiences to be fascinating and their insight of the evolution of several forms of music into what has commonly become referred to as rock-and-roll and rhythm and blues educational.

Having defined clear objectives for the book, in truth its title came as a result of the initial interviews that I conducted with artists. As one after another began to describe exasperation over the amount of incorrect facts that somehow came into existence, started to be accepted as fact, and continued to be touted as historical information regarding the music, its period, and their respective careers, the interesting play on words came into being.

I cannot adequately thank those artists who afforded me the time to be interviewed, to correct facts, and to add a new dimension to stories that have been considered legendary for years. Whether backstage before and/or after a performance, in a hotel room or lobby, or while eating an ice cream cone in a North Wildwood, New Jersey vintage ice cream parlor, their candor, pride, willingness to assist me, and genuine warmth made this project a reality.

Carl Gardner, founding member of the legendary Coasters, was perplexed one Sunday morning in April 2005 as we spoke quietly at a dining room table in a hotel in Islandia, New York. As one after another of his countless fans noticed him sitting there and came over for an autograph, the music legend turned to me and pondered, "I am happy to sign an autograph but then they just seem to want to stand there and talk and talk. I just don't understand it." I explained to the humble Gardner that as a fan of the music it was very clear to me. When a fan sees him they not only acknowledge his music and career but are in fact transformed back to the first time they heard one of his songs, met and danced with a boyfriend or girlfriend, or recalled a specific place and time from their youth. It goes well beyond the music itself. Through the music of these pioneering artists, we all gain an opportunity relive a very special period of time in our lives, a time that was perhaps simpler, less chaotic, and carefree.

Listen now to the words of the recording artists that helped shape a generation and develop the unique blend and style of music that is both powerful and timeless. Given their impact on the music industry and society itself, it is only fitting that when it comes to their respective stories, we *set the record straight.*

The location and date of each interview conducted for this book is listed beneath the respective artist's name and photo.

The original Crickets Joe Mauldin, left, and Jerry Allison, right flank Sonny Curtis. Curtis performed with Buddy Holly prior to the formation of the Crickets and joined Mauldin and Allison after Holly and the group parted ways.

Jerry Allison
Joe B. Mauldin, Sonny Curtis
(The Crickets)

Wildwood, New Jersey   **October 15, 2005**

While the band's front man and rock-and-roll icon Buddy Holly would die much too young in a tragic plane crash, the Crickets have continued to play their own brand of music for fifty years. A pioneering force of rock-and-roll bands, the group continues to enjoy legendary status both in the United States and abroad.

The group's name has an interesting origin, since it was created to allow Buddy Holly, Joe B. Mauldin, and Jerry Allison to release their first hit recording, "That'll Be the Day," on the Brunswick Records label. It occurred while Holly was under contract with another label. "Buddy had a recording contract with Decca Records in 1956 and went to Nashville to cut four sides," Allison remembered. "'Blue Days, Black

Nights' and 'Love Me' were released and sold well under a million copies. We went back during the summer school break and recorded 'That'll Be the Day' and three other sides."

When Decca failed to release "That'll Be the Day," a tune composed by Allison and Holly, their manager suggested creating a group, the Crickets, and releasing the song on the Brunswick label. The idea was to release it sans Buddy Holly's name as the recording artist, although he is clearly singing the song. Since Brunswick was a subsidiary of Decca, the strategy didn't cause a rift or legal action, and the rest is history.

The Crickets are documented as being one of the first rock-and-roll acts to be self-contained and responsible for writing, playing, and recording their own original material. But as for producing, Allison said that they never handled the technical end of the recordings, as is widely believed. "We didn't actually record our own material," Allison said. "For 'That'll Be the Day' we drove about ninety miles to Norman Petty's studio in Clovis, New Mexico, and he was the engineer for the recording. You had to buy five demo records for each song at three dollars each, so that session cost us fifteen dollars.

"We initially sent the demo to Roulette Records to try to get a deal but they already had Buddy Knox and Jimmy Vaughn, so they turned us down," Allison added. "After that we sent it on to Brunswick. We only did two cuts and felt it was good enough for a demo, but once Brunswick heard it, they released it as is."

Allison said that the group could technically be considered the producers since they paid to record "That'll Be the Day" and no one told them what to do or when to quit. "Ironically, Petty eventually started having more to do with actual production, getting the recordings slicker and slicker, and they sold less and less," he said.

In 1957, the Clovis sessions featured background vocals by a group other than the Crickets. "The group that sang on 'That'll Be the Day' was made up of some friends of ours: June Clark; her cousin Gary Tollett and his wife, Ramona; and Niki Sullivan, who was with us on that first record and stayed with the group for about six months," Allison said. "It was a two-take live deal and for some reason everyone always thought that the Crickets was a vocal group. We weren't; we were always a band."

So uninformed or duped was public perception that the Crickets were actually named Vocal Group of the Year in 1957, an award that went unchallenged since television appearances in those days were strictly lip-synced performances to records.

"When we did the Dick Clark Show they didn't go to any trouble setting up instruments or any of that stuff, so we'd just stand up there and pantomime," Allison recalled. "It wasn't really a Milli Vanilli deal, since we never said that we sang on the records."

When "That'll Be the Day" hit the charts, the Crickets headed out on a four-month appearance tour in support of the record, having only three days off during the period. They did, however, record a few songs on the road, in one case at Tinker Air Force Base in Oklahoma City, Oklahoma, where Petty joined the group for an impromptu session at the officers club. "Norman played with a trio that was performing at the club and he brought along some equipment so that we could record four or five songs to finish up *The Chirping Crickets* album," Allison said.

Allison recalled that at that time, Petty secured the services of the Picks, a vocal group that the Crickets never met, and overdubbed their voices onto the album's recordings. "All of a sudden the Picks thought that they were the vocal group of the year," Allison said.

An interesting piece of trivia is that a black group named the Crickets existed before the Buddy Holly ensemble, and some of its members would eventually go on to gain musical fame as the Cadillacs. Allison recalled first learning of them when they toured together later on, and the Cadillacs playfully told the Crickets that they stole their name. In reality, "That'll Be the Day" became a bigger hit on rhythm and blues charts than it did on the pop charts.

One of the Crickets' biggest hit records went through a name change at the request of Allison. "Buddy had started writing a song named 'Cindy Lou,' one with a calypso-Latin feel, and I had known this girl in high school that I really liked and she moved to California," Allison explained. "I asked Buddy to change the name of it to 'Peggy Sue' and he said okay, and so we changed the feel of it and finished it. When we went in to record it I messed up the first time through and you couldn't punch in (edit) material later on in those days. Buddy said, 'Okay, if you don't get it right this time we're changing it back to 'Cindy Lou.' We got it right the next time, it came out as 'Peggy Sue,' and now she's more famous than Princess Di. That's what she said anyway."

The real Peggy Sue moved back to Texas and Allison eventually married her.

After charting with early releases, the Crickets began a grueling schedule of one-night performances on a bus tour that covered many miles. For some artists it was a challenging time. Allison had a different recollection of the experience.

"It was like going to heaven," he said. "Everyone we loved was there, and I mean all our favorite artists, like Chuck Berry and Fats Domino and Eddie Cochran. Buddy Knox and Jimmy Vaughn, who we knew from Texas were there. The Diamonds, the Drifters with Clyde McPhatter; all told about twenty acts toured together. We got in on the ground floor and were booked for four months."

The Crickets were also booked into predominantly black venues such as the Apollo in New York, the Royal Theatre in Baltimore, and the Howard Theatre in Washington, D.C., as they were often mistaken for black recording artists, sometimes even confused with the black Crickets group. The fact that "That'll Be the Day" received significant airplay on black radio stations and climbed the rhythm and blues charts provided the Crickets with a sense of familiarity at those venues. "I think there was a bit of surprise at first when the curtains rose at our early shows, but after performing seven shows a day at those theaters, word got around about us white guys," Allison recalled.

Following the Crickets' appearance on the nationally broadcast *Ed Sullivan Show*, Niki Sullivan left the group. It remained a trio throughout its tour of England and for the most part until it disbanded following an October 1958 appearance on Dick Clark's *American Bandstand*. Allison adamantly dispelled rumors that attribute the breakup to creative differences, internal strife, or any reason other than Holly's desire to relocate to New York. Allison and Mauldin simply preferred to stay in Lubbock, Texas.

"Buddy had gotten married and I had gotten married (to Peggy Sue) and that's been the ruin of many a group," Allison said. "Things just were changing and with Buddy's wife coming from New York and my wife from Texas, priorities shifted."

Allison recalled a discussion that he, Holly, and Mauldin had over the decision to stay in Lubbock. "We weren't fighting but it wasn't a real easy feeling," he said. "We'd all decided to go to New York, but when we got back home we had second thoughts. We sat out in front of Norman Petty's studio and Joe B. and I told Buddy that we weren't going to move to New York. He tried to convince us that we could do a lot better up there because Petty didn't want us to be in any films like the Alan Freed movies, which we were jumping up and down to be in. Whenever we got an offer like that Petty turned it down, saying that he was going to get a real movie for us, but we were tired of all that." Holly tried to persuade the pair to relocate to where the music industry and publicity existed, and that was New York not Clovis, New Mexico. Warily, they declined.

The Crickets asked Sonny Curtis, another Lubbock native and one with musical ties to Holly, to become the group's new lead guitarist and singer. Curtis had begun performing as a teenager on the local *Buddy and Bob Radio Show*, one of Holly's earlier ventures in the industry. Together with another disc jockey at the station, Waylon Jennings, they performed at a local movie house during intermissions. Curtis joined Holly's pre-Crickets group, the Three Tunes, in 1956 and eventually left to tour with Slim Whitman before going solo in 1958.

When the Crickets stayed in Texas, Allison struck a deal with Holly to retain the group name while Buddy recorded as a solo act. Documented reports, however, state that Holly subsequently formed a backup group consisting of Waylon Jennings, Tommy Allsup, and Carl Bunch and billed them as the Crickets. Allison disputed that claim.

"Actually Buddy didn't do that," Allison said. "Buddy and I were the best of friends and he said, 'You guys work as the Crickets and I'll work as Buddy Holly.' It wouldn't be like Buddy to say that and then use the name Crickets. And anytime I ever heard him questioned about being a Cricket, I always heard Waylon say, 'I never was a Cricket. I worked with Buddy Holly but the Crickets are Jerry Allison and Joe B.,' and Buddy told him that."

The last tour that Buddy Holly performed on, the fateful Winter Dance Party, did in fact bill the act as Buddy Holly and the Crickets, but Allison attributes that billing to the promoter, not Holly. The tour would claim the lives of Holly, Ritchie Valens, and the Big Bopper when, on February 3, 1959, the plane Holly charted to fly to the next engagement in Moorhead, Minnesota, crashed in a blinding snowstorm. Allison recalled first hearing the tragic news when he returned to Lubbock from Clovis, New Mexico.

"We were living in Clovis, New Mexico at the time and had come back home and were staying at my folks' house," he said. "Sonny was sleeping on the couch, when a neighbor from across the road came over and told him and my mother what had happened. Sonny came and woke me up, as it was very early in the morning."

Allison recalled that since Allsup had given Holly his wallet to hold on the flight in order for Buddy to pick up a telegram for him, initial accounts reported that Allsup was killed in the crash.

When Buddy Holly's plane crashed, killing the three major recording artists, a subsequent decision was made to continue the Winter Dance Party tour. Promoters made repeated requests on a local radio station for bands to fill in for the fallen legends on that sad night. As such, when the curtain came up at the Moorhead venue, fifteen-year-old Bobby Vee and his group the Shadows served as replacements on the bill. As fate would have it, Vee would join the original Crickets in 1963 to record several singles and an album, *Bobby Vee Meets the Crickets.*

"We had a friend who was a disc jockey in Texas named Snuffy Garrett, who moved to Los Angeles, and when we left Coral Records, Snuffy helped us to sign with Liberty," Allison recalled. "He was into producing by then and hooked us up with Bobby Vee for some recording work."

By the end of the 1960s, Mauldin decided to leave the Crickets. "I didn't feel like I was getting ahead at the time," he recalled. "It seemed to me like the Crickets weren't working as much as I wanted to and I had an opportunity to go into another business, so I just kind of bowed out for a while. I missed it but it was a career decision at the time."

A footnote to the Crickets career and music is the fact that the group recorded and released "The Ballad of Batman" and "Batmobile," but did so under the name the Camps. Sonny Curtis recounted how that came about. "We had a friend in Laverne, Minnesota, named Jimmy Thomas, who called me in 1966 and told me that a Batman television series was going into production," Curtis said. "I was picking with the Everly Brothers at the time in Seattle. Jimmy said that we needed to get a record out fast to beat everyone to the punch so that when the Batman series came out we'd be sitting on the ready line with it."

Curtis quickly wrote the "Batman and Robin" song and raced into a studio to cut a demo, which was eventually sent to New York for review. Back in Texas for Christmas that year, he and Allison drove to Odessa, where Tommy Allsup owned a recording studio. There, the pair produced a finished recording of the tune and sent it on to New York. When it was ready to be released, label officials decided to call the group the Camps due to the fact that "camp" was considered a hip word at the time.

"What happened on that deal is that we had everybody beat hands down, but Snuff Garrett called us from New York and he was doing some deal on Batman and advised us not to release our record because the television show would sue us," Curtis recalled. "I called my entertainment lawyer in Los Angeles and after talking with him, I told our label not to release the single until after the show was on the air. The label backed off and, of course, Snuff put his record out, Neal Hefti had a big hit with the theme song, and we put ours out and it flopped."

In 1965 the Crickets appeared in the motion picture *Girls on the Beach*, with the Beach Boys and Leslie Gore. "It was a lot of fun hanging out with the Beach Boys," Allison said. "They would do a scene and then have to change clothes and do it again. When they came back, whoever had long pants on during the first take wore short pants, and so on. The producers ended up assigning someone to make sure everyone had the same outfit on for each take. The Beach Boys were just having fun with it."

Allison explained that the Crickets had a surf version of "La Bamba" out when the movie was being made, but because the film producers couldn't hear the spoken lines over the music track, they shut off the recording and instructed the group to lip-sync to nothing. "Our mouths were so out of sync that we'd be on the second verse while they were at the bridge," he said. "But when you see the movie, it doesn't matter anyway because they had us set up seven miles away," Curtis added with a laugh. "It was a fun experience but embarrassing to look back at."

The Crickets were unanimous in their opinion of the 1978 widely acclaimed Columbia Pictures big-screen biography *The Buddy Holly Story*, starring Gary Busey. "It was about like flagging down a freight train with a candle," Allison said. "It was all jive. They took a book written by John Goldrosen, who did a lot of research and came to Nashville to talk to all three of us. So his book is pretty accurate, but there wasn't anyone involved in the movie that was ever on the road with us. And Gary Busey played me in a movie called *Not Fade Away*, so he was reading a script from that."

Allison referred to one specific scene that had Buddy Holly and the Crickets performing at the Apollo Theatre in New York. "In the first place, to show you how accurate the movie was, they had Sam Cooke there," he said. "We never, ever worked with Sam Cooke. They called Joe B. Ray Bob, and called me Jesse."

The career longevity that Allison, Mauldin, and Curtis share is a tribute to their fifty-plus-year friendship, one that began in high school and continues in 2006, where the three musicians live within thirty minutes of each other in Tennessee. They still maintain the ability to pack concert halls, and their good-natured manner and fun-loving attitude is matched by their firm place in rock-and-roll history. Each shared a deep pride in their respective career accomplishments.

"I like all the names we can drop," a playful Allison joked. "I couldn't have been any prouder to be leaving Lubbock, Texas; not that I didn't like Lubbock, but to be going on the road with all these people that I had idolized—and now I was hanging out with Fats Domino and Little Richard and playing the Paramount in New York for ten days."

"I don't mean to make it sound like a joke but I'm kind of proud that we're still working and there are people out there who look a lot like us who seem to get it," Curtis added.

The Crickets were never far from Holly's mind and heart. In fact, on the fateful Winter Dance Party tour, Holly asked backup musician Jennings if he would like to tour England with him. During the discussion, he shared his intention of reuniting with Allison and Mauldin for the tour.

Billboard Top 40 Hits by Buddy Holly and the Crickets

Date	Pos	Wks on Charts	Record Title	Label/Number
Crickets releases				
08/19/57	01	16	That'll Be the Day	Brunswick 55009
12/02/57	10	13	Oh, Boy!	Brunswick 55035
03/10/58	17	08	Maybe Baby	Brunswick 55053
08/04/58	27	04	Think It Over	Brunswick 55072
Buddy Holly & the Crickets releases				
11/11/57	03	16	Peggy Sue	Coral 61885
06/09/58	37	02	Rave On	Coral 61985
08/11/58	32	04	Early in the Morning	Coral 62006

Lee Andrews
(Lee Andrews and the Hearts)

Philadelphia, Pennsylvania   **November 28, 2005**

During the 1950s and 1960s, a number of communities throughout the country seemed to breed musical talent. New York City; Los Angeles, California; and Pittsburgh and Philadelphia, Pennsylvania, served as primary centers of creativity. The latter city boasted solo artists such as Bobby Rydell, Frankie Avalon, Fabian Forte, and Chubby Checker as well as major chart-topping groups such as the Turbans, the Tymes, the Dovells, the Orlons, and Lee Andrews and the Hearts.

Born Arthur Thompson and using his two middle names to form his own identity, Lee Andrews grew up in South Philadelphia and formed a vocal group, the Dreamers, while attending Bertram High School. While no specific recording group of the time served to influence the Dreamers' sound, Andrews' personal idol was Nat Cole. His father, a one-time member of the legendary Dixie Hummingbirds, Andrews, and a friend, Butch Curry, sang in a gospel group for a brief time before shifting music styles to a more contemporary sound.

The founding members of the Dreamers consisted of Andrews, Curry, Roy Calhoun, Jimmy McAllister, and John Young.

In late 1953, the Dreamers started to become serious about their aspirations in music and the following year they visited Philadelphia radio station *WHAT* and its popular on-air personality Kae Williams in hopes of an audition. Andrews said that Calhoun became aware of Williams's radio show and arranged for the young group to get into the studio to meet the disc jockey.

"The kids used to go to the station after school and they were allowed to dance in another studio while Williams was on the air," Andrews said. "After the show ended he'd come in and talk to everyone. We sort of laid in wait for him, cornered him when he came in, and wouldn't let him out until he heard us. He seemed to be quite happy when we sang. He liked what he heard.

"The songs we performed for him were the very first ones that we eventually recorded for Rainbow Records, that being 'Maybe You'll Be There' and 'The Bells of St. Mary,'" Andrews added.

Around the time the group prepared for their first recording session, they learned that a West Coast contingent had already claimed the Dreamers' moniker. It required a swift name change for the Philadelphia group. "The secretary at Reco-Art Studios suggested the name Hearts," Andrews recalled. "When the first record was released Kae took it upon himself to put it out as Lee Andrews and the Hearts. He might have been thinking in terms of two for one, eventually breaking me out as a solo artist."

An enthusiastic Williams brought the recording of "Maybe You'll Be There" to Rainbow Records and in May 1954 it was released with the group's second offering, "Baby Come Back," as its flip side. But within a month's time, the more established and popular vocal group, the Orioles, also recorded and released "Maybe You'll Be There."

"For some strange reason the Orioles release didn't really affect us," Andrews recalled. "But during that same time Clyde McPhatter [and the Drifters] covered our recording of 'The Bells of St. Mary.' I don't know if it was a coincidence but it's usually the other way around, where you have a new artist covering an established artist."

While another artist attempting to break into the tough music industry might have taken offense or been discouraged by being faced with the competition of an already-established artist covering his recordings, Andrews said that he was honored. "I loved Clyde McPhatter and loved his voice as a pure first tenor," he said.

Following a stall of the Hearts' version of "The Bells of St. Mary," primarily due to the popularity of the Drifters' single, the group left Rainbow Records and began to work the club scene in the Philadelphia area. In early 1955, Jimmy McAllister left the group for military service and another teenager from the Woodland Avenue section of town, Ted Weems, replaced him.

Around that time, with gigs becoming scarce and the group's recording prospects all but nil, Andrews and Calhoun secured employment with Gotham Records, pressing records. "Ivan Ballin, who owned the Gotham label, also owned a factory that pressed records," Andrews said. "Since we weren't entertaining much, he gave us jobs in the factory for about a year and a half." In addition to pressing records for Gotham, the factory produced product for the Grand, Southern, and Champagne labels.

Having become aware that the contract they signed with Williams was not legal due to the fact that its members were underage when it was drawn, the group was free to approach a new label. It was for that reason, Andrews said, that he and Calhoun accepted any form of work they could get at Gotham. "Lee Andrews and the Hearts were pretty well known in the Philadelphia area by that time, so it was just a matter of letting Ballin know that we were looking for a new contract," he said.

Signing with Gotham in 1956, the Hearts grew frustrated with the label rather quickly when it continued to record various sides for the label but none were ever released. Toward the end of its association with Gotham, Young decided to leave the Hearts and the group replaced him with Calhoun's brother, Wendell.

They then approached another popular Philadelphia radio personality, Douglas "Jocko" Henderson. Already aware of the Hearts' sound, Henderson sent the group to audition for Barry Goldner, his partner at Mainline Distributing Company. When they recorded "Long, Lonely Nights" in the spring of 1957, Henderson originally took it to Atlantic Records to distribute the record nationally. But after hearing it, Atlantic officials told him that they wanted their own artist, Clyde McPhatter, to record the song. Henderson offered the recording to Chess Records, sold the master, and informed its executives that Atlantic intended to re-cut and release the song by McPhatter.

"During those days it was good to have a little competition battle with artists," Andrews recalled. "Initially Clyde's record sales on that song [were] higher than mine, but over time it was my version of 'Long, Lonely Nights' that became the classic."

When researching the writer's credit for the Hearts' first national hit song, one might actually believe that the tune was a collaborative effort by several people, those listed on the record including Andrews, Henderson, Uniman, and Abbott. In reality, Andrews was the sole writer of the song. Henderson; Mimi Uniman, the wife of another major Philadelphia DJ, Hy Lit; and Abbott aka DJ Larry Brown, though sharing writing credit had nothing whatsoever to do with composing the song. Andrews explained the practice of crediting other names to a song's origin as "moonlighting."

"That was the deal in those days," Andrews said. "You could not hope that someone was going to play your records unless he'd realize some things out of it."

Having scored a national hit with "Long, Lonely Nights," the Hearts' life changed drastically as requests for appearances from all over the country began to come in. In July 1957, Lee Andrews and the Hearts appeared at the legendary Apollo Theatre in Harlem, New York, along with Lloyd Price, the Moonglows, and the Teenchords.

"We were just petrified," Andrews recalled about the appearance. "It was the great Apollo Theatre and we had never entertained on that scale or level before. After the second or third show, we began to finally settle down and perform more at ease."

Andrews attributed the fact that having a current hit with "Long, Lonely Nights" at the time made it easier to appear before the Apollo audience, famous for embracing and rewarding an artist's quality performance but never shying away from showing distaste for a less-than-credible performance.

"When appearing at the Apollo, it was always your shoes to mess up," he said. "If you were terrible and messed up, the audience would let you know it."

Lee Andrews and the Hearts were known for a slick stage presence, one that included a trademark and perfectly timed tug in unison on the French cuffs of their shirts. Andrews and Calhoun always dictated how the group would dress and developed its classic stage act. "At that time there were a lot of smooth groups out there," Andrews said. "It's not like hip-hop, where anything goes. In those days the first thing you thought of as an artist was to look sharp. We looked the part. That's how show business should be. If people are coming out to see you and you look just like they do, what's the point?"

The Hearts were similar to other black groups of the period who, despite their national success and fame, endured some challenging and somewhat threatening experiences on the road, especially when touring the Southern states. One such incident involved Andrews and Curry, who were stopped by police in Birmingham, Alabama, and ordered to get off the streets and not to be seen again that night. "I had just explained to the police officer that we had just performed at a Jackie Wilson tour that closed that night and we were in the process of leaving town," Andrews said.

Generally accepted reports of the incident incorrectly state that Curry and Calhoun (not Andrews) were arrested at gunpoint, but Andrews said that while he didn't face the barrel of a gun, it very well could have happened at a moment's notice given the climate of the time. "I can say that if you know what fear is like, that's how we felt," he said. "While he didn't pull his gun, he easily could have. It would have been par for the course. People that are evil may do you a favor by speaking to you first about it; but if you don't heed their word, anything could happen."

The Hearts followed "Long, Lonely Nights" with an even bigger hit, "Teardrops," and the group's third release, "Try the Impossible," also charted. But only one month after re-recording "Maybe You'll Be There," Andrews left the Hearts.

"I was at the point of leaving the group after we released 'Try the Impossible,'" Andrews said. "Sometimes people don't handle popularity and success too well and we weren't handling it. We had a lot of internal strife at the time."

Andrews went on to record "I Wonder" on the United Artists label, a single that was released as Lee Andrews with the Hearts. "I actually went back with the Hearts three times to try to see if we could do it again," Andrews explained. "I'd try to reform with them and after a few months it was the same old nonsense." The United Artists' release was a recording that Andrews made while solo, but, in an attempt to rekindle the Hearts' magic and sound, credited it as "*with* the Hearts" rather than "*and* the Hearts."

Andrews explained that after "Try the Impossible," all singles he recorded, despite featuring the Hearts on background vocals on a number of them, were solo projects.

When Grand Records struck a deal with the Gotham label to release some of the old sides of Lee Andrews and the Hearts' that never surfaced through the years, Andrews made a last attempt to reform the group, but it was short lived. A subsequent album recorded for Lost Nite Records at a club in Fairless Hills, Pennsylvania, pictured Andrews on the LP cover but featured none of the original Hearts' lineup. "I had a fellow by the name of Richard Mason and another, Bobby Bell, that were friends of mine and also sang with me after I left the Hearts," Andrews said. "They were on that album."

Eventually retiring from music and opening a successful dress shop, Andrews returned to the industry to form Congress Alley, a group that included his wife. The group recorded two singles and an LP for AVCO Embassy. "We focused on five-part harmony similar to a Fifth Dimension style of music," Andrews said. His last stab at the music industry came full circle as Andrews, his wife, son, and daughter performed familiar tunes for twenty years as an incarnation of Lee Andrews and the Hearts.

Now retired, the last performance Lee Andrews gave was on PBS's first televised doo-wop special, *Doo Wop 50*, in 1999.

Billboard Top 40 Hits by Lee Andrews and the Hearts

Date	Pos	Wks on Charts	Record Title	Label/Number
12/09/57	20	10	Teardrops	Chess 1675
06/16/58	33	1	Try the Impossible	United Artists 123

Vito Balsamo
(The Salutations)

Patchogue, New York   **September 24, 2005**

In the early days of vocal-group harmony, neighborhoods throughout New York City's borough of Brooklyn turned out countless numbers of singing ensembles who honed and perfected the five-part harmonic sound. Groups like the Mystics, the Passions, the Classics, the Chimes, and the Salutations got their early start in music by singing in underground subway stations, tunnels, and school rest rooms, where the acoustics that resonated off the tiled walls produced an almost angelic echo and sound.

It has long been documented that the formation of one of Brooklyn's finest groups, Vito and the Salutations, came as a result of Bob DePallo and Barry Sullivan harmonizing in a subway station. When a passerby, Linda Scott, heard the duo singing and recommended them to producer Dave Rick, an audition was scheduled for later that week. The pair realized that they needed to organize a group rather quickly.

Vito Balsamo, who became the group's lead singer, recalled a different scenario. "I used to hang around with Bob's [DePallo] younger brother John," Balsamo recalled. "At the time I had recorded a demo with Eddie Pardocchi, Charlie DiBella, and two other guys and we called ourselves the DelVons. We sang in a railroad tunnel near Our Lady of Loretto Church in East New York, Brooklyn, to get an echo effect."

Balsamo soon moved to Church Avenue in Brooklyn. "I was teaching Bobby's brother and some other guys how to sing during rush hour at the Church Avenue subway station," Balsamo said. "A lady was passing by and gave John DePallo a card, which he took to his brother Bob, who had a band with Barry Sullivan, a first tenor."

While both Bob DePallo and Barry Sullivan played instruments, they had a hard time organizing a band and decided to get involved with vocal-group harmony. When the younger DePallo handed his brother the business card, he recommended Balsamo as a potential singer for the group that needed to be formed.

"When Bob approached me and I agreed to join them, I told them I knew a baritone from East New York, Bobby Mitchell, and he joined the group," Balsamo said.

The teenagers selected the group's name based on the popular disc jockey of the time Douglas "Jocko" Henderson, whose standard radio sign-on was "Ooh-pooh-pa-doo, how do you do? Greetings and salutations!"

In December 1961, the Salutations recorded several tunes at ODO Studios. "We went into the studio with two demos that Dave Rick wrote, 'I Look at the Moon' and 'Hey, Hey Baby,'" Balsamo said. "After we recorded them Rick said, 'We have a little time left. Hey Vito, do that song 'Gloria.'" The song was already a classic hit as recorded by the Cadillacs and later by another Brooklyn group, the Passions.

The Salutations cut a version of the song and it served as their first single, in February 1962. While a New York favorite, Rayna Records' limited ability to promote and distribute the single stifled its exposure beyond the immediate geographic area.

Shortly after the release of "Gloria," DePallo, Solomon, and Mitchell decided to leave the Salutations, leaving Balsamo to reform its lineup. "I was the youngest of the group members," he said. "One was getting married, another had a family to support, and the money just wasn't there. Being so young, I was able to stick it out. Even though the managers took the credit, I went around and recruited three new guys, that being Shelly Buchansky, who in turn knew a brilliant man, Frankie Fox, who was the bass and baritone; and this crazy Irishman, Ray Russell, who lived in Queens."

While he attended Thomas Jefferson High School, Balsamo recalled that neighbors called the police time and time again as he took to singing on the corner of Jamaica Avenue and Dexter Court, outside Franklin K. Lane High School. He cited Earl "Speedo" Carroll and the Cadillacs as having been a big influence on him at the time.

After recording "Your Way" on the Kram label, Rick got the group to record for Herald Records. Their single of "Unchained Melody" featured exaggerated bass and falsetto parts and became a huge hit. Balsamo recalled how the Salutations' arrangement of the song came about.

"We were driving upstate to a gig one day and heard Al Hibler on the radio singing a slow version of 'Unchained Melody,'" he said. "While we were listening, Frankie and I started mimicking the song, with him doing bass and me singing tenor. By the time we got to the gig and back home, we had arranged the song."

The group's follow-up single, "Extraordinary Girl," got immediate airplay but suffered from Herald's limited promotion, a fact that Balsamo attributed to the record company's failing business. "Herald was a pretty big label with the Dixie Cups and the Turbans," he said. "When we hooked up with Herald we thought that we were going on to success, but it turned the other way. What company paid in those days? Everybody got robbed. We were actually looking for another label at that time."

Of the many shows that the group performed on, which included Murray the K and television spots with Clay Cole and Dick Clark, Balsamo cited the ten appearances that the group made at New York City's Radio City Music Hall as personal favorites.

Balsamo also recalled a performance that the Salutations gave at Roosevelt Theatre in Harlem, one in which a then-unknown blind guitarist named José Feliciano backed them. "We did a show in Harlem on a Wednesday night when the Lowe's Theater held amateur night and featured one known group," Balsamo said. "John Zacherley [who later gained fame as television's 'Cool Ghoul,' the host of television's *Shock Theatre*] was the MC that night and Vito and the Salutations were promoting 'Our Way' at the time. Our guitarist didn't show up and I was sitting in the auditorium. José Feliciano was a contestant, and was sitting next to me. They called me to rehearse and I didn't know what to do without a guitarist."

Feliciano asked the singer sitting next to him if he was Vito and wanted to know what the Salutations planned to perform. "I told José that we were only going to do two numbers, 'Gloria' and 'Unchained

Melody.' He says, 'If you want me to do it, I'll do it for you.' When he told me that he knew the songs, I took him to rehearse for five minutes and he was the greatest thing in the world."

When the Salutations disbanded in 1965, Balsamo joined the Kelloggs, a group formed to appear on a morning television show in Philadelphia, similar to the then-popular Clay Cole format. As luck would have it, the show never materialized.

The Salutations reformed in the early 1970s but legal haggles over the group name caused Balsamo to perform under his own name, while Pardocchi became Vito in a new lineup. "What happened was that I just had enough of it and went down South for about eight years," Balsamo said. "I left the business and Eddie became Vito with the same manager while I was away. Eventually I came back and stepped in again."

Balsamo currently performs at various oldies concerts as a member of the Chaperones as well as with Golden Group Memories. Still boasting his familiar vocal range, he continues to be a crowd favorite.

Tony Butala
(The Lettermen)

Wildwood, New Jersey   **July 6, 2005**

I f one vocal group defined surviving the test of time and continued
to tout its close harmonies and high level of success throughout
decades of continual change in audience preference of musical styles
and trends, the Lettermen is that group. But the origin of the group has
been the subject of conflicting stories. One version states that Brigham
Young University students Jim Pike and Bob Engemann began singing
together and soon joined a lounge singer, Tony Butala, in 1960. Given
Butala's advanced career in music at a young age, a different story
cites the group's formation as evolving from a Butala-led vocal group
originally named the Fourmost, with the Lettermen's well-documented
debut appearance occurring in Las Vegas in 1958.

Butala began singing professionally at seven years old and a year
later he started performing on radio in Pittsburgh, Pennsylvania. "I
had a large family and I am number eight of eleven children," Butala
said. "We used to perform for each other around the dinner table on
Sunday afternoons because we couldn't afford movies. My brother was

a comedian, my mom played the organ in church, and my dad was in the choir, so music was part of my life."

Butala remembered going to the movie theater with his mother and three brothers on Saturday afternoon, where for five cents you could watch fifteen Gene Autry films. "I used to come out afterward and my family would be astounded how after hearing Gene Autry sing songs just once, I could remember and sing them all. It was almost as if I was a novelty. My Uncle Tony took me to all the local bars, put me on a stool, and asked them to let me sing. I'd sing a song and they'd buy him a beer."

Coming from Pennsylvania, Butala's introduction and eventual membership into the Mitchell Boys Choir came as a result of his mother's need to travel to California to assist an ailing relative.

"My mother's cousin moved to California, and when her husband was transferred to Saudi Arabia, his wife and six children under twelve years old were left in Hawthorne alone," he said. "When she subsequently got pneumonia, she wired my mom [a nurse] to help her out with the kids. My dad suggested that I accompany Mom and possibly audition for a band. While there, I auditioned for the Mitchell Boys Choir and I made it."

Within two weeks, Butala found himself appearing in the motion picture *On Moonlight Bay* with Doris Day and Gordon MacRae. Having worked in several motion pictures with the choir, he cited the finale of *White Christmas* starring Bing Crosby, doing the voice of the Lost Boys in *Peter Pan,* and singing tunes for child actor Tommy Rettig in *Lassie* as his favorite memories.

"He (Rettig) couldn't carry a tune in a bucket," Butala recalled. "When he sang, it was my voice he was mouthing to."

Of his ability to perform with the likes of a music legend such as Crosby, Butala explained, "We sang at Good Shepherd Church in Beverly Hills and that was Bing Crosby's church along with Loretta Young, Vera-Ellen, and Danny Thomas. When you're a young kid you get used to hobnobbing with these people."

While in high school Butala formed a vocal group named the Fourmost. "When I formed that group there was no such thing as rock-and-roll," he said. "The big groups of that era were the Modernaires, the Four Freshman, and the Hi-Lo's, so I patterned myself after that style, not thinking that it was commercial. When rock was coming in, the girl that sang with us, a classmate named Concetta Ingolia, said, 'Tony, get with it. I have a chance to do a television series and I think our group has had it.' So she left, went on to become Cricket on *Hawaiian Eye* and became famous as Connie Stevens."

Leaving him with an all-male trio, Butala decided not to resist change any longer. "We began to do harmonies like the Platters and that's kind of how the Lettermen sound was born," he said. "When Connie left, me, Jimmy Blaine, and Dan Witt were left and a kid named Mike Barnett replaced Dan and his wife came up with the name Lettermen. I thought that if we had that name we could wear letter sweaters as a visual aid for people to remember us, more so than the other ten thousand groups trying to make it."

On February 28, 1958, the group opened at the Desert Inn in Las Vegas for the first time as the Lettermen, playing the part of the Rhythm Boys with the Paul Whiteman Orchestra. The revue included Buster Keaton and Rudy Valee, and Butala played the part of Bing Crosby in the Rhythm Boys. The Lettermen recorded for the first time in 1959 with Butala and a new contingent of singers, and in 1960 he drafted Jim Pike and Bob Engemann for a third lineup that became very focused on their recording work.

After releasing "The Magic Sound" and "Their Hearts Were Full of Spring" on the Warner Brothers label in 1960, the group shifted to Capitol Records in 1961 and recorded "That's My Desire." But instead of the song climbing the charts, its flip side, "The Way You Look Tonight," generated airplay and entered *Billboard*'s Top 20 charts.

"It was an absolute phenomenon and wasn't supposed to happen," Butala recalled. "The reason we put 'The Way You Look Tonight,' a really slow, melodic, pretty ballad, on the B-side is because it would not in God's green earth be a hit as far as anyone at the label was concerned. Let's put the dog on the B-side so people won't flip it over and they'll concentrate on 'That's My Desire.' 'Desire' went to number forty and stopped dead, and a disc jockey, J. P. McCarthy on WJR in Detroit, was the first known guy to flip it over to play the soft, pretty ballad side. That shows that the listeners know more than anybody else."

The Lettermen were labeled by that very recognizable sound, one that has served them well for more than forty-five years.

The group followed with a number-seven hit record, "When I Fall in Love," and while Butala sang lead on most of the group's recordings, his efforts at composing songs was never featured. "I've written two hundred and fifty lousy songs and that is why the Lettermen are still around, because we know they're lousy," he said. "We look for the best writers like Irving Berlin, George Gershwin, Dorothy Fields, Cynthia Weill and Barry Mann, and Paul Anka. We knew that the main thing was the song and we outlasted a lot of groups that had to write their own stuff."

In 1962, the group's third album was simply named *Jim, Tony, and Bob*, a fact that Butala explained as an intentional attempt to phase out the Lettermen name. "The Lettermen was a lousy name," Butala said. "We loved it, for the fifties. But everyone around us was being called Iron Butterfly and the Beatles and Mac Truck. The name was passé. It wasn't when we first named the group but it was later on."

Having gained name recognition by that time and experiencing huge chart success as the Lettermen, the attempt was futile. "Show business has two words: show and business," he said. "When we realized that we couldn't change the name and that Capitol wouldn't let us anyway, we decided that we'd make the name mean us and not us mean the name."

As a result of the group's continuous string of hits, they toured with major names such as Bob Hope, Frank Sinatra, Sam Cooke, Debbie Reynolds, and Jerry Lewis. Of all the shows that they performed at, Butala cited one as being the most memorable.

"There is one show that was beyond and above every show in my amazement," he said. "When Jim Morrison of the Doors did that indecent-exposure show in Miami and dropped his drawers, the city of Miami wanted to get rid of that taste in the press and they had what they called a decency rally, with Anita Bryant, Jackie Gleason, and the Lettermen," Butala said. "A lot of groups wouldn't do it. We were so squeaky clean, with no drugs, we decided to be part of that. Well, one hundred and four thousand people crammed into the Orange Bowl and Jackie Gleason walked on stage. It was like a hush came over all those people and everybody was so respectful. He was Mr. Saturday Night. He talked and got them laughing and then he introduced the Lettermen.

"I'd been on stage with Frank Sinatra and Dean Martin and all these people, but the most bizarre thing was seeing one hundred and four thousand people in a hush like they were in church. It was amazing!"

Among the appearances that the Letterman made on various television shows, Butala recalled that the group performed some fifty times on *American Bandstand*. A surge in area record sales was easily attributed to an appearance on that specific show.

"We gave Dick Clark a letter sweater our first time around and made him the fourth Lettermen," he said. "Anytime that we came through Philly, he always wanted us on his show. Immediately, three or four days after appearing on *Bandstand*, record sales in that area would spike."

During the late 1960s, while other groups' sound and appearance began to lean toward hard rock, a dressed-down look, and drug-oriented material, the Lettermen maintained their clean-cut image. "I guess it took away some of our audience because some of the guys thought we were real square," Butala said. "We didn't care because we had the girls buying our stuff. You play the rock stuff at the beginning of the party but what happens at the end when people start coupling up? They put on Johnny Mathis and the Lettermen.

"Joey Reynolds, a disc jockey out of New York, told me during an interview recently that he really didn't dig the Lettermen and preferred the harder stuff, but then realized that you couldn't get a hickey playing the twist," a laughing Butala said. "In the end, he reverted back to the Lettermen."

Butala's early work with the Mitchell Boys Choir served him well when the Lettermen began to perform worldwide and record songs in fourteen different languages. "You can sing in any language you want; you don't have to know the language," he said. "When I was in the Mitchell Boys Choir we sang in twenty-seven languages. Paul Mitchell was a linguist who read Latin, Greek, and Hebrew, and he spoke all the [Romance] languages, so when we learned songs they were with the correct pronunciation."

In 1979, the Lettermen formed a recording company, the Alpha Omega label, and continue to release at least one new CD each year.

Personnel changes in the Lettermen lineup through the years have not compromised the sound or the quality for which the group has become famous. With Butala serving as the group's mainstay from day one, members other than Bob Engemann and Jim Pike that have sung with the group through the years include Gary and Donny Pike (Jim's brothers), Mark Preston, Ernie Pontiere, Bobby Poynton, Don Campeau, Chad Nichols, Donovan Tea, and Darren Dowler.

To date, the group has recorded more than seventy albums and CDs, sold more than twenty million records, and remains one of the most revered vocal groups in history. With classic hit singles such as "Theme from a Summer Place," "Put Your Head On My Shoulder," "Hurt So Bad," and "Shangri-La," the distinctive Lettermen sound is as fresh today as it was in the late 1950s. In 1967, on the Capitol album *The Lettermen ... and Live,* the group released one of its better-known hit recordings, "Goin' Out of My Head/Can't Take My Eyes Off of You," the first of its kind to integrate two songs as one.

In 1997, after serving as the unofficial source for vocal-group information, Butala fulfilled a longtime ambition and founded the

Vocal Group Hall of Fame, in Sharon, Pennsylvania. It serves to honor the greatest worldwide vocal groups, and unlike other musical hall of fames and museums, it includes groups from all genres of music including rock, rhythm and blues, country, gospel, big band, pop, doo-wop, folk, and jazz. A non-profit organization, it opened its museum doors in 2001. The first groups inducted into the hall in 1998 were the Ames Brothers, the Andrews Sisters, the Beach Boys, the Boswell Sisters, the Five Blind Boys of Mississippi, Crosby, Stills and Nash, the Golden Gate Quartet, the Original Drifters with Clyde McPhatter, and the Mills Brothers. Subsequent inductions have included the Coasters, the Moonglows, the Marvelettes, and the Dells.

"Back in 1963 I was working at the Riviera in Las Vegas with George Burns," Butala said. "I had three or four albums and several hit singles by then and I was feeling pretty good about myself and blessed by God. I was having dinner at the gourmet restaurant with George Burns and his manager, Irving Fein, and the busboy came to change our butter and relish trays, recognized me, and we said hello to each other.

"I found out that three years earlier, that busboy was the lead group singer on the number-one record in the country," Butala continued. "The group had one hit and its second didn't get much attention. They started to break up since the record company was vacillating, and when they dissolved the record company stole their name, bought it without their knowing it, and he couldn't get a job and ended up doing busboy work."

Horrified by the experience, Butala said that he felt there was something very wrong with that picture and committed to finding a way to give something back. "I said to myself right there that somehow, somewhere, sometime, I was going to start a place to honor guys like this, the greatest individual singers of the greatest vocal groups in the world."

While he has vowed never to reveal the busboy's name, Butala realized his dream with the opening of the Vocal Group Hall of Fame.

"We're doing a lot of good work for individual vocal-group singers who might be down on their luck," he said. "We're planning a retirement home and a hospital for them. A lot of groups got screwed out of their royalties. We have inducted ninety-five vocal groups into the Hall of Fame through 2005, but we are very different than the Rock and Roll Hall of Fame. If you've had a hit record, your stuff can be included in our museum. So even if it takes years or maybe never being inducted to the hall, you are still being honored by having your memorabilia on display in the museum."

Butala has also taken an active and vocal stance with regard to current efforts to push through legislation that would prevent bogus lineups from performing as legendary vocal groups but without any original members.

"We're trying to help out," he said. "I've always protected myself by copywriting and trademarking things and I've never had a problem. But so many groups out there have problems and we are supporting bills that have been passed in six states so far, titled the Truth in Music. We are trying to get it passed in all fifty states."

Billboard Top 40 Hits by the Lettermen

Date	Pos	Wks on Charts	Record Title	Label/Number
09/25/61	13	09	The Way You Look Tonight	Capitol 4586
12/04/61	07	11	When I Fall In Love	Capitol 4658
03/10/62	17	07	Come Back Silly Girl	Capitol 4699
07/17/65	16	05	Theme From A Summer Place	Capitol 5437
01/06/68	07	11	Goin' Out of My Head/Can't Take My Eyes Off of You	Capitol 2054
08/16/69	12	10	Hurt So Bad	Capitol 2482

Earl Carroll
(The Cadillacs)

New York, New York   **June 8, 2005**

While various facts are cited as having influenced the Cadillacs' breakout hit single, "Speedo," one fact that remains undisputed is its distinction as being the first rhythm and blues record to enter *Billboard*'s pop charts before appearing on the R&B charts. Recorded in September 1955, the single went unnoticed for months before catapulting up the charts and becoming one of the biggest hit records of that era.

In the early 1950s, Earl Carroll, LaVerne Drake, "Cub" Gaining, and Robert Phillips formed the Carnations, performing at school dances in their Harlem, New York, neighborhood. While the group's primary influence was the Orioles, Carroll favored the gospel sounds of the Five Blind Boys of Mississippi and the Swanee Quintet.

"Most of the groups in those days had bird names, like the Cardinals, the Flamingos, the Robins, and quite a few others," Carroll said. "We wanted to be different and thought that we would go to flowers and came up with the Carnations."

The Carnations joined other groups from Harlem, such as the Harptones and the Five Crowns (later to become the New Drifters), at impromptu "battle of the groups" sessions, on 118th Street and Eight Avenue. It was there that they were discovered by Lover Patterson. "We all knew Patterson, who was a couple of years older than us, and we knew that he was in the music business and had connections with record companies that were downtown," Carroll said. "He introduced us to a young lady, Esther Navarro, and she took us to Jerry Blaine of Jubilee Records, which we went on to record for."

Before their first recording, Gaining decided to leave the group and Patterson replaced him with James Clark (of the Five Crowns) and Johnny Willingham.

Carroll said that Navarro wasn't thrilled with the name Carnations and told the group to "go back to the woodshed and come up with something that might be a little more appealing. We thought of what the best car that America had to offer was, came up with Cadillac, and the rest is history," Carroll recalled.

In July 1954 the Cadillacs recorded their first single, "Gloria," and it proved to be a regional success. "'Gloria' was an old standard and we heard it sung by the Mills Brothers, and another rendition by Charles Brown," Carroll recalled. "We put a little doo-wop flavor to it. Low and behold, it's like the national anthem of the doo-wop era now."

Following the group's next release, "Wishing Well," Clark and Willingham were replaced by baritone Earl Wade and tenor Buddy Brooks. Carroll recalled that while the addition of Wade and Brooks provided the Cadillacs with the ability to perform beautiful ballads, the record company preferred that they concentrate on up-tempo songs.

In early 1955 the Cadillacs recorded "Speedo," a song that would define their career and solidify their distinctive sound. But the song's origin, its true composer, and the basis of Carroll's lifelong nickname from that point on have remained a matter of debate. One account credits the composition to Carroll, while another lists Navarro as its writer. A third version states that it was copied from a song that was performed at the Apollo Theatre by a group named the Regals.

"Esther Navarro was a fantastic manager and was very good at what she did, but she wasn't a songwriter," Carroll said. "We weren't into publishing and copywriting, so most of the stuff she put her name on it and that's how that came about. As for the name 'Speedo,' we were performing at a sold-out show at an armory in Massachusetts with the Moonglows, Connie Francis, the Flamingos, and a couple of other artists and a riot broke out. After the engagement, we were on our way to our car in the parking lot and there was a great big bombshell outside of the armory.

"Bobby Phillips was the ham of the Cadillacs and they used to tease me quite a bit because my head was kind of pointy," Carroll said. "He hollered out, 'Hey Speedo, here's your torpedo,' and the guys just rolled on the ground and thought that was the funniest thing that was ever said. Now, I was a little upset and I told Bobby, 'Listen, my name is Earl; Mr. Earl, as far as you're concerned. It ain't no Speedo.' We all got in the car and the Regals had a song out called 'I've Got Your Water Boiling Baby' and they sang something like 'wamp-wamp-shoo-be-do' and by the time we got to New York we had written 'Speedo' in the car. We went in the studio the following day and recorded it. "I was Speedo from that point on."

The Cadillacs was one of the first vocal groups to incorporate choreography into its stage act. It set them apart from many of their contemporaries. Cholly Atkins, who, with partner Honey Cole, was a popular dance act at the Apollo Theatre, received high praise from Carroll, who attributed the group's stage presence to his guidance.

"Navarro introduced us to Cholly Atkins, who had an act called Atkins and Cole," Carroll said. "These guys were so good that it looked like one person dancing. They were so graceful. Atkins took us under his wing and he had a business office at the old Ed Sullivan Theater, and we'd go there and work for twelve hours a day."

Atkins went on to work for Motown and is responsible for all the choreography done by its major acts during the 1960s, including the Temptations, Gladys Knight and the Pips, and Smokey Robinson and the Miracles.

The Cadillacs have performed as part of many concert tours and on the bill of many major shows through the years. Carroll reflected on the group's work at some of Alan Freed's now-legendary shows.

"It was a gas and so very exciting," he said. "Alan Freed was such a gentleman and a beautiful person. We broke Sinatra's attendance record down at the New York Paramount Theater and we had lines all around the block. Those were the days, working with Count Basie's band and Joe Williams, Al Sears, and Sam 'the Man' Taylor. We had the best musicians in the world. Those were times I'll never forget."

Carroll eventually left the Cadillacs, citing management problems, and joined the Coasters for about twenty years. "When I first saw those guys, they were acting," Carroll said. "Not only did they have number-one hit songs but they acted on stage and everyone had a role to play. Without patting myself on the back, we were so good that Billy Guy, the

MC of the Apollo, had to come out and try to calm down the audience after we performed. It was a huge thrill."

During that period, Navarro enlisted a new Cadillacs' lineup and continued to issue singles sans Carroll. He claimed that a reference to a group named Speedo and the Pearls, featured in existing music biographies, is inaccurate. "I never sang with that group," Carroll said. "They tried to use my name but it was actually just Howard Guyton and the Pearls. I don't know what ever happened to them."

In 1979 Carroll, Wade, Phillips, and Johnny Brown joined to do a Subaru commercial. That lineup, with the addition of Gary K. Lewis, remained intact as the Cadillacs for a significant period of time. Despite several personnel changes since, the group maintained a loyal following and continued to serve as crowd pleasers at appearances in 2006. Carroll speculated on reasons for the group's longevity and success.

"It's a classy cat," he said. "We were always well dressed on stage, and acted like gentlemen. I'm proud of all the entertainers that I have met and worked with like Fats Domino, Ray Charles, Jerry Lee Lewis, Paul Anka, and the Everly Brothers. God has been good to me."

Billboard Top 40 Hits by the Cadillacs

Date	Pos	Wks on Charts	Record Title	Label/Number
02/04/56	17	05	Speedo	Josie 785
01/12/59	28	03	Peek-A-Boo	Josie 846

Chubby Checker
("The Twist")

Wildwood Crest, New Jersey   **October 16, 2005**

With the introduction of a new style of music called rock-and-roll, a sound that was geared toward and embraced by an enthusiastic teenage audience, came the evolution of some equally unique dances developed to augment the energized and uninhibited music. Philadelphia, Pennsylvania, undeniably served as the dance capital of the early rock-and-roll movement due in large part to a local television show, *American Bandstand*, one that was set on a dance floor filled with teenagers moving to the beat of the latest hit records of the day.

It's no surprise that Philadelphia-based groups that came into existence during the late 1950s and early 1960s and recorded on the local Cameo-Parkway label reacted to the call for new dances and dance-oriented tunes. Groups such as the Dovells and the Orlons benefited from working with the label's master songwriters, Dave Appell and Kal Mann, in turning out huge dance-oriented records such as the "Bristol Stomp" and the "Wah Watusi." But clearly, if the city was indeed the capital of the rock-and-roll dance movement and its talent led the nation in recorded dance tunes, then one Philadelphia artist, Chubby Checker, served as the unrivaled king of the growing dance craze.

Born Ernest Evans, the soon-to-be recording artist was a contemporary of other Philadelphia solo artists of the time such as Bobby Rydell, Frankie Avalon, and Fabian Forte. But in Evans's case, his unbridled energy and natural stage presence, coupled with carefully produced dance tunes and an aggressive promotion schedule, thrust the young entertainer to the forefront of the dance craze.

The motivation to become an entertainer came early for Evans, following his attendance at performances of people such as Frankie "Sugar Chile" Robinson and Ernest Tubb. "When I saw these people play I thought that was the only thing in life that a human being should do," he said. "There were people watching them and they were singing and looking like they were having such a good time and everybody was so motivated and happy. I thought, oh my, if I could do something like that."

At eleven years old, Evans formed a street-corner vocal group in his inner-city neighborhood. He cited the Moonglows, the Drifters, the Dells, and the Turbans as having served to influence the sound that his group tried to emulate. While attending high school, Evans worked at a local poultry market and began to entertain customers by singing and telling jokes. At one point the market owner had him record a novelty version of "Jingle Bells" as a holiday gift for *American Bandstand*'s Dick Clark, who was a friend.

"My boss had a friend named Kal Mann and they were partners in the business and Kal was a songwriter too," Checker said. "That's how I ended up getting onto Cameo-Parkway. Kal was told about me singing in the store and I also did impressions, which they needed for the 'Jingle Bells' recording."

When the producers at Cameo-Parkway heard his recording of "Jingle Bells" they got Evans to record an original novelty song "The Class." "I did Elvis, and Fats Domino, and the Coasters, and the Everly Brothers, and we did a take-off on Fabian and Frankie and Ricky Nelson, who was very popular at that time. They were teen throbs. It was the first record I ever recorded and we had a hit."

While it's been generally accepted through the years that Dick Clark's wife suggested Evans's name change to Chubby Checker, one reference credited Tony Anastasi, Evans's boss at the poultry market, as giving him the name.

"Tony gave me the name Chubby," he recalled. "Then when they took me to the studio to do the 'Jungle Bells' recording, Dick's wife said, 'Is that Chubby? Chubby like Fats, and Checker like Domino. And that's how that came to be."

In 1959, Checker recorded a cover of a song released a year earlier by Hank Ballard and the Midnighters called "The Twist." But Cameo-Parkway executive Bernie Lowe was initially opposed to recording the tune after its earlier release by Ballard was perceived as racy and vulgar.

"I did Hank Ballard's version of his song because radio stopped playing it," Checker said. "It wasn't like Hank Ballard had a record that was going on the charts and I came in and decided to cover him. That wasn't what I wanted to do at all. They just weren't playing it. And no one was ever going to see the dance that the kids made up to that song and no one was ever going to hear the song.

"When we put it out, Bernie Lowe thought that 'Toot,' the B-side, was the main side," Checked continued. "We went to Pittsburgh to do a record hop for a man named Porky Chadwick and he said that he was going to turn the record over and play 'The Twist.' At that point Bernie Lowe lost his power."

The song was so strong that "The Twist" climbed to number one in late 1960, remained on the charts for four months, and then did what no other hit record had done before. In late 1961, the record reentered the charts and climbed to number one again.

"Zsa Zsa Gabor did the twist at the Peppermint Lounge and that revived interest in the song and it climbed the charts again," Checker recalled.

"But 'The Twist' and dancing apart to the beat is the biggest event in show business," he said. "You can compare it to Thomas Edison's discovery of electric lights, to Alexander Graham Bell's invention of the telephone, to Walt Disney's animated cartoons, and to Henry Ford's invention of the V-8 engine. When these men did those things, that form became the way of life 24-7. And the same thing with Chubby Checker and 'The Twist' and the way we dance apart to the beat. At that very moment it became a 24-7 activity all over the world.

"If that isn't so, why is 'The Twist' the only song to be number one twice?" he continued. "If it's not the biggest event in show business, why did we have five albums in the Top 12 all at once? If it wasn't the biggest event in show business, why do we have nine double-sided hit songs? If it wasn't the biggest event in show business, why was the first platinum ever given to Chubby Checker for 'Let's Twist Again'? It was the biggest song of the 1960s and we had a lot of big stars in the 1960s. In about forty-two months, it's believed, that we sold about 250 million pieces of music."

To be sure, "The Twist" quickly developed into a phenomenon, and soon "Twist" T-shirts, shoes, ties, dolls, and even chewing gum flooded the marketplace. Television stations featured Checker giving personal instruction on how to do the dance during five-minute intervals, televised at the end of normal half-hour programs. In short, there was little chance that any living person wasn't aware of "The Twist" during that period of time.

Checker readily admits that the huge surge in popularity did not only affect him in 1960, but continues to affect him in 2005. "If you go to the supermarkets, drug stores, and convenience stores today, look at all the twist products that are on the shelves," he said. "They're making a fortune."

While Checker does not benefit financially from any of the retail products associated with "The Twist," he recently introduced his own line of snack products and anticipated moving over 150 million pieces of it during 2006.

Checker followed "The Twist" with other dance tunes such as "The Fly," "The Pony," "The Limbo Rock," and "The Hucklebuck." "We took what we saw in the streets and put it to music," he said. "The Bible says that nothing is original and everything's been done before. There was dancing apart to the beat since the beginning of time, but no one put it together and no one called it anything. If you wave your hands in the air, you're doing 'The Fly.' If you're doing 'The Fly,' you've got to be doing 'The Shake.' And 'The Pony'; what does a pony do? He hips and he hops. This is what hip-hop is; they do 'The Pony.' 'The Hucklebuck' is a nasty dance; we know what it is."

Checker has a simple analogy for the dance-tune formula. "These things are put together like a keyboard and after the keyboard is there, you can do anything," he said. "We brought to light the dancing keyboards that give us dancing apart to the beat, which we call 'let's go out and do the boogie.' Before Chubby, the boogie wasn't here."

Checker has appeared on the bills of countless shows and venues and was perhaps the most aggressive performer in support of his string of hit records during the early 1960s. But when asked if one show throughout his career stands out as a personal favorite, his answer was a telling attribute about the consistent crowd-pleasing performer. On October 15, 2005, Checker visited Wildwood, New Jersey, to have a street named in his honor and to headline a star-studded lineup in concert at its convention center. The community has served as a springboard for many rock-and-roll acts including Checker, Bobby Rydell, Danny and the Juniors, and Charlie Gracie.

"The only show that stands out would be the one that we did in Wildwood, New Jersey, last night, because I got the highest honor that I've ever received since I've been singing on stage," he said. "It goes back to when I was eighteen years old playing Wildwood in 1960."

In addition to his hit recordings, Checker appeared in two motion pictures, *Don't Knock the Twist* and *Twist Around the Clock*. He spoke about the experience.

"In those days I wasn't able to really be a movie star like I should have been," he said. "What I do like about the films is that you can watch them today and nobody's offended. I once asked Ali why he made *Freedom Road*, with them calling him that dirty name through the entire movie and him being the greatest boxer that ever lived. He lived to see the day when it came on television and he told me that I was right."

When Ali's name came up in the interview, Checker said that he was the one who advised the legendary boxer to call his rounds, a trademark promotion for every bout throughout his career. "He came to me during the early part of his career when he had just won an Olympic gold medal and he wanted to be a champion," Checker explained. "He said, 'I'm too young and no one's going to listen to me.' I asked him how good he was and he answered that he was the best in the world. I asked him if he could name his rounds and if he said, 'You goin' to go in four,' could he do that. He said he could and I told him if he could do that he'd be the man."

While Checker is happy with the production of all the recordings he has made throughout his career, he is less than pleased with the airplay that he got and continues to get today. "'Twist and Shout' is the biggest twist record played today," he said. "That's not right." He balked at speculating as to why that situation exists.

In 1982, Checker had two disco-flavored hit records, "Running" and "Harder than Diamond." But he contends that in consort with earlier times, neither recording received the airplay it deserved. "Jimmy Buffett hasn't had a record in twenty-five years but he sells the house out and that's because he gets airplay," he said. "We don't get airplay."

In 1988, Checker recorded "The Twist" again, this time on the Fat Boys' rendition of his greatest hit. It climbed to the Top 40 charts.

"Fat Boys said, 'We want to do "The Twist," Chubby,' and I said well go do it," Checker recalled. "He said, 'No, no, no, we want to rap and you can sing the song.' I said, whew I like that, and we had a big hit that went to number fourteen on the charts. It was great and they were great."

It almost seems an inconceivable feat that Checker had five albums in the top twelve at the same time given the time necessary to produce the product while he maintained an extremely high level of appearances during the early 1960s.

"We were making records every week at Cameo-Parkway, and then when Zsa Zsa went on stage and did that dance we already had the records recorded, so we were ahead of everybody," he said.

Checker pondered the effect that his early work with a series of dance tunes has had on subsequent dance fads and styles through the years.

"The biggest dance in the world is not 'The Twist'; it's just recognizable," he said. "It's 'The Pony.' Everyone knows how to do it. It's two on one side and two on the other side, over and over, and they are still doing it.

"When I think about what we've done and what is still being done as a result of us being on the planet, our work is not like anyone else's," he continued. "When you think about Chubby Checker—and I don't want people to think that I have a big head but I'm just telling the truth—the biggest event in the music industry is what we did, and it's still going on.

"What bothers me a lot is that the historians try to cover me out," he said. "I don't like the fact that the historians have given the Beatles my success by playing 'Twist and Shout' for young people on rock stations, making young people think that the Beatles did 'The Twist' in 2025. They are diluting my fame and what I've done in the music industry. It's a very carefully, shady, underhanded, and dark orchestration of deteriorating a man who gave the world the greatest gift in the music industry."

Chubby Checker continues to maintain a busy schedule of appearances, and, given the surrounding throng of fans that enthusiastically greet him following each performance, his contributions to music and dance are respected, appreciated, and alive and well in the minds and hearts of those people that remember the significant impact his body of work has had on music and dance.

Billboard Top 40 Hits by Chubby Checker

Date	Pos	Wks on Charts	Record Title	Label/Number
06/15/59	38	02	The Class	Parkway 804
08/08/60	01	15	The Twist	Parkway 811
10/31/60	14	09	The Hucklebuck	Parkway 813
01/30/61	01	14	Pony Time	Parkway 818
05/01/61	24	04	Dance the Mess Around	Parkway 822
07/03/61	08	15	Let's Twist Again	Parkway 824
10/02/61	07	11	The Fly	Parkway 830
11/20/61	01	18	The Twist (reissue)	Parkway 811
12/25/61	21	03	Jingle Bell Rock (with Bobby Rydell)	Cameo 205
03/10/62	03	12	Slow Twistin' (with Dee Dee Sharp)	Parkway 835
07/07/62	12	07	Dancin' Party	Parkway 842
09/29/62	02	17	Limbo Rock (double-sided hit)	Parkway 849
09/29/62	10	09	Popeye the Hitchhiker	Parkway 849
02/23/63	20	08	Let's Limbo Some More (double-sided hit)	
03/23/63	15	07	Twenty Miles	Parkway 862
06/01/63	12	07	Birdland	Parkway 873
08/03/63	25	05	Twist It Up	Parkway 879
11/23/63	12	09	Loddy Lo (double-sided hit)	
01/11/64	17	08	Hooka Tooka	Parkway 890
04/04/64	23	05	Hey, Bobba Needle	Parkway 907
07/11/64	40	01	Lazy Elsie Molly	Parkway 920
05/22/65	40	01	Let's Do the Freddie	Parkway 949

Jimmy Clanton
("Just a Dream")

Waterbury, Connecticut   **March 11, 2005**

I n 1959, disc jockey Alan Freed produced the second of his two rock-
and-roll movies, *Go Johnny Go*, a film that starred Jimmy Clanton,
a recording artist from Baton Rouge, Louisiana, who scored a breakout
hit on the Ace record label just one year prior. Clanton's boyish charm
and honest demeanor in the film was immediately embraced by its
audience, and despite the film's celebrated cast, which included Chuck
Berry, Jackie Wilson, the Flamingos, the Cadillacs, Eddie Cochran, and
Ritchie Valens, Clanton became the subject of much attention.

Given the teen-idol boom that was developing during that time,
Clanton was a natural to join the ranks of Fabian, Frankie Avalon, and
Bobby Rydell. But Clanton brought a greater element to the mix, one
that made him unique among his peers. An avid enthusiast of rhythm
and blues and a white artist who actually composed the songs that he
recorded, a rarity in those days, he held a more serious stature than
other artists of the era did.

While virtually all biographies state that Clanton formed his first band, the Dixie Cats, he adamantly disputed that fact. "The Dixie Cats were our New Orleans-jazz-type band and I was in junior high school," he said. "When I got into late high school and the first year of college age, that's when we started a group called the Rockets. With the Rockets we were able to go and play high school dances, while the Dixie Cats were okay but didn't have the good players that the Rockets did. We were the first, and in another year or two John Fred and the Playboys came upon the scene."

Clanton credits pianist Dick Holler as being the catalyst who opened the doors of his career, of realizing his talent, and who enabled him to enhance and embellish upon his climb from a background guitar player to a front man who learned how to handle himself in that role. "If it wasn't for Dick Holler at that time allowing me to do that and giving me the opportunity to grow in that respect, who knows where I'd be. He was definitely a tremendous influence on me.

"I've got to be truthful about my compositions," Clanton said. "For the sake of promotion I told everybody that 'Just a Dream' was my first record, but that's not true. Actually, I didn't want to be a singer; I wanted to be a guitar player, but I noticed that you could make more money on one-nighters if you could sing as well. So I went from five dollars a night to ten to fifteen, and eventually I was making forty dollars a night."

Clayton was part of the first white rhythm and blues band in Baton Rouge and the surrounding area, and one night a member of the group told the others that he learned of a recording studio in New Orleans where they could make a dub, or demo, of their songs.

"We go down there and record and, as much as it sounds like a script from *Happy Days,* the guy that was doing the recording told us that we had about seven minutes left that we had paid for and asked if we had anything else to record," Clanton recalled. "The piano player didn't have any material and turned to me and asked if I had anything. Well, I'd been going with this girl, my first love, and she kind of dumped me and I was sitting in my house and wrote a song in about twenty minutes. I didn't tell anybody but that night I said, 'Well, I do have this song.'"

Encouraged to lay down the track, Clanton got his guitar and sang, "I trusted you for such a long, long time and now you're telling me bye bye," and the tune was recorded. "We go back to Baton Rouge and a couple of weeks go by and I get this phone call and it's Johnny Vincent from Ace Records saying that he wanted to talk to me. Come to find out, just to show you how things go, that this recording studio was the hub for all the major artists of the South like Ray Price, Fats Domino, Smiley Lewis, Little Richard, and all of the major, major black soul artists recorded there."

As such, Vincent produced all his Ace records at the studio, and by chance, while walking through headed for a scheduled session, he heard the playback of Clanton's demo. The call he placed to Clanton was to initiate action to sign the young musician to the label, which was accomplished a short time later.

"We went back into the studio and rerecorded the song with a New Orleans group and put out the record," Clanton said. "I was the first white rhythm and blues artist in that area to have a record and I'll never forget the first time I heard it on the radio."

The song became a local hit, and after a few months Vincent called Clanton and told him that they had to do another session. "Well, this same girl and I, we just had a stormy relationship and I ended up writing 'Just a Dream' in about twenty minutes too," he said. "I went back and did the session and I did a play-through on the song. I'll never forget Red Tyler, the baritone sax player, looking at me and saying, 'That's a hit!'"

Shortly after recording the song and going home, Clanton got another call from Vincent instructing him to put some clothes together and prepare to travel.

"Now mind you, I got hayseed all around me. I mean I talk with a twang; never been out of Louisiana in my life," Clanton recalled. "I mean I didn't know nothing from nothing, y'all. I just could sing it."

Vincent informed the youngster that he had landed him a spot on a new television show that was broadcast from Philadelphia, Pennsylvania, called *American Bandstand*. "I get up there and do a lip sync of the record and he gets orders for a hundred thousand copies the next day," an amazed Clanton said. "It was April 1958, and from then on it was just like barnstorming. It was just like a video fast-forwarded of life. Before I knew it I'm in New York, I'm signing with a major agency, I'm barnstorming around the country. Alan Freed fell in love with me. He loved my honesty. I became his favorite white male artist and Jackie Wilson was his favorite black male artist. Jackie and I always did the shows with Alan whenever he put them on."

Clanton traveled around the country with the disc jockey on a series of package tours that boasted some of the biggest names in the industry. He reflected on those experiences.

"There is just no way to put into words what it was like, but I will tell you that there was a big difference between the 1950s and the

1960s," he began. "Even though I came onto the scene late, in 1958, I was able to come right in at a time when acts from the early 1950s, with Bill Haley and the Comets, Bobby Day, Clyde McPhatter, and LaVerne Baker, were still predominant in the late 1950s and I was able to grab hold of their spirit and their soul and their expressions. They all liked me and helped me so much. We would travel together and it would break my heart because I didn't realize that we'd go to a town and go in to eat together and we couldn't even do that. I mean, they couldn't even go to the same restroom. This was still going on in '58 and '59.

"They all took me under arm and really protected me, and groomed me because they realized that I was so innocent from all of that," he continued. "Those shows were electrifying because they enabled me to bond to these people and it was tremendous. It was little things, for instance, like LaVerne Baker. She had an interesting hobby. We all traveled on the tour buses and when we boarded we had long hauls and on these several-hundred-mile trips we'd fall asleep in various stages. She had one of the first Polaroid cameras and she took pictures of everybody in various states of appearance while they slept. The way you found out about it was, with no warning, everyone would get up and LaVerne had taped the photos along the top of the bus. We roared."

Clanton withheld the person's name, but recalled that the manager of one of the acts on a bus tour taught him how to play craps—but when Clanton participated in one game, the dice were loaded and he was taken.

As for playing the part of Johnny Melody in the Freed movie *Go Johnny Go*, Clanton shared a memorable story that occurred during a scene near the end of the film.

"I had one scene where I had to throw a brick through the window of a jewelry store," he said. "I was aware that the set was fragile and so I held back on how hard I threw the brick at it. All of a sudden Freed yelled 'cut' and came over to me and said, 'Jimmy, you're throwing the brick like a girl. You have to throw it hard.' Every time I tried to explain, Mr. Freed cut me off and insisted that I throw it like a macho guy. When they called action I reared back and threw it as hard as I could."

Almost immediately, Clanton, the cast, and crew began to hear a creaking sound. Within seconds, he said, the entire set collapsed to the floor of the studio.

"Jimmy, what did you do?" Clanton recalled Freed calling out. "It took two hours for the crew to reconstruct the set."

In the early 1960s Clanton began recording more and more songs that were written by other composers such as Doc Pomus and

Mort Shuman. "I think what a wake-up call was for me, and it was unfortunate, was that Johnny Vincent at Ace Records got in over his head," Clanton said. "He was really just a promo man. He had no idea how to produce; he just got so lucky with me and Huey 'Piano' Smith and the Clowns and a couple of things with Frankie Ford. He didn't know what to do. He got hold of a lion by the tail and didn't know how to tame it. He pretty much just left it to us."

When Clanton got out and began to hear other productions and started meeting people like Neil Sedaka and Pomus and Shuman and became friends with them, he was asked to consider working with New York musicians. Initially refusing these overtures in favor of musicians in New Orleans, he came to the realization and understanding that the music in New Orleans was starting to sound all the same to him.

"If you listen to my real early songs, technically speaking the musicians went as far as they could go," he said. "They gave me what they could, but little by little I felt that I was growing and there was more that I could do. So I let some of my friends talk me into it, and that's why I began working with those composers."

In 1962, the British Invasion kicked in, a period of great challenge for most American recording artists. As the decade came to a close, the Woodstock generation motivated significant changes in musical taste and culture, and the ongoing Vietnam War served to affect public opinion. In the course of ten years, the world and the music industry in general experienced huge shifts in acceptance and taste.

"We suddenly had the voices of the English; we've got the voices of the teenage girls who still love the teen idols; we've got the anything-goes crowd that subscribe to the notion that if it feels good, do it; and it's like a whirlwind and there's nothing concrete," he said. "DJs don't know what to do. Some DJs want to go all English, some don't. I kind of panicked, as some of the artists did, and I just started grabbing for straws. I began to think that maybe I should try anything so that I could stay in the mix, and that's why during that era people might wonder why I did this or why I did that. I was trying to find where I was going to fit with all of these different voices around."

During this time, Clanton went into military service. Contrary to reported accounts that claim he was drafted, Clanton readily admitted to having joined the National Guard to avoid the draft. In fact, he had just landed the starring role for a television series to be produced in California and based on the comic book character Archie. "I shot it and did a decent job because remember I'd already done Alan Freed's movies, so I had a little experience," he recalled. "I landed the part in the series and I'm on the set, and a guy comes up to me and says there's a long-distance call for you and it's super important. I take the phone and it's a friend in Baton Rouge, and he tells me to grab a plane and get back home quick. He told me that my National Guard unit was activated and I was in full service; I was in the army."

Clanton came to find out that his guard unit happened to be a crack communications group. "I thought these were all of my beer-drinking buddies and they don't know from nothing," he laughed. "How can they be a crack unit for anything? I go from the set of a television series and the next thing I know I'm in a military truck and they haul me to a train on my way to Fort Lennonwood, Missouri, for basic training. I'm talking about overnight."

For the next year, Clanton was completely out of touch with the music industry, his career, and any prospects that he had when he left for the military. Meanwhile, Vincent was desperate to keep Clanton's music and image alive during his absence but was ill-equipped to accomplish the task. He tried by releasing singles that had been recorded early in Clanton's career.

When his military commitment ended, Clanton traveled to New York and hooked up with his favorite writers, Howie Greenfield and Neil Sedaka, who wrote the Top 20 hit "Another Sleepless Night" for him. Thankful to be back on the scene and with a hit record, he visited Alden Music to review some potential material for his next release.

"You've got this stack and you've got that stack," he recalled. "This stack is one that all the artists have looked through and everybody's turned it down. Over here you've got fresh stuff. So I go through the fresh stuff and nothing's hitting home. I thought, 'All right, let me go through the other pile,' and I picked one to listen to. I listen to the opening bars and said, 'Howie, that's a catchy one.' Howie said to forget it and threw it to the side. He told me that everybody had looked at it and nobody took it, so forget it. I left it alone and ended up listening to a couple of other things, and I said that I wanted to do the one I liked as a throwaway."

When he went to do the recording session, one that included horns, he readied himself to lay down his favorite of the tunes reviewed and Carole King was there to do the musical arrangement for the session. The song was "Venus in Blue Jeans," and once released the record was the fastest-climbing record Clanton ever had.

"An interesting story is how that horn section came to open 'Venus in Blue Jeans,'" he said. "Carole King said, 'We paid for the musicians

44

and we're going to use them." I said fine. And that's how that came to be."

Clanton became a disc jockey during the 1970s and developed a lounge act that chronicles his amazing career, complete with vignettes of his experiences that serve as crowd pleasers. He continues to perform and resides in Texas.

Billboard Top 40 Hits by Jimmy Clanton

Date	Pos	Wks on Charts	Record Title	Label/Number
07/21/58	04	15	Just a Dream	Ace 546
11/17/58	25	05	A Letter to An Angel (double-sided hit)	
12/01/58	38	02	A Part of Me	Ace 551
08/17/59	33	06	My Own True Love	Ace 567
12/21/59	05	11	Go, Jimmy, Go	Ace 575
05/30/60	22	06	Another Sleepless Night	Ace 585
09/01/62	07	10	Venus in Blue Jeans	Ace 8001

Lenny Cocco
(The Chimes)

Harrison, New York   **March 19, 2005**

The history of the Brooklyn, New York, vocal group the Chimes is another of the era's classic street-corner-to-Top-20-recording-artist stories. In began in 1957 when Lenny Cocco formed a singing group originally named the Capris. Given his father's work as a professional accordion player, Cocco was exposed to music standards made famous by Tommy Dorsey and Eddie Duchin. As a result the group concentrated on that style of music, and peppered the tunes with their own blend of doo-wop harmony.

A pool hall located over a neighborhood supermarket had one of the few pianos available for public use and quickly became the group's rehearsal center. By 1960, having achieved tight harmonies and a growing confidence, the group decided to make a demonstration record in a professional studio. Cocco believed that the group's sound had the potential to adapt to the 1937 Dorsey hit "Once in a While" and arranged it to fit a five-part harmony.

When the group recorded the song, a studio engineer was so impressed he called a friend at Tag Records, who went to the studio to hear it. By fall of that year, they had a Top 20 hit record that sold one million copies.

Given the large number of vocal groups that formed in New York City during the era, Cocco learned that another group, friends of his, had already claimed the name the Capris and he quickly came up with the Chimes for his outfit.

"We used to sing on the beach together with Nicky Santo and his group [of 'There's A Moon out Tonight' fame] and when I found out that they already had the name Capris I dropped it right away and picked the Chimes." In reality, a number of groups at the time used the name the Chimes, but in Cocco's case, when "Once in a While" charted, his group secured it as their own.

"For our first recording, my dad said that I should pick out a good standard," Cocco recalled. "I selected 'I'm in the Mood for Love' for our follow-up release because the record company told me that they wanted me to record something in the same vein as our hit record. I arranged both tunes to fit our harmonies."

"We started out practicing at the Cactus Poolroom on Rockaway Avenue and Fulton Street," Cocco recalled. "Soon after we recorded 'Once in a While,' we were driving in the car on Eastern Parkway on our way to rehearsal and heard it played on the radio for the first time. We stopped the car in the middle of the parkway and got out. It was such a thrill."

Cocco recalled receiving huge support from friends in Brooklyn; some even drove to Baltimore to support the group when it played the Howard Theater. The Howard, a predominantly black venue, was one of several included in what was known as the "chitlin circuit." The circuit included the Regal in Chicago and the Apollo in New York and served as early venues for the Chimes, who, because of their sound, were perceived as black recording artists.

"What happened was we had a black sound and people never saw us," Cocco explained. "The first big job that we had was the Regal Theater in Chicago. While we were there we shared the bill with Roy Hamilton, and his manager, Bill Cook, had an idea. He told me that he wanted to work something out with me and get me a few more gigs. The five of us came out on the side of the stage and we sang a song called 'The Pal That He Loves Stole the Gal That He Loves, That's Why They're Not Pals Anymore' and the spotlight was on us. All of a sudden Roy Hamilton came out and we went into 'bomp bomp bomp bomp.' He began singing 'You Can Have Her' and that's how he was introduced. We ended up getting more work from that routine."

At one point during the group's early days, its bass singer, Pat McGuire, was killed in a tragic car accident. The incident affected Cocco so deeply that he decided to keep the Chimes a quartet from that time in honor of his fallen friend, never replacing the bass singer.

"I knelt at Patty's coffin and I swore to him that there would never be a fifth person to take his place and there never has been," Cocco said.

In 1986, Cocco formed Freedom Records and recorded a contemporary tune, "New York City Lady." He also acquired all of the Chimes' original master recordings and issued a compilation record.

"The project went well," Cocco said. The lineup that performs with Cocco in 2006 is a fine-tuned contingent of musicians and vocalists. "The guys I have with me now are super," he said. "The second tenor, Rocky Marsicano, is with me more that twenty-one years; my trumpet player played with Blood, Sweat, and Tears for fifteen years; and my baritone sax player backed Tito Puente for seventeen years. They're all pros."

In addition to maintaining an aggressive schedule of performances, Cocco hosts a weekend oldies radio show on the Long Island station WNYG.

Billboard Top 40 Hits by the Chimes

Date	Pos	Wks on Charts	Record Title	Label/Number
01/16/61	11	06	Once in a While	Tag 444
05/15/61	38	01	I'm in the Mood for Love	Tag 445

Joe Cook
(Little Joe and the Thrillers)

Framingham, Massachusetts   **August 18, 2005**

A nother product of the City of Brotherly Love, South Philadelphia's Joe Cook got involved in music early, forming his own gospel group, the Evening Star Quartet, when he was twelve years old. Being blessed with a good sense for music and a natural ability to please an audience, Cook's taste in music shifted from gospel to the popular rhythm and blues of the early 1950s and he joined Farris Hill, Richard Frazier, Donald Burnett, and Henry Pascal to form the Thrillers.

Known for his high-pitched falsetto voice, Cook became a local favorite and after the Thrillers developed a tight harmony, he secured a recording contact with Okeh Records in 1956. The Thrillers' first single, "Let's Do the Slop," was released later that year and became an East Coast favorite, in conjunction with an original dance.

The group released a follow-up single in October 1957, "Peanuts," a song defined by Cook's falsetto lead. Rising nationally to number twenty-two on *Billboard*'s Top 40 charts, the record is said to have been the first one in history that climbed the charts as a result of television exposure. That exposure came when the group appeared on Philadelphia's own *American Bandstand* broadcast.

During the 1960s, Cook formed a girl group made up of his daughters, called the Sherrys. The group charted with one single before fading from the industry.

"When I was born, my grandmother raised me because my mother sang on the road at carnivals with artists like Bessie Smith, Ethel Waters, and Big Maybelle," Cook said. "We went to church every night and listened to the music. Although I never really knew her, I guess I developed singing from my mother. Living with us in a big house were my two cousins, and I began to teach them and a friend of mine harmony and we sang all the time."

Cook said that when the family attended church services on Sunday his grandmother would get up and announce, "Here is a selection by the Joe Cook Quartet," and the four youngsters would sing a cappella in front of the congregation. "When my grandmother died, her church had a gospel group called the Morning Star, and so I decided to call ours the Evening Star Quartet," he recalled.

Upon the death of his grandmother, Cook's mother ended her music career, settled down in Philadelphia, and was determined to ensure that her son did not stray from the "music of the righteous." In fact, she was so adamant about it that when Billy Ward (of the Dominoes) came looking for Cook to offer him one hundred dollars a week to join the group, Cook's mother instructed his wife not to tell him about the offer. Cook had met Ward while singing at a battle of the quartets at his aunt's church.

"When Ward decided to go into doo-wop-blues, he knew that I could sing," Cook said. "When he formed the Dominoes he came to the house in the daytime while I was working to make the offer. My mother wouldn't let my wife tell me about it. In fact, I never knew about it until after my mother passed away." Ward went on to draft Jackie Wilson to join the group.

As a teenager, Cook frequented a Philadelphia showplace, the Mint, where a number of top acts such as Count Basie, Lionel Hampton, Duke Ellington, Dinah Washington, and Billy Ekstine performed. He quickly earned the nickname "Jitterbug Joe" due to his ability to shine on the dance floor. "I didn't have any money," Cook recalled. "But because the guys there knew that I could dance they'd always ask me if I was going to the show. When I told them that I had no money, they'd pay my way in. I used to dance in the middle of a big circle of people, doing splits and throwing two girls over my back." During the next decade, Cook would score hit records and introduce two dances, the Slop and the Bicycle Bounce.

Cook eventually met four street-corner singers that he would mentor and form into a popular vocal group. At first he did not sing with the quartet but rather coached them in singing and style. "They used to come to my house to rehearse and I was teaching them along with Little Jimmy and the Sparrows," he said. "I got those guys (the Thrillers) singing so tight that I told them that we should perform at every party in Philly. We'd find out where there was a party and crash it to perform.

"One night while the group was singing, I heard a girl say, 'They thrills me,' and the name just popped into my head," Cook said. "From then on they were the Thrillers.

"When I felt they were ready, I went up to the Diamond Horseshoe nightclub and told the man that I had a group that could fill the place," he recalled. "He asked how much we wanted to perform and I told him twenty-five dollars a man, and that included me. They put flyers out and we packed the place every Friday night. After a while I asked if we could perform on Saturdays and we started doing that too."

As a result of the group's growing popularity in Philadelphia, an executive from Columbia Records listened to the Thrillers at the Diamond Horseshoe and shortly after visited Cook's house one day during the group's rehearsal. When he asked to hear an original tune, they sang "This I Know," a song that motivated swoons from the girls at the nightclub. When the executive asked for more, the group sang "Peanuts," "Let's Do the Slop," and "Echoes Keep Calling Me."

"He asked if I could have the boys in New York the next day," Cook said. "I told him that I could but I knew the guys had no money. I had no money. And I couldn't ask my wife for money because we had two little girls. Somehow I scraped up enough to get us all to New York."

In Manhattan, the group went to Columbia's recording Studio B, where an array of New York musicians, including sax player King Curtis, were scheduled to accompany them. While Johnny Mathis recorded in Studio A, the Thrillers recorded their four songs onto a tape so that an arranger could prepare sheet music for a formal session.

"They gave us five hundred dollars and told to get lost until two o'clock," Cook said. "When we returned all the musicians were there and it took two takes to lay down 'Let's Do the Slop.'"

But the mentor and singing instructor was thrust into the position of lead vocalist when Hill, the group's first tenor, flubbed the lyrics on one of the songs. After making a mistake on the lead for "Peanuts,"

Cook stepped in to demonstrate how it was done. The producers liked what they heard and told Cook that they preferred his voice on the recording. "I told them that I didn't want to sing no rock-and-roll at first."

He recorded the tune but still considered Hill the lead vocalist for the Thrillers. That is, until the group's first appearance at the legendary Apollo Theater. "In the dressing room before we went on, Ferris turned to me and said that he was too chicken to sing lead," Cook said. "I had to end up singing lead from then on."

His first appearance at the landmark Harlem venue was both exciting and nerve-wracking. "All the groups were backstage and the Apollo's owner, Mr. Shipman, said that he wanted everyone down for the lineup of the first show," Cook said. "He announced that Little Joe and the Thrillers would open the show. Then he told the G-Clefs they were next and went down the list. When we walked on the stage the girls fell out, and when we did 'The Slop' they went crazy. We did our dance routines, and when we ran off the stage the audience yelled for more. We had to come back and do the same two songs again."

Just before the second show began, Shipman called the acts together and told Cook that the Thrillers would perform just before Big Maybelle and the headlining act, the Drifters. "I got mad because I liked to open up the show," Cook said. "I asked Mr. Shipman why he was moving us and if we were bad or something. He told us that we were great and too strong an act to open the show."

Little Joe and the Thrillers didn't balk when they were moved again before the third show, this time in the slot just prior to the Drifters.

Cook recalled that the lyrics for "Peanuts" came to him by accident. "I was sitting by the window of my house and this little girl was outside," he said. "She couldn't talk and just kept saying, 'Ah ah, ah ah.' All the while her older sister was yelling at her, 'Peanuts, get back here!' and the girl keep saying, 'Ah ah, ah ah.' I wrote the song in five minutes."

But, despite gaining fame through the success of "Peanuts," Cook was dealt a bad hand in collecting royalties on the song. "After we had the record out, a music publisher called," he said. "He asked how much I wanted for the copyright of 'Peanuts.' I asked what that was and he said it was something legal that I wouldn't understand about the music. He told me that it would still be my song and I signed it over to his publishing company." Cook eventually got the publishing rights back years later when he learned more about the business and the song became available.

As their songs charted, Little Joe and the Thrillers toured the country with many of the top acts of the era. "It was beautiful," he said. "We went on our first tour with Bo Diddley, Screamin' Jay Hawkins, the Orlons, and Lee Andrews and the Hearts. In those days they had to have a whole bunch of groups to make up a good show."

Unfortunately, following significant success, internal strife in the group caused Cook and the Thrillers to part ways. "When I was training them, they all agreed that when we got to rolling I would get 25 percent," Cook said. "Our first gig at the Apollo, I faced them with that, and Richard (Frazier) and Farris (Hill) protested that they didn't think it was right that I get 25 percent. They said we should split the money. What they didn't know is the record company already told me that they wanted to record me by myself, so when we got back to Philly and they told me they didn't need me, they played right into my hand. Columbia didn't want them."

Cook ended up hitting the road again, but this time as a solo act, playing the Apollo, the Regal, and the Howard Theaters to favorable reviews. While he has fond memories of the performances and camaraderie with other artists on the road, his experiences in the studio, and specifically his turbulent relationship with Columbia president Mitch Miller, is a different story.

"When Mitch Miller took over at Columbia, they had me dying," he said. "They had me record other people's songs, and then didn't even release a lot of my records. I got a list of all the songs I wrote with them and they didn't put them out."

A particular sore point for Cook is a recording he made of the Maurice Williams and the Zodiacs song "Stay." While he recorded the tune before Williams, Columbia sat on it and ended up costing Cook a hit record. "I had just come back off a tour and (radio disc jockey) Joe Niagara called me and told me he had a guy trying to imitate me on a record that he had and he thought it would be a hit for me," Cook said. "I drove over to the radio station in Camden, New Jersey, and liked the song. We recorded 'Stay' and when Maurice's label heard that I did it they started making promotional deals. They gave out free records if you bought so many. My label told me we couldn't do that. Mitch Miller is a jive turkey. We were set to go on *Bandstand*, and if that happened, it would have been all over."

In the early 1980s a friend called Cook in Philadelphia and urged him to relocate to Massachusetts, where radio stations were giving his tunes good airplay. After the friend helped to connect Cook with a local booking agent, he made the move. In 2005, Cook celebrated his twenty-third year of regular weekly appearances at the Cantab Lounge in Cambridge. The club is located in the center of town, most appropriately in Little Joe Cook Square, across from City Hall. Some might be surprised to see the audience that Cook, now in his early eighties, draws.

"The young kids line up outside the lounge and they charge eight dollars to get in," a proud Cook said. "We had another club on the block that had free admission and they went out of business."

Cook performed five nights a week at the Cantab until he suffered a stroke, at which time he limited his appearances to Friday and Saturday evenings. As for his falsetto, Cook is extremely proud of the fact that he still sings "Peanuts" in the same key in which it was originally recorded.

Billboard Top 40 Hits by Little Joe and the Thrillers

Date	Pos	Wks on Charts	Record Title	Label/Number
10/07/57	22	09	Peanuts	Okeh 7088

Judy Craig
(The Chiffons)

New Haven, Connecticut   **April 29, 2006**

While the 1960s female vocal group the Chiffons charted three Top 10 singles between 1963 and 1966 and became extremely popular during the decade, in truth, becoming a musical act was the last thing that Patricia Bennett, Barbara Lee, and Judy Craig had in mind when then began singing together.

"Originally, the young man that wrote the song 'He's So Fine,' Ronald Mack, is the one that got us all together," Craig said. "We all grew up together, and Ronnie was trying to become a songwriter and he asked us to sing his songs so that he could take them around to different places. We did the demos and he took them around and he got turned down at a lot of places."

But on one visit, a male vocal group with significant success of their own that had branched out into record production liked what they heard. "He (Mack) ran into the Tokens; they liked how it sounded and asked us to come in and record. That was it."

Since the three teenagers had no intention of performing, they did not have a group name. With their debut single soon to be released, that changed. "When we first started singing, we didn't have a group name," Craig said. "In fact, we didn't pick the name until right before the record ('He's So Fine') came out. Barbara picked it because she thought it was a good name for us because of the fact that we had sweet little voices and didn't have the church sound like most groups."

Existing biographies cite a group named the Chiffons as having covered the Shirelles song "Tonight's the Night" on the Big Deal record label in 1960. In 1961, another recording credited to the group appeared on the Wild Cat label, titled "Never Never." And, in 1962, "After Last Night" was released on Reprise Records. Craig said that she, Bennett, and Lee had no association whatsoever with those recordings.

"We never knew who that was on the recordings," she said. "We didn't even know that there was another group out there called the Chiffons. We would have never called ourselves the Chiffons if we knew about another group having the name."

In 1962, Sylvia Peterson became the fourth Chiffon and the quartet recorded a demo for Mack of a new song he wrote, entitled "He's So Fine." Upon hearing the demo, the Tokens invited the girls to record a more finished pressing of the song. A longstanding myth regarding the tune's signature introduction was set straight during the interview with Craig. It stated that the now famous "doo-lang, doo-lang" sung by the girls at the beginning of the recording was actually the result of a last-minute suggestion made by a studio technician.

"No, no, no," Craig said. "Ronnie did everything. He made up the background and everything. It was all him from the very beginning. It [the unique introduction] was on the demo and that's what caught the Tokens' attention—the 'doo-lang, doo-lang'—because no one ever did that before."

When the single began to climb the charts in March 1963, spending four weeks in the number-one slot, the Chiffons' lives changed dramatically. "It was exciting," she said. "We got to go to a lot of different places that we probably never would have gone to if we hadn't started singing. It was really a nice experience."

"When we first got started it was a little overwhelming because, like I said, we weren't really trying to be a singing group; we were just trying to help Ronnie out," she added. "When it all came down on us, we had to start moving around and getting clothes, so it was a little overwhelming. But when we got the hang of it, it was great."

The Chiffons' next big hit record is the subject of several variations in biographies regarding the actual production of "One Fine Day." The first states that the Tokens used the backing track of a demo recorded by the song's composer, Carole King, and simply placed the Chiffons' vocals on top of it. Another credited the background vocals to another girl group, the Cookies, with Craig's lead vocals added in. And a third version says that a last-minute change had Craig replace Paterson on lead and actually record over a background track that also included her voice. Craig provided the true story.

"Little Eva actually did the song for Carole and she [King] brought it to us and asked how we liked it," Craig said. "Everybody liked the song and she said if you don't mind we'll go ahead and just use the same musical track so you don't have to go and get musicians and go through the whole thing again. Really it was in Little Eva's key, but I did it even though they didn't bring it down to my key. After I did it, they said, 'Let's try Sylvia doing it,' so Sylvia did it too and they were weighing which one of us they were going to put out. Everybody liked my vocal better, so they put mine out."

But, Craig said, some records that feature Sylvia's lead vocals exist and she has heard it played on the radio. "Sometimes if I am listening to the news in the morning, sometimes they play old songs and stuff," she said. "They played 'One Fine Day' with Sylvia's lead. The single is not really out there but I guess when they asked for 'One Fine Day' from the record company, they just gave them a copy with Sylvia's lead."

Another biographical fact that Craig disputed was one that reported the girls' dismay over their first album cover for the "He's So Fine" LP. The report stated that because the album was put together so quickly, the record company used picture cutouts of each member of the group on its cover.

"It wasn't that it was done that quickly, but that's just the way they wanted to do it," Craig recalled. "To tell you the truth, we didn't know what they were doing. We saw the cover and said, 'Okay, what the heck.'"

While Craig confirmed that the 1963 recordings of "A Love So Fine" and "When the Boy's Happy," credited to the Four Pennies were really the Chiffons singing, she denied reports that claim the group also recorded under the names the Penny Sisters and the Cinnamon Angels.

"We just recorded under the name the Four Pennies," she said. "Sylvia led on all the Four Pennies records and I led on all the Chiffons things. They were trying to get a two-different-group thing going. The Four Pennies never hit and we never performed under that name."

In 1963, the Angels ("My Boyfriend's Back") covered "He's So Fine." Many theories cite that because the group's sound is markedly different on that recording that it was actually the Angels' voices dubbed on top of the Chiffons' original demo of the song. Craig said that she had no knowledge of that having occurred.

As stories are passed down through the years, they seemingly take on an authenticity and credibility that has the most knowledgeable people citing it as fact. Such is the case with the longstanding account that the Chiffons remained busy throughout 1964, touring with the Beatles and the Rolling Stones. In reality, they never even met the bands.

"We never toured with the Beatles or the Rolling Stones, ever," Craig said. Amazingly, within an hour of the interview, the master of ceremony at a concert the Chiffons performed at included the widely accepted fact in his introduction of the group.

While the Chiffons won a lawsuit filed against their production company, Bright Tunes Music, over the use of profits from the group's hit recordings, Craig said that reports that the girls were hard-pressed to secure a recording deal with another label because of the litigation were false. "We never really tried to get a deal with another company," she said.

From 1966 through 1969, the Chiffons recorded for Laurie Records and scored a Top 10 hit single with "Sweet Talkin' Guy." When the group subsequently left the Laurie label, Craig decided to leave the group.

"I was tired of moving around," she said. "They didn't replace me and went on as a trio at that point."

In 1971, the Chiffons were thrust into the spotlight when the estate of Ronald Mack, who had passed away shortly after the release of "He's So Fine," filed a plagiarism lawsuit against Beatles member George Harrison. The suit claimed that Mack's composition "He's So Fine" was infringed upon by Harrison with his song "My Sweet Lord." Craig said that while the group received attention due to their obvious part in the alleged action, no member was involved with the trial. "Ronnie's family was involved with that lawsuit," she said.

Craig rejoined the Chiffons in 1994, after a long absence from the group and the music industry. "When Barbara [Lee] passed away they asked me to come back," she said, "I came back, and then Sylvia and Pat decided that they weren't going to sing any longer, so now I'm singing with my daughter and my niece."

In reflecting on the success that the group had in the 1960s and the ongoing appreciation of their music that exists in the twenty-first century, Craig pondered her proudest accomplishment. "I think I am proud of the fact that people remember the songs that we put out and it brings back good memories for them," she said. "They seem to be very happy when they hear the songs, and I'm proud of that."

Billboard Top 40 Hits by the Chiffons

Date	Pos	Wks on Charts	Record Title	Label/Number
03/09/63	01	12	He's So Fine	Laurie 3152
06/08/63	05	09	One Fine Day	Laurie 3179
10/19/63	40	01	A Love So Fine	Laurie 3195
01/04/64	36	02	I Have a Boyfriend	Laurie 3212
05/28/66	10	07	Sweet Talkin' Guy	Laurie 3340

Joey Dee
(The Starliters)

Patchogue, New York   **March 26, 2005**

Born and raised in Passaic, New Jersey, Dee formed his first group, the Thunder Trio, while in high school. It came in second place on a 1954 television broadcast of *Ted Mack's Amateur Hour.* "My godfather Sam, unbeknownst to me, sent in an application to Ted Mack's show and we got selected to perform," Dee recalled. "We came in second to a seven-year-old little Irish boy who sang 'Danny Boy,' and I had all my relatives call in. I got the entertainment bug after we did that show."

While playing a gig at nearby Garfield High School, Dee met David Brigati, the lead singer of another group the Hi-Fives. Dee sang background vocals on a few songs with Brigati's group and soon the pair joined forces to form the Starliters. "He sounded fantastic and he went on to have a hit record with the Hi-Fives," Dee said. "After they broke up and I needed a lead singer, I went out and got him to join my group."

Dee attended high school with members of the popular girl group the Shirelles, who encouraged him to contact Florence Greenberg of

Scepter Records in the hope of getting a recording contract with the label. The meeting was fruitful. "That had everything to do with our recording future," he said. "Florence Greenberg came from Passaic, and her son Howard was also a student at my school. He went to his mother, along with the Shirelles, and asked her to give us an audition and she did. They signed us to a one-year contract."

The group recorded "Face of an Angel," a song Brigati wrote with Chuck Jackson. While Brigati sang lead on the recording, Dee joined the Shirelles for the track's background vocals.

While biographies state that the Starliters' "1-2-3 kick, 1-2-3 jump" dance routine, one that eventually became known as the Peppermint Twist, was developed in consort with the group's recording of "Shimmy Baby," Dee disputed that fact.

"We did the 'Shimmy Baby' song, which is miles away from the 'Peppermint Twist' sound," Dee said. "When we did the 'Peppermint Twist,' which I wrote with Henry Glover on a Sunday afternoon in the lounge, we came up with the dance at that particular time with original Starliters David Brigati and Larry Vernieri."

Dee recalled his fascination with the new dance craze the Twist. "'The Twist' was a major portion of our stage act, although it wasn't our whole act," he said. "I used to frequent a place called Ben's Cotton Club in Newark, New Jersey, and Hank Ballards' 'The Twist' was on the jukebox. We put it into our show at the Peppermint Lounge and our closing number was the Isley Brothers' 'Shout.' We were a Top 40 band at the time."

During a performance at Oliveri's, a Lodi, New Jersey, nightclub, an agent discovered the group and arranged a weekend engagement for them at a Manhattan club called the Peppermint Lounge. When newspaper columnists Earl Wilson and Cholly Knickerbocker reported that actress Merle Oberon and Prince Serge Oblinski had danced into the wee hours of the morning to the Starliters' captivating sound, the weekend gig turned into a wild and celebrity-filled thirteen-month engagement.

Celebrities that stopped by the Peppermint Lounge during the year included Shirley MacLaine, Judy Garland, Truman Capote, and Ted Kennedy. The lounge became so famous during the Starliters' engagement that the Beatles stopped by during their first tour of the United States in 1964.

"Being from a blue-collar family in New Jersey, it was like catching the brass ring on the merry-go-round or hitting a grand-slam homerun in the World Series," Dee said. "It was special for us. All these people that were idols of mine were actually coming to see Joey Dee and the Starliters, and I was humbled by that."

While offered contracts by both the Capitol and Atlantic Record companies, the Starliters signed with the Roulette label and on December 4, 1961, Joey Dee and the Starliters scored a number-one hit single with "Peppermint Twist—Part 1."

"I spoke to all three record companies and I knew that expediency was of the utmost importance," Dee recalled. "We had to get the record out quickly because the phenomenon was becoming so hot that I figured the first one out was going to have a hit and everybody else would fall by the wayside. Morris Levy from Roulette promised me a release within a week, and true to his word, he had it out."

In 1961, the group recorded "Peppermint Twist," and soon after, the *Doing the Twist at the Peppermint Lounge* album was released. The single quickly rose to number one on the charts.

"It gave us quite a bit of airplay at the time," Dee said. "It seemed like I never walked into a house that someone didn't have a copy of *Doing the Twist at the Peppermint Lounge* live album. We had three Top 10 singles from that album and the mystique about it was that these were live recordings of the 'Peppermint Twist.' 'Mashed Potatoes,' 'Shout,' and 'Ya Ya' were all live, and each one of those songs made the charts."

The group went on to appear in two motion pictures. "Being in the movie *Hey Let's Twist* was a wonderful experience for us," Dee said. "I got to work with Teddy Randazzo, a dear, dear friend of mine and a superstar; unfortunately, gone now. He played my brother in the film and he had experience because he was in all the Alan Freed movies. He was handsome, very talented, and a great songwriter, and he and I got along famously. That experience alone was worth the effort.

"We also did another movie called *Two Tickets to Paris*, and in that movie we needed a love song and Johnny Nash wrote me a song called 'What Kind of Love Is This,' which is my favorite Joey Dee and the Starliters song." Dee attributed the song's even greater success on the charts to Morris Levy's keen ear for a hit recording and subsequently releasing it on his Roulette label as a single.

When the Starliters embarked on a European tour in 1963, a local group was selected as their opening act. That group soon became household names as the Beatles.

"They were great guys," Dee recalled. "We worked with them in Stockholm, Sweden, but I never knew that they were going to be such a success at the magnitude that they became. When I heard them they were just playing reruns of American songs by the Everly Brothers,

Little Richard, and the Isley Brothers. They asked me what I thought of their possibility of making it in the States. I told them that we already had Little Richard and the Everly Brothers there, so their chances were probably nil to none."

Following the release of the group's last charting single, 1963's "Hot Pastrami with Mashed Potatoes—Part 1," Dee recorded eight songs with a trio of girls that had danced with the Starliters at the Peppermint Lounge and later became the Ronettes.

Dee recalled the night that Veronica and Estelle Bennett, and their cousin Nedra Talley, known as the Ronettes, joined the Starliters on stage at the Peppermint Lounge. "The girls were great and they had so much charm and so much energy," he said. "When they came to the Peppermint Lounge they must have been fifteen or sixteen years old and they got up on stage and sang a song with my band. I took them to Wildwood, New Jersey, for their first professional engagement, and while we commuted back and forth to Wildwood during one trip I turned on the Murray the K show on the radio and heard 'Be My Baby.' Unbeknownst to me, Phil Spector had heard of them and he was recording them. I was very happy for them."

In 1964, Dee curtailed recording but continued to tour with various Starliters lineups. One contingent included Felix Cavaliere, Gene Cornish, and David Brigati's younger brother, Eddie. Soon after, the trio was joined by Dino Danelli to form the Young Rascals. Another Starliters lineup included a young guitar player named Jimmy James, who went on to change the face of music in the late 1960s as Jimi Hendrix.

Dee reflected on the Starliters' impact on the music industry and influence on other artists through the years. "I think we were the only act ever to make a nightclub famous and at the same time [make] ourselves famous," he said. "We were a band that motivated the audience and I still think we do that. My goal every time I get on stage is to get the audience involved. So far, so good!"

In 2005, original Starliters Joey Dee and David Brigati were joined by new member Bobby Valli, brother of Four Seasons lead singer Frankie, and perform about one hundred dates each year.

Billboard Top 40 Hits by Joey Dee and the Starliters

Date	Pos	Wks on Charts	Record Title	Label/Number
12/04/61	01	14	Peppermint Twist—Part 1	Roulette 4401
03/03/62	20	04	Hey, Let's Twist	Roulette 4408
03/31/62	06	09	Shout—Part 1	Roulette 4416
09/15/62	18	06	What Kind of Love Is This	Roulette 4438
06/01/63	36	01	Hot Pastrami with Mashed Potatoes—Part 1	Roulette 4488

Cleveland Duncan
(The Penguins)

Waterbury, Connecticut   **March 11, 2005**

The 1954 hit record "Earth Angel" by the Penguins is one of a distinct few songs from that period that has served to define the doo-wop era and has stood the test of time as a classic representation of that style of music.

The Penguins was an aggregation of four students that attended Los Angeles, California's Freemont High School. While Cleveland Duncan was the group's lead vocalist, tenor Curtis Williams served as its leader. The pair was joined by baritone Dexter Tisby and another tenor, Bruce Tate.

Shortly after they formed, the group signed with an independent label, DooTone Records, and planned to release the up-tempo "Hey Sinorita" as it's first single, with "Earth Angel" as its B-side. But when the single was released, Los Angeles radio stations began to receive many requests for "Earth Angel" rather than the intended feature tune. As such, given significant airplay in the area, the B-side became the favorite and by December 1954 the newly formed Penguins had a hit record.

Shortly after "Earth Angel" was released, baritone Randolph Jones replaced Tate, who decided to leave the group. They continued to record for DooTone through 1956 when they shifted to Mercury Records, and shortly after to the Atlantic label.

In 1959, the group disbanded and a brief incarnation in 1963 made up of Duncan, Tisby, and two new vocalists released "Memories of El Monte," a song written for them by future Mothers of Invention members Frank Zappa and Ray Collins. When the record failed to revitalize the group, Duncan returned to fronting various lineups to perform at oldies shows. Tisby joined the Coasters for a brief time.

"My earliest recollection of being attracted to music is when I was a child through gospel choir, glee club, and boy's chorus at Freemont High School," Duncan said. "After I joined with three other Freemont friends to form a vocal group, I picked the name. It came from the 'Willie the Penguin' mascot on the pack of Kool cigarettes."

While "Earth Angel" thrust the newly formed group into the limelight, the composer of the classic song and how the Penguins came to record it has been a matter of debate through the years. Some credit the song to another area vocalist, Jesse Belvin, while others state that Penguins member Curtis Williams wrote the tune. Two other accounts exist, the first claiming that Williams and Belvin co-wrote the song and the second crediting the composition to Gaynell Hodge, member of a doo-wop group called the Turks. In 1956, Hodge won a lawsuit that gave him co-writing credit. Duncan *set the record straight*.

"As far as I'm concerned, Curtis Williams wrote the song," he said. "I had the pleasure of writing the music for the song but Curtis Williams actually wrote it for his wife."

Duncan reflected on how the song, slated to be a flip side, actually became the huge hit that it did. "We thought that 'Hey Sinorita' would have been a likely choice," he said. "But after they turned it over it became history."

The lead singer recalled the first time he heard himself singing the tune on the radio. "I had such a sense of pride and amazement," he said. "I can't explain hearing my own voice on it and I just knew that it would be a hit. We all figured it would be."

After recording for the DooTone label for a couple of years, the Penguins signed with Mercury and then Atlantic Records, where they recorded 'Pledge of Love,' a song that was well received. But despite the attention it received, the group soon disbanded.

"We broke up in 1959," Duncan said. "None of the other members stayed in music. Dexter Curtis left the group for other employment. I always stayed with the group with different lineups. Curtis Williams and Bruce Tate have passed away."

When a fan approached him prior to a performance in Connecticut and requested that he autograph an old 78 RPM recorded by the Penguins, Duncan explained how the variety of distinct color labels used for each song came about. While collectors treasure all things original, many times causing its individual value to rise significantly over reissued material, Duncan's story of how the label variations originated proved to be a much simpler explanation than one might expect.

The record presented to him at the show featured a maroon label, one that Duncan identified as the company's original and standard issue. But as each record sold and the firm's standard color stock was depleted, the company owner simply used whatever was available. "Whenever the original color labels that were printed ran out he just started pressing the records with, in this case, blue labels," Duncan said.

Having worked as a supervisor for an aluminum siding company in California through the years, Duncan continues to lead his latest Penguins lineup to perform at up to two dozen oldies shows nationwide each year. And "Earth Angel," the song that defined the doo-wop era, continues to be played regularly on oldies-format radio stations.

Billboard Top 40 **Hits by the Penguins**

Date	Pos	Wks on Charts	Record Title	Label/Number
12/25/54	08	15	Earth Angel	DooTone 348

Norman Fox
(Norman Fox and the Rob Roys)

Uncasville, Connecticut   **January 15, 2006**

In 1956, three white DeWitt Clinton High School schoolmates, Norman Fox, Robert Thierer, and Marshall "Buzzy" Helfand, joined two black students, Bob Trotman and Andre Lilly, to form a vocal group called the Velvetones. Trotman and Lilly had previously sung with another group called the Harmonaires.

One of the earlier integrated vocal groups of the time, the Bronx teenagers honed their unique blend of harmonies and were influenced by popular groups such as the Heartbeats, the Cleftones, the Teenagers, and the Harptones, all New York contingents. Fox became attracted to music while listening to popular 1940s artists but soon joined other youngsters in embracing the new style known as rock-and-roll.

"When I was a kid my uncle used to listen to Bing Crosby and Frank Sinatra and those guys on his car radio, and he'd drive us around," Fox said. "That was my earliest introduction to music. After that, in terms of my own personal taste, it was when Alan Freed came on the air in the mid-1950s with the *Moondog Show* and I was just bowled over by that."

The Velvetones became serious about their potential to elevate themselves in the music industry. "I guess we were entrepreneurial types of kids and we were imitating all these groups like the Cleftones and the Cadillacs," he said. "Through the nature of a process of elimination, we were able to come up with the voices over a period of time that blended together and were able to take it to a group level where we could sing together."

In early 1957, the group was auditioned by Don Carter at Buddy's Record Store in the Bronx. Carter was the New York agent for Duke/Peacock Records, and after meeting and auditioning the new group he signed them to a recording contract with the label, which was based in Texas and primarily produced gospel music.

"Bob Trotman knew the owner of a record store at 145th Street and Third Avenue, whose name was Buddy Dunk," Fox recalled. "He held auditions in his record shop and he introduced us to Don Carter, who was there. We did the audition there in the store and he liked what we sounded like and picked us up."

Around the same time the Velvetones entered the studio to record their first single, they changed the group name. "Don Carter didn't like the name the Velvetones so Buzzy Helfand and I came up with the Rob Roys," he said. "It was a drink, and we were kids and it was sophisticated sounding."

In April 1957, the Rob Roys went to Bell Sound Studios to record their first single, "Tell Me Why," on Peacock's affiliate, Backbeat. An original tune penned by Helfand, who provided strong bass background on the record, the writer's credit was listed on the label as Helford-Carter. Released during the summer of 1957, "Tell Me Why" received significant airplay in New York and Philadelphia, but lackluster promotion by the label hindered any chance for national attention.

"They didn't promote it at all," Fox said. "I had a relationship with Alan Freed, who happened to be a neighbor of mine. I didn't know at the very beginning that he lived in my building. He gave us a certain amount of spins but there was no promotion of the record, which is why it didn't take off nationally."

Fox explained why the writer's credit on the "Tell Me Why" record label cited Helford-Carter as the tune's composers, rather than Helfand, who in fact wrote the song alone. "Carter put his name on a lot of things because that is what happened in those days," Fox said. "Buzzy wrote the song 'Tell Me Why' and I wrote the middle part of it, but because the name of the group was Norman Fox and the Rob Roys I gave them credit for it. We were only kids, and who cared about or even knew anything about a contractual thing?"

When "Tell Me Why" started to get good airplay in New York, the group began to perform, primarily at black venues in Harlem. Fox recalled the experience. "It was an interesting situation because we did play a lot of black venues at the time," he said. "[New York City disc jockey] Jocko gave us a lot of airplay and his audience was primarily a black audience. We also did the Audubon Ballroom in Harlem a couple of weeks before Malcolm X was shot there."

Other early integrated groups like the Del-Vikings and the Crests have commented through the years on how the makeup of their respective group somewhat limited the exposure and promotion they received on a nationwide scale due to the politics of that period. Some cited limited television exposure, while others recounted inferior treatment regarding promotion in specific locations throughout the country. Fox said that it was difficult to determine how that might have affected his group.

"I don't know really," he said. "We were so naïve and really didn't have a handle on the workings of the business. We didn't have managerial people who could handle us and show us the way around. We were basically out there on our own."

The Rob Roys' follow-up single, the Thierer/Trotman composition "Dance Girl Dance," further spotlighted Fox's ability to sing lead, but the record suffered the same fate as the group's earlier effort. Quite simply, the label was ill-prepared to market the tune and it soon faded into obscurity. Frustrated over the lost attempts, the Rob Roys ventured to the offices of Capitol Records in late 1958, armed with two original Fox compositions, "Pizza Pie" and "Dream Girl."

"Backbeat didn't promote our records and we didn't get any royalties, so we decided to go elsewhere," Fox said. "It was actually a mutual thing because Capitol also approached us and it would have been great if it worked out."

When Capitol recorded and released "Dream Girl" and "Pizza Pie," executives from their former label, Backbeat, produced an existing contract with the Rob Roys, which prompted Capitol to halt the single's distribution and promotion. "We thought we were released from Backbeat," Fox said. "At that point we had gotten an agent and he told us to go ahead and sign with Capitol. We were kids and didn't know anything about the legalities and signed with Capitol, not realizing that we were still bound to Backbeat. Capitol wouldn't fight it and they just dropped it."

Fearing that Backbeat's action would all but destroy future efforts for them, the Rob Roys agreed to record five original songs for the label, with the stipulation that upon completing them they would be released from their contract. While the decision had the ability to benefit the group as well as both record labels involved, when the five Fox originals were laid down for Backbeat, they were never released. Ironically, Capitol never issued "Pizza Pie."

"I believe that Backbeat probably didn't have the funds to release and promote anything because they had the Casuals ['So Tough'] after us, but I don't know that they had any other groups on their label," Fox said. "As for Capitol's decision to not release 'Pizza Pie,' they were a big company and didn't want to get involved with any kind of lawsuit. They were interested in Frank Sinatra."

In 1962, the Rob Roys moved to the Time label and recorded "Aggravation" and "Lonely Boy." But, similar to their past experience, the records were never released. "I think that the owner of Time Records ran out of money and couldn't do anything with the single," Fox said.

The group disbanded a year later, but when New York City disc jockey Gus Gossert invited them to reunite in 1971 for a rock-and-roll revival show at the Beacon Theater, the group joined for a one-time performance.

"Gus was great and he brought it back," Fox recalled. "I was involved in business at that time and I thought it was a joke and didn't take it seriously. I should have taken it more seriously because Gus oversaw all of this type of revival thing. We did the show and enjoyed it very much."

In 1986, at the urging of Thierer, Fox helped to form a new lineup of Rob Roys, one that in 2006 continues to perform at oldies shows. "I was getting to a point in my life where I was getting nostalgic about the music and the people who I ran into were fans of mine and loved the music," Fox said. "I thought it might be fun and I tried it a few times and absolutely loved it.

"I am most proud that we came back to start to build a repertoire with the people that I am close to in this group that we have today," he added. "We went from having a couple of songs to being entertainers and we are still striving, and that makes me proud. And, as far as I'm concerned, it's only the beginning."

Original members Norman Fox and Robert Thierer, second
and third from left, reformed the Rob Roys in 1986.

Joe Frazier
(The Impalas)

In 1959 three young aspiring singers, Tony Carlucci, Richard Wagner, and Lenny Renda, formed a street-corner vocal group in Brooklyn, New York. The group practiced every chance it could and on one occasion a young man, Joe Frazier, happened to hear them sing and offered to assist them with their harmonies.

"My mother always told me that I sang all the time as a child," Frazier said. "I guess my first exposure was at talent shows in school when I was six years old."

But music nearly gave way to another career, as Frazier once attended Cathedral College, having aspirations of joining the priesthood. "I thought I had the calling to become a priest," he said. "Then I met a girl and the rest is history.

"Tony, Richard, Lenny, and I all lived in the Canarsie section of Brooklyn when we were young," he recalled. "I was actually in another group, the Dreamtones, and we were doing a lot of rhythm and blues stuff. I used to come home at night and those three guys were trying to get it together on the corner, and they weren't quite connecting. One night I stopped and told them that I'd help them get their notes straightened out and get some decent harmony. I started working with them and they started sounding good."

Frazier explained how he came to use the name 'Speedo,' which he described as a "left-handed compliment to Earl 'Speedo' Carroll" of the famous vocal group the Cadillacs. "At the time people I knew said that there were certain things about me that reminded them of him," Frazier said. "He's a heck of a nice guy but believe me we are two entirely different individuals. They must have seen something and they tagged me with the name, although I was a pretty fast runner."

Eventually assuming the lead tenor role from Carlucci, Frazier was quick to dispute many documented accounts that cite the group's first recording as being the Hamilton Records single "First Date." According to Frazier, their actual entry into studio work was the song that thrust them into the limelight, "Sorry, I Ran All the Way Home."

"Number one, I've seen that fact written [about the Hamilton recording] and I don't have the faintest idea how the story started," Frazier said. "I was never on that record. When I saw that fact, I often asked myself who those guys were. I do remember that later on, years after 'Sorry' was out, there was another group made up of guys who were in the Canarsie section of Brooklyn. They put a group together and called themselves the Impalas and they worked for quite a while as the 'Sorry, I Ran All the Way Home' Impalas. They also did a couple of other recordings, which went nowhere." That group might in fact be the one heard on the recording of "First Date."

Frazier said that he never took legal action against the fake group simply because it just played itself out. But one radio appearance that the false Impalas' lineup made motivated Frazier to attempt to set the facts straight. "By the time this started I had actually gotten out of that type of music and I moved on to soul and rhythm and blues, with a different type of band and going in a different direction, and it didn't bother me," he said. "But then one night I was riding home from a rehearsal or a gig, and I was listening to [New York disc jockey] Norm N. Nite on the radio and he had the Impalas on as guests. I turned up the volume. When Nite asked the group whatever happened to Joe 'Speedo' Frazier, they said that 'he retired and doesn't sing anymore.' I said, 'Oh, really!' That kind of hit a nerve and I called Norm N. Nite and told him what the real story was."

Soon after, Nite had Frazier on his show as a guest and he refuted the entire group and the story that they told on the earlier broadcast.

"It didn't bother me until they said that on the air," he said. "I knew they were performing as the Impalas, but since I wasn't doing it I just said, 'Okay, no problem.' But when they said that, they went too far."

Just prior to recording "Sorry," the group worked to find a unique name that would make them stand apart from other vocal groups. But a widely accepted story on how the group name originated served as one more sore point of bad information for Frazier and the group's history. "The way we came up with the name Impalas is another myth I have to explain now," Frazier said. "The Impalas were not named after the car. Richard Wagner, our second tenor, actually came up with the name, and while we were looking at cars, we saw the animal named the Impala and thought it was beautiful. We thought, 'Okay, we'll be the Impalas.'"

One night, while rehearsing on a Brooklyn Street corner, two men approached the Impalas and asked if they would be interested in recording a new song that they wrote, one called "Sorry, I Ran All the Way Home." The composers were Artie Zwirm and Aristides (Gino) Giosasi, the latter of the two having already gained some success in the music industry as half of Gino and Gina, a duo that scored a Top 20 hit single with "Pretty Baby" in 1958. After visiting with the pair, the Impalas set out to record the tune.

Frazier recalled how a meeting with Alan Freed shortly after agreeing to record the Zwirn/Giosasi song resulted in the group's contract with the Cub label. "We met Freed through his personal representative named Jack Cook," he said. "We had recorded a demo of 'Sorry,' got it to him, and he played it for Alan Freed, who liked it. We had a meeting with him, he took it to MGM, and they decided to release it."

When Frazier experienced a miscue during the recording session for "Sorry," it turned into an unmistakable trademark for the song through the years. "We were recording the song and in those days everything, including the band, was done live," he said. "We sang, 'Sorry, sorry, oh so sorry,' and the conductor cued me and I missed it. I said, 'Uh ooh.' Morty Craft, who was the A&R man and sitting in the booth, said, 'You know something, let's take it again and this time leave 'uh ooh' in there. And that's how the 'uh ooh' was born."

Once released, the record climbed on both the pop and rhythm and blues charts, and in the summer of 1959, it became a Top 40 hit in England. Off the success of the single, life for Frazier and the other members of the group changed quickly as demands for appearances skyrocketed. "It got to a point where it wasn't just an occasional record hop or other appearance," he said. "We went out on the road and for about six months we were as busy as could be."

Frazier praised Freed for always being upfront and honest with the group and has fond memories of playing two of the disc jockey's famous shows at the Brooklyn Fox Theater. "When we played the Brooklyn Fox, that was really our first professional gig," he said. "We were happy to be there and scared to go on stage at the same time."

Following the success of their first hit, the group was enthusiastic about their follow-up recording, another Zwirn/Giosasi tune, entitled "Oh What a Fool." But when Cub received advanced orders for the record in excess of one hundred thousand copies, it mistakenly decided that a full-blown promotional effort wasn't necessary and gave the release minimal attention. The record stalled at number eighty-six on the charts as a result of the ill-fated decision.

"It was a lot of the overconfident thing and also it might have had something to do with the fact that it was just around the time they were trying to get Alan Freed," he recalled. "We were in Chicago at the time and received a telegram that said, 'Congratulations, you've got another hit with a hundred thousand advance sales.' It got on the charts and all of a sudden everything with MGM went dead. They had a station in New York, WMGM, and they didn't even play it. We never knew why but they just wouldn't play it."

The group went on to record two more singles and one album for Cub, titled after their only hit, and then moved to 20th Century Records, where a sole record failed to gain attention or airplay. Following the failed attempts to chart with another record, the Impalas began to splinter and the last recording made by the group, a cover of the Rogers and Hammerstein classic "There's Nothing Like a Dame," found Frazier as the only original member in the lineup. "At that point, maybe it was burnout but I wasn't into music, and I knew I wasn't putting my all into it, so I just stopped until sometime in 1969 or 1970. I just went to work and completely got away from music."

In 1973, Frazier formed a soul and rhythm and blues group named Love's Own. The group was made up of Frazier and two female vocalists, and following some studio work and a promise for a single's release in Europe, a snag encountered by one of the members caused the group to miss its overseas engagements.

"We were ready to leave for Europe and one of the girls screwed up [her] passport and we could not get into the country," Frazier recalled. "That was the end of that." The group missed their bookings and disbanded.

Following the breakup of Love's Own, Frazier remained in music, reforming the Impalas after a stint with another Brooklyn vocal group, Vito and the Salutations.

"I knew the guys in the Salutations, and one night they were short and I went on the stage and helped out," he said. "All of a sudden, for a while I was actually part of Vito and the Salutations. I guess technically you could almost say that I was Vito because I used to sing 'Gloria' [in absence of Vito Balsamo, who had left the group by that time]. Eddie Pardocchi was in that group, and that's how he eventually became a real Impala." Pardocchi had been one of the members of the Impala lineup that appeared on the earlier Norm N. Nite radio show, one that upset Frazier and motivated him to inform Nite's audience that he was still actively performing.

Of the many shows and venues that the Impalas have performed at throughout the years, Frazier is split on a particular favorite. "For the original Impalas the show that stands out the most is one we did in Flint, Michigan," he said. "We played a theater that had a sound system that, from what I understand, was one of the first stereophonic systems ever. When we heard ourselves back from the monitors it blew our minds. I never heard a sound like that coming out of the speakers. Other than that, a few years back we played the Palm Palm Revue in Atlantic City, New Jersey, and we were part of a variety show. We represented the music of the 1950s. It was very nice."

While the Impalas recorded alongside other Cub label acts such as the Five Satins, the Harptones, the Velours, and the Wanderers, Frazier's own preference toward musical style centered on older groups. "At the time I liked the Dells and the Flamingos, but my own personal taste was for groups like the Mills Brothers, Ink Spots, Ravens, and I loved the Hi-Lo's."

While he will forever be known for singing lead on "Sorry," Frazier listed other songs that serve as a sense of personal pride for him and his career in music. "When I was with the original Impalas, we recorded a song called 'Goodbye Everybody,' which I thought was very good," he said. "The last recording we did was 'I'm On My Way,' which I liked. There were also some songs on the Impalas album that could have been good except for the way MGM recorded it in the space of about four days at three and four o'clock in the morning. I had no voice. When I hear them today I get sick listening to it. There is no way that you could release something like that today."

Despite health issues in recent years, Joe 'Speedo' Frazier continues to front an Impalas lineup that thrills audiences and prompts them to join him in singing the famous opening of "Sorry." During a 2005 concert appearance in Connecticut, the sold-out arena beat Frazier to the punch by singing out 'uh ooh' in unison before he could get the words out of his mouth.

Billboard Top 40 Hits by the Impalas

Date	Pos	Wks on Charts	Record Title	Label/Number
04/13/59	02	11	Sorry (I Ran All the Way Home)	Cub 9022

Harvey Fuqua
(The Moonglows)

Waterbury, Connecticut   **March 11, 2005**

During the course of interviewing many recording artists for inclusion in this book, the two primary vocal groups that were cited as having influenced most of them are the Flamingos and the Moonglows. The latter of the two groups, though only in existence for six years, left a legacy that in many ways can serve to define the pioneering period of a musical sound that would evolve into rock-and-roll and rhythm and blues.

Born into a family that included an uncle that was the guitarist for the renowned Ink Spots, Harvey Fuqua showed both talent and an early desire to carve out a career in the music industry. "I always wanted to be in show business," Fuqua said. "When I was in the fourth grade the teacher had a group sing-a-long every morning with a song named 'Old Dog Tray.' One morning while we were singing, she cut us off in the middle and told us to go back through it and do it again. I just wasn't paying attention when she cut everybody off and I just had my head back singing away. Suddenly I realized that everyone had stopped singing and she told me I should've been paying attention. I was made to sit in the corner with a dunce cap on. I was so embarrassed." That, Fuqua said, was the first recollection he has of wanting to sing in public.

Moving from Chicago to Louisville, Kentucky, Fuqua learned to play piano and with Bobby Lester, a high school friend, began to perform at local dances. "There was a talent show in Louisville and we would always try to get on every show we could find," he said. "I wrote a song and Bobby would always sing it. I would play the piano and he was good at improvising; we made a great team. We won the contest and the local paper came in to take pictures. Well, I was sitting at the piano and Bobby was grandstanding for the camera. Anyway, that's how we started out."

Following both their military obligations, the duo joined bandleader Ed Wiley, where they were exposed to singing jump and blues. But with low earning potential, the pair soon split and Fugua relocated to Cleveland, Ohio.

With music still very much a part of his life, Fuqua formed a trio that consisted of an army buddy, Danny Coggins, and a neighbor who sang gospel music, Prentiss Barnes. Eventually, Lester was recruited into the group. Called the Crazy Sounds, they were known for what was then termed vocalese, or the art of using their voices to mimic the sound of instruments. "Actually it became known later on as scatting," Fuqua said.

In 1952 they came to the attention of a Cleveland disc jockey who soon would play a major part in changing the face of music. His name was Alan Freed, and upon auditioning the vocal group he was so taken with their harmonies that he renamed them the Moonglows, recorded them on his own Champagne Records label, and assumed management of the group.

"We were singing in a club and unbeknownst to us a friend of ours called Alan Freed when he was on the air," Fuqua recalled. "He came backstage afterward and told us that Alan Freed wanted to see us and suggested we go the following night. We went down to the studio and sang two songs for him and he said, 'I'm going to record you guys on my label.' He asked us what our name was, and when we told him the Crazy Sounds he said, 'Nah, can't have Crazy Sounds.' We threw a few names around and he said, 'My nickname is Moondog. How about the Moonshines?' Well, we were definitely not going to be called the Moonshines. Well, he thought a little and finally suggested the Moonglows. I said, 'Yeah, that's it.'"

After recording a couple of sides for Freed, including a Lester original named "I Just Can't Tell No Lie," the group landed a deal with Chance Records, a label that already touted among its acts the Flamingos and the Spaniels. But in October 1954, after recording numerous ballads and a few jump tunes for the label with little luck, the Moonglows moved to Chess Records.

"When we first got to Chicago we met a guy named Hubert Abner from Chance Records," Fuqua said. "We did eight sides for them including a Doris Day thing, 'Secret Love,' and they put them out." When the records didn't receive much attention Fuqua became disenchanted with the label.

"I went around the corner from Chance's offices to meet with Phil Chess of Chess Records," Fuqua said. "Phil was at the recording session the Moonglows did for Alan Freed. Phil wasn't there at the time but his brother Leonard was," he added. "Phil had told him about our session with Alan Freed and he asked to see what we had. We pulled out all the stops and whatever we had we started singing, and he said he liked it."

But with the Moonglows already signed to Chance Records, Leonard Chess was concerned about moving forward with the group. "I told him that if he gave Chance Records five hundred dollars they'd let us out of our contract," Fuqua said. "He gave us five hundred dollars and we went back around to Chance and they gave us a release. A couple of days later we rehearsed with the band at Chess and laid down thirteen songs. We did it all on one track too. Everyone would stand around the mike, and if you were too loud they'd tell you to come out a little bit and sing a little softer.

"We had a lot of songs by that time," Fuqua said. "We recorded only two of them for Alan Freed's label and they became fairly popular regionally. Alan was giving shows twice a month in places like Akron and Toledo, and so we were appearing on those. All of a sudden he got this big job in New York and said, 'Well guys, I'll see you later.'"

One song among the thirteen sides recorded for Chess was a Fuqua composition (regardless of the fact that the record's label credits it as having been co-written with Freed) titled "Sincerely." It became one of the label's biggest-selling records. Charting in December 1954, it knocked the Penguins' "Earth Angel" out of the number-one slot on the R&B charts one month after its release. It eventually would score a number twenty pop chart hit and sell more than two hundred and fifty thousand copies.

"Sincerely" was so well received that the Moonglows became one of the earliest rhythm and blues acts to have its record covered by pop artists. When the white female vocal group the McGuire Sisters recorded and released the song, it climbed the pop charts to its number-one slot and sold more than a million records. Fuqua considered the song's crossover success flattering.

"That was great," he said. "In the beginning everyone was yelling that they covered my song and thought I was upset about it. I said, not me, I wrote it. Their success with the song did well for me with royalties."

With Freed behind the breakout recording group, the Moonglows began to perform at many of the disc jockey's high-profile and multitalented package shows throughout the country. While they never achieved another pop-crossover hit song like "Sincerely," the group produced some memorable recordings such as "Most of All," "Foolish Me," "Starlite," and "In My Diary." Around 1956, the Chess label began to issue singles by both the Moonglows and the Moonlighters, the latter being primarily sides cut by Fuqua and Lester. And both lineups performed at various shows together. Fuqua explained the label's theory.

"As the Moonlighters, they released 'So All Alone,' which was a big record, and another song, 'Sho Be Do Be Do,' which sounded a little like the part in 'Life Could Be a Dream' [by the Diamonds]," he said. "As far as performing together, we always did that because we were booked as the Moonlighters and the Moonglows. Bobby and I would come out and do two songs and then go back, and later on the four of us would come out and perform as the Moonglows."

The Moonglows made appearances in two Freed-produced full-length motion pictures, *Rock, Rock, Rock* and *Mr. Rock and Roll*, appearing with an array of popular acts of the day, including Chuck Berry, the Flamingos, and Frankie Lymon and the Teenagers. The experience was recalled fondly by Fuqua. "It was fabulous," he said. "Actually, *Mr. Rock and Roll* is the one I liked the best. We did a Mexican/Caribbean song and we wore big sombreros and danced, and that was my favorite of all of them. Of course, the one that I did alone was nice too. But it was great appearing with all those acts because we all knew each other."

The exposure that the group received from a combination of the package concert shows and film appearances should have been enough to give it star status, but internal strife, primarily between Fuqua and Lester, caused the Moonglows to splinter by 1957.

Despite that fact, "The Ten Commandments of Love" was released in 1958 and featured Fuqua in its spoken verse. The record climbed to number nine on the rhythm and blues chart and number twenty-two on the pop chart. But rather than being credited as the Moonglows, the label read Harvey and the Moonglows. A matter of much debate among recording buffs for years after its release surrounded who actually provided the background vocals on that recording.

While some accounts credit the vocals to a group named the Marquees that featured a young Marvin Gaye, other reports state that the vocals were actually provided by the same Moonglows lineup that is featured on sides recorded before the group's breakup in 1957. Fuqua offered to set the record straight.

"It was actually the Moonglows that sang on that recording," Fuqua confirmed.

Fuqua continued to work with Harvey and the Moonglows as well as doing solo projects under his full name, and appeared in Freed's final rock-and-roll screen offering *Go Johnny Go*. As time passed, his ambition focused more on the creative side of the music industry rather than his performing role. He soon joined Motown as executive-in-charge of new talent development and also became more involved with songwriting and producing. His influence at Motown can be attributed to many of the label's shining stars in both vocal arrangements and stage presence.

Fuqua's career as a songwriter and label operator, and his work as an executive at Motown Records, is best documented in a series of connect-the-dots scenarios.

While recording and performing with the Moonglows, Fuqua also sang some duets on the Kent label with his then-girlfriend Etta James. Around 1960, he helped James secure a contract at the Argo label, a subsidiary of Chess.

During the same period that the Moonglows were hitting it big at Chess, a Detroit songwriter, Billy Davis, also worked at the label and in 1956 produced two sessions for a local quartet, the Four Tops. The songs did little for the group and Davis went on to collaborate with another Detroit music aspirant, one Berry Gordy. Together the pair scored with hit singles by Jackie Wilson, LaVern Baker, and Etta James with each of the records released on various labels. Gordy's sister, Gwen, co-wrote some of the songs and was in fact engaged to Davis at the time.

Together with her sister Anna, Gwen ran a photo stand at one of Detroit's most prestigious black nightclubs, the Flame Showbar. Ambitious and in the company of many music industry types at the club, Gwen soon borrowed fifteen thousand dollars from Leonard

Chess and formed Anna Records with Davis as a partner. But fate has a way of changing things.

Fuqua and a young baritone from Washington, D.C., named Marvin Gaye, who sang with the last lineup of Moonglows before the group formally disbanded, came to meet Gwen and Anna Gordy and began dating them. Fuqua had established the Tri-Phi label and signed area talent such as the Spinners and Junior Walker and the All Stars. Eventually Fuqua and Gaye married the Gordy sisters. Subsequently, having turned down his sister's offer to join her Anna label, Berry Gordy borrowed eight hundred dollars from his parents and formed Talma Records, touting among his earliest talent the Miracles. It became apparent rather quickly that Berry Gordy's business interests were the most solid of the family's multiple music interests.

Acquiring both the Tri-Phi and Anna labels along with some other local labels, Berry Gordy consolidated them into one company, named Motown. Fuqua would join the new label as a promoter and later executive in charge of talent development.

"After we [the Moonglows] disbanded I kept Marvin because he was so talented," Fuqua recalled. "We both moved to Detroit and I went to work for Anna Records, which was a subsidiary of Chess. I was actually doing A&R work for Chess after the Moonglows broke up, and so they told me to go to Anna and watch out for everything and give them all the help they needed. I had already met Berry and his sister way before that because we wrote a few songs together like 'Don't Be Afraid to Love' and 'See Saw.' When Marvin and I got there, he fell in love with Berry's sister, Anna. So there wasn't anything for me to do but fall in love with the other one, so that's what I did. He got married first and then we got married."

While many accounts of Fuqua's work at his Tri-Phi label specifically cite him as having actually sung on recordings made by the first group that he signed, the Spinners, he disputed the claim. "They say that it's me but it's not," he said. "He [lead singer Bobbie Smith] just interpreted what I was teaching him word for word and he emphasizes the same places that I did, which was fine. And that's why everybody said that it was me singing. But it wasn't."

Fuqua said that record distributors in those days were slow in making payouts and it was important to have two or three hit records in a row to maintain an operating cash flow. Tri-Phi never had that level of success with charting singles, but Gordy's label did, which lead to an offer that called for Gordy to assume the Tri-Phi label in return for stock options and a position doing promotion for his record company. Fuqua initially wasn't keen on the offer.

"I didn't want to work for nobody," he said. "I didn't care if he was my brother-in-law or not, except my wife sort of talked me into it and I finally said okay. I went over as a promotions person because I knew all the disc jockeys and I'd go around and distribute the records and talk to them. And I'd take the acts out on the road."

The first act Fuqua took on the road was the up-and-coming female trio the Supremes. "I remember sitting in the station wagon with them and taking the records around, with Gwen along with us," he said. "We had a great time, but eventually I told them (Motown) that what their acts needed was some tutoring, some development. My acts, like the Spinners, were always put on as openers because we didn't have a hit record, compared to others on the bill like Stevie Wonder and the Temptations. Well, we opened and we killed them because we rehearsed and rehearsed and rehearsed ten and twelve hours a day for about six months. We had skits, and show presence, and we use to kill the other acts."

When Gordy agreed, Fuqua traveled to New York to see Cholly Atkins, Maurice King, and Maxine Powell, a team that, with Fuqua, would be responsible for developing a professional, slick, and polished stage presence for Motown acts from that time forward.

"Maxine Powell was there for the girls," he said. "She'd teach them how to walk, how to talk, how to do makeup. Maurice King, an arranger, taught them harmony along with me. And Cholly did the choreography. We would work with them four hours at a time and the groups loved it because they wanted to be wonderful. We did that sometimes seven days a week. When we worked with the Supremes, we worked longer than four hours because we were grooming them for the Copacabana, and we succeed in that. They were the first group for us to go pop."

Marvin Gaye would soon follow the Supremes in that status, before a bevy of the label's acts did likewise, including the Four Tops, Martha Reeves and the Vandellas, and Stevie Wonder.

Fuqua has enjoyed an exceptional career in music as a performer, songwriter, producer, promoter, record company executive, and a talent development coordinator. In addition to his smash hit composition "Sincerely," he cited his 1956 ballad "We Go Together" as his favorite song. Appropriately, when his wife Gwen joins him on stage during recent occasional appearances, they perform that song together.

Billboard Top 40 Hits by the Moonglows

Date	Pos	Wks on Charts	Record Title	Label/Number
03/26/55	20	01	Sincerely	Chess 1581
10/13/56	25	01	See Saw	Chess 1629
10/20/58	22	04	Ten Commandments of Love (Harvey and the Moonglows)	Chess 1705

Carl Gardner
(The Coasters)

Port-St.-Lucie, Florida   **April 21, 2005**

I f ever a vocal group earned the status of being called "legendary," then certainly the Coasters are among that distinct class. One of the first groups to augment its musical performance with a carefully orchestrated comedic stage act, the Coasters became one of the most popular acts of the late 1950s due to a number of factors.

First, the group benefited by having recorded a series of incredibly well-written songs composed by the successful writing team of Jerry Leiber and Mike Stoller. Second, their well-rehearsed and polished stage act complemented the lyrics of their songs to a T and provided their audience with a visual entertainment that up to that time had not been experienced. And the sheer talent and musical ability of each member in the group proved to be a winning combination.

The Coasters were an off-shoot of a popular Los Angeles, California, vocal group the Robins, which began recording in 1949 and developed an association with Leiber and Stoller in 1953. "Around 1952, I left Texas for California to start my career in music, but not with a group,"

Gardner said. "I was into the Johnny Mathis-type stuff; that's the kind of music I really wanted to do. I met Jerry Leiber and Mike Stoller and had a chance to sing with the Robins and decided to do it. Grady Chapman had to leave the group and they had no lead singer and asked me to replace him. We practiced and they liked it. I sang with them, but without any money."

In 1955 the talented writing duo presented the Robins with a new composition, "Smokey Joe's Café." After recording and releasing the single, it was apparent rather quickly that it had become too successful for Leiber and Stoller's small Spark record label to properly promote and distribute it. Atlantic Records cut a deal with the pair to assume the record's distribution, along with the Robins's future.

In return, Leiber and Stoller secured an independent contract as producers and composers with the major record label. Shorty after, with some members of the Robins, somewhat unsettled over the new arrangement the group, disbanded. Its lead tenor, Carl Gardner, and bass Bobby Nunn formed a new group, the Coasters, and added baritone Billy Guy and second tenor Leon Hughes to the lineup.

According to Gardner, a certain contingent of the Robins remained intact but saw little success in subsequent years. It was Gardner who selected the name for the group that he and Nunn formed.

"I always wanted to go from the West Coast to the East Coast," Gardner said. "I thought about that and came up with the name Coasters for the group."

Backed with the powerhouse compositions of Leiber and Stoller, the Coasters recorded "Down in Mexico" and its B-side, "One Kiss Led to Another," in 1956. While both sides hit the charts, "Down in Mexico" reaching number eight on the rhythm and blues charts, Gardner said that he was somewhat distressed at not being able to record the style of music that he preferred at the time.

"I was very mad because I wasn't doing the songs I wanted to do," he said. "I loved Billy Ekstine and Nat Cole and never got a chance to do that kind of material."

While busy launching their own career, the Coasters provided background vocals on another 1956 Top 20 hit record, LaVern Baker's "Jim Dandy." Gardner explained how the Coasters came to provide the vocals on Baker's recording.

"We were in the studio in Los Angeles and LaVern Baker had a session scheduled that day," Gardner recalled. "They needed background vocals and the only ones around were the Coasters. Leiber and Stoller asked us to sing on the record."

In May 1957 the Coasters scored a double-sided single with "Searchin'" and "Young Blood." But later that year when follow-up singles failed to match their debut's success, a decision was made for Leiber and Stoller, along with the Coasters, to relocate to New York, where Atlantic Records was based. Hesitant to do so, Nunn and Hughes left the group and were replaced by bass Will "Dub" Jones and second tenor Obie Jessie. However, Cornell Gunter stepped in to replace Jessie after a brief period.

Nunn and Hughes decided to leave the Coasters as the group was preparing to leave for a performance in Hawaii. The group's manager quickly located two replacements for the pair, but time constraints prevented them from rehearsing with the group prior to taking the stage. The results, however, and the impact of the two new voices in the group enhanced its sound, Gardner said.

"It made it a little better," Gardner recalled. "We were on our way to Hawaii and our manager, Lester Field, asked Cornell and Dub to join us for the performance. When we were short singers he'd just go find them. He told me that they were both good singers and I said, 'Okay, but we're going on without any rehearsals.' We met them in California, flew straight out to Hawaii and did a show, and it came out very good."

The first recordings made with the new lineup were "Yakety Yak" and "Zing Went the Strings of My Heart." While "Yakety Yak" became the Coasters' first number-one hit record, the latter tune was a distinct departure from their quickly established and recognizable sound.

"Leiber and Stoller knew that I always loved pop music and they selected 'Zing' for us to record," Gardner said. "But Cornell Gunter sang the high part on that record, not me."

"Charlie Brown," the Coasters' next recording turned out to be their biggest hit single in England. "I remember traveling to England to support the song over there and we couldn't say the words 'spit ball' in the song," he recalled. "They didn't allow that. They came up with some replacement lyrics for us to sing but it wasn't 'spit ball.' It was a very well done record, though."

The Coasters followed with other hits including "Along Came Jones," "Poison Ivy," and "Little Egypt." Shortly after the success of the latter song, Gunter left the group and was replaced by Earl "Speedo" Carroll, the former lead singer of the Cadillacs, who remained with the Coasters for two decades.

Gardner reflected on the period following Gunter's departure from the Coasters, and the effect that Carroll's addition had on the group. Interestingly enough, the Cadillacs were perhaps the closest vocal group to the Coasters with regard to a stage presence that was both energetic and entertaining.

"Our stage act was powerful," Gardner said. "When we performed at the Apollo, sometimes with people like Ray Charles, after we entertained nobody could come on for fifteen minutes. When Earl Carroll joined us he became part of the act. We had one scene where a guy got shot for messing with somebody's woman. While we sang the song, we acted the scene out and I ended up shooting Earl Carroll in the butt. That used to be Will Jones's part. It was so funny and the audience loved it."

The Coasters charted one last song in 1971 with a cover of "Love Potion No. 9," but by that time Gardner was the sole remaining original member of the group.

After recording "Along Came Jones" and "Poison Ivy," the Coasters recorded "What About Us," a song that was a serious social statement, reflecting the mood and somewhat turbulent atmosphere of the 1960s.

"Leiber and Stoller were such good writers," Gardner said. "They would sing it to me first and give me the right to take a song or turn it down. When I heard 'What About Us' I just liked it, so we recorded it. There was another song they wrote, 'I Ain't Here,' that I thought was too racial and I told them that they wouldn't get me to sing a song like that. When we turned it down they gave it to Peggy Lee."

A documented fact about Gardner's reported departure from the Coasters during one of its tours, to be replaced by a young Lou Rawls, was soundly rejected as yet another myth that has flourished through the years.

"I never in my life left the Coasters," Gardner said. "I went on vacation one time. I knew Lou Rawls from hanging out at the Theresa Hotel near the Apollo Theater in Harlem. I told Lou that I was tired and needed to get home for a little vacation and I asked him if he'd take my place and he said, 'Sure.' He went to Boston and some other places with the group. But I didn't take more than a week, and met them back in New York and took my job back."

The Coasters, for all their success, have been the subject of one of the most complicated and intertwined internal legal situations in the history of the music industry. In 1960, Gunter formed his own lineup of the Coasters. Nunn did likewise and Jones and Billy Guy formed another. Gardner, who to this day is the sole legal owner of the group's copyrighted name, has continued to perform with his Coasters lineup. The legalities, if not the sheer confusion of audiences that have experienced a number of different lineups appearing as the original

Coasters at various shows through the years, has been a constant source of dismay and frustration for Gardner.

"In that era, no one was making any money," he said. "Everybody got out and tried their own way of doing things but they had no right to do it under my supervision. But they got away from me in Los Angeles and started performing as the Coasters."

Even as original and/or second-generation Coasters members leave or pass away, different variations of performers have continued to perform as the original group, unbeknownst to the unsuspecting audience. Of those members that even had credible ties to the original group, albeit in the absence of legal rights to perform as the Coasters, Nunn died of a heart attack in 1986, Gunter was murdered in Las Vegas in 1990, and Jones passed away in 2000, leaving Gardner as the sole surviving original member.

In 1987, the Coasters were honored by having the distinction of being the first vocal group inducted into the Rock and Roll Hall of Fame. Most appropriately, in 1999 they were inducted as part of the second class into the Vocal Group Hall of Fame.

Billboard Top 40 **Hits by the Coasters**

Date	Pos	Wks on Charts	Record Title	Label/Number
05/20/57	03	22	Searchin'/ (double-sided hit)	
05/20/57	08	11	Young Blood	Atco 6087
06/09/58	01	15	Yakety Yak	Atco 6116
02/09/59	02	12	Charlie Brown	Atco 6132
06/01/59	09	08	Along Came Jones	Atco 6141
09/07/59	07	11	Poison Ivy/ (double-sided hit)	
09/21/59	38	01	I'm A Hog For You	Atco 6146
01/25/60	36	01	Run Red Run	Atco 6153
02/27/61	37	02	Wait a Minute	Atco 6186
05/29/61	23	06	Little Egypt	Atco 6192

Paul Giacalone
(The Fireflies)

Brooklyn, New York   **May 21, 2005**

Biographical information in existence today regarding the vocal group the Fireflies is made up of numerous inaccuracies and a string of loosely tied anecdotes that have for years left its origin and its founding lineup in question. From its formation in the late 1950s through the group's final recording in the mid-1960s, its chronological history and membership on the eight singles released by the group remains clouded.

Perhaps the most glaring inaccuracy regarding the Fireflies is the fact that virtually every biography lists them as having formed in Philadelphia, Pennsylvania, in 1957. "We're all from Brooklyn, New York," Giacalone confirmed. "Ritchie was from Ridgewood, Carl came from Maspeth, Lee came from East New York, and I came from Williamsburg. Lee was born in Tennessee but he grew up in Brooklyn.

"The original lineup consisted of Lee Reynolds, Ritchie Adams, and Carl Girosolli," he said. "When the group recorded 'The Crawl' in 1958 on Roulette, they just had two guitars and a bass. I joined the group as a drummer after that session."

The Fireflies had the distinction of being one of the few vocal groups of that time period to be self-contained, every member having been proficient on an instrument. It served the group well at gigs and personal appearances.

"The Fireflies were a vocal group but we were also excellent jazz musicians," Giacalone said. "I played drums, Ritchie played guitar, Carl played guitar, and Lee played bass guitar. When Carl decided to pack it in we added a sax player, John Viscelli. But we were basically musicians before we were singers. Because of that, it was easier for us to do a lot of things at engagements."

The group moved to Ribbon Records to record their second single, a song that would put them in the limelight. But varying accounts regarding the Fireflies Top 40 hit "You Were Mine" credit either Ritchie Adams or the song's composer, Paul Giacalone, as having sung lead on the record.

"I don't know how that confusion started but Ritchie Adams was the original lead singer of the group and he sang 'You Were Mine' and 'I Can't Say Goodbye,' which I also wrote," Giacalone confirmed.

Another longtime matter of confusion related to the group's recordings named a background singer referred to only as Granahan, having no ties whatsoever to the group itself. As it turns out the background singer was in fact Jerry Granahan, who went on to experience significant success as a singer, songwriter, and as one of the more influential producers of pop-rock on the East Coast from the mid-1950s through the 1960s. Granahan not only charted with his own 1958 hit records "No Chemise Please" and "Click Clack" (as Dicky Doo and the Don'ts) in 1958, but he also produced major hits for, among others, the Angels ("My Boyfriend's Back") and Jay and the Americans ("Cara Mia").

"Gerry Granahan was the A&R man who put the recording together for us," Giacalone recalled. "He also dubbed his voice in as a soprano but he was never a member of the Fireflies, but was more of an added attraction as a background singer."

Like many compositions, the Fireflies' hit record was based on a true life experience. "I wrote 'You Were Mine' in memory of a youthful crush," he said. "I met this girl in Canada and she gave me the inspiration to write that song. The Paulette Sisters came out with an answer record to 'You Were Mine' later on called 'I Was Yours.' Unfortunately, nothing big came of it."

After releasing the record the group was invited to appear on Dick Clark's *American Bandstand*. But the story behind that experience has a bit of a twist to it.

"Originally, the flip side of 'You Were Mine' is the one that we were going to try to push as the hit," he said. "It was called 'Stella's Gotta Fella.' But when Dick Clark heard 'You Were Mine' he flipped it over, and I have to thank him for triggering it out in Philadelphia. On the show they had the Top 10 survey and we made number eight with the song. And Murray the K was the guy that triggered it for us in New York.

"Appearing on *Bandstand* was a turning point in our lives because it was a nationwide television show," he said. "And if it wasn't for a guy like Dick Clark that loved the song and pushed the record it might not have happened."

The Fireflies performed at a variety of venues including the Apollo Theater in Harlem, where the group shared bills with the likes of Jackie Wilson, Bobby Lewis, Sarah Vaughan, and Lloyd Price. While the Apollo was a black venue, its audience had a reputation of seeing beyond color barriers if the music performed was of high quality.

"One of the greatest times of our lives was working the Apollo Theater with those great acts," he said. "They loved us and we were the only white act there. We got some tremendous ovations and Jackie loved us. In fact, at night after we finished the show we all used to go together to the Palm Café and hang out for a drink or two."

Giacalone described the feeling of fellowship backstage at the shows. "I was nineteen years old and the youngest member of the group, and hanging out backstage with these guys was fabulous," he said. "They treated us like we were a part of their organization. It was a pleasure to work with them."

The group's follow-up single for Ribbon was "I Can't Say Goodbye," which failed to generate attention. At that point, Adams decided to leave the group for both solo work and to concentrate on songwriting. With nearly four hundred songs to his credit, Adams composed tunes for the novelty groups the Banana Splits and the Archies, penned two huge hits ("Tossin' and Turnin'" and "After the Lovin'"), and sang lead on "Love Is Living in You," the only Archie's single that does not feature the voice of Ron Dante.

"Ritchie decided to try and make it on his own," Giacalone said. "He came out with five different songs and wrote quite a few songs. He had more success as a songwriter than he did as a singer. Two years ago when the Fireflies performed at a show, he was in the audience. We invited him up to sing 'You Were Mine' and it sounded great."

After Adams left the group the Fireflies splintered, with Reynolds holding the remnants of the lineup together. In 1960, the Fireflies released two singles on two different labels. The first, "My Girl," served as their last Ribbon release, while "Marianne" was recorded on the Canadian American label. When the Fireflies moved to Taurus Records in 1962, the label tried to revitalize interest by recording a play on their only Top 40 hit single, releasing "You Were Mine for a While." It received virtually no airplay, as did the group's final four attempts on Taurus and Hamilton Records.

Giacalone reformed the Fireflies in 1992. "I heard Marco [Gueli, current lead singer] sing and I thought he sounded a lot like Ritchie Adams," he said. "From there we got together with a few different members and the harmony was a good blend. I was out of the business until then, and when I heard how it sounded I thought it would be good to put it together. It's worked!"

Billboard Top 40 Hits by the Fireflies

Date	Pos	Wks on Charts	Record Title	Label/Number
09/28/59	21	10	You Were Mine	Ribbon 6901

Jerry Gross
(The Dovells)

Cherry Hill, New Jersey   **December 7, 2006**

Forming in 1957, the original members of the all-male vocal group that evolved into the Dovells consisted of Jerry Gross (aka Summers), Len Borisoff (aka Barry), Mike Freda (aka Dennis), Arnie Silver (aka Satin), and Jim Mealey (aka Danny Brooks). The Brooktones, were named after Overbrook High School in Philadelphia, Pennsylvania, where the group's members attended and where the quintet began to perform at school functions.

Gross showed an early interest in music. "I started playing drums at five years old," he said. "When I was twelve or thirteen my influences in music were Little Richard and Elvis Presley."

He explained how, along with some school friends, he helped to form his first vocal group. "Overbrook was a school where you either played basketball, you sang, or you got beat up," he said. "Singing on the corner was the thing and I really enjoyed it. I formed a group with Mark Stevens, Alan Horowitz, and Roland Scorinchi called the Gems and we sang at school. And there was the Brooktones, a group formed by Len Barry and four other guys, and we used to have a battle of the groups and we'd go to each other's place and sing."

Odd as it might seem, every member in the group changed their respective names, as referenced above. "We did that because we were stupid," Gross laughed. "That's the easiest answer, but I guess it seemed like the show biz thing to do. It was just the thing to do."

Rehearsing at each other's homes and at John Madara's record shop, the teenagers worked on their harmony. Madara eventually became known for his composition "At the Hop," a Top 10 hit song recorded by another Philadelphia group, Danny and the Juniors.

The Brooktones, led by Barry, eventually landed an audition with the Cameo/Parkway label. Signed to a recording contract in late 1960, the group was experiencing problems with its harmony, and at Barry's request Gross agreed to formally join the group and brought Freda back with him.

In March 1961, Cameo/Parkway released the now-renamed Dovells' debut single, a re-recorded version of their original composition, "No, No, No." The original track of the tune included Gross and Freda, during a period that saw the Gems and Brooktones harmonizing together. Gross explained that his and Freda's involvement with the Gems was a sporadic thing and that they frequently swapped off with the Brooktones.

"Lenny had a couple of guys in this group that couldn't sing and he asked me to come on board," he continued. "He told me that he was having trouble with the harmonies and I went to one of their rehearsals. He was right; the guys couldn't sing, so Lenny convinced me to join the group."

Gross agreed to join if he could bring either Freda or Stevens along, but as it turned out Stevens preferred to work solo at that point. "I called Mike [Freda] from the rehearsal and gave him the part over the phone," he said. "We went to Mike's house and rehearsed and he just fell in and the harmonies were just spectacular. Unfortunately, Cameo/Parkway never captured what we could really do. The label was all about doing it on the fly, doing it cheap, and getting it out."

The Brooktones officially changed their name to the Dovells when the record label's owner, Bernie Lowe, returned from a vacation in Miami Beach, Florida, where he stayed at the Deauville Hotel. "Bernie Lowe came back from Florida and said that he had the best vacation at the Deauville," Gross recalled. "He said that all the groups out back then had L's and that was the sound. There were the Shirelles, Rondells, this dell and that dell. He said, 'You're going to be the Deauvilles.'

But nobody would know how to spell it that way so we changed it to Dovells."

Still, even with the change in spelling, Gross wasn't and still isn't fond of the name. "I thought the name stunk then and still do," he said. "We wanted to be called something that people would remember and not blend into everything else."

After the release of "No, No, No," the Dovells returned to the studio to record "Out in the Cold Again." But another tune, composed in response to a new dance that was discovered by the label's promotion man at a teenage sock hop in Bristol, Pennsylvania, became the A-side on the single.

The song "The Bristol Stomp" didn't do too much at first, but it soon blazed a trail straight up the charts. "Nothing happened with it after they released it, and all of a sudden Bernie Lowe called and told us we had a hit record," Gross said. "An order for 100,000 records came in from a distributor in Chicago. After that, we were on *American Bandstand* in a matter of a day or two, and then it just took off."

Gross claimed that the songwriters responsible for the Dovells material lifted much of it from other tunes. "They stole 90 percent of the tunes that all the artists had," he said. "For 'Bristol Stomp' they actually put on 'Every Day of the Week' because Billy Harper came in and said here's what they're stomping to at the Goodwill Fire Hall in Bristol, Pennsylvania. He put on 'Everyday of the Week' and he put on Curtis Lee's 'Pretty Little Angel Eyes.' If you play 'Bristol Stomp' and 'Every Day of the Week,' it's the same beginning."

Following the success of "Bristol Stomp," the Dovells began recording a series of dance-related songs, all composed by Parkways' master songwriters Dave Appell and Kal Mann. But the group did not chart again until 1964's "You Can't Sit Down."

"There was a tune that we recorded called 'Stompin' Everywhere,' which is on one of our albums, and it should have been the second release," Gross said. "It is probably one of the best-written, melodic tunes that we've done. It was a great song but they decided that we couldn't jam the same song down the people's throat twice. We had a big argument over it and Bernie Lowe decided to go with 'Do the New Continental' because it was another dance that was breaking and that started the tensions."

"Do the New Continental" climbed to number thirty-seven on the pop charts. "I'm convinced that 'Stompin' Everywhere' would have been another number-one or number-two record," Gross said.

Like many groups of that time, the Dovells provided background vocals for other artists, most prominently on the Chubby Checker single "Let's Twist Again." The group also backed Checker as well as Fabian and Jackie Wilson at multi-talent package shows at the Brooklyn Fox Theater in New York.

Given the sound projected by the group on records, it is no surprise that the Dovells' first major appearance came at the Fox Theater in Detroit, Michigan. Along with New York's Apollo Theater, and the Howard Theater in Washington, D.C., the Fox catered primarily to a black audience.

"We were received fine there and our hit single was big there, but that show was such a mish-mash," he recalled. "Besides us it was Ray Charles, Timi Yuro, Johnny Mathis, Fabian, and others that were just a strange mix of acts. But it went over great and sold out." Fabian was a familiar face to the Dovells since he, Frankie Avalon, and Gross lived within a block of each other in South Philadelphia.

In 1962, the Dovells appeared in the rock-and-roll movie *Don't Knock the Twist*. "I loved making that film," Gross said. "It was a lot of fun. We were on the road and Lenny said, 'I need a vacation; let's go to Miami.' I'd never been to Miami, so Mike, Lenny, and I jumped on a plane, checked into a hotel right next door to the Deauville, and were down there for four or five days having a ball. Our manager called one morning and told us to come right home. Lenny answered the telephone, told him we were on vacation, and hung up. When I asked Lenny what the call was about he said, 'Ah, some stupid movie.' I called back and found out that we had to leave the following day for California to do a movie with Chubby Checker."

That same year, the Dovells had a harrowing experience while on tour. Near Atlanta, Georgia, the bus that carried the concert tour's acts came under fire. "We were there with James Brown and passed a truck driver," Gross recalled. "It was right after the Rosa Parks incident and they were part of the Freedom Riders. Lenny was yelling out the window and the guy reached for his shotgun and he shot at the bus."

In 1964 the Dovells recorded a cover of a previously unreleased song, "She Loves You," but Cameo/Parkway stalled in putting it out in time to beat the Beatles version, which became a huge hit single. "One of the South Philadelphia labels had the song and brought it into the studio to us," he said. "They said that it was by a group that was really making some noise in England and Bernie said, 'Yeah, let's record it.' We did and they sat with it and sat with it. Then the Beatles released 'I Want to Hold Your Hand' and I remember going in and telling them to get the record out fast. They screwed around with other things and recorded other acts. They weren't very good at moving quickly, and then the Beatles came out with it and it was all over."

Gross said that the lost opportunity wouldn't be the only one the label experienced. "We were in Studio A recording something and we walked out into the hall and this girl singer was next door and we went into the control room to listen to her," Gross said. "She was phenomenal. I walked into Bernie's office and told him that he should sign her because she was incredible. Bernie said, 'Nah, just another girl singer.' It was Barbra Streisand."

On December 29, 1963, on Gross's birthday, growing strife within the group boiled over in the Dovells' dressing room prior to a Christmas performance in Miami Beach. "We were at the Deauville Hotel with Dick Clark and we got there and went to rehearsal," Gross recalled. "Knowing that we'd be in Miami Beach, we had some charts done. They were some standards like 'A Foggy Day in London Town,' 'A Lovely Way to Spend an Evening,' and some ballads. We figured that we'd play to the audience that was there and then work our records in. Lenny said that he wasn't doing that stuff and we argued about it. He wanted to open with 'Locking up My Heart,' which is a screamer by the Marvelettes. I told him that we were going to bomb if we did that and he said that was the only way he would go on stage."

Disgusted, Gross informed Barry that once the show was over, he was leaving the group. When they performed the songs that Barry insisted on doing, the audience response was exactly as Gross had predicted. "We went on with a big band doing rhythm and blues and screaming black music and the people sat there and their mouths dropped open," he said. "It was great music and what I liked to do, but not for that audience. The applause was almost nil. People were holding their ears, and when we came off I asked Lenny if he was happy with that. He said, 'Screw 'em, that's what we do.' At that point I told him that I wasn't going to go onstage to be embarrassed and I was going to quit and go to medical school."

One by one, the rest of the Dovells followed Gross's lead and informed Barry that they were leaving the group. Stunned by the reaction, Barry told the group that he would leave and perform the music that he preferred doing. Upon returning to Philadelphia, the group called Lowe and informed him that Barry was out and the Dovells were now a trio.

The Dovells left for a tour of Japan, which lasted two months, and when they returned to the United States the British Invasion had hit its stride, all but stifling any effort made by American groups. Wanting to change the sound of the group in an attempt to survive the onslaught from England, the Dovells developed a new style.

The group recorded a few singles that Gross contends had all the ingredients necessary to become hit records but for Cameo/Parkway's failure to release or promote them. "They were falling apart at that point," he said. "Bernie Lowe was in competition with Berry Gordy and he couldn't win. They lost some of their key promotion people, who left to promote British acts at other labels. He started to really stretch, so we asked for our release and got off the label."

Working the nightclub circuit, the Dovells were able to secure regular work. In 1968 while driving home from a gig in New York, Gross and Freda began to play with some lyrics based on a skit he'd seen on the popular television show *Laugh-In*.

"We were driving on the New Jersey Turnpike and I said that we should do a tune on 'Here Comes the Judge' from *Laugh-In*, which was getting really big," Gross said. "Mike and I started working on it during the drive and ran into the studio overnight. We brought this girl Jeannie Yost in; we called her Jean Hillery on the record. She did gospel singing. We recorded it right away."

Following an all-night mixing session, Gross and Freda took a train to New York carrying a fifteen-inch tape of the song and searched for a record company. Based on the fact that Gross's parents' initials were MGM, the pair headed for that company's office.

"We walked into MGM and I asked the girl there who ran the place," Gross said. "She told us and we went down to his office while she protested that we needed an appointment. We just walked right in. He was in a meeting at the time and I remember he looked up and said, 'And you are?' We told him that we were the Dovells and we had a hit record for him. I said, 'Do you want it or not?' He kept us waiting for a half hour and came out."

Looking skeptical at the reel of tape handed to him, the executive played it for thirty seconds before asking Gross and Freda how much they wanted for it. "We didn't know what we wanted," Gross said. "We gave a ridiculous number and he cut it in half. We asked for half the publishing and we got it. We made more money on 'Here Comes the Judge' than on any Dovells record, because the record companies ripped us off."

But the recording was released under the name the Magistrates. "Why we didn't call it the Dovells, I don't know."

The deal was made on a Wednesday, Gross said. That Saturday, while driving over the George Washington Bridge to a gig in Connecticut, the group heard the song played on WABC radio, the number-one station in the country. "We did a half-million records sold overnight," Gross said. "We got an advance payment from BMI. We got paid by the record company. It was great.

"Mark tried his Bobby Darin thing and while it didn't work for him on record, he was a great live act," Gross said. "We went to see him and he was phenomenal on stage. In 1966, I wasn't sure of the band that was going to back us at a gig and invited Mark to play guitar. He rehearsed the band, played guitar, and eventually started singing the fourth-part harmony with us."

In 1969 following a two-week break in the Dovells' schedule, Freda approached Gross one night just prior to a nightclub gig in Manhattan. "He was growing his hair longer and longer and he walked in wearing a white robe and had grown a beard and looked like Jesus," Gross said. "He said that he'd seen the light and had to leave the group. I told him we were on stage in thirty minutes and to get ready and he said that it would be his last performance with us. When we finished, he said 'God bless you' and he left."

With Freda gone and another gig scheduled for the following weekend, Stevens put his guitar aside and joined rehearsals as a full member of the Dovells. It not only worked out, Gross said, but "it came together very well."

"Mark was always crazy," Gross said. "With him out front, comedy started developing a lot more than we had. It became pretty insane comedy and it was working. We starting getting more and more work, and then we did a showcase in Atlanta, Georgia. We didn't know it, but this girl that was sitting up front was the wife of the entertainment director of the Flamingo. We did twenty minutes and she was laughing so hard she was crying. They booked us for two years, three times a year for a month at a shot with options. We went out to Vegas and just lit that strip up."

Three years after the group started generating rave reviews in the trades, ones that likened the act to the old Jerry Lewis-Dean Martin routines, Silver gave the group two weeks' notice that he would be leaving. Gross and Stevens played their first gig as a duo the following night and it all came together beautifully.

During the 1980s, the pair formed the Gross, Stevens Organization in addition to performing as the Dovells. The company produces shows and corporate events and does marketing and promotions. At the time of this interview, Gross and Stevens were in the process of putting a motion-picture production company together.

"We're working more now than ever," Gross said. "This past summer we've done more than fifty dates. I'm proud that we can get on stage and take people back to the time that I consider was some of the best years of this country. They forget their problems and they laugh and come to see us after the show and tell us what a great time they had."

One of the biggest highlights of the Dovells' career, Gross said, was performing at Bill Clinton's inaugural ball. "Three days before the 1992 election, Bill Clinton was coming into the area," Gross said. "Since we were into promotion, a friend of mine asked us to put together a press party at the Garden State Track. Clinton planned to stop there after he visited the Meadowlands. When he arrived we were up on stage playing and he came up and said, 'Man, you guys are great.' We introduced ourselves and after a while he grabbed a sax and played with us."

When Clinton complimented the group as the finest he'd heard on the campaign trail, Gross asked to be invited to the inaugural ball if he won the election. "You got it," Clinton promised. "We rewrote the words to 'You Can't Sit Down' for the ball," Gross said. "After Greg Allman finished playing and the Secret Service swept the stage, they announced that Clinton would do the first dance and he cut the band off, turned to us, and said, 'Come on up, guys.' We all went up, he grabbed a sax, and we went into the tune and he was on stage with us for fourteen minutes. That to me was the highlight."

Billboard Top 40 **Hits by the Dovells**

Date	Pos	Wks on Charts	Record Title	Label/Number
09/18/61	02	14	Bristol Stomp	Parkway 827
03/03/62	37	02	Do the New Continental	Parkway 833
06/03/62	27	05	Bristol Twistin' Annie	Parkway 838
09/15/62	25	07	Hully Gully Baby	Parkway 845
05/11/63	03	11	You Can't Sit Down	Parkway 867

President Bill Clinton joined Dovells Mark Stevens, left, and
Jerry Gross, right, to perform at his inaugural ball. Gross
considered the performance a highlight of his career in music.

Barbara Harris
(The Toys)

Elmsford, New York   **March 22, 2005**

Barbara Harris was born and raised in Elizabeth City, North Carolina, and in 1956 she moved to St. Albans, New York. Harris gained an early appreciation for music from listening to and attempting to emulate gospel singers at a local church during her youth.

"When I was a child we had a church at the end of my block and you could hear the music all the way down to my house," Harris said. "When I was about six or seven I'd go down there and watch because I loved the way they used to get the Holy Ghost and they would dance. So I started picking up the tambourine and tried to imitate the ladies that played it, and then I started singing the songs. Somebody heard me one day and asked if I would sing in church on Sunday. I said yeah and after that I sang every Sunday and every Wednesday night at Bible meetings. My mother always knew where to find me; I'd be in church."

Following her relocation to New York, Harris attended Woodrow Wilson High School, where she became friends with Barbara Parritt, who was also originally from North Carolina, and June Montiero. The

113

two girls performed with a local vocal group called the Charletts and soon asked Harris to join them.

"Barbara Parritt was the lead singer and had the group formed before I even came to Woodrow Wilson," Harris said. "One of the girls was giving her trouble and she asked me if I'd fill in for her. I said yes and that's how I got in the group."

Harmonizing and honing their talent on street corners, the Charletts were discovered while performing at a local talent show by Eddy Chase, a scout who worked for the group's soon-to-be manager, Vince Marc.

"I remember going to the city all the time, even after school," Harris said. "I would have to come home first and fix dinner because my mother told me to do that before I went anywhere. We weren't very successful with it, but shortly after, we met our manager. Before that, a guy named Eddy Chase saw us in a talent show and said he wanted to introduce us to somebody and took us to meet Vince Marc. Shortly after that we started doing background work.

"When we met Vinnie, he introduced us to Sandy [Linzer] and Denny [Randell] and they had each one of us sing a song to see what they wanted. After Barbara and June sang, they tried me, and when I sang they looked at each other as if my voice was what they were looking for. I had the most commercial sound. Barbara's voice was deep and rich and great. June's was just a little light, so mine was right in the middle."

Harris said that she felt bad over the producer's choice because her friend Barbara was hurt by it, and in reality, she enjoyed singing background vocals. When the group met and were signed to Bob Crewe's DynoVoice Records, their fate would change for the better with a prolific and creative team and producer behind them.

"Bob Crewe was a real cool, sweet guy," she said. "I think we were doing some background work for Diane Renay and he was working with her. When he heard us he said that he'd like to put us on his label. He tried to help us in every way, with clothes, by taking us around to get us the best setting for our album, and [he] tried to make sure we got whatever we needed."

When the Charletts signed a recording contract with Crewe, Marc changed the name of the group to the Toys. Harris reflected on how that came about.

"He just picked it out of thin air I guess, but he went by the way we behaved," she recalled. "We used to laugh a lot, had a lot of fun together, and I guess we acted like kids. When he said that we should be called the Toys we didn't like it but it stuck."

Linzer and Randell took a common piano classical finger exercise, Bach's "Minuet in G" and added a more contemporary Motown beat to it and came up with "A Lovers Concerto." The Toys recorded the tune and in September 1965, the record climbed to number five on the rhythm and blues charts, crossed over to number two pop, and climbed to number five in England. With a million-selling hit record to their credit, the Toys began to appear on the *American Bandstand, Shindig,* and *Hullabaloo* television shows, went on a concert tour with Gene Pitney, and made an appearance in the American International Pictures feature-length beach party movie *It's a Bikini World.*

Harris recalled the latter experience. "We got out to Los Angeles at night and they had us up at six o'clock in the morning because we had to be at the set by six thirty," Harris said. "We were so sleepy because we had stayed up half the night with our friends. We had lines under our eyes and they had to keep sending us into makeup and fixing us up. It was cool, though. They had us in a dragon's mouth. It was exciting because it was a movie."

Ironically, Harris was skeptical about "Lovers Concerto" and didn't pay too much attention to the song. "We practiced those other songs over and over again," she said. "As for 'Lovers Concerto,' I didn't think it would work. It sounded like just a regular little school song, and that's the way we took it and we just sang it down one time. Shows you how much I know. It was different. Wherever we went people would say, 'This is a concerto piece.' They were amazed."

While the Toys considered the tune a simple school-type song, its quick rise on the charts wreaked havoc at another label. The impact of "Lovers Concerto" was so huge that reports of Motown Records' near obsession with composing and recording a similar-sounding tune resulted in the Toys hit single being played in its Detroit, Michigan, offices and hallways all day long. Soon after its release, the Motown power songwriting team of Holland/Dozier/Holland had churned out "I Hear a Symphony," which became a hit for the label's star act, the Supremes.

"The Isley Brothers told us that the Motown folks took our record and played it over the loudspeakers for weeks until they came up with one to match it," Harris said. "We were thrilled about hearing that and thought it was great."

"We used to follow the Supremes," she said. "There was a club in Detroit called the Rooster Tail and we came in right after they were there. Then there was another place in Washington, D.C., and we came in right after they had appeared. We were like following them around."

Harris said that the two girl groups got to know each other during the course of touring and making various appearances.

"We met all three of them," she said. "We just loved Florence and Mary. They were so great. Diana was doing her own thing and didn't have too much time for us. Mary and Flo would sit with us and try to give us pointers on what we should do. They were so nice."

Of all the television appearances the Toys made, their first spot proved to be a significant learning experience for them. "*American Bandstand* was the first one that we did," she recalled. "I remember that we didn't know how to put on makeup too well, and when we saw ourselves after, oh my God, we had to get somebody to make us up. We looked all greasy.

"*Where the Action Is* was really cool too but there was one television show in England called *The Top Of the Pops* and they had a setting where you had to walk down these long, winding stairs while you were singing the song, and I loved that," she added. "That was one of the best shows we did because of that set."

Harris tried to explain how the sudden burst in popularity and fame affected the three young girls from Queens, New York, and how a decision to embark on a long concert tour overseas after "Lovers Concerto" hit big might have hampered their potential for success with their debut album.

"We were real excited," she said. "Our manager used to say that we didn't realize what we had, and we didn't. We were just having fun with the glitter and the glamour and we were just enjoying it and loving it. We didn't realize that we should have been taking care of our business at the same time. We should have been back here in America doing the album. The label was upset with us and kept telling our manager to get us back home. I guess he was making his money with us over there touring, and they got into a lot of arguments and we were right in the middle. I think that's why we left the company. He took us away from them."

The Toys eventually went back into the studio and recorded the remaining tracks for *The Toys Sing a Lovers Concerto* and *Attack* albums.

"I thought the albums were great but they just came out too late," she said. "We should have been back to do it instead of staying away and touring Germany, England, and Australia."

In 1968, after recording a cover of a Brian Hyland song "Sealed with A Kiss," the Toys parted ways with Harris, taking time for marriage and raising seven children. However, her passion for music remained very much alive and she continued to perform occasionally at area clubs, most recently with a group called Rhythm and Babs.

"I stopped performing after I had my children," she said. "I went to a gig with my husband [musician Kenneth Wiltshire], who played bass for some friends of his in a group called Raised on Blues. When they found out who I was they asked him if I'd come up and sing a song. I got up and did a blues song and they asked me if I would join the band."

From there Harris began to include rhythm and blues in the group's repertoire, and when its founding member departed, she renamed it Rhythm and Babs. "It's still R&B, and that's how it started and we are still going today," she added.

In 1988 Harris reformed a new lineup of the Toys to perform at oldies shows, and ten years later she recorded a new CD entitled *Barbara Now*. She composed all but two of the songs on the CD. The project was a family production.

"My sons helped me with the CD," she said. "They're into computers and were making real good money, and they financed it. We built a little studio in our home and my husband and I put it all together. I tried to do gospel and jazz and blues on it."

Composing songs for the CD wasn't exactly a new experience for Harris, who said that when the Toys signed with Musicor Records, all three girls began to write tunes for the group. While most of the songs they composed were never released, one did make it onto the B-side of "Sealed with a Kiss."

Another project that Harris was involved with was performing with Joe Rivers as half of the popular 1950s duet Johnnie and Joe. The duo recorded a Top 10 hit single for Chess Records in 1957 titled "Over the Mountain, Across the Sea."

"Joe was such a sweet man," Harris said. "It was a pleasure being up on stage with him. He's just a gem. When I couldn't do it, Barbara Parritt took over for me and she was a perfect match for him. I'm a little on the wild side and like up stuff. Joe liked ballads and Barbara does too."

Harris makes a point to perform at a number of benefit concerts on a regular basis, including the From the Heart show that raises funds for needy musicians, and another, the Rolling Thunder Review, which donates its proceeds to Vietnam veterans. "We always try to give back when we can," she said. "It's not always about money. God gave me the gift, so why not use it."

The three original Toys remain close friends and maintain regular contact. Harris reflected on how she would like her and the Toys to be remembered in years to come. "I would like to be remembered as someone who just took the love of the music and gave it to the audience," she said. "When I'm up there on stage, I feel for the people out there. I look at the faces and some would be crying. They tell me that a particular tune was their wedding song. I met guys that were in Vietnam when one of our songs was out and they tell me that we brought a little bit of home to them. Those kinds of moments can't be compared to anything. That means the world to me."

Harris continues to hear from fans worldwide in letters and e-mails. She said that reading their comments brings a huge sense of joy to her.

Billboard Top 40 Hits by the Toys

Date	Pos	Wks on Charts	Record Title	Label/Number
10/02/65	02	11	A Lovers Concerto	DynoVoice 209
01/01/66	18	06	Attack	DynoVoice 214

Original Dixie Cups Rosa Lee Hawkins, left, and Barbara Anna Hawkins, right, with current member Athelgra Neville Gabriel at a recent concert.

Barbara Ann Hawkins
(The Dixie Cups)

Tampa, Florida   **November 15, 2005**

In 1963 sisters Barbara Anna and Rosa Lee Hawkins, and a cousin, Joan Marie Johnson formed a vocal group called the Meltones in their hometown, New Orleans, Louisiana. Having sung together in church the three girls formed the group in order to participate in a school talent show.

Barbara Ann Hawkins was born in New Orleans on October 23, 1943. Her earliest introduction to music, like many other artists of that era, began in church. "As kids, Rosa and I sang in church with my mom, so I have to say that gospel music influenced me at that time," Hawkins said. "My mom was also a singer and she sang at home and we used to join her."

Hawkins explained how, with her sister and a cousin, the foundation was set for what would eventually become the vocal group known as

119

the Dixie Cups. "As for Joan [Johnson], we didn't know that we were related at the time," she said. "She asked me to sing in a group because there was a talent show at St. Augustine High School in New Orleans. They had one every year. One of the guys in the group had to fall out to take care of his family because his mom was ill. I told Joan that I had a person that could sing bass, which was Rosa, and that's how she got in the group."

Hawkins said that due to the limited number of girl groups in existence at the time, no one specific group influenced their sound; rather, it was their personal love for music that helped them to develop their own harmonies.

There are conflicting reports about the name the group performed under at the talent show. One states that it was the Meltones, while another says it was Little Miss and the Muffets. "We were called the Meltones when we performed at the show," Hawkins said. "Little Miss and the Muffets was a name that the record company wanted to give us when we signed the recording deal, but we didn't like it."

Another New Orleans artist, one that had already gained fame after charting with the 1960 hit single "You Talk Too Much," Joe Jones, discovered the group at the talent show and offered to manage them. When Jones took the trio to the famous Brill Building in New York City, the girls experienced first-hand the workings of the center of the music industry at that time.

"It was all new to us," Hawkins said. "We had never been exposed to anything like it. We had only heard the different groups on the radio. We were only teenagers and didn't know anything about the business. It was very exciting but we were nervous because Joe had taken us to several different record companies and each one wanted to record us. But he wanted a special deal. We thought that he was looking out for us but he was looking out for himself."

What Jones sought in the way of a deal was basically front money, and not in any way funds that would go to the girls. He subsequently negotiated a recording deal for the trio with songwriters Jerry Leiber and Mike Stoller, who were in the process of starting their own record label, Red Bird.

Upon signing, the group was presented with a song that was composed by three of the biggest names in the business at the time: Ellie Greenwich, Jeff Barry, and Phil Spector. The song was named "Chapel of Love."

"We didn't like 'Chapel of Love' when we first heard it," Hawkins recalled. "When Jeff and Ellie played it for us we looked at each other and said, 'You want us to sing that?' We didn't like the way they sang it and they told us to sing it any way we wanted to. We went off into the corner and came up with it the way it is."

"Chapel of Love" was already recorded by two of Spector's groups, the Ronettes and the Crystals. But it was released by the Dixie Cups as Red Bird's first single and quickly climbed to number one on the charts in May 1964. Hawkins explained how the group transformed from the Meltones to the Dixie Cups upon recording their first song.

"When we signed with Red Bird we were the Meltones," she said. "After they decided to record us, they told us that they wanted to change the group's name. Their suggestion was Little Miss and the Muffets and we didn't like it. We picked the Dixie Cups based on the fact that in the 1960s groups had weird names like the Beatles and the Rolling Stones. We wanted to be in the mix, and Dixie Cups came from the land of Dixie because New Orleans is the land of Dixie, and Cups was just cute."

Upon the release of "Chapel of Love," its immediate and huge success had a significant impact on the trio, who for the most part were ill-prepared for the onslaught resulting from instant fame.

"After we recorded 'Chapel of Love' we went back to New Orleans," she said. "After it was released and it was being played so much, Jerry Leiber and Mike Stoller called us and told us that we were moving to New York because our record was definitely going to be a hit. We needed to start working and everything, and things changed for us. We were no longer at home doing whatever, like going to school. We moved to New York and started doing gigs."

The Dixie Cups had three more Top 40 hit singles with "People Say," "You Should Have Seen the Way He Looked at Me," and "Iko Iko," the latter tune one that the girls routinely sang during breaks at recording sessions.

"The song is something that we had heard all our lives when our grandmothers sang it to us," she said. "It's about the Indians in New Orleans, so it's something that everybody has their own version of. We were doing our version with our words at the sessions. It was something that we were planning on recording at some point later on."

With a string of hits, the Dixie Cups were contracted to perform at a variety of shows and played many of the leading venues in the United States and abroad.

"I really loved performing in Hawaii because I had never been there before and the people were so great," Hawkins said. "I also liked England because we met the Beatles and the Animals and those artists. That tour was a little different for us than here in America. When the people over there like something that you do, they truly love you. In other words, once you're a hit with them, you're a hit, period. It's different from here, when you don't have a hit on the charts and people say 'the Dixie what?' Over there they know the Dixie Cups and they know what we did. If we come out with another one, fine; and if we don't, they still love what we did."

Johnson eventually left the Dixie Cups and New York because of ongoing problems with Jones. She was replaced by Beverly Brown, another New Orleans singer who performed with a band in area clubs. After Brown's departure, Dale Mickie was recruited to round out the trio.

Upon Red Bird Records closing shop in 1966, the Dixie Cups moved to ABC-Paramount Records but did not chart any hit singles with the label.

When the Hawkins sisters left New York in 1974, all accounts state that they both went into the modeling industry. "Rosa was a model but I never got into that," Barbara Hawkins said. "After she finished modeling school, she was a model in New Orleans for different department stores. Then she taught modeling at two different venues and we both became representatives for fashion companies."

Hawkins addressed a longstanding myth that the Dixie Cups disbanded when the girls returned to New Orleans. "To be perfectly honest, we never left the music industry," she said. "What happened was, we had problems with Joe in New York and we had to leave New York. We left, moved back home, and were working with a booking agent named Ron Peters, who was based in the Carolinas. We worked through Ron.

"When we left New York, Joe, who was a very, very ugly person, told us that we didn't own the name and we, being youngsters, didn't know anything that he was talking about," she said. "But we do own the name and we have always owned the name because we created the name. If it weren't for us, there would be no Dixie Cups. We are the Dixie Cups."

Because Jones frightened the girls at that time, they changed the spelling of their group name, Hawkins said. "The original was the Dixie Cups," she said. "When we got back to New Orleans we changed it to the Dixi Cups, and you'll see it spelled that way in some material. But talking to our lawyer, he told us that Joe owned nothing and we had already incorporated our name, so we shouldn't be afraid to use what was ours. That's when we went back to the original spelling of the name, and maybe that's where people assumed that we'd come back.

"I have to tell the truth," she added. "Joe discovered us in New Orleans at the talent show and he told us that our name would be in lights. He said that everybody would know our name and that we would be the number-one group in the world. And he said that we would travel. He never said that we would make money, which we didn't.

"I am most proud that when we do a show we can make the people forget their problems, if they have any, for a small amount of time and enjoy what we're doing," she said. "They become a part of us and we become a part of them, and when we leave the stage and they walk away, they've enjoyed us. We make them remember what was going on at the time when our song was out—hopefully something happy. If we can bring a smile to everyone's face with our music, we have done our job."

The Dixie Cups continue to perform on the bills of many oldies shows despite losing their homes in New Orleans as a result of Hurricane Katrina, which devastated a huge portion of the city in 2005. The group joined other New Orleans musical luminaries such as Fats Domino to perform at a benefit relief concert at New York City's Madison Square Garden following the disaster. Athelgra Neville Gabriel, sister of the famous Neville Brothers, joined the Hawkins sisters in recent years to round out the trio.

Billboard Top 40 Hits by the Dixie Cups

Date	Pos	Wks on Charts	Record Title	Label/Number
05/16/64	01	11	Chapel of Love	Red Bird 001
08/01/64	12	07	People Say	Red Bird 006
11/21/64	39	01	You Should Have Seen the Way He Looked at Me	Red Bird 012
05/01/65	20	05	Iko Iko	Red Bird 024

Ray Hildebrand
(Paul and Paula)

Islandia, New York   **November 12, 2005**

When Jill Jackson was offered an opportunity to host a fifteen-minute show on a small, local radio station, Ray Hildebrand, a student at Howard Payne College in Brownwood, Texas, joined her in the endeavor.

On one of the broadcasts, the duo sang a song that Hildebrand had just written, titled "Paul and Paula." The motivation for the composition came as a result of one of Hildebrand's friends whose girlfriend left him. By chance, a disc jockey from the same radio station lifted the tape of that broadcast and began to play the tune on his show the next day. When an endless stream of calls came in to the station in response to the song, Hildebrand and Jackson decided to set out and make a recording of it. That recording would become one of the most recognizable and beloved tunes of the era.

Ray Hildebrand was born and raised in Harlingen, Texas, the son of school teachers. "In the late 1950s while I was in high school in the Rio Grande Valley of Texas, a friend of mine and I started singing and doing some other things and I began writing poetry," Hildebrand said. "Then I started putting melodies to them. It really wasn't until junior college that one of the guitar pickers in a band taught me how to play guitar a little and I began to sing. My favorite artist is those days were the Everly Brothers because of their harmonies. I would always get with one of my friends and we'd harmonize just like the doo-wop guys did, but we only used two guys. It didn't take that many guys in Texas."

Hildebrand said that he loved the 1962 number-one hit song "Hey Baby" and that the composition served as a heavy influence for his own original tune "Hey Paula."

"Had it not been for the song 'Hey Baby' by Bruce Channel from McKenny, Texas, there would have been no 'Hey Paula,' because this fellow that was the producer, Major Bill Smith, would not have had the money and would not have been taking chances in the music business," Hildebrand said. "I just loved that song and we did it on our first Paul and Paula album in honor of Bruce."

In college, Hildebrand joined a band, the Prisoners, one that performed popular songs of the day recorded by acts like the Everly Brothers and the Kingston Trio. "We were just a college band playing local dances and we had a motto," he said. "We literally wore striped prison uniforms that we got someplace and our motto was 'We're a bunch of guys behind a few bars looking for the right key.' One of the local girls in Brownwood, Texas, where Howard Payne College was located, would get up on the stage and sing like Julie London, and she was so beautiful of both form and face. The college girls were all jealous of her."

One summer after Hildebrand broke up with his girlfriend Judy, he was alone and working toward his degree in college. The local girl was offered an opportunity to host a fifteen-minute radio show in Brownwood after she raised the most money at a cancer fund charity show. The station's owner had lost a young son to cancer and in appreciation he offered the girl the radio show. That girl was Jill Jackson, soon to become known worldwide as Paula, half of the famous recording duo Paul and Paula.

"She knew who I was because I sang and I knew who she was because she sang," he said. "She was a drop-dead beauty who looked like Annette Funicello a little bit. The coach had given me a chance to stay there and finish my degree by letting me be the manager of the swimming pool on the college campus. Jill had a chance to do this local radio show and she didn't want to do it by herself. She saw me at the swimming pool one day, knew that I played guitar, and asked if I would help her. I said okay, and we went ahead and did the *Jill and Ray Show.*"

At the same time, Hildebrand was working on a song. "One day after Judy had left and everybody had gone home for the summer and I was lonely, I was sitting there writing this little song for this guy Russell, who had a girlfriend named Paula," he said. "It was meant to keep her from running away from him like Judy had done to me. I finally finished the song, but the feelings in the song were really about Judy. I was missing my girl that I had broken up with because I didn't have any money to marry her and she wanted to get married.

"I pulled the song out one day and told Jill that we could do it together," he said. "It was a boy and a girl song. Her mother really liked it and Jill agreed. We did it and the disc jockey that was the manager of the station, a fellow named Ronnie Jordon, loved that song. Unbeknownst to us, when we went back home he took the tape of just the guitar and she and I and started playing it during drive time in the evening, along with Frank Sinatra and Bruce Channel and all the big names. They started getting calls about that little boy and girl song."

The song entered the Top 40 locally and became hugely popular. "Ronnie called us one night at home and asked, 'What's the most popular song in Brownwood, Texas, tonight?' Hildebrand recalled. "We said 'Elvis Presley' and he answered, 'It's Paul and Paula.' That was the original name of the song, 'Paul and Paula,' by Jill and Ray. Jill's mother's antenna went up real high and by the following Saturday we were headed for Fort Worth, Texas."

Driving to Fort Worth in November 1962, the duo hoped to get an audition with Major Bill Smith, an independent record producer who owned LeCam Records. Upon arriving at the studio, they were informed that Smith was preparing to record another artist, one Amos Milburn Jr., and would not be able to see them. But their determination and decision to hang around the studio for a while paid off when Milburn failed to show for the recording session, leaving Smith with five paid musicians and nothing to record.

When he was informed that two youngsters were in the outer office and wanted to perform some of their material for him, Smith summoned Hildebrand and Jackson to the studio and asked them to play what they had. It took but a few strums of Hildebrand's guitar and the accompanying vocals to his new song "Paul and Paula" before Smith stopped them and ordered a recording of the tune be made immediately.

"Amos never showed up, thank God," Hildebrand said. "Major Bill Smith had these musicians sitting around getting paid and he wasn't happy. He had this loud voice and I remember him yelling out, 'We're gonna record something tonight if it's the 'Star Spangled Banner.' Along with my song, Jill had a little love song for her boyfriend named Bobby. It ended up being on the flip side and it's a beautiful song. It sounds like Linda Scott or Annette Funicello, and girl singers in those days were hot items."

When the session was over the duo was asked what name they went by, to which they answered Jill and Ray. Thus, all original pressings of the record label on LeCam had it listed that way. After pitching the record to the bigger Vee Jay label with no luck, Smith decided to release it on LeCam in November 1962.

Hildebrand cited one of Major Bill Smith's co-workers, Marvin Montgomery, for molding the song into what was eventually recorded. "Marvin Montgomery is really the one that made the song what it is structurally," he said. "When I wrote the song I wrote an epic. As a matter of fact, the chorus of our second song, 'Young Lovers' (no. 6 pop—3/63) was part of that original 'Hey Paula' song. He took that part out and considered it way too much material for one song. He whacked it off right in the studio."

"Paul and Paula" by Jill and Ray was pressed locally by Smith on his LeCam Record label and it quickly began to get huge airplay in places like Waco, Texas, ironically enough the home of Judy, Hildebrand's former girlfriend. After the record sold sixteen thousand copies in one day, Smith received a telephone call from Shelby Singleton of Mercury Records with an offer to buy the master tapes. When the deal was made with Mercury Records and its subsidiary label, Philips, for marketing purposes the song's title was changed to "Hey Paula," and Jill and Ray became Paul and Paula.

The decision was not to the liking of Hildebrand and Jackson, who, with a hit record to their credit, felt that nobody in Texas would know it was them. They relented and the record was pressed with the new name.

"They told us that there were too many names and they couldn't have it," Hildebrand recalled. "Major Bill called us about a month later and said, 'You got a cotton-pickin' smash.' We didn't know what to even think. We had forgotten all about going to Fort Worth. He told us he was sending us five hundred dollars each for clothes, and that was a million dollars in those days. He said, 'Your song is "Hey Paula," you're now Paul and Paula, and you're sweethearts, so act like it. In one week we're heading for Baltimore, Washington, Boston, New York, Atlanta, and Nashville for promotional deals, so get it together.' And we went from fans to famous in less than four months."

When the song was released on the Philips label, it climbed to number one on both the pop and rhythm and blues charts, something that rarely occurred in those days. It remained in the Top 40 charts for twelve weeks and sold nearly two million copies. Their follow-up single, "Young Lovers," hit the charts in March 1963 and climbed to number six, while their third single, "First Quarrel," reached number twenty-seven on the pop charts in June of the same year.

Hildebrand and Jackson were suddenly thrust into a limelight that was at times overwhelming. "Everybody wanted to talk to us at the same time, even your friends," he said. "We were little fish in a big pond. We were hardly ever home and found ourselves on the road constantly. We were literally catapulted into fame and it was exciting and a hoot, but we never got any sleep."

Hildebrand said that the duo didn't even have an act at the time. "We sang some little harmonizing songs on a radio show and went our separate ways," he said. "We didn't sing together. Our very first show that we did with anyone professionally as Paul and Paula was in Sweetwater, Oklahoma, at a big coliseum, with the Smothers Brothers. They had been doing their act since they were itty bitty kids and were so polished. It was like Frank Sinatra and Tiny Tim. I felt so stupid but they loved it, and singing that little song at the end always saved us."

While the duo traveled worldwide to promote their recordings and perform at a variety of venues, their appearance on *American Bandstand* is the one single appearance that stands out as a favorite.

"We got *American Bandstand* in Harlingen and Brownwood, Texas, and so to be on the show and having family and friends see it was cool," he said. "It was a little disappointing how small the studio was, because it's not anywhere near as big as you think it is. Dick Clark was the sweetest and neatest man. The second time that we were on his show, he was presenting us with our million-selling award and he dropped it. He interviewed us for a long time because he felt bad about dropping the award."

During a trip to England, Paul and Paula had the distinction of bumping a soon-to-be mega star band, the Beatles, from a spot on a popular British radio show.

"We bumped a bunch of people off of different things traveling around because we happened to be there and they were locals and kind of regulars there," he said. "They [the Beatles] were kind of slowly getting some airplay like we did in Brownwood, Texas, and nobody had any idea that they would be that big, but they were very nice to agree to get bumped and they wanted our autographs and took photos with us. That was their idea to take the picture."

On one of Paul and Paula's many concert tours, Dick Clark's Caravan of Stars, Hildebrand, without warning left notes at the artists' hotel for both Jackson and Clark in effect notifying them that he was leaving. He disappeared in the middle of the tour.

"It was all about morals and values and ethics, and, of course, the girl," he said. "I had broken up with Judy once and because of 'Hey Paula' we had gotten back together. In my heart, she was really Paula. I basically ran away from this tour because we were hot items and I was never home and it never let up. Judy and I were back together, with her back home and RCA was trying to get us to move to the East Coast, and to jerk us away from Major Bill. They told us that Major Bill was ham and eggs and they were going to go big time with our own television show and be like Steve and Edie.

"Jill had wanted to be in that business all her life but I really didn't plan on doing it; it just happened," he said. "I love music but I didn't want to do that, so it just came to a head one day in Cincinnati, Ohio, and I was dying and on my knees. I had the Gideon Bible out of the drawer and [was] praying to God to show me what to do. I said, 'Lord, I love this occupation and it's all great but I can't hurt Major Bill. He brought us to the dance. He may be a klutz and a terrible manager but I can't do that to him.' It was an ethics thing, generally, about the morals of my Christian faith. That and I knew if I traveled much more I was going to lose Judy again, and I wasn't going to do that. Plus, some of the parties they had after the shows were getting crazier and crazier. As I prayed, all I could hear was 'Get out of here.' So I packed my bags and I left."

Hildebrand said that the decision to leave couldn't even be shared with his partner and friend, and he simply left a note under Jackson's hotel door and walked away.

"I went to Oregon and joined some friends to haul hay and cleared my mind in the beautiful Pacific Northwest," he said. "Then I went back to Major Bill and he cried because he knew what was going on but he couldn't do anything about it. RCA was a powerful force."

Hildebrand said that Smith wasn't the only one that felt powerless when it came to dealing with the record industry. The artists, at least those who were the subject of a label's focus and promotion money, were often manipulated.

"A record company can't push all of the acts the same amount," he said. "You have to get the one that's really doing it for you and spend more money and time on them. Well, we were their first call but the responsibility of that is that we had to be gone all the time and I didn't want to pay that price."

As for Jackson, after Hildebrand departed, a decision was made to keep the act on the bill, and Clark sang the part of Paul for the remainder of the tour. Hildebrand said that Clark seemed to understand his inner struggle and ultimate decision, being aware of the grueling nature of show business and its touring demands. Jackson, he said, wanted to be in show business so badly but was also experiencing homesickness at the time. She eventually forgave him for leaving as well.

Hildebrand assumed that when he walked away from the music business in Cincinnati, Ohio, his career was finished. But while a few lawsuits resulted from his action, it didn't prevent Paul and Paula from picking up jobs again after a brief period.

"We performed in Atlantic City, New Jersey, and Japan, and so it wasn't over," he said. "But they got scared of Paul and Paula after that. We didn't work on Sundays already, but now they viewed us as unstable. They'd say, 'He ran away from a Dick Clark tour; don't book them.' We didn't get that many gigs and slowly but surely we kind of went different ways because we had different ideas."

Hildebrand married Judy and moved onto the same block as Smith in Fort Worth, Texas, working for him as a songwriter and A&R man for the LeCam label. He also began to compose contemporary Christian music during that period. A recording company in Waco, Texas, heard some of Hildebrand's new music and recorded him. In 1967, he relocated with his family to Kansas.

The ever-savvy Smith continued to send recordings to Hildebrand in Kansas, ones that Jackson had sung on in Fort Worth. Once he added his vocals to the tracks, Hildebrand returned the tapes to Smith in Texas, where they would be released as a new Paul and Paula album.

"He turned out a bunch like that," Hildebrand said of Smith. "He had kind of turned himself into Colonel Tom Parker, who was his hero. Major kept in very close touch with me and used to tell me what he was doing. He put out some of the craziest stuff. But as a producer he took a chance. Three years in a row, in 1962, 1963, and 1964, he had three number-one songs by three different artists. Now, there aren't very many independent producers that can do that. That old boy, for a guy who didn't have an ear for music, he was mighty lucky."

While Jackson eventually moved to California and continued to perform as a solo act, Hildebrand went to work for the Fellowship of Christian Athletes. "Everybody there knew me from the 'Hey Paula' thing and that put me on an equal [footing] with these athletes because in my field I had already been there," he said. "I began to lead singing at some of the events, crusades, and meetings and I was also the head of all the high school groups from the Christian athlete clubs, so I was very busy for fourteen years."

In 1983, Hildebrand met a fellow contemporary Christian musician, Paul Land, at a coffeehouse event. The pair did so well performing together that they developed an act and continue to perform and record Christian music, based in Kansas. Hildebrand also recently began hosting a weekly radio show that focuses on the growing entertainment options in Branson, Missouri.

When nationwide oldies shows began to generate a significant fan base, Hildebrand and Jackson began to get calls from concert promoters asking them to perform as Paul and Paula. Hildebrand remained distant from the business but gave Jackson permission to recruit a new Paul (actually several came and went), and they performed at shows locally and as far away as Australia. Around 1995 Hildebrand and Jackson decided to pair up again to perform at the oldies reviews. They continue to make appearances to enthusiastic and appreciative audiences into the twenty-first century.

"It's so much fun," Hildebrand said. "We would love to do twenty or thirty minutes sometime but we only get to do one song or two. I guess that's the way it's got to be on these big shows or you'd be there for six hours."

Hildebrand reflected on his body of work in music through the years. "As I look back, of course the most famous thing that I've written would be 'Hey Paula,' and it's amazing that I can still make a living off of that song," he said. "I'm most thankful [for] that song, one that is about boy and girl love. But the older I get I realize that God loved us first so that we'd know what love was. I have a song called 'Say I Do' that has been recorded by more people than 'Hey Paula' will ever be, and that song was written in about three hours on a Sunday afternoon in Texas. It was done by Ray Price, a country singer, a number of years ago and went to number six in the country. You're talking about two things: a love of God and a love of a woman. So 'Hey Paula' and 'Say I Do' are my two favorites."

Billboard Top 40 Hits by Paul and Paula

Date	Pos	Wks on Charts	Record Title	Label/Number
01/12/63	01	12	Hey Paula	Philips 40084
03/23/63	06	08	Young Lovers	Philips 40096
06/22/63	27	04	First Quarrel	Philips 40114

Ray Hildebrand (Paul) and Jill Jackson (Paula) continue to entertain appreciative audiences nationwide.

Terry Johnson
(The Flamingos)

Islandia, New York   **April 9, 2005**

There is no telling just how many vocal groups the incredible harmony of the Flamingos has influenced, but suffice it to say that a huge number interviewed for this book cited them and the Moonglows as having a significant impact on their sound.

The foundation of the group came together in 1952, when cousins Jake and Zeke Carey met Paul Wilson and Johnny Carter at the Church of God and Saints of Christ, a black Jewish church in Chicago, Illinois. The Careys had relocated from Baltimore, Maryland. While the quartet began singing Jewish hymns together in the church choir, they soon started to blend their harmonies in a rhythm and blues style. Around that time, they met, Earl Lewis, the boyfriend of the sister of one of the group members. With his addition to the group, they selected the name the Swallows but quickly dropped it when it was discovered that a group in Baltimore already claimed the name.

Carter came up with the El Flamingos, which soon became the Five Flamingos, and eventually they agreed on the Flamingos. When Lewis left the group to join the Five Echoes, he was replaced by a new lead singer, Sollie McElroy. The group subsequently signed a recording deal with Chance Records and recorded singles that gained little momentum. After the Flamingos moved to the Parrott label with similar results, McElroy bailed out and was replaced by Nate Nelson.

In 1955, the group signed with their third label, this time Checker, a subsidiary of Chess Records. After two failed attempts the Flamingos scored a hit single with "I'll Be Home" in 1956. While the song climbed the rhythm and blues charts, a cover of the tune by white recording artist Pat Boone stifled any hopes the Flamingos version had of becoming an even bigger hit for the group.

In October of that year, during an engagement at the Royal Theater in Baltimore, Maryland, Terry Johnson, a member of the recently disbanded Whispers, sat in the audience. Having known Jake Carey as a child growing up in Baltimore, Johnson stopped backstage after the show.

The Flamingos were facing a challenge since both Zeke Carey and Carter were recently drafted into military service. When Nelson asked the sixteen-year-old Johnson if he knew someone who was both a tenor and a guitarist to replace the pair, he needed little time to consider the question. The following day Johnson, with guitar in hand, showed up to audition for the group. He left assured that he had impressed them.

Terry Johnson was born and raised in the same Baltimore, Maryland, neighborhood that boasted musical talent such as Sonny Til of the Orioles and Earl Hurley of the Swallows. He also attended the same church as Zeke and Jake Carey.

Perhaps due to the influence of the recording artists that he called neighbors, Johnson displayed an early interest in music. By fourteen years old he purchased a guitar and began to learn to play rhythm and blues. He also harmonized with his friend Billy Thompson, who with Johnson attended Douglas High School. Soon, the pair decided to form a vocal group and enlisted Eddie Rogers (bass), Bill Mills (tenor), and Eugene Lewis (second tenor).

"We were all friends from school and the neighborhood, and I put the group together," Johnson said. "I was a lover of the Orioles and Ravens because they had that real sweet harmony."

Legend has it that the group got their name, the Whispers, when someone remarked that they could whisper and still sound great. Having honed their harmonies on street corners, the group began to perform at local talent shows throughout the Baltimore area. Soon, Rogers was replaced with James Johnson, a roommate of Mills.

In late 1954, the Whispers traveled to Philadelphia, Pennsylvania, in hopes of landing an audition with Gotham Records. Not only did they audition but also Gotham owner Ivan Ballen was so taken with their sound that he immediately set up a recording session. "We recorded four songs," Johnson recalled. "I sang 'Are You Sorry' and 'Fool Heart,' Billy Thompson sang 'We're Getting Married,' and Bill Mills wrote and sang 'Don't Mess with Lizzie.'"

Johnson got into songwriting with "Fool Heart" and co-wrote and arranged "Are You Sorry." "When I play my guitar I can just hear music," he explained. "As for arranging music, that is simply God's gift."

While Gotham rushed the Whispers into a recording studio, for some reason the label dragged its feet in releasing and promoting the four sides. Since Johnson and Mills were still in school and underage at the time, the group's engagement schedule was extremely limited. After experiencing internal conflicts among its members, the Whispers faded into the history books.

By the time Johnson auditioned for the Flamingos, the group had added second tenor Tommy Hunt to its lineup. It wasn't until December 24, 1956, that Johnson heard from the Flamingos with an offer to join the group. The only catch was that he had to join them the next day in Philadelphia. Not one to pass up an opportunity, he met the group and thus began a fifty-year association with them.

He went on to write, arrange, and sing on "Mio Amore," "At the Prom," "Heavenly Angel," and "Lovers Never Say Goodbye," providing lead vocals on the latter song.

After some legal entanglements with Chess Records, the Flamingos signed with Decca, where they recorded "The Ladder of Love," a song that Johnson arranged. "Decca put out a press release and hosted a big party with all the big wheels and DJs, and they were really going to put big money behind us," he said. "Nate still had a few more months with Lenny Chess of Chess Records and they threatened Decca with a lawsuit if the record was released. Nate sang lead on 'Ladder of Love.'" With the promotion halted, the group departed to join George Goldner's End Records and recorded "Lovers Never Say Goodbye," a Johnson composition. A year later they scored their biggest hit single, "I Only Have Eyes for You," which climbed to number three on the rhythm and blues charts and number eleven on the pop charts. They continued their hot streak with the 1960 single "Nobody Loves Me Like You," a Sam Cooke composition.

"First of all, to set the record straight, I am singing lead on 'Lovers Never Say Goodbye"; myself and Paul Wilson," Johnson said. "My wife and I were listening to Internet radio the other night and at the end of the song the disc jockey said, 'That was Nate Nelson singing 'Lovers Never Say Goodbye' and that's Terry Johnson doing a beautiful tenor.' I said, 'No, I'm doing the lead.' Just to get it straight, I'm singing lead on all the duets that Paul and I did."

"Lovers Never Say Goodbye" was not only a hit on the rhythm and blues charts but it also crossed over and became the Flamingos' first pop-chart success.

"What I really liked about it was that I had brought my sound from Baltimore with the Whispers," Johnson said. "I just heard those chords, taught it to Paul, and presented it to the guys. They really fell in love with it. As for its crossover success, when I joined them the group was really upset that Pat Boone covered 'I'll Be Home' and made a hit out of it. But the Flamingos did it first. So I felt very good that a composition of mine was able to cross over."

That same year, the Flamingos backed Bo Diddley on the ballad "You Know I Love You." It was an unusual song for Diddley to record, especially having been backed by the Flamingos. "I don't know how we got involved with that production," Johnson said. "It was a surprise but we just did it."

When Carter returned from military service in August 1958, Jake Carey and Wilson rejected his reentry into the group. He would eventually join the Dells. That same year, when Zeke Carey was discharged from the army he received the same treatment from the group he helped to form. Had it not been for Johnson's interjection on the issue, the decision would have stood. Johnson taught Zeke Carey to play bass guitar and the Flamingos now boasted six members.

Johnson explained how "I Only Have Eyes for You," a tune that he arranged, was selected for the Flamingos. It was a cover of a 1934 Eddy Duchin hit recording.

"Richard Barrett and George Goldner wanted us to be more like the Platters because they knew we had another style other that the doo-wop sound," Johnson said. "As a matter of fact, there was no such thing as doo-wop in those days; it was rhythm and blues. They chose the songs and it was just something that I heard with that song. Nate was influential with me and he said, 'Let's change it around, Buzzy [Johnson's nickname].' I went off by myself to my room and kept playing on my guitar and it just came to me.

"When I showed it to the guys, they looked at me as if I was nuts," he added. "But they couldn't hear the whole arrangement. I showed them the harmonies of what I wanted them to do. I was singing lead on it at first and Nate and I had a little altercation. I was the baby of the group and I let Nate sing it. I can't tell you how many times I've kicked myself in the butt, because that was our biggest song because it was so different and unique."

From 1959 to 1961 the Flamingos released four albums and five singles, making it the group's most prolific period of production and success.

"George Goldner was really putting money behind us during that time," Johnson said. "I had a personal relationship with him myself. I could go into his office and he'd tell me what he wanted. He wanted a lot of old standards. The Platters were the number-one group and he wanted us to be the next Platters. He knew that I could update the old standards and he loved it."

While Carter appeared with the Flamingos in the Alan Freed rock-and-roll movie *Rock, Rock, Rock*, Johnson appeared with the group in another Freed film, *Go Johnny Go*. Their appearance was described as being akin to a private sound check.

"We just came in and performed our number for the movie," Johnson said. "We didn't even know what the story was about."

The Flamingos also made regular appearances at many of Freed's live concerts at the Brooklyn Fox and the Brooklyn Paramount theaters. They also performed on Dick Clark's *American Bandstand* in 1958, 1959, and 1960.

Johnson's influence and musical input into many of the Flamingos' hit singles is a stark contrast to the misconceptions regarding his involvement with the group. Some accounts state that he was simply a guitarist that accompanied the group. He believes that much of the tainted information was generated by Zeke Carey as a result of bitterness over Johnson's leaving the group. He spoke about the myths and inaccuracies that have unfortunately been accepted by many as fact through the years.

"When I left the group I think Zeke had something against me and Tommy Hunt," Johnson said. "When Tommy Hunt recorded 'Human,' that's what really started things, because he didn't let us know. We heard it on the radio and said, 'That sounds like Tommy's voice.' The disc jockey said, 'That's Tommy Hunt and his new release 'Human.' Zeke freaked out and he started telling me about what we were going to do and not do, how we're going to live our life, and who you were going to be with, who you can't be with. Even though I may have been younger than all of them, I'm still a man and you can't tell me who I'm going to be with. I had to break up with them. Then Nate lost his mind and started yelling, 'Are you crazy to let Buzzy go?' None of them could write. Paul started drinking very heavy after I was gone and they dismissed him. At that point Nate asked them to call me to see if they could get me back and they wouldn't do it. They told Nate, 'If you like Buzzy so much, why don't you go with him?' Now they are getting rid of their main lead singer. Nate said, 'The hell with you.'

"Nate called me up when I was in Philadelphia with a group I put together, Terry Johnson and the Modern Flamingos, and we joined forces," he said. "We had the sound. I was the lead singer on 'Lovers,' 'But Not For Me,' 'Time Was,' and all those beautiful songs that Paul and I sang and I would also sing the repeat tenor parts, which a lot of people don't know. Everybody thinks it's Nate but it was me."

Johnson, now in partnership with Nelson, traveled to Pittsburgh with the group, now named Terry Johnson's Flamingos featuring Nate Nelson. When they arrived, Joe Rock, a local producer who recorded, among other groups, the Skyliners, approached them with an offer to record the group.

"He asked us if we had any original songs," Johnson said. "I told him we did, and later on Nate asked me what songs. I said, 'Come on, let's write one.' We came up with 'Let's Be Lovers,' they liked it, and we recorded it in one or two takes."

Because the group obviously could not release a single as the Flamingos, they came up with a new name, the Starglows.

"I always loved the Moonglows," Johnson said. "The Moonglows had that sound. Nate came up with the Flaming O's. He figured it was spelled the same way as Flamingos. We both respected the Moonglows and so we came up with Starglows."

But when Goldner heard the new record, he immediately recognized the two familiar voices and protested to Atlantic Records. Faced with a dilemma, Atlantic stopped all promotion and the single faded away.

While still performing with the group, Johnson joined Motown as a production partner to Smokey Robinson. He recalled the experience of working with many of the label's outstanding talent.

"Working in that environment let me know that I'd been producing all the time and not getting paid for it," he said. "I was already doing it and didn't know. Working with groups like the Temptations, Four Tops, Supremes, and Miracles opened my head up to how artists take a song that you give them and say, 'Okay, I'm going to go live with it.' They take it home and study it while they're doing whatever they're doing around the house. They play it until they hear what they want to do with their voices."

Johnson said that Marvin Gaye and Levi Stubbs in particular would take a song home and when they came back to the studio they'd sing it as if it was a new song. He explained that what they were accomplishing was putting their own soul into it, projecting what they felt inside. He recalled that on occasion Gaye or Stubbs would come in and lay down a track that sounded fabulous. But invariably they'd want to take it back home and work with it some more. "It's the passion," he explained.

While Johnson originally joined Motown as an artist, aside from one release his work was restricted to production. He explained why.

"I still had Terry Johnson's Flamingos when I was at Motown," he said. "But Smokey wasn't really interested in recording us because they already had so many artists. They put out a record of me, 'Baby What You Gonna Do,' that was a strong song. Smokey wrote the lyrics and he's a great lyricist. They put my record out when they put out records by the Supremes, the Miracles, Stevie Wonder, Gladys Knight and the Pips, Marvin Gaye, Junior Walker and the All Stars, and Martha and the Vandellas."

Johnson made his first appearance on the television show *Soul Train* in support of the single. That was his sole promotional performance. "They [Motown] had to put their real money and concentration into their main acts," he said.

With the onslaught of the British Invasion of the 1960s, the Flamingos, like many other American recording artists, struggled to maintain their popularity.

Fortunately, Terry Johnson's Flamingos continue to thrill audiences at oldies shows nationwide in 2006 with soothing harmonic vocals that seemingly transcend the decades and present a fresh and current flavor, while maintaining its distinctive and unique sound.

Billboard Top 40 Hits by the Flamingos

Date	Pos	Wks on Charts	Record Title	Label/Number
06/08/59	11	11	I Only Have Eyes for You	End 1046
05/23/60	30	03	Nobody Loves Me Like You	End 1068

Larry Kassman
(The Quotations)

Patchogue, New York   **March 26, 2005**

The all-male vocal group the Quotations consists of four street-corner singers from Brooklyn, New York, whose single "Imagination" cast them into the limelight in 1961. The quartet recorded only four sides for the Verve label, one that lacked an elementary understanding of the new wave of music style called rock-and-roll. It's fair to attribute that fact as having stymied the group's potential for greater success.

Ironically, the weather played a significant role in the group's origin. Originally made up of three schoolmates from Brooklyn's James Madison High School, first tenor Richie Schwartz, second tenor Lew Arno, and baritone Harvey Hershkowitz, the group sang primarily at the local train station, on the boardwalks of Manhattan or Brighton Beach, and along Kings Highway. But a rainy day in 1958 forced the singers indoors.

It was during that fateful rehearsal at Barney's Pool Room, a location that provided excellent acoustics due to its tile walls, that things seemed to come together for them. Struggling with three-part harmonies that didn't seem to resonate in absence of a lead singer, the trio was approached by a young baritone who listened briefly and then asked if he could sing with them. The baritone was Larry Kassman and he would soon become the lead singer the group so desperately needed to fully develop their unique harmony.

"I didn't know the guys at all," Kassman said. "I heard three guys singing harmony and I asked them if I could sing a song. The rest is history. We actually had a fifth member, Mike Rose, who sang bass. He had a bad heart and died from a heart attack at seventeen years old. The group never replaced him."

Soon after Kassman's arrival, the now-quartet selected the group name, the Quotations, from one of the songs that they liked to sing, "Quotations of Love." In 1959, they recorded three demos and secured a management agreement with Helen Miller, who worked for the legendary producer Don Kirschner. Approaching numerous recording companies in New York in search of a record deal for her new group, Miller eventually landed one at Verve Records. While the label focused heavily on jazz and blues rather than doo-wop and rock-and-roll, the group remained optimistic.

In 1961, the Quotations reworked an up-tempo version of a classic tune, "Imagination," as their first recording. Their effort was encouraged by the success that the Marcels had with "Blue Moon." The formula worked very well for them.

"Helen Miller wrote songs with Howie Greenfield when we met her," Kassman recalled. "A mutual friend of hers and a member in the group introduced us, and the next thing we knew, we were in the studio recording 'Imagination.'"

The single was submitted to the extremely popular Murray the K radio show, one that had gained a reputation as a barometer for potential hit recordings and when it was named record of the week, the song beat out "The Wanderer" by Dion. Life changed quickly for the Quotations when that happened.

"We were walking on air at that point," Kassman recalled. "Murray the K used to take a song a day. At the end of the week listeners would vote for their favorite song and it became the record of the week. Tons of people must have called in for our song and that's how we beat out 'The Wanderer.'"

The group became the focus of much attention when their debut release hit the airwaves, securing engagements for personal appearances at a variety of venues along the East Coast. But it became apparent rather quickly that the Verve label was helplessly ill-equipped to capitalize on the strength of the group and their popular single. The record company executives' inability to fully comprehend and react to the energized and ever-growing rock-and-roll marketplace proved to be a detrimental factor in the Quotations' promotion and, sadly, its level of success.

Kassman spoke about the decision to record on the Verve label. "We were originally supposed to record on MGM, but they didn't have recording time for us so they threw us on a jazz label," he said. "That's what turned the group around, because we didn't belong on a jazz label. If we'd have been on the MGM label rather than the Verve label maybe things would have been different."

The Quotations are said to have a very distinctive sound and Kassman elaborated on that subject. "We had a very unique and very different sound," he said. "Richie, our first tenor, sang it in his own little kinky way and you knew immediately that it was the Quotations singing."

The group's follow-up single to "Imagination" was one of the four sides that were recorded during their only session at Verve, a tune called "This Love of Mine." The song failed to get much airplay despite its similarity in structure to the group's hit record. The Quotations did, however, perform the song at a concert appearance at Palisades Amusement Park in New Jersey, a venue frequented by many of the top acts of that era. Popular New York DJ Cousin Brucie Morrow hosted the show.

"We performed 'This Love of Mine' at Palisades with a broom," Kassman said. "We dressed the broom up with hair and everything and I was jumping all over the stage singing 'This Love of Mine' to a broom."

"We performed at a lot of shows in Pittsburgh, Baltimore, and all over the East Coast," he added. "We were kids at the time and I had to get permission from my mother to go to all these places. We hadn't even turned eighteen years old yet. It was a big thrill to appear with all these major groups."

The group's third effort, "See You in September," despite being recorded in April and intended to be a summertime release was issued in August and received little to no attention from DJs. Following the Quotations' fourth and final recording for Verve, "In the Night," the group's disenchantment with the label's ineptness in promoting or even having a basic understanding their style of music caused its original lineup to splinter in 1962. Kassman said that their decision to disband wasn't limited to the growing frustration over Verve's failure to properly promote them. "We just started going our own ways," he said. "We got back together in 1970 just to sing, and then WCBS-FM radio began playing oldies in 1972. We started to rehearse and put the group back together."

While various lineups augmented by original members performed as the Quotations for more than forty years, the original four singers came together in 1988 to record a CD and have been together ever since. "I was in the transportation business, another went into printing, one became a graphic designer, and one is a financial planner," he said. "We have remained close friends for all these years. Two members moved to New Jersey, two went to Long Island, and I remain in Brooklyn. I'll never leave Brooklyn. I like it too much and it's my hometown."

Of the four sides recorded by the Quotations on the Verve label, and despite scoring a hit record with "Imagination," Kassman cited that single's B-side, "Ala Men Sy" as being his personal favorite.

"The recording should have never been a B-side," he said. "That definitely should have been an A-side single. They needed a song for the B-side to 'Imagination,' we recorded 'Ala Men Sy' in eight minutes, and they put it on the flip. It's still my favorite of everything we did."

Kassman displayed a huge sense of pride over one lasting fact. "I enjoy performing with all the old groups," he said. "I remember singing with them in Brighton Beach on the boardwalk with Jay and the Americans, the Mystics, the Passions, the Classics, and all the Brooklyn groups. These guys are still around. *But*, my group is still the original four guys from 1959, still going strong in 2005."

Founding member Dee Dee Kenniebrew, center, reformed a new lineup of Crystals and continues to thrill audiences at shows nationwide.

Dolores "Dee Dee" Kenniebrew
(The Crystals)

Uncasville, Connecticut   **August 7, 2005**

Originally a quintet of high school students from Brooklyn, New York, members of the Crystals began singing in church. Organized by their soon-to-be manager, Benny Wells, the original lineup consisted of Barbara Alston, Dee Dee Kenniebrew, Mary Thomas, Patricia Wright, and Myrna Gerrard.

"Actually, I was the first member that Benny Wells had for the group," Kenniebrew recalled. "He knew my mother from the school, where she worked in the office, and he was allowed to use the music room to rehearse groups. He'd been a musician himself and was Barbara Alston's uncle, and he put her in the group too. She brought in two friends, Mryna Gerrard and Mary Thomas."

The group's name, Kenniebrew said, was inspired by Wright's niece. "Her brother-in-law was writing original songs for us and his four-year-old daughter's name was Crystal," she said.

In 1961, Wells took the group to the Celebrity Club in Long Island for their first stage appearance. "I can't recall exactly what we performed that night but we were rehearsing things like 'Mr. Lee' and material by the Shirelles and the Chantels," she said.

Eventually Wells secured work for the group at the legendary Brill Building in New York City, where they provided background vocals for other artists and cut demonstration records for the music publishing firm of Hill and Range. During rehearsal for one of the demos, producer Phil Spector, who had just formed his own Phillies Records label, heard them and approached Wells about recording them.

Prior to the encounter, Gerrard left the Crystals and was replaced by La La Brooks, who assumed the role of singing lead in the group. But Spector preferred Alston in that role and made the switch.

"Phil Spector happened to be at Hill and Range while we were there working one day and overheard us singing," Kenniebrew said. "He talked with us after we were finished singing and asked if we would be interested in recording for him. He took us into the studio at Mira Sound and recorded 'There's No Other (Like My Baby).'"

In September 1961, the Crystals had their first hit with the single, but "There's No Other" was actually intended to be the B-side for "Oh, Yeah, Maybe, Baby." "'There's No Other' became the A-side because of Jerry Blavat," Kenniebrew said. "He claimed that they gave him the record with 'There's No Other' as the side to push. He told me later on that he said to Phil, 'If you had any ears you'd know that the hit was 'There's No Other', not 'Oh, Yeah, Maybe, Baby.' He [Blavat] was pumping 'There's No Other' and he had a lot of influence at the time. He was right."

The single soared into the Top 20 pop charts and reached number five on the rhythm and blues charts. In support of the hit recording the Crystals made their first professional appearance at the Apollo Theater in Harlem, New York. Being high school teenagers at the time, the experience was somewhat overwhelming.

"I had heard about the Apollo but that was the first time I'd ever been there and it was a bit scary," she said. "We were just so green and that was the first show I ever saw. It was scary and exciting at the same time because when you don't know what to expect, having never seen a live show, you go on. We had worked out all of our choreography and had our new clothes on. They called our name and we just walked out on stage."

The Apollo audiences had a reputation for being extremely critical but most appreciative when an act performed well. For that reason, many artists both longed to perform there and were apprehensive at the same time. "We were received very well because I guess they knew we were so green that they were very forgiving," she said.

In early 1962 the Crystals recorded "Uptown," a song composed by the team of Barry Mann and Cynthia Weil that featured both a lush sound, due to its accompaniment of a full string section, and lyrics that boasted a relevant subject matter about life in the ghetto. It climbed to number thirteen on the national pop charts and established a more sophisticated and socially conscious type of material that would set the stage for future recordings in the rock-and-roll movement.

Following the release of "Uptown" the Crystals recorded "He Hit Me (But It Felt Like a Kiss)." But the single was met with controversy given its lyrical content that focused on infidelity and physical abuse and, suffering poor sales and limited air time, the Carole King/Gerry Goffin tune was eventually withdrawn from the market.

"None of us liked it at all," Kenniebrew recalled. "We didn't particularly care for it and we wanted to do something more funky, or groovy, or soulful, and just did not like the whole thing."

The next single released under the Crystals name turned out to be a Spector innovation of sorts, when the producer recorded a number-one hit record by the group, but without any of its original members. Spector returned to the West Coast and decided to record a Crystals single at Gold Star Studios in Los Angeles, the same place that he recorded his own 1958 number-one hit single with the Teddy Bears, "To Know Him Is to Love Him." But since he owned the Crystals name at that point, he decided to use a studio group, the Blossoms, to record the tune "He's a Rebel." Kenniebrew reflected on that time and what actually transpired between Spector and the group.

"Actually our voices might have been on those recordings because we never knew what he did once he left the studio," she said. "What really happened was that our first recordings, 'There's No Other' and 'Oh, Yeah, Maybe, Baby,' went national, and they'd even been released overseas because I remember seeing an article in the trades. But we didn't get paid for it. He told us it was just because all the receipts weren't in and so on and we decided that we weren't going to record anymore until we got paid."

The group was finally talked into returning to the studio to record "Uptown," Kenniebrew said. "We went in and did 'Uptown' and we were still waiting to be paid for 'There's No Other.' We were really in turmoil with him and there were a lot of things going on, and while we rehearsed, we said we weren't going into the studio with him anymore. He just wouldn't pay us.

"When he recorded 'There's No Other,' it was not supposed to go on his label," she continued. "He was the producer but he was doing it for Liberty Records. Instead, he went to Lester Sill and got Lester to get the money together and they formed a record label, Phil and Les Records. And he put 'There's No Other' out as his first release on their new label. But he didn't pay us. Then we went back into the studio with the second one and again he didn't pay."

At that point, Spector moved to California. "We didn't know that he had any connections in California outside of living there for a while," Kenniebrew said. "He decided, 'Well, it's time for a new Crystals record,' and the next thing we know we've got a record out on the air. We're in the car one day going to a gig and hear, 'Here's the latest Crystals record.' Well, what were we going to do, not sing our new record?"

Kenniebrew said that the Crystals ended up firing Wells for allowing them to sign a contract that stated that as long as they were under contract to Spector, he had the use of the name the Crystals for recording purposes. The group had signed the deal, which bound them by the agreement for seven years.

"We realized that he was just a thief and wasn't going to pay us," Kenniebew said. "I remember him telling us once that acts don't make money from recordings; they make it from going on the road. But [in the] meantime, we still had to go from a studio apartment on Fifty-eighth street and Eighth Avenue to two apartments on the Upper East Side, but we should not be paid. His attitude was that we should be lucky we had a hit record. So he went and got some studio girls, recorded them, and put it out under our name."

Being faced with a tough situation, the Crystals had no choice other than to perform the hit singles at shows despite the fact that another contingent of singers' voices, led by Darlene Love were heard on the recordings.

"We began to have a lot of discord amongst the group because we had no way to get rid of him [Spector]," she said. "But we got rid of that manager. We were only school kids and he [Wells] took the contract to an attorney, but you don't just take it to any attorney; you go to a show business attorney.

150

"What I did not realize until recently, because I guess I never went back to look at the contract, is that our parents never signed that contract," she said. "By the time we signed it, Myrna Gerrard had left and La La Brooks had come in. We signed it in 1962 and when he did the first record with us, we didn't even have a contract with him for 'There's No Other.' There was no Phillies label. So by the time we signed the contract right after recording it, he got the record label, put us on there, and he began to get really high and mighty and full of himself. But prior to that, he was easy enough to work with and he wasn't really much older than we were. But those few years make a difference when you're fourteen and fifteen and others are twenty-two."

In early 1963, Spector scored another Top 20 hit with Love's vocals on a single released as the Crystals on "He's Sure the Boy I Love." In May of that year, the real Crystals, featuring Brooks on lead vocals, released the number-three hit single, "Da Doo Ron Ron," which became the girls second huge hit in England. Along with "Then He Kissed Me," the group's follow-up to "Da Doo Ron Ron," the Crystals became one of the hottest groups in England, at a time that barely preceded the British Invasion in the United States.

The Crystals seventh single, "Then He Kissed Me," is considered by many to be the song that established Spector's Wall of Sound, the legendary record production style he developed and used on subsequent recording sessions. "Even before that record he started using a lot of musicians and overdubbing to the point of even losing the original generations because everything was done in mono in those days," Kenniebrew recalled. "He'd go in and lay down beautiful vocals and backgrounds, and by the time he'd go in and overdub and overdub with more musicians he'd bury the original song. You didn't hear the finished product until he was finished with it. We'd lay down the basic track and then he'd take it and then you'd hear the finished track and you got so buried on it. There were some songs that he put out that were just so awful but he'd pull them off right away so it looked like he didn't have any failures.

"We had done a few other records before we did 'And Then He Kissed Me' that were just mish-mash because it was just too much," she continued. "But we were paying the cost. He could stay in the studio for a week because it was coming out of our money and he wasn't paying for it. Well, coming out of your money if he ever decided to pay you."

Despite the success that they were achieving, the Crystals were entangled in a growing tension with Spector. At a time that saw the group appearing constantly at a wide variety of venues and on concert bills, the fact that they were obligated to perform songs that were actually recorded by Love and the Blossoms grated on them. As time passed, Spector's attention began to shift toward other acts such as the Ronettes and the Righteous Brothers. Legal issues also surrounded Spector as he broke ties with business partner Lester Sill. A court-ordered settlement between the two former partners resulted in, without doubt, the most bizarre recording ever made by the Crystals.

To fulfill the terms of the settlement, Spector was required to pay Sill a share of the proceeds generated from the next Crystals' single. The recording, "(Let's Dance) the Screw," featured Spector speaking the lyrics with the members of the Crystals singing its background vocals. Not appropriate for release, of the few singles produced one is said to have been forwarded to Sill as a parting shot from the exceedingly eccentric producer.

Kennibrew recalled recording the controversial song. "That was what he gave his partner and shows you what a beautiful person he [Spector] is," she said. "Lester Sill was so sick of him and his behavior and his attitude. Now he was on a roll and was the golden boy, so to speak, and he's wonderful and great. Lester just wanted out of the partnership and asked Spector to just give him the proceeds from the next Crystals record because he knew that we were on a roll and would more than likely have a hit. At that point, he'd let Spector have the label.

"So he [Spector] had us go into the studio and do an instrumental and it's called 'The Screw,' and he's screwing his own partner who helped get the funds for him to even have a record label," she continued. "We really didn't know what was going on at the time. And remember, at that time we didn't have any choice over what we recorded, because part of our contract with him said he had total artist control. He would just say, 'We're going to do a record; this is how the song goes,' and then do this and that was it."

The practice, Kenniebrew said, resulted in a number of Crystals recordings never being released, some of which went on to become huge hits for other artists, one being Leslie Gore's "It's My Party." "We didn't record 'It's My Party' because it wasn't finished yet, but Carole King first brought it to us as a ballad," she said. "She also brought us 'Chains.'"

In 1965, becoming increasingly tired of Spector's indifference and inattention toward them, the Crystals bought out their contract and shifted to the Imperial Records label, but failed to find success there.

Eventually signing with United Artists, they disbanded after releasing just two singles.

"There was a lot of frustration amongst the group at that time because when you're young and you have a hit record and become famous, you're traveling around the country, but you're not getting paid—he starts pitting one against the other. He told La La Brooks he was going to record a single with her and he just used us to line his pockets, and if you're a kid you're going to go for it. After a while we started to disintegrate one by one. Mary left, and then Pat left. People just can't take the abuse and no respect; you just want out. You're expecting that you're going to make money and do lots of things and this guy is taking everything he can from you. With no recourse, you just walk away."

Five years passed before the strength of the rock-and-roll revival period prompted a Crystals reunion. A 1971 Richard Nader rock-and-roll concert stimulated Kenniebrew to reform the Crystals. But while some accounts state that the original core of the group performed together for a few years, Kenniebrew disputed that fact.

"We only came together to perform at that one show," she said. "Actually, I had stayed with the group and worked with two other girls down in the Islands but I was the only original left. Richard Nader called my mother's house and said he was interested in doing the show. We were due to come back after a few months [of] performing, and the lawsuit against Phil Spector was going to trail around the same exact time as the Nader concert. We came up to New York and I called the girls together and we did that one show. Barbara, Mary, and me did a few shows after that but La La had two kids by then and she never worked with us again."

Two hit singles that the Crystals recorded, "Da Doo Ron Ron" and "Then He Kissed Me," were re-issued and became hits in England in 1974. "I have no idea what motivated those songs to be re-issued but that is the only money I ever got from him [Spector] because he approached the guy who was our booking agent at the time and said that he wanted to record us again," she said. "I guess he knew that he was going to re-issue the songs at the time. He was with Warner Brothers then, as Warner-Spector, and said he'd give me, as the only one left with the group, some upfront money. I agreed and he gave me the money against royalties, but I doubted that Warner or anyone would work with him. He's got to be in total control and thinks that nobody's got a brain cell working but him. I knew that Warner Brothers wouldn't

153

put up with him and I was right. For one whole year, which is what the contract was for, he never recorded one thing.

"When the year ended and it was time for the next advance payment, he didn't want to pay it," she said. "It wasn't my fault he didn't record during that year, and since he wasn't paying the next advance, I said forget it. That was the end of that deal."

Kenniebrew continues to lead the Crystals in 2006 at performances throughout the country. Now based in Georgia, she reflected on her career in music through the years. "I guess that I am proud to have been in the industry for so long and never got involved in drugs or alcohol, and I've always stayed responsible to my audience.... I would never sing or come on stage in any way that wouldn't find me dressed nicely and give people something to look up to," she said.

"A lot of people are out there looking at you, and while we don't have royalty in this country, people look up to stars and follow you," she said. "When you go out there dressed like a bum, overexpose yourself, or sing something really bad it becomes, especially for young children nowadays who are very much into music, a bad signal. A lot of people say, 'Well, I'm singing reality.' People see reality every day. Why would you go to a show and pay money to see what you can on a street corner in a ghetto. You have to bring people up, not down."

Billboard Top 40 **Hits by the Crystals**

Date	Pos	Wks on Charts	Record Title	Label/Number
12/11/61	20	07	There's No Other (Like My Baby)	Phillies 100
04/28/62	13	08	Uptown	Phillies 102
10/06/62	01	12	He's a Rebel	Phillies 106
01/19/62	11	08	He's Sure the Boy I Love	Phillies 109
05/11/63	03	10	Da Doo Ron Ron	Phillies 112
08/31/63	06	09	Then He Kissed Me	Phillies 115

**John Kuse
(The Excellents)**

Brooklyn, New York   **May 21, 2005**

The local and sometimes intense rivalry between residents that lived in two New York City boroughs, the Bronx and Brooklyn, was in its heyday during the 1950s due to the fierce competition and loyalty shown to their respective professional baseball teams. While Brooklyn fans wholeheartedly embraced their beloved Dodgers, Bronx fans boasted the legendary and world champion (many times over) New York Yankees.

Musically, the two boroughs had an equally competitive spirit, each turning out many of the era's top vocal groups. Among the huge representation were Brooklyn's the Classics, the Mystics, the Chimes, and Little Anthony and the Imperials and Bronx groups that included Dion and the Belmonts, the Channels, and the Excellents. Ironically, the latter Bronx contingent would record a hit song that served to both epitomize street-corner harmony as well as unify, at least musically, teenagers in both boroughs. The song, recorded by the all-male Bronx group, was about a girlfriend in Brooklyn, titled "Coney Island Baby."

When friends from Christopher Columbus and DeWitt Clinton high schools came together to form the Premiers in 1960, the group included baritone Joel Feldman, falsetto Denis Kestenbaum, second tenor Phil Sanchez, bass Chuck Epstein, and the Kuse brothers, John (lead singer) and George (first tenor).

"During the early 1960s, I lived in a private neighborhood in the Bronx and we just started singing among ourselves," Kuse said. "Then Phil Sanchez, my brother George, and I ventured over to Pelham Parkway, which is a neighborhood full of kids, and they had a lot of shows going on. I ran into three other fellows at a dance there that were also in a group. Before you know it we all sang together; the three met the other three and became six. And that was the start of the Excellents."

They soon selected the group name the Excellents, but Kuse said that while a story has floated around for years on how the name was chosen, he really didn't have the faintest idea if it was true. "They said that we were sucking down White Castle hamburgers and someone said, 'Boy, this is excellent.' That's a great story but I really can't say one way or another if that was the reason the name Excellents was picked."

The unusual number of singers in the group's lineup differed from other vocal groups of that time who sang a four- or five-part harmony. Kuse explained how the extra member enhanced the sound the Excellents were able to achieve.

"It was a very full sound," he said. "It was everything you could possibly ask for in a group. You had a baritone, bass, second tenor, first tenor, a falsetto, and then you had a guy floating around into baritone plus doing the bass with a riff. As far as I know, the Wrenditions [a more current a cappella group] tried to follow us because they have six guys too, and they always liked that idea."

Kuse credits Sanchez as being the songwriter in the group, having composed a number of tunes through the years.

In 1961, when a local record producer, Vinny Catalano, heard the group sing he offered them an opportunity to record on his Sinclair label. The group entered the studio to lay down tracks on an up-tempo version of an Al Jolson tune "Red Red Robin." The single was released on the Mermaid Records label with a flip side that featured another cover tune, the Jesters' "Love No One but You."

"That song ['Red Red Robin'] originally came out in 1931, and how we ever put it together is beyond me but we did a great job on it," Kuse said. "It was a very tinny record, a great arrangement, and it could really be redone nicely. But it was done on the Mermaid label and Mermaid was a subsidiary of Sinclair Records. Sinclair had the Whale, Blast, and Mermaid labels." He recalled how the group came to Catalano's attention.

"You knocked on doors and brought your demos around," Kuse said. "We knocked on their door and they said, 'Come on in.' That was it." When the group went back into the studio in 1962 to record "You Baby You," Catalano and Peter Alonzo presented them with a song that they wrote called "Coney Island Baby." Kuse recalled first hearing the tune.

"I thought it was pretty good," he said. "When we put down our rendition of the Cleftones' 'You Baby You' we really had nothing else that they were interested in. At that point they said, 'Hey, try this.' Imagine that. But this is how it goes. We went out into the bathroom, where you could get an echo, practiced and came back to record it."

The song was originally intended as the B-side to "You Baby You." But when disc jockeys began to flip the record and it gained attention, Blast Records initiated some high-profile promotions in support of it. "I actually remember seeing a plane flying overhead with a banner that said 'Miss Coney Island Baby Contest.' They were actually going to try and have the contest, but whether it went through or not, I don't know."

Like many new records issued at that time, it became the focus of the WINS Murray the K radio show's record of the week contest. And while "Coney Island Baby" won the contest, other New York stations considered the voting process skewed.

"The reason they say that the record really didn't fly back in those days is because too many votes came in from concentrated areas in the Bronx," he recalled. "WINS played it and had their call-in voting and WMCA (another major New York station) said that they didn't want to play it that much because they found that the votes from the WINS contest just came in from the Bronx. They played it a little but it never went any further than that until WCBS-FM started their oldies format."

Despite a questionable perception regarding the voting process when the song became the number-one record of the week on WINS, the Excellents began to make appearances in support of it, albeit they were limited. Kuse attributed that to promotional ineffectiveness by the label. "The manager at Blast Records didn't handle it the right way," he said. "We were very disillusioned about that."

Two years later, the Excellents went to court over some recording issues and learned that "Coney Island Baby" had actually climbed to number fifty-one on the *Billboard* charts despite WMCA's earlier doubt.

With a hit record on their hands, the Excellents' future looked promising. But when they were booked to perform on the popular Dick Clark's *American Bandstand* television show, circumstances encountered by the group prompted the label to send a different Excellents lineup to appear in their place. Devastated by the action, the Excellents would never return to the recording studio.

"We sang at the Steel Pier and we had to drive to Atlantic City [New Jersey] ourselves," Kuse said. "The company was just terrible. They never even asked us how we were getting there. They were our manager and they didn't even come to the Steel Pier. After that show, I got a call two days later saying that they wanted us on *American Bandstand*. It was just ridiculous. I was nineteen years old and had a girlfriend and didn't want to leave her. Our past experience with the way they handled us had us wondering how we were going to get to Philadelphia. It was crazy. They needed my parents' consent, and some of the guys were locked up in school and couldn't make it.

"It came down to a Monday when the company called my mother at work and said if I didn't come they would sue her for five hundred thousand dollars," he added. "But we found out that they couldn't do that. I should have just gone down, because they just wanted the guy who sang the lead."

When Kuse and the other group members balked at going to Philadelphia, Sinclair Records brought in replacements to make the appearance and to record songs as the Excellents. Since none of the members of the Excellents owned the group's name and the label eventually secured it, Kuse and friends were left out in the cold.

"They got some other guys to record 'I Hear a Rhapsody,' 'Why Did You Laugh,' and 'It Takes Two to Fall in Love' and credited it to the Excellents," Kuse said. "That was really the Ultimates, who became the Excellents."

In 1964 Bobby Records released "Helene," a single that included the voices of all the original Excellents, but the song was actually recorded during the group's original session at Sinclair. The record was released as being performed by the Excellents.

"We were very, very soured on what we'd gone through at the time," Kuse said. "We thought we'd stay small and do some local gigs, and that's how it was for twenty years. We never had anybody come after us to be another manager and we had soured with those guys [Sinclair] by walking out. They needed to push the other records they had, so they hired the Ultimates, whose members came from all five boroughs in New York City."

During a trip that Kuse made to visit his parents in Florida in recent years, he was invited to be interviewed on a local doo-wop radio show. He used the interview to set the record straight regarding a longstanding disagreement involving Chuck Epstein, the Excellents original bass singer, and Dave Strum, the bass singer that was part of the group's replacement lineup. "They both were Excellents," Kuse said. "I sang a couple of songs on the show, and then explained that whole story on the air. When I went back to Chuck's house that night he hugged me and said that it came out perfect. Now Dave knows that Chuck was an original Excellent and Chuck knows that Dave was a succeeding Excellent and it worked out really good."

In the late 1980s, Kuse reformed the Excellents and added Jerry Pilgrim and Les Levine to the lineup. "For the longest time I was doing little private gigs and we weren't really out there promoting the name as far as professional shows go," he said. "At that time another group was but I didn't know about it and we were just doing our thing. We were still calling ourselves the Excellents and have never stopped.

"Finally, in 1987, we were appearing on the Don K. Reed radio show and were set to do a show at the Westbury Music Theater, and out of the woodwork someone came by and tried to stop me," he added. "And then I found out that this other person was out there with another group. Slowly but surely word about me came out. Now I finally got my recognition that I made that song."

In 1996 Kuse left the Excellents to join Cathy Jean and the Roommates to perform at oldies shows. "I had a falling out with some of the guys we had then and decided to branch out," Kuse said. "Performing with Cathy was the greatest experience of my life. I loved singing with her and I loved singing her songs. I got the opportunity to sing 'Give a Little, Take a Little' and all of the songs that she made. They sought to get a first tenor and lead, and she thought my joining them was a great idea. I sang my songs and she sang hers and I absolutely loved it."

In 2000, Kuse and the Excellents released a CD titled *You'll Always Be My Coney Island Baby* on Crystal Ball Records. It was a compilation of Kuse's career in music through the years. The recording included his work, along with Cathy Jean's songs, and the original tracks laid down by the Excellents in the early 1960s.

Kuse cited Tony Passalaqua of the Fascinators as his personal favorite recording artist from the early era. "I saw him singing with the

Legends of Doo Wop a few weeks ago and I loved it," he said. "For me, Passalaqua singing 'Oh Rosemarie' and 'Chapel Bells' is the best. And I try to imitate Vito Picone [the Elegants] when he was younger."

In 2005, John Kuse and the Excellents continued to perform at about twenty shows a year throughout the New York tri-state area.

Brenda Lee
("I'm Sorry")

She is known as "Little Miss Dynamite" but despite her diminutive four-foot-eleven-inch height, Brenda Lee became one of the most successful recording artists in both rock-and-roll and country music throughout a career that spans more than fifty years.

Born Brenda Mae Tarpley in 1944 in Atlanta, Georgia, Lee displayed a gifted vocal talent by the time she was three years old. "I was born in a charity ward at Grady Memorial Hospital," she said. "A lot of Southerners were. We were poor, from the South, and proud of it."

She sang gospel music in church as a youngster and at five she represented Conyers Grade School at an annual talent show that was held among the area's schools. There has been a longstanding debate on which song she actually performed at the show, one that gained her first prize. Lee set the record straight.

"The first song that I ever sang was 'Take Me Out to the Ballgame,'" Lee said. "But at my first talent show I sang 'Slow Poke' and 'They Try to Tell Us We're Too Young.' As for the ballgame, my mother was a big

Dodgers fan and my dad was a Yankee man. He was an amateur baseball player too, so at out our house it was an argument every year as to who was going to win that pennant."

While Tarpley won the prize at the talent show and soon began to secure various radio and television engagements, her compensation came in a most unusual form.

"When I won the talent show the prize was an appearance on a local television show called *John Farm and the TV Ranch Boys*," she said. "I was on that show and it was sponsored by Borden's Ice Cream, so I didn't get paid but I could eat all the ice cream that I could hold on Saturdays, when the show was on."

She soon became a regular on the show and began to travel with its band performing at a number of small venues in the area. She also sang with a gospel group called the Master Worker's Quartet and performed at shows with the group. "My raising was in gospel," she said. "It was a natural thing for me to sing."

Lee's father died in a tragic accident in 1953, and when her mother remarried in 1955 and the family relocated to Cincinnati, Ohio, Tarpley began to perform the country music hits of the day on Newport, Kentucky's WNOP radio, a show that originated from the Jimmy Skinner Record Shop. Later that year the family moved to Augusta, Georgia, where the youngster continued to wow audiences with appearances on WJAT-TV's *Peach Blossom Special* show as well as on WRDW radio, where she sang from a record store her step-father had opened, and one that bore her name.

It was during her work on the *Peach Blossom Special* that Tarpley's name was changed to Lee. "The producer of the show, Sammy Barton said, 'Why don't we shorten your name from Tarpley to just Brenda Lee?' so we did," she said. "He felt that Tarpley was too hard to remember."

During a visit to Augusta, Georgia, to perform, country music legend Red Foley heard Lee sing and became an instrumental part of her future and career in music.

"He came to my hometown to do a show and a DJ friend of mine took me over and asked him if he would listen to me sing and let me sing on the show," Lee recalled. "He graciously obliged, liked what he heard, and at that point in time he had a network television show out of Springfield, Missouri, called the *Ozark Jubilee*. He asked me if I'd like to come and be on that, and of course I said yes. I became a regular and got my contract with Decca Records and went on to do all the big variety shows. Red was pretty much a great mentor of mine."

As she became known and her popularity soared, she appeared on other television shows including Ed Sullivan and Perry Como.

In 1956 Lee signed a recording contract with Decca Records and recorded her first single, "Jambalaya," when she was ten years old. While the record received good airplay, it failed to reach the charts. A year later she charted with "One Step at a Time." Though it didn't go higher than number forty-three on the pop charts, it entered the Top 20 country music charts. Upon the release of her follow-up single, 1957's "Dynamite," she gained the nickname "Little Miss Dynamite."

Lee credited Owen Bradley as being a significant influence in her recording career. "Owen and I were a team," Lee said. "Whatever sound I have, Owen is pretty much responsible for it other than what comes out of my throat. That's my thing and God's own creation, but his technique and the way he worked in the studios, the musicians that he chose to work with and all, made it the Brenda Lee sound."

In December 1957, at twelve years old and with two singles already released, Lee made her first appearance on the Grand Ole Opry at the legendary Ryman Auditorium in Nashville, Tennessee. Another young artist that would soon take the world by storm, Elvis Presley, shared the bill with her.

"What a sweet guy," Lee recalled. "We remained friends until he passed away. He didn't go over so well that night on the Opry, by the powers that be. The crowd loved him, but the powers that be told him to keep his day job. We all make mistakes, don't we?"

Her early singles were well received in Europe and as a result she toured France in 1959. But promotions for at least one tour stop, in Paris, advertised the American artist as a thirty-two-year-old midget. "That's true," she confirmed. "I had a hit record there because I had covered 'The Stroll.' It was a hit for me there but they had never seen me; they only heard my voice. They wanted a picture for the tour and we sent one over. I was twelve years old and they kept calling back saying that they needed more recent pictures and we said, 'These are recent.' It's what I looked like.

"My manager actually started this thing that I was a thirty-two-year-old midget, and *La Figaro*, the big Parisian newspaper there, picked it up and it was great," she added.

In February 1960, one of Lee's singles finally climbed the American charts with her recording of "Sweet Nothin's." Her popularity began to gain momentum. "I had had a lot of songs out before then but really didn't do anything. Some charted, some didn't. Some were played, some weren't. There was nothing to establish me as a viable recording artist.

But when 'Sweet Nothin's' became my first Top 10 record, it really got me out there." The record climbed to number four on the pop charts. During the next thirteen years, Lee would chart eleven singles in the Top 10, two of which hit number one, "I'm Sorry" and "I Want to Be Wanted."

A bit of information regarding "Sweet Nothin's" for music trivia aficionados is the fact that Louis Nunley of the Anita Kerr Singers is the voice whispering in the background on the recording. While Lee did a few recordings backed by the legendary Jordanaires, she accomplished most of her singles with the Anita Kerr Singers.

Lee went on to attend the Hollywood Professional School in 1960. "I went out to California in my sophomore year of high school and was there for the tenth, eleventh, and twelfth grade, and it was a very colorful place," she said. "I went to school there with Mickey Rooney, Kathy Young [of the Innocents], Kurt Russell, and a lot of actors and actresses. It was a lot of fun."

In June 1960, when Lee's recording of "I'm Sorry" scaled the charts and reached number one, she became an international star. Throughout her career she has performed through the United States, Canada, and some seventy foreign countries.

"I sure did enjoy my travels overseas," she said. "It was a wonderful thing because I'd only seen those places in books and pictures and I never dreamed that I'd be getting to go over there much less to go over there and sing and get paid for it."

Following "I'm Sorry," the biggest hit recording of her career, Decca released "That's All You Gotta Do," and then "I Want to Be Wanted." The latter single would become Lee's second single to reach number one on the charts. "That was a wonderful song and was from the musical 'Never On Sunday,' written by a wonderful Greek writer. It was sent to us and of course we had to put English lyrics to it. It was one of my biggest records."

In 1960, "I'm Sorry" was named the number-six song of the entire year. It would be one of six Top 40 hits for Lee that year. Lee reflected on that year and the significance of her work and what it meant to her career.

"That song 'I'm Sorry' changed my life," she said. "It changed my family's life, my siblings' life, my mom's life, and it was just a blessing for all of us. That was a busy year for me. I started traveling nonstop, working eleven months out of the year and in the studio the other month. It was hectic. That year I bought my mom our first home. A lot of things happened in 1960."

A song that Lee recorded in 1958 and that exploded onto the scene in December 1960 has become a perennial holiday favorite. It is named "Rockin' Around the Christmas Tree," a tune composed by Johnny Marks, who also wrote "Run Rudolph Run," "Holly Jolly Christmas," and "Rudolph the Red-Nosed Reindeer."

"They say it was the first rock-and-roll Christmas song," Lee said. "It was released in 1958 and again in 1959, and it didn't do a whole lot. But when it was released again the Christmas right after I had a hit with 'I'm Sorry,' it took off great guns and it just never ceases to amaze me every year what it does."

Lee has included the song in her stage act regardless of the time of year. That decision came after years of fan requests.

"I sing that song at every show, all year long," she said. "If I don't, they ask why I didn't. So I started putting it in, and it's something when you're at a fair in July and it's one hundred four degrees outside and you're doing Christmas stuff."

"Dum Dum," a Jackie DeShannon composition, entered the Top 5 charts in 1961 for Lee. "Jackie wrote a lot of my stuff," she said. "She used to send me the best demos. Her demos would be like a record and it just made you want to go in the studio and record them. She was and is a great writer."

In January 1962 Lee charted a number-four hit single with "Break It to Me Gently." "I loved that song," she said. "That was my first foray into that kind of a bluesy sound. That record was good to me."

While touring England in the early 1960s, Lee saw a local group perform and was so taken by their sound that she brought a tape of the band back to the United States with her and asked her record company to give it a listen. That group was the Beatles, one of only three acts that would eventually top Lee in charted singles during the 1960s.

"I brought back a demo and a picture of the group, but my record company rejected them," she said. "They said that their look was way too different and the sound would never make it. I toured with them again and told them that I had taken their material to my company. About a year later they came out with 'I Want to Hold Your Hand.' The rest is history."

Lee was named as one of five American artists who best survived the British Invasion of the 1960s. While many American recording artists struggled to maintain their popularity and adapt to the changing sound and preference of music fans during that period, Lee continued to flourish. She theorized on why that might have been the case.

"I think that was because I wasn't trying to compete with what was happening from the British shores," she said. "I was completely different. At that point in my career I was not so much rock [as] I was pop, and their sound was truly rock. I think it was just a no-competition type thing."

In the early 1970s, Lee began to chart hit singles, this time in the country music marketplace. Her first hit, a Kris Kristofferson composition called "Nobody Wins," preceded the extremely popular "Big Four Poster Bed," the latter written by Shel Silverstein. Bradley originally wanted to trim the song, encompassing more than four minutes in length and considered unusually long at the time, for commercial reasons.

"When Owen Bradley told Shel that he wanted to cut it down, Shel said that if anything was cut out we couldn't have it and couldn't record it," Lee recalled. "We took a chance and did it and it was a Top 5 record for me."

Throughout the 1980s and 1990s Lee continued to chart Top 10 country hits with songs that include "Tell Me What It's Like," "The Cowgirl and the Dandy," and "Broken Trust," a tune she recorded with the award-winning country artists the Oak Ridge Boys.

"I loved working with the Oak Ridge Boys," she said. "I traveled with them on the road for a couple of years and had a ball. 'The Cowgirl and the Dandy' was a Bobby Goldsboro song. I think he's one of the most creative people I know."

Lee has recorded songs in, among other languages, German and Japanese. When performing in the various countries she sings in the native language.

"I've had hits in six languages, and at first I learned them phonetically, but then as I toured the countries year after year, I pretty much learned to speak the language," she said. "It was original material, not my hits that I had in the States. I had a big hit in Japan called 'One Rainy Night in Tokyo.' It's a pretty language when you sing it."

As for having been cited as the number-one female recording artist of all time, Lee responded. "Well, that's what they say," she said. "I know that Mariah Carey is way up there, and Madonna is. I don't know if I still hold that record or not but I'm going to take your word for it."

Before Lee turned twenty years old she had recorded two hundred fifty-six sides. She is credited with having more double-sided hit singles that any other woman in the history of pop music. She achieved a greater number of hit chart recordings than any female in the history of music, and in a myriad of genres including pop, rock, country, rhythm and blues, and easy listening. During the 1960s Lee was the female leader in charted songs and overall only three other artists topped her, Elvis Presley, the Beatles, and Ray Charles.

Her biggest hit, "I'm Sorry," has sold more than fifteen million records worldwide, and "Rockin' Around the Christmas Tree," which has become a perennial holiday favorite, has sold nearly ten million copies.

In recognition of an outstanding career and body of work in music, Brenda Lee has the distinction of having been inducted into both the Country Music Hall of Fame in 1997 and the Rock and Roll Hall of Fame in 2000. She continues to perform at a variety of venues in 2005.

Billboard Top 40 Hits by Brenda Lee

Date	Pos	Wks on Charts	Record Title	Label/Number
02/15/60	04	15	Sweet Nothin's	Decca 30967
06/06/60	01	18	I'm Sorry/	
06/20/60	06	09	That's All You Gotta Do	Decca 31093
09/19/60	01	13	I Want to Be Wanted	
10/31/60	40	01	Just a Little	Decca 31149
12/19/60	14	03	Rockin' Around the Christmas Tree	Decca 30776
01/16/61	07	09	Emotions/	
02/06/61	33	02	I'm Learning About Love	Decca 31195
04/03/61	06	10	You Can Depend On Me	Decca 31231
06/26/61	04	10	Dum Dum	Decca 31272
10/09/61	03	12	Fool #1/	
10/16/61	31	03	Anybody But Me	Decca 31309
01/20/62	04	12	Break It to Me Gently	Decca 31348
04/28/62	06	08	Everybody Loves Me But You	Decca 31379
07/21/62	15	07	Heart in Hand/	
07/21/62	29	04	It Started All Over Again	Decca 31407
10/06/62	03	12	All Alone Am I	Decca 31424
02/16/63	32	03	Your Used To Be	Decca 31454
04/20/63	06	10	Losing You	Decca 31478
07/27/63	24	06	My Whole World Is Falling Down/	
07/27/63	25	05	I Wonder	Decca 31510
10/12/63	17	05	The Grass Is Greener	Decca 31539
12/28/63	12	08	As Usual	Decca 31570
03/28/64	25	05	Think	Decca 31599
10/31/64	17	07	Is It True	Decca 31690
06/26/65	13	08	Too Many Rivers	Decca 31792
11/13/65	33	03	Rusty Bells	Decca 31849
10/29/66	11	08	Coming On Strong	Decca 32018
02/11/67	37	02	Ride, Ride, Ride	Decca 32079

Bobby Lewis
("Tossin' and Turnin'")

Islandia, New York   **November 12, 2005**

ollowing the opening soulful strains of his number-one hit song
came perhaps one of the most recognizable lines in a rock-and-roll
recording as Bobby Lewis sings an energized: "*I couldn't sleep at all last
night.*" The song, a Ritchie Adams and Malou Rene composition titled
"Tossin' and Turnin,'" became one of the biggest hits of the 1960s, rode
the charts for twenty-three weeks, and reached the Top 10 slot two
separate times. It also accomplished a rare feat for that time, climbing
to number one on both the rhythm and blues and pop charts, selling
more than three million copies.

Despite the fame generated from his long career in music,
biographies about Lewis are plagued with inaccuracies regarding his
early influences and eventual entry into the music industry.

Bobby Lewis was born in Indianapolis, Indiana, on February 17,
1933, and was raised in a local orphanage. While biographies on Lewis
begin by stating that he showed an interest in music at an extremely

young age and had the aptitude to learn how to play a piano at five years old, that story is only half true.

"I couldn't have played piano at age five," Lewis said. "The orphanage didn't even have a piano to play on. In fact, it didn't have any instruments at all and we had to make our instruments. We used a big, empty corn flake box that we got at the grocery store and used it for a drum. We used a kazoo and spoons and a harmonica and vinegar jugs for a bass. We also used a wash tub as a bass. We would turn it over, knock a hole in it with a hammer and a nail, and then tie a wire between it and a broom handle. We played it just like a bass fiddle."

Another source of misinformation cites Lewis's moving from the orphanage to live with a foster family in Detroit. It goes on to state that after becoming disenchanted with the almost abusive rules of the home, those imposed by his foster mother, he decided to run away when he was fourteen years old. Again, the statement is half true.

"I didn't run away from Detroit; I ran away from my foster parents' house, in Indianapolis," he said. "They were something like [comedian] Flip Wilson's foster parents and they were pretty rugged. The man was fine but the lady was a little ambitious and she had us always cleaning and washing things. Once a month she would have me washing the windows upstairs, and on the front of the house there was an overhang over the porch like a steeple. She would have me stand on that steeple and wash windows and I was frightened. It was high and the tiles were smooth. When I told her that I was afraid I would fall, she used to always yell at me."

When Lewis finally ran away, he didn't get too far before re-thinking his decision and returning home. Greeted at the back door by his foster father, a man that Lewis described as "nice, but henpecked," the man would not allow Lewis to enter the house, fearing the wrath of his wife. At that point, Lewis headed out again but was soon picked up by the state troopers, who, upon determining that the teenager didn't want to go back to the home, had him placed with a new foster family.

"She was worse than the first woman," Lewis recalled. "She didn't use lights, didn't use heat, and what I had as a bed was a tiny bunk with one cover. She told me that if I got home later than five o'clock in the evening I wouldn't be able to get in. One night I got home at five thirty and she wouldn't open the door."

Finding himself on the road again, Lewis stayed with friends, slept in a park or in the back of a car, and shined shoes to earn money for food. Being able to play harmonica fairly well, he started to attempt to pick up gigs wherever he could.

"I couldn't get work otherwise, so I was doing weekend shows," Lewis said. "I worked with the guitarist Wes Montgomery and his brother Monk. They are from Indianapolis and everybody gravitated to an area we called the main stem. It was a black neighborhood that had the bars, restaurants, and laundries. I walked into this club, the Music Bar, one day and Wes Montgomery was up there playing with a trio. One guy went up there and just started singing, so I asked Wes if he wanted me to do a number because I could sing a little bit. He told me to come on up and when I finished the song and got some nice applause, he asked if I wanted to do another one. I did a couple of tunes. My favorites were songs by Joe Turner and Doctor Clayton."

Lewis said that performing came natural since, even though only seventeen years old, he had already worked with a number of road shows that included a shake dancer, a female blues singer, a comic (who performed in blackface), and a magician.

"We did okay with the crowds but we only made about ten bucks," he said. "It was all a learning experience, but I didn't realize it at the time. I just wanted to sing and entertain and make a living."

The impromptu performance with Montgomery resulted in Lewis securing a weekend engagement at the club, which paid twenty-five dollars.

Greatly influenced by acts such as the Mills Brothers, Billy Ekstine, and Bing Crosby, Lewis said that he looked for a song that featured a good storyline. "I would do mostly rhythm in those days because most people didn't care for slow ballads," he said.

"After I worked with Wes Montgomery for three or four months the owner of the club, Mr. Vance, told me that his brother was an entertainment manager and handled Lucy Johnson," he said. "She had a beautiful voice and was the featured vocalist with Duke Ellington. He told me that I had done as much as I could at the small club and offered to mention my name to his brother, who was coming to town in a week."

The following week, Vance told Lewis that his brother had indeed stopped by and heard him sing but couldn't stay to speak to him. Lewis was informed that the manager wanted him to meet him in Detroit a week later, where he planned to pick up a recently purchased Chrysler Imperial. He and Lewis would drive together to a scheduled Duke Ellington engagement, he was told.

"I left Indianapolis and took a bus to Detroit and he met me with the new car," Lewis recalled. "When he greeted me he informed me that we would head straight out to San Diego, California, and said that

I could help him drive. I didn't say anything to him but I hadn't had much experiencing driving and didn't have a driver's license, but I said okay. We stopped in Texarkana in Texas and Duke did his gig there."

The experience is memorable for Lewis in that he got to perform a song with the legendary entertainer at that location. "They were finished setting up in this ballroom and I was standing on the floor by the stage looking up at them and Duke said to come on up," Lewis said. "I turned around, thinking that he was talking to somebody in back of me because he certainly couldn't be talking to me. He looked right at me at said, 'You, come on up.' Well, I guess he was told that I could sing and I shot up there."

When Ellington asked the youngster what he wanted to do, Lewis responded with "boogie blues in E." "I did this rockin' thing by Joe Turner, 'Feel So Fine Today,' and Duke loved it," he said.

The pair's next stop was Los Angeles, where Lewis got to attend multiple performances by Billie Holiday. Around that time Lewis began to clash with the manager over Johnson. "He was molesting her and they were having a little fallout and I butted in," Lewis recalled. "He told me at that point that we would be leaving for New York and we drove across the country. After arriving in New York, I stayed for about a week, when he told me that there was nothing he could do for me. He gave me money and I went back to Detroit."

Once there, the resilient Lewis secured an engagement at a music bar on Hastings Street and soon found himself earning ninety-five dollars a week at the Flame Show Bar, the premier venue in the town. It was during his engagement at that club that Lewis met Nat Tarnopol, who eventually managed Jackie Wilson. Tarnopol approached Lewis with an offer to manage him. That association led to Lewis recording "Mumbles Blues" for Parrott Records.

"We went to a recording studio in Detroit and I laid down a tune that I wrote called 'Mumbles Blues,'" he said. "They liked the recording but I didn't care for it too much. I was too inexperienced, I didn't like the band and they didn't have acoustics. It's hard to sing or do anything without feedback. I did it anyway because I was anxious to get a record."

The song was inspired by a girl that Lewis courted for a short time while living at the first foster home in Indianapolis. "I went with a girl who couldn't talk," he said. "She was a nice kid but I didn't even know that she couldn't talk until after about a month. She never said anything and never had to say anything. The song went, 'I got a girl; they call her mumbles mum. She can't speak a word, but she sure ain't dumb. She says mumumu, baby, you my desire. Don't you know, sweet baby, you set my soul on fire.'"

Spotlight Records took over the recording of "Mumbles Blues" and subsequently turned it over to the Mercury label. When it was released, it got good airplay and attention in New York, Detroit, and Cleveland. But ultimately, the song's lyrics were considered too controversial, and this limited its exposure.

"The censors wouldn't let it go any farther," Lewis said. "When I got to Chicago I was with Della Reese to promote the recording. We got to the radio station and a guy was looking at me and shaking his head no while Nat was urging him to put me on the air. Nat told me later that they wouldn't play the record because they thought it was too suggestive."

Despite the censor's restrictions, the song gained enough attention to get Lewis a series of gigs at venues such as the Howard Theater in Washington, D.C., the Royal in Baltimore, the Regal in Chicago, and the Apollo in New York. It was during one engagement at the latter venue that Lewis visited the offices of Beltone Records.

"During my third or fourth appearance at the Apollo, I performed with Jackie Wilson and the Fireflies," he said. "We got along great and talked a lot before the shows. When I left the Apollo about six weeks later, I made up my mind that I had to get a record. I wasn't making any money out there and in those days you paid your own rent, food, and fare to get there, so it was tough. I went over to 1650 Broadway looking to get a record and planned to knock on every door. I had my songs in my hand and wanted an audition. I started at the second floor, and when I got up to the sixth floor and got off the elevator I saw a sign for Beltone Records. I thought that maybe that was an omen since I used to have a quartet that sang religious songs that I called the Beltones."

When Lewis walked into the Beltone office, Ritchie Adams of the Fireflies was standing there. After greeting him, Lewis told Adams that he was looking for an audition.

"We went into the music room and Ritchie introduced me to Joe Rene, the A&R man, and Les Kahan, the president of the company," Lewis said. "I took out my sheet music and played two songs, and Ritchie said that they were nice but he wanted me to look at one that he wrote. He took sheet music out of his briefcase and on the top it read 'Tossin' and Turnin'.' I tried to think of what that could refer to. If it said squirming in the bed I'd know what they were talking about, but I had never heard that term."

Adams began to play the song with its mellow opening, and then went into a more upbeat rhythm. "He sang, 'I could not sleep a wink last night, just thinking of you; things wasn't right. I was tossing and turning, tossing and turning, tossing and turning all night. I threw the blankets on the floor.' I said, 'Wait a minute, Ritchie. Now, the intro is good. But you can't say wink. That is so outdated.'"

With that, Lewis improvised new words for the song and then suggested changing the eighth notes in "tossing and turning" to whole notes, much to the approval of the three men. Once again Lewis questioned another line.

"You said you threw the blankets on the floor," he told Adams. "Now that's not what you really want to do, because the next line is 'turn my pillow upside down.' Now you got a hand full of pillow; how you gonna throw the blankets on the floor? What you want to say is 'I kicked the blankets on the floor.' It's more vivid and more dramatic."

By this point, Lewis had captivated the entire room with his quick redo of the song's lyrics and beat, adding significant rhythm and bass lines to it. "They were all nodding and smiling, and the next thing they asked is if I wanted to record it," Lewis said. "'You know damn well I want to record it,' I told them. I asked, 'How about the front money?' I was standing there with about thirty-five cents in my pocket."

Lewis was instructed to return in two days to sign a contract, which he did. When he arrived, another of the label's recording artists was in the midst of a dispute with the company's owner.

"When I went to sign the contract, Chuck Jackson was in there huffin' and puffin' and arguing," Lewis said. "He said that he didn't want to be with Beltone and asked the company owner to give him his contract back. He had another deal going and wanted out. Kahan refused, telling Jackson that he had him signed. When Jackson left, Les asked me if I thought I should give him his contract back. I said, 'Listen, that's bad luck holding somebody against their will. The man don't want to be here. Give him back his contract.' He said okay and the next thing I heard was that Chuck had a hit with Faye Treadwell called 'I Don't Want to Cry.'"

Lewis recorded "Tossin' and Turnin'" and its B-side, "Oh Yes, I Love You," a song that he said he would love to re-record because it wasn't recorded at Beltone "with the feel and expression that a good song like that deserves." Lewis recalled that it took about two months before "Tossin' and Turnin'" started to get any significant airplay. But the company sent Lewis on the road immediately to promote the single.

"When they put me on the road I went to Chicago, Baltimore, Washington, Cleveland, and Detroit," he said. "I also did an appearance on *American Bandstand* in Philadelphia. That appearance had all kinds of impacts. Dick Clark was very, very friendly and tried to help me in any way he could. I remember that they didn't even have dressing rooms yet at the studio. We were dressing in locker rooms with the cameramen and floor director."

In addition to the *American Bandstand* appearance, Clark booked Lewis on his popular Caravan of Stars tours. "I went out with the Shirelles, Chubby Checker, Johnny Tillotson, Freddy Cannon, and Del Shannon," he said. "They weren't long tours. It only lasted three or four gigs at a time."

While he thoroughly enjoyed performing on the tours, Lewis recalled one negative encounter that had a significant impact on him.

"One time I did a show in Akron, Ohio with Del Shannon and after the show some of us went into this little restaurant and were about to order when Del left to go to the restroom," Lewis recalled. "We sat there waiting for the waiter to come and all of a sudden Del came back and said, 'I can't go to the restroom.' I asked what was wrong and he said that they wouldn't let him use the restroom. I got up from the table and walked over to see what the problem was. The waiter told me that Del couldn't go in his restroom. When I asked him why, he said because he was Jewish.

"I told him that he must be out of his ever-loving mind," he added. "I said, 'If he can't go in there, I ain't going in there, and I ain't going to eat here." As Lewis and Shannon started to walk out of the restaurant, a police officer entered. After talking to the restaurant owner, he approached Lewis and asked what the problem was. "When I told him how I felt about what the man said about Del, the cop got up in my face like a drill sergeant and gave me holy hell." After the officer finished yelling, Lewis and Shannon simply turned and walked out.

It wouldn't be the only time Lewis came to support a fellow artist. At a gig in Detroit, he assisted a young and nervous vocal group from New York who showed up ill-prepared for their first large-scale engagement.

"The Cleftones did their first major gig with me at the Fox Theater in Detroit," he said. "They were looking nervous while they waited to rehearse and I felt bad that they seemed so forlorn, so I approached them and started to talk to them. When they told me they were from New York I told them about all the venues that I performed at there. Then I asked Herb Cox if he had their charts since I didn't see any in his hand. When he said he didn't have charts I told them, 'This is professional stuff and you need charts. It's not like high school or a bar on the corner.' It just so happened that the band leader, Maurice King, was the house band leader at the Flame Show Bar, so I knew him quite well. I went over and said, 'Hey Maurice, see those kids? They're out of New York and just teenagers and they have this record, "This Little Girl of Mine." They seem like nice kids but they don't have charts with them. Can you do me a favor and do what you can to help them out?'"

Lewis said that from that day on he has never been without a friend named Herb Cox. "He tells everybody that story," Lewis said.

Nat Tarnopol secured a spot for Lewis on the Alan Freed show at the Brooklyn Fox Theater. "By that time Nat wasn't managing me but he always looked out for me," Lewis said. "Jackie [Wilson] used to always look out for me too. If Jackie was going out on tour, I was on it too. He was like my brother. I knew his mama and she would welcome any entertainer, and she always had a pot of food on the stove. Nobody went hungry when they came to Jackie's house."

"Tossin' and Turnin'" was one of the first songs ever to cross over and chart on both the pop and rhythm and blues charts. Lewis speculated on why that might have occurred.

"I credit that to the A&R man," he said. "He had a knack for doing good arrangements. If he'd have followed my suggestion and did it in a more rhythm and blues flavor, it may not have got as much play on the pop chart as it did. If you listen to that song and all the others on my first album, the pop comes out even stronger than the blues. But the blues was there and that audience heard it, and the background singers were singing heavy blues, so it went rhythm and blues as well as pop."

"Of everything I have done throughout my career I am most proud of my fidelity to quality," Lewis said. "I've always been on time; in fact, I've been as much as three to four hours early. I've kept my character and haven't let fame go to my head. I'm just proud that I've had the opportunity to be in this business. For me it's the best business in the world and I'm just glad that I had a chance to be part of it."

"Tossin' and Turnin'" was recognized as the number-five single of the entire decade of the 1960s, a fact that Lewis remains extremely proud of, as well he should.

So lasting was the song that it was included in the soundtrack of the 1978 feature-length motion picture *Animal House*. Just prior to the movie's release, *Billboard Magazine* named the song the fifth-highest-selling single in the history of rock-and-roll.

Lewis continued to record well into the 1970s and continues to perform at oldies concerts nationwide in 2005.

Billboard Top 40 Hits by Bobby Lewis

Date	Pos	Wks on Charts	Record Title	Label/Number
05/29/61	01	17	Tossin' and Turnin'	Beltone 1002
09/11/6	09	07	One Track Mind	Beltone 1012

Marshall Lytle
(Bill Haley and the Comets)

Uncasville, Connecticut   **August 6, 2005**

While the majority of recording artists recognized for having pioneered the evolution and introduction of the music style known as rock-and-roll were solo acts or vocal groups, the self-contained band that has been widely regarded as the first of its kind to champion and develop the new sound is Bill Haley and the Comets.

Bill Haley has been long credited as the first leader to form a rock-and-roll band, but Marshall Lytle, its bass player, said it was more an aggregation of the work of Haley and the group that eventually became known as the Comets.

"It was not so much Bill himself but the original Saddlemen that I was part of," Lytle said. "There were just four of us in the band in the beginning. Bill played rhythm guitar and sang and he also taught me how to play the bass fiddle. When I sang, he would play the bass fiddle. So he and I switched off a lot. Billy Williamson played the steel guitar, and Johnny Grande played the accordion at that time. We were playing cowboy music, country and western, western swing, and we were experimenting with different types of music."

The Saddlemen first formed in 1949, and their eventual shift from country and western came about through the inclusion of unconventional aggregations of instruments into the band and blending the beat of both rhythm and blues and country.

For the most part, country and western bands of the era featured guitars, a steel-pedal guitar, and an upright bass. And while an occasional piano, fiddle, or accordion might augment a group's sound, drums and horn instruments were never employed to achieve the desired sound of that style of music. In most cases, the bass player in a country group would use a percussive technique called "slap bass," one that somewhat served to provide the beat to each song.

Conversely, a rhythm and blues band almost always included guitars, keyboards, saxophones, and drums, but absent were accordions and steel-pedal guitars.

By blending these two distinct styles of music, the Saddlemen developed a unique sound, which came to be known in those days as country-blues or rockabilly.

In June 1951, the Saddlemen recorded a cover of the rhythm and blues song "Rocket 88," one done earlier by Ike Turner and His Kings of Rhythm. Limited to a regional hit, it served to encourage the band to explore further options in merging the two sounds. Within months, the band added bass player Marshall Lytle to a lineup that already included guitarist Bill Haley, keyboardist and accordion player Johnny Grande, and steel-pedal guitarist Billy Williamson. It was that lineup that would rename itself the Comets in late 1952.

The Saddlemen performed on a live daily radio show from noon to one o'clock to promote scheduled appearances in the coming weeks. A disc jockey on the station that had a show called *Judge Rhythm's Court*, which featured rhythm and blues music, approached the group one day and told them about an rhythm and blues song that was the most requested one on his show. He encouraged them to learn it for future gigs. Haley liked the idea and the group learned it. The song was "Rock the Joint."

"We recorded the song and it became quite a territorial hit," Lytle said. "The record company sent us to Cleveland to promote the recording because that was one of the record hubs. If you could have a hit in Cleveland you had a pretty good hit somewhere else. We went there and met a young man named Alan Freed, who was at that time known as 'King of the Moondogs.' He played rhythm and blues music and he played our record. We all sat around a big round table with a microphone in the middle of it and he had a switch on the wall to allow him to turn the microphone on and off while the records were playing. While 'Rock the Joint' was playing, he kept yelling 'Rock-and-roll, everybody, rock-and-roll.' Pretty soon the telephone started ringing and people called asking him to play that rock-and-roll song again. Every time he'd play the song he'd say, 'Here's that rock-and-roll song one more time.' He kept playing 'Rock the Joint' over and over and over.

"I truly believe that that was the night that rock-and-roll got its name," Lytle said. "Although he coined the phrase at other times, he really promoted it that night with 'Rock the Joint.'"

Encouraged by the success of that recording, Haley composed "Rock-A-Beatin' Boogie," a song that featured a similar rhythmic beat and became popular at the group's live shows. While two other groups, the Esquire Boys and the Treniers, recorded the song in 1952 and 1953, respectively, the Comets didn't wax the tune until 1955.

Lytle recalled how the Saddlemen eventually changed their name to Bill Haley and the Comets. "We were known as Bill Haley and the Saddlemen and while we were doing a radio show, the program director of WPWA in Chester, Pennsylvania, came through the lobby and he said that we should change our name to Haley's Comet because of the comet that just went across the sky," he said. "Bill said, 'Haley's Comet, that's pretty good. What do you guys think about that?' We said, 'Yeah, let's do it.' We were really looking to get out of the cowboy clothes, take the hats and the boots off, and become a regular band. We decided that day that we were going to become Haley's Comets."

Eventually the name was changed to Bill Haley and the Comets, and then Bill Haley and His Comets.

In 1953, when the band recorded "Real Rock Drive" and "Stop Beatin' Around the Mulberry Bush," the sides had the distinction of being the first ones that they recorded with drums. They also became the first record labels to credit the name Comets. The group's follow-up single, "Crazy Man Crazy," co-written by Haley and Lytle (although the record label credits only Haley), became their breakout hit. The single was the first rock-and-roll record to make the *Billboard* charts, climbing to number fifteen. Despite its success, Lytle remains upset that he never received writer's credit.

"I got very angry at that because Bill Haley and I wrote that in his kitchen," Lytle said. "One day, we were promoting the song 'We're Gonna Rock This Joint Tonight' at a high school in Eddystone, Pennsylvania. We wanted to take our music to where the kids were because they were the ones that we had to please on our records. After the assembly that we performed at one day, we were loading the instruments into Bill's car because Bill and I rode together, and these kids all gathered around us. Bill asked them, 'Hey, how did you guys like our music?' One kid said, 'That's crazy, man, crazy.' Bill wrote that down on the palm of his hand. We went to his house and his wife was making lunch for us and he grabbed a guitar and starting singing, 'Crazy man, crazy; crazy, man, crazy.' I'd throw lines in like, 'When I go out and have a treat, I find me a band with a solid beat.' Then he'd throw in another line and we wrote the song that day.

"At the record session, after the recording was all finished the A&R man, Dave Miller, asked who the writer of the song was," Lytle continued. "Bill said, 'It's just Bill Haley.' I overheard that and said, 'Bill, you know damn well that you and I wrote that song together. What's the matter?' He said, 'Oh Marshall, I want to take this one by myself. I'll take care of you on later songs. Don't worry; I'll take care of you.'

"Bill was my hero when I went to work for him because he was seven years older than me and I kind of looked up to him," he said. "But at that moment his 'going to take care of me' was in the wrong direction and I really felt that I was getting a raw deal. I resented it from that point on because you just don't do that to someone that you have great respect for. My legacy of helping to write that song just went down the drain."

Having already succeeded in changing the instrumental makeup of a band during the period, one additional component was added to the Comets' sound when sax player Joey Ambrose joined the group. The groundbreaking conglomeration of instruments gave the Comets a sound unlike anything heard before. The introduction of Ambrose into the Comets and his subsequent friendship and professional association with Lytle also resulted in a high-energy stage presence that can easily be credited with having influenced a number of major acts decades later.

The musicians worked closely to develop a stage act that quickly became popular with fans. During a rousing number, Lytle would toss his upright bass over his head, or lay on top of it while sliding across the stage, without once missing a beat. Ambrose augmented the act with his own spirited antics while playing sax.

"In 1953 when Joey came with the band, he was just seventeen years old and I was eighteen," Lytle recalled. "Joey got his training playing saxophone in the bars in Philadelphia and he used to walk on the bar and go out and honk at people in the audience. We started playing these teenage dances and one day we were doing an instrumental called 'Straightjacket' and Joey just walked out into the audience and started honking at these girls and they were screaming. So I'm standing up there playing the bass and figured I'd see if I could do something to make them scream.

"I threw the bass up over my head and started playing it like a nut and they screamed at that," he continued. "I said, 'Oh, that's good.' Then he did something else, and I thought I'd try to do something better and I laid on top of the bass, and they screamed again. It was kind of like a 'can you top this?' thing. One day I sat the bass down and told Joey to sit on it. When he did I slid him across the floor and they went crazy for that. Then we started going out into the audience and I'd slide him around on the bass and he sat there honking his horn."

During a performance at a theater in Chicago, Lytle recalled that when the duo went up and down the aisles as fast as they could, they experienced a mishap. "I ran the bass into a seat and the bridge fell off the bass, and the strings were all hanging," he said. "We went back on the stage and I didn't have a bass to play, so I used the house band's bass. I played it gently because I knew it was an expensive bass, but its owner watched me and thought I was going to hurt it and was on the side pulling his hair out. I had to assure him that I wasn't going to sit on it, stand on it, or anything, and he was okay with that."

Interestingly, when Lytle recounted his reputation for destroying a few bases throughout the years, I couldn't help but recall one Peter Townsend and his stage act in the early days with the British group the Who.

Audiences at rock shows in the late 1960s would marvel at the stage theatrics of guitar master Jimi Hendrix and cheer the interplay displayed by Bruce Springsteen and the E Street Band's sax player Clarence Clemons. But it's hard to know how many were aware of or appreciated the fact that the energy-filled performance had actually been developed years earlier by two original members of the Comets.

The act became such a trademark at the Comets' shows that when the duo left to form another group, Haley instructed all succeeding band members to imitate Lytle's and Ambrose's actions during each performance.

"I feel so honored that it's difficult to put into words how good it makes me feel that I was able to influence these people," Lytle said. "The whole band feels humbled that the Beatles say that we were a big influence on them being in show business. John Lennon said that until he heard 'Rock Around the Clock,' he had no idea of ever getting into the business. Graham Nash said in an interview on the *Tonight Show* that what made him go into the business was when he went into the theater to see Bill Haley and the Comets. He said he heard a voice that said, 'See you later, alligator,' and the curtain opened and Bill began singing the song. Graham said that he's gone through several wives, has lost houses, and lost everything in his life but he still has that ticket stub. That's quite an honor."

Perhaps one of the most glaring myths that surround the band is one that incorrectly states that the Comet's signature single, "Rock Around the Clock," was in fact a cover recording. The inaccuracy cites an earlier recording of the song by a black rhythm and blues group from Philadelphia, Pennsylvania, called Sonny Dae and the Knights. And while that group did indeed record the song a short time before the Comets' release, its intent and version needs further clarification.

Written specifically for Bill Haley and the Comets, the group initially could not record the song due to what Lytle termed "music industry politics that involved an existing record contract." He explained what really occurred.

"The guy that owned Essex Records, Dave Miller, had a kind of ill feeling toward James Myers, who owned Myers Publishing Company," Lytle said. "Miller felt that he [Myers] was too pushy and was trying to get us to record something that he didn't like. So he would never let us record 'Rock Around the Clock.' When our contract with Essex Records expired, Dave Miller was so busy he didn't realize that it was time for him to pick up the option. When he let the option lapse, Jimmy Myers, who was a good friend of Bill's, told Bill that he could get him with a bigger label. Bill told him to take 'Crazy, Man, Crazy' to New York and get the group on a bigger label."

The first label that Myers approached with the song was Decca Records. The label's executives loved the song and agreed to sign the Comets to a recording contract, and provided them with a significant advance. A recording session was scheduled quickly. That session, despite a shaky start due to the tardiness of the group's arrival served to produce the one song that is considered the foundation of rock-and-roll.

"We were late getting to our first session because the ferry boat going across the Delaware River got stuck on a sand bar," Lytle said. "We had to wait for them to pull another one over and transfer us so we could get to New York and meet our obligations at the record company. When we got to Decca Records, we were late and only had three hours left to do the session. They gave us a song called 'Thirteen Women and

Only One Man in Town' but we had no arrangement for it and hadn't even heard it before we got there, so we spent two and a half hours on an arrangement for the song and finally got it in the can. With thirty-five minutes left, Milt Gabler of Decca told us that we could now 'do that rock thing that you were gonna do.' That was his attitude. He didn't even know what we were gonna do but he knew we had a rock-and-roll song."

Danny Cedrone, a guitarist who preceded Franny Beecher in the Comets, was at the session since he played on all the group's recordings. Cedrone had a group in Philadelphia, Pennsylvania, called the Esquire Boys. While Haley and the Comets had rehearsed "Rock Around the Clock" the night before the Decca session, Cedrone wasn't a part of that.

"Bill always wanted a guitar solo on all the recordings," Lytle recalled. "So Danny Cedrone was fooling around with what he was going to play and trying to figure out some solo to play on 'Rock Around the Clock.' We were really pressed for time and I told Danny to just play the great solo that he played on 'Rock the Joint.' He wasn't sure it would fit, but I encouraged him to try it. The next take we did, Danny came in with it and it became the greatest guitar solo that was ever put on a recording and became quite famous as the years went by."

Lytle addressed the longstanding myth that the Comets' recording of "Rock Around the Clock" was a cover version of a song previously waxed by a black rhythm and blues group from Philadelphia.

"It was not a black rhythm and blues group at all but one called Sonny Dae and the Knights," he said. "They were a group that did novelty songs and they did 'Rock Around the Clock' as a demo record. After we recorded our single, they put the demo out on the market and everyone thought that Sonny Dae and the Knights recorded it first. But when we got it, it was a demo, and James Myers, who wrote the song, had them record the demo so he could peddle it to other people. Theirs was a totally different arrangement and had a nursery rhyme in its melody."

Another bit of trivia is the fact that the supposed black group billed as Sonny Dae and the Knights was actually made up of Italian Americans, led by one Pascal Vennitti.

When the Comets finally recorded the song in April 1954, it received only mild attention. That is, until the nine-year-old son of actor Glenn Ford overheard his father discuss a new movie, *Blackboard Jungle*, with its director. An avid music fan, when the youngster became aware that the director was looking for a song for the film that would reflect the day's teenage spirit he immediately suggested "Rock Around the Clock."

Upon its inclusion in the film's soundtrack, the song's impact on teenagers motivated a series of outbursts and dancing in the aisles at movie houses. The record company quickly reissued the song, and in July 1955 the single became the first rock-and-roll record to reach number one on the charts. It became such a huge hit that it actually motivated studio heads to release a rock-and-roll feature-length movie, and title it after the song. Bill Haley and the Comets performed in the film.

While the original Comets are all represented on the "Rock Around the Clock" recording, in late 1955 Lytle, Ambrose, and Richards left the Comets to form their own group, the Jodimars (the name derived from the trio's first names, JOey, DIck, and MARShall). Replacements for the three musicians subsequently appeared with Haley in the 1956 film *Rock Around the Clock*, as well as the group's second motion picture in 1957, *Don't Knock the Rock*.

"I spoke to James Myers, who co-wrote and published 'Rock Around the Clock,' about three weeks before he died in 2002," Lytle said. "He told me that of the many recordings that were made of the song through the years, it had sold two hundred million copies worldwide. He thinks that our particular recording of it sold over eighty million copies, and it's known as the best-selling single ever recorded."

Upon further reflection, Lytle recalled an ironic fact regarding his role in that mega-hit single. "I made forty-one dollars and twenty-five cents for making that record," he said. "That was the three-hour record session union scale in those days. That's what musicians worked for."

In June 1954, the Comets recorded a cover of Big Joe Turner's "Shake, Rattle and Roll." "Decca Records had some reluctance in letting us record it because of the lyrics," Lytle recalled. "Joe Turner's record of it had blue lyrics and we were trying to sell rock-and-roll to the young kids. They said we had to change the lyrics, so Bill and another writer went out in the hallway and changed the lyrics to clean it up a little bit and it was our first million seller."

During the following year, Bill Haley and the Comets performed on stage, radio, and television and in May 1955 they became the first rock-and-roll act to give a concert at the prestigious Carnegie Hall in New York City. The venue had long been a premier concert hall that featured the world's finest luminaries in classical music.

"When we played that particular venue, it was a time when there were a lot of things going on," Lytle said. "I remember that we just did okay there and didn't knock them dead the way we wanted to. In fact, there were a few places where we played and didn't knock them dead. One I recall was a show we did with the Four Freshman at the big auditorium in Los Angeles. The Four Freshman just knocked us out and you would've thought it would be the other way around. We were just having a good time doing what we did and they really went at it. It was really a mismatch because we should have never been on the same show because they drew a jazz crowd and we drew a rockabilly crowd or a rock-and-roll crowd."

Beyond the paltry sum of money that the Comets received for recording sessions, specifically the one that resulted in the groundbreaking hit single "Rock Around the Clock," Lytle and the other group members received a weekly wage to perform with the group.

"We had a dispute back in 1955 when the band was making big money," he said. "The big royalty checks were rolling in for 'Rock Around the Clock' and 'Shake, Rattle, and Roll' and the other hits and three of us were on a salary, making a small amount of money in comparison to what the others were making. We felt we wanted a little fifty-dollar-a-week raise and they refused us. Well, we decided that we were going to start our own band and we did. Joe, Dick, and I left Bill that year and formed a group called the Jodimars, and we recorded for Capitol Records and had a couple of minor hits. They liked us so much over in England that they named a magazine after one of our songs, 'Well Now Dig This.' We had a good sound with that group and it's a shame that we just never had the right promotion on it, because when we were with Capitol it seemed like every artist on the label had a smash hit. We recorded in New York City and the heart of Capitol Records was in Hollywood, California. We were out in left field in New York and we didn't get the promotion that we felt we deserved."

Among the Jodimars' singles was "Clarabella," a song named for Lytle's sister. It became a favorite of Paul McCarthy, who would gain fame in later years as a member of the Beatles. "I never met Paul McCarthy but always wanted to because he's been one of my favorite entertainers," Lytle said. "Paul is an absolute genius in writing himself, and because I was the co-writer and the singer of 'Clarabella,' I feel honored that he chose that song to perform with the Beatles. His rendition of it is a little bit different than the one we did, but it's an honor to have had him copy one of our songs."

Despite the trio having parted ways with Haley, Lytle said that the decision was made with no animosity toward the leader of the Comets. "When we left Bill we gave him the right amount of notice," he said.

"We gave him three weeks so that we wouldn't leave him high and dry. He hired four guys to take our three places and he became a seven-piece band instead of a six-piece band."

In addition to specifically replacing the three departing members, Haley brought Beecher into a regular full-time role, his prior association with the Comets being limited to recording studio work.

As younger artists such as Elvis Presley, Jerry Lee Lewis, and Chuck Berry began to emerge on the rock-and-roll scene, Haley took his Comets to tour England, becoming the first rock-and-roll band to do so. That exposure to the new form of music would serve to influence a myriad of budding musicians in the audience, including many future recording artists that would be a part of the soon to come British Invasion.

By 1963, all of the original Comets had departed the group, leaving Haley to tour with a series of revolving lineups, estimated to include some one hundred musicians through 1981, when the music legend passed away at the age of fifty-five.

Lytle reflected on a career in music that has personally served to influence musicians that followed the Comets through the years. "I am so lucky to be able to have caused a lot of people to enjoy the bass fiddle, the old slap bass" he said. "In Europe I really get such admiration from the bass players that come to me and say that I'm their idol and without me they never would have gotten into music."

He recalled one specific meeting with a fan following a more recent Comets' performance during a European tour. "One of the biggest thrills I got when somebody paid an honor to me was in Paris, France," Lytle said. "We were doing a show there with about three thousand people in the audience, and after the show we always go to the autograph table to meet and shake everybody's hand and thank them for keeping our music alive. This one gentleman in his twenties came over and put his arm down on the table, and right there on his arm was a picture of me standing on the bass fiddle tattooed on his arm. Right underneath it was my signature.

"I knew how he got the picture, with a camera, but I asked him how he got my signature on there," he said. "He told me that last year when we performed in Paris he came through the autograph line and put his arm out and asked me to sign it. He went home, had his pictures developed, and decided to have the one with me on the bass tattooed on his arm, above my signature. When I asked him why in the world he would ever do that he told me, 'You don't understand, do you?' He told me, 'I'm a bass player and you are the inspiration and the most copied bass player in the world.

"Bill is the one that taught me how to play slap bass," Lytle recalled. "He had a special sound that he was looking for because we did not have drums; he said that he needed me to drive the band with the beat. He showed me how to play a shuffle slap style that is still very prevalent on all of our recordings. The engineer on 'Rock the Joint' captured that sound and that became kind of our signature for other recordings."

Lytle said that through the years he has seen many tattoos that portray Bill Haley's image. One in particular is a full-size head shot of Haley on the back of a woman in England. She also has tattoos of Chuck Berry and different pioneering rock-and-roll artists on her shoulders and arms.

The original Comets lineup reformed in 1987 and has performed together since that time. Five surviving members continue to thrill audiences with the same level of musical intensity and stage presence for which they initially became famous. At a 2005 performance in Connecticut, Lytle played his bass while lying on top of the instrument, while Ambrose provided his accompanying flair while playing his sax. And true to form, neither missed a beat. The 2005 Comets range in age from seventy-two to eighty-four years old, but when they perform they defy both imagination and restrictions that typically plague the octogenarian set. In short, they still rock-and-roll!

"For a bunch of old guys we have a lot of fun," Lytle said. "I guess that's the secret to our longevity. We enjoy what we do and we do what we enjoy. We are what we call the originals and it's very unusual to have all original members in a band more than fifty years later.

"Our guitar player, Franny Beecher, is eighty-four years young, and I'm one of the babies in the crowd at seventy-two," he added. "Joey Ambrose, our sax player, is seventy-one and our drummer, Dick Richards, is a wild man himself; he's eighty-one years young and he plays one of the meanest set of drums you've ever heard. Johnny Grande plays the keyboard and has been with Bill Haley since 1949. There are others that claim to be the originals, but we're the ones that made all the recordings.

"We just signed the greatest contract of our lives," Lytle added. "We're going to be at Branson, Missouri, for the full season of 2006 at a brand-new venue called Dick Clark's *American Bandstand* Theater. We're gonna do a show at ten o'clock in the morning so that people can start their day with 'Rock Around the Clock.' It's going to be wonderful."

Billboard Top 40 Hits by Bill Haley and the Comets

Date	Pos	Wks on Charts	Record Title	Label/ Number
11/20/54	11	15	Dim Dim the Lights	Decca 29317
03/05/55	17	08	Mambo Rock/	Decca 29418
03/19/55	26	02	Birth of the Boogie	Decca 29124
05/14/55	01	24	Rock Around the Clock	Decca 29552
07/23/55	15	04	Razzle-Dazzle	Decca 29713
11/19/55	09	13	Burn That Candle	Decca 29791
01/14/56	06	15	See You Later, Alligator	
04/07/56	16	05	R-O-C-K	Decca 29870
04/07/56	18	05	The Saints Rock'n'Roll	Decca 30028
09/01/56	25	04	Rip It Up	
11/24/56	34	03	Rudy's Rock	Decca 30085
04/21/58	22	06	Skinny Minnie	Decca 30592
05/25/74	39	01	Rock Around the Clock	MCA 60025

Bill Haley's original Comets, from left, Franny Beecher, Marshall Lytle, Johnny Grande, Dick Richards, and Joey Ambrose still "Rock the Joint" after all these years.

Johnny Maestro
(The Crests, The Del Satins, The Brooklyn Bridge)

Flushing, New York   **October 22, 2005**

Having the good fortune to have sung with three popular vocal groups throughout his career in music, John Mastrangelo, better know to his legion of fans as Johnny Maestro, started out as the lead singer of the Crests.

The group was not unlike others of the time in that they were mistaken, because of their sound, for an all-black aggregation. In reality, the group consisted of two black, one Puerto Rican, and one Italian male singer and a female black vocalist. First tenor Talmadge Gough and second tenor Harold Torres were students at Public School 160 Junior High in the Chinatown section of Manhattan when they joined bass singer Jay Carter, who lived on nearby Delancey Street, to form a singing group.

While documented biographies of the group cite female tenor Patricia Van Dross, who also attended PS 160, as singing with the group when they joined Carter, the fact is that she was recruited after Maestro came on board.

Another inaccuracy that is documented in various biographies on Maestro state that he was a member of a vocal group prior to the Crests, one that was said to include a young Tony Orlando. Maestro set the record straight. "I was never in a group with Tony and don't know how that story got out there," he said.

Maestro credited popular 1950s disc jockey Alan Freed as having served as his early influence and interest in music. "I would listen to his Moondog show religiously," he said. "I would love listening to the Flamingos, and Harptones, the Moonglows, and just loved that harmony sound. I also listened to Johnnie Ray on the pop stations. He and Frankie Layne were my favorites."

Maestro, who lived on Mulberry Street in the Little Italy section of Manhattan, recalled first meeting the vocalists that he would eventually join and form the Crests with, at the Henry Street Settlement. "I had been trying to form a vocal group in high school and I had a couple of guys and we sang together for a few months but it just didn't work out," he said. "I was still looking in the neighborhood that I was living in, downtown Manhattan. I guess word got around and these three guys approached me one day and said they were just learning gospel harmony and asked if I wanted to join them for rehearsal and sing with them to see if we meshed.

"I agreed since I'd been looking and thought that maybe this is what I was looking for," he continued. "We went up to this apartment at the Al Smith projects downtown and a man by the name of Mr. Morrow was teaching them how to sing gospel harmony. We started singing together and everything really clicked, the blend was beautiful, and that's how it all began."

At that point, Maestro said the group consisted of a quartet. "We wanted to have a bass singing with us, and J. T. Carter was singing baritone at that time," he said. "We started searching for a first tenor and I believe it was J. T. who knew Patricia [Van Dross], and he brought her to a rehearsal. Once again the sound clicked."

The group's name, Maestro recalled, was selected without rhyme or reason but quickly stuck. "It came up one evening when we were going to perform," he said. "We hadn't had a name at that point because we weren't performing live at all. I really don't know who suggested it but someone said the Crests sounds right, as that was the top, the peak, and we agreed. We wanted to stay away from any 'tones,' like the Crestones or any other variations like that."

Maestro recalled how the Crests first met and eventually auditioned for music arranger Al Browne. "We would perform everywhere we went be it on a street corner, on a train, and in the train stations, and that's where we met up with a woman I believe was Al Browne's wife," Maestro said. "We were singing on the train itself in a little compartment between the train cars and she heard us and liked what she heard. At the station when we were about to get off she gave us a card and said, 'Please call this man and he may be able to help you.'"

The card read "Al Browne and Orchestra" and the group quickly contacted him to arrange an audition. As it turned out Al, Browne was a music arranger who had worked with, among other groups of the era, the Heartbeats.

In June 1957, the group recorded two sides, both original compositions by Mastrangelo, who around that time shortened his name to Maestro. The tunes were "My Juanita" and "Sweetest One," and while most savvy listeners would have selected "My Juanita" as the side to promote, when the single was released on the small Joyce Records label, "Sweetest One" was the side that was pushed. The beautifully done ballad entered the Top 100 national charts.

Maestro reflected on his early days of composing songs. "We started composing tunes immediately when we met Al Browne," he said. "Up to that point we were doing cover tunes. He told us that we couldn't do other group's songs so we had to try to come up with some new material. At that point we started rehearsing and I came up with 'Sweetest One' and 'My Juanita.' That was my first attempt at composing a song."

While the Crests' follow-up single, "No One to Love," failed to generate significant attention, the group continued to get gigs at local sock hops and church dances. But when the engagements that were secured started to require travel beyond the local area Van Dross, who was younger than her male counterparts, was forced to leave the group as her mother refused to let her tour with the others. Van Dross's younger brother Luther, who frequented the Crests' rehearsals, would gain his own level of fame in later years as a top recording artist and performer.

Following the release of "No One to Love" the Crests were introduced to music publisher George Paxton. "At that time, Joyce Records was about to go out of business," Maestro recalled. "One of the arrangers for Joyce Records was Billy Dawn Smith and he had been working with George Paxton and Paxton Music as a songwriter. Paxton, at that time, had decided to start a record company, and, of course, Billy Dawn was involved with him. Billy knew us through Joyce Records and he knew that the label was folding so he offered to take us to George Paxton and his new label for an audition."

Having founded his new Coed Records label, Paxton signed the group and released another Maestro original as their first single, "Pretty Little Angel." It did fairly well in the local market, but the group's follow-up record would finally gain them the attention they'd been hoping for.

When the group recorded and released "Besides You," its B-side, "Sixteen Candles," started to get airplay and soon became a huge hit and eventually served as the Crests' signature song. "When the single was first released, 'Beside You' was the A-side," Maestro said. "I believe it was Alan Freed who started playing the flip side. He was always different, so he decided to play 'Sixteen Candles' and it clicked immediately. The rest of the stations then started playing it."

Upon the strength of the hit single, the Crests were invited to perform at Freed's Christmas Party show at New York City's Loew's State Theatre. Maestro described how the local group reveled in the experience, appearing on the same bill as many of the acts that they had idolized and emulated a short time earlier.

"That had to be the highlight and just blew me away," he said. "Here I am just singing on the street corners one day, and the next week I'm performing at the Loew's State Theatre with the Moonglows, Jackie Wilson, the Platters, and this was mind blowing. These are the people that I grew up with and that I admired."

As for sharing the backstage area at the show with the legendary acts, Maestro described the experience. "It was rock-and-roll back then," he said. "Everybody was partying backstage. We shared a dressing room with Dion and the Belmonts. We started at the same time and our records charted at the same time."

Maestro cleared up a longstanding story that claimed that during the Crests first meeting with Dick Clark, the popular disc jockey and host of *American Bandstand* ended up with a black eye, the result of the group's horsing around backstage.

"Actually, there wasn't a black eye and that wasn't the first time we met Dick Clark," he said. "The first time was in Philadelphia, when we performed on his show *American Bandstand*. But a year or so later, we were performing at a benefit and as Dick was coming into our dressing room, somebody was opening the door at the same time and accidentally hit him on the side of his head. But he didn't get a black eye from it."

The Crests toured extensively from 1958 through 1960 and scored hit records with "The Angels Listened In," "Step By Step," and "Trouble in Paradise." But despite that success, the Coed label appeared to be courting Maestro to leave the group and embark on a solo career. The group's last recording on the label was "I Remember" in reality a cover of the Five Satins' "In the Still of the Nite."

Maestro eventually did leave the group, and Gough also left and relocated to Detroit, Michigan, where he went to work for the automotive manufacturer General Motors. Replacing Maestro with James Ancrum on lead, the Crests continued to perform but failed to chart any more hit recordings. They would sign with Selma Records, where hits and airplay eluded them.

"What they had told us toward the end [was] they felt that record sales were diminishing," Maestro said. "They felt the reason for that was that we were not able to be seen nationally on television because of the integration in the group. They told us that a lot of the major stations like NBC and CBS shied away from integration and we couldn't perform on these shows. And that was their reason for breaking the group up. They said that they couldn't do anymore with us as we were."

After attempts at a solo career, Maestro would record "Over the Weekend" with the Tymes, and then "Try Me" with studio background vocalists. However, accounts state that the latter recording was actually done by the Crests, a fact that Maestro soundly disputed.

"That song was produced by J. J. Jackson and the background voices included him, his partner, and I might have sung background too along with studio guys," he said. "They may have tried to release it as being the Crests but I had no legal right to the name, so they couldn't do that. The three remaining singers of the Crests had the name. After they disbanded, I believe that J. T. Carter legally got the name."

Maestro went on to perform with the Del-Satins, a group that experienced regional hit status as well as gaining fame as having provided background vocals on all of Dion's solo recordings after he left the Belmonts.

"I was not with the Del-Satins when they backed Dion," he said. "I joined them after that time. I was doing a solo act from 1961 on and had crossed paths with the Del-Satins quite often during that time. They were going through lead singers very quickly, and the last singer they had was being drafted I believe. They had approached me a number of times to join the group, but I wasn't ready for a year or two after they first asked me. Finally I decided to give it a shot and try something different."

In 1966, in an attempt to enhance the group's sound with additional instruments, the Del-Satins staged an audition. Upon hearing a horn group called Rhythm Method, the foundation for what would become their distinctive sound during the late 1960s was born.

"We were performing as the Del-Satins and really didn't have a backup band," Maestro recalled. "We had a guitarist and a drummer. The rock-and-roll sound was getting bigger, so we decided that we needed to augment the instruments; so we held an audition on Long Island in one of the clubs that we performed at often, the Cloud Nine. One of the groups really stood out, a seven-piece horn group; three horns and a great rhythm section. We liked the sound and got together with them after the auditions, went to our manager's office, and discussed the whole thing. We decided to merge the two groups and became the Brooklyn Bridge."

A year after the two groups merged, the Brooklyn Bridge charted with "Worst That Could Happen," a cover of a song originally recorded by the Fifth Dimension. "I selected that song for the group to record," Maestro said. "When we signed to record for Buddha Records, they were producing mostly bubble gum music like the 1910 Fruit Gum Company and that type of thing. These are the types of songs that they gave us to record. The first song was called 'Little Red Boat by the River' and then they gave us 'From My Window,' and they were both in that same vein. It wasn't exactly what we were looking for, with the horns and all that.

"We wanted more of a Chicago or Blood, Sweat, and Tears sound but with big vocals," he added. "I went to the office and asked them to let us record one more song before they put those records out. I told them that I had a song that I thought would be nice and they told me to go ahead and rehearse it. We did. The way the Fifth Dimension recorded that song was a basic rhythm section and the lead singer. I thought maybe if we put our vocals, our horns, and a big arrangement to it, this would be a great tune. We recorded it and the label loved it and put it out."

The Brooklyn Bridge has sold in excess of ten million records of hits that include "Welcome Me Love" and "Blessed Is the Rain," but Maestro stopped composing tunes after he left the Crests.

"I don't know if it was that I didn't have time or just lost interest in it but I may have wrote one or two songs after the Crests, but nothing that was major," he said.

Maestro attempted to explain how the Brooklyn Bridge has both achieved and sustained longevity and star status in an industry that is largely dependent on a continuing string of hit recordings to stay popular.

"I think the important fact is that we've been together for such a long time," he said. "Also, we have tried not to rearrange, update, or change any of the songs like a lot of groups do, because when the people hear us they want to hear what they remember. They want to hear what they heard on the records, not how you can do it better or arrange it to a more contemporary style. That's what we like to do: keep it as it was, and I think that's what helped to sustain us."

Given a career that has spanned three popular groups and achieved hit recordings that continue to receive significant airplay in 2005, Maestro reflected on what he is most proud of. "I am most proud of the fact that I'm still singing," he said. "There are a lot of vocalists that started back when I did and, unfortunately, whether it be sickness or abuse, they lost what they had. I am very, very fortunate and I thank God that I still have the voice that I have. I've enjoyed everything I did from the Crests on up and there's not one song or one record that I can say I don't want to hear anymore. I'm proud of everything I did, of where I am now, and I'm proud of the fact that our audiences are still coming to see us."

In 2005, four of the original members continue to perform with the Brooklyn Bridge at a large number of shows nationwide. Along with Maestro, Les Cauchi and Fred Ferrara, both from the Del-Satins, and the group's bass player, Jim Rosica, remain active members.

Billboard Top 40 Hits by the Crests

Date	Pos	Wks on Charts	Record Title	Label/ Number
12/22/58	02	14	Sixteen Candles	Coed 506
04/13/59	28	07	Six Nights a Week	Coed 509
09/14/59	22	09	The Angels Listened In	Coed 515
04/04/60	14	08	Step By Step	Coed 525
07/18/60	20	08	Trouble In Paradise	Coed 531

Billboard Top 40 Hits by the Brooklyn Bridge

Date	Pos	Wks on Charts	Record Title	Label/ Number
01/04/69	03	10	Worst That Could Happen	Buddha 75

Fred Parris
(The Five Satins)

Uncasville, Connecticut   **August 6, 2005**

In 1956, a male vocal group from New Haven, Connecticut, recorded a song that would come to define the music of that era, titled "In the Still of the Nite." The song's composer and the group's lead singer, Fred Parris, formed the Five Satins in 1954 after singing with two other local groups.

"When I was about three years old I lived in Milford, Connecticut, and on the radio I would hear Glenn Miller play 'Little Brown Jug' and things like that, and it was that kind of sound that first attracted me to music," Parris said. "Later on, I embraced jazz and that still remains my favorite kind of music. But of course, when you're a teenager you go with what's going on, and that how I got started. Groups were very popular when I was sixteen and seventeen years old. That was the fad, and the style of the day.

"That's how I ended up going into that type of music instead of jazz," he added. "I was lazy and should have gone to my piano lessons, but it was easier to sing doo-wop, doo-wop."

Parris first joined a vocal group called the Canaries. But while documented accounts state that he parted ways with the group when he didn't care for its direction, Parris had an entirely different story.

"The Canaries were current and we did material by the Orioles and the Four Buddies," he said. "But I didn't leave the group because of their direction; I left because they asked me to. One of my friends, Al Denby, and I were both in the group but we also had jobs and couldn't make all the rehearsals when the others wanted to. Plus we weren't as good as the guys that they got to replace us."

At that point, Parris said, he and Denby formed another vocal group and named it the Scarlets. "We admired the Red Robin label people like the Velvets and the Vocaleers, and the New York groups like the Crows and the early Drifters with Clyde McPhatter," he said. "Even the ones in California like the Penguins and the Robins."

After practicing with the Scarlets, Parris traveled to New York in search of a label to record the group. There, he met Bobby Robinson of Red Robin Records. "Bobby Robinson owned Red Robin Records and he also owned Bobby's Record Shop on 125th Street," he said. "After my group started we were mostly covering other people and didn't have original material at first. I went to New York but didn't know where the record companies were located and didn't know you had to go downtown, and I got off the train in Harlem. I walked on 125th Street and at that time they used to have the speakers outside the stores that played the records out to the street. Bobby had that same setup and you got a chance to hear all the music in the street.

"I stopped at a department store that was playing music, went in and walked to the record counter, and there was a guy standing behind it," he continued. "This is how naïve I was. I told him that I had a group and I wanted to make a record. I asked him if he could direct me to a record company and he said that he owned one. He told me that he owned Jax Records. Here he was working behind the counter but I didn't know that in those days you couldn't make it on just the record label."

The record label owner asked Parris if he had a demo recording so that he could hear what the group sounded like. While Parris didn't have one, he offered to make one with the group. "The guy said, 'Well, whatever you do, bring it back to me. And whatever you do, don't go down to Bobby Robinson down there,'" Parris recalled. "When I heard that Bobby Robinson of Red Robin Records was right there, I never saw that guy again. I went right down to Bobby Robinson. It was a very small shop and he was up on a ladder putting records up and I told him who I was and what I wanted and he asked for a demo too. He told me to bring him a demo so that he could hear us. My heart started beating as if I was already a star. I got back on the train, went back to New Haven, got the guys together, and we made a demonstration record and I took it back to him."

When Parris brought Robinson the demo, a recording of "Dear One," he was not overly impressed. And when he asked Parris what song he had for the other side of the single and learned that the group only had one tune, Robinson told him he needed another song. Paris returned to Connecticut and wrote "I've Lost."

Upon his return with the newly recorded tune, Parris said that Robinson still failed to display any enthusiasm toward the group. Weeks passed by and Parris made repeated calls to the record shop. Robinson finally called to inform them that he had arranged a split recording session with another local group, the Velvets. The arrangement called for each group to record two songs.

"The reason that the session came to be was because Bobby's brother, Danny Robinson, liked us," Parris said. "Danny owned Everlast Records and urged his brother to record us. Bobby finally compromised by arranging a split session with the Velvets."

In late 1953 the Scarlets entered Sunset Studios on 125th Street in Harlem to rehearse their material. "The next day we got on the subway and went downtown to Bell Studios to record 'Dear One' and 'I've Lost.' When the single came out in February 1954, within a couple of weeks it was doing well in New York and California."

As a result, the group began to get engagements, sometimes performing with top acts of the time. One such gig found them contracted to perform on a cruise along the Hudson River with the famed Cadillacs.

"It was a thrill because mambo music was very popular at the time," Parris said. "Joe Loco, Tito Puente, and Tito Rodriguez were big then. On that boat ride, all of these mambo bands were there too and it was a big thing. There were eight bands and twelve groups, like the Cadillacs and the Solitaires. But unfortunately, only one or two groups got to perform that night."

As Parris described it, the enthusiastic crowd on the boat became somewhat unruly and quickly erupted into a near riot. As a result, pandemonium broke out and the boat quickly returned to shore, with members of the Scarlets separated in the confusion as patrons hastily exited the vessel.

"That was our very first big gig and there was so much commotion going on that we never got to perform," Parris said.

Parris soon formed the Five Satins and eventually wrote a composition that would come to define the doo-wop era as a classic and enduring song. That tune, "In the Still of the Nite," remains one of the most requested songs on radio shows that play an oldies format. But a longstanding story that he wrote the song in the basement of a church in New Haven is incorrect, as is the origin of how the group first came together. Parris happily set the record straight.

"I formed the Five Satins in 1955 while I was already in the military," he said. "A fellow I knew, Marty Kugell, who wanted to get into the record business, had a partner who was an engineer who knew all the ins and outs with tape recorders and stuff and he was from Connecticut. When I would come home on the weekends, he would try to get in touch with me because he knew about the Scarlets. But by then the Scarlets were all spread around since we all went into the service together. He kept bugging me to write a song and to record something for him, so finally when I came home I got some guys I knew from the neighborhood and put the Five Satins together.

"The first thing that we recorded was 'Oh My,' and 'Rose Marie' was on the flip side," he continued. "The main side, 'Oh My,' was a cappella and 'Rose Marie' was accompanied by a piano. We did 'Oh My' a cappella because the band didn't show up. We didn't want to waste the time. We recorded it at a VFW hall and it was hot and we left the doors open. At the end of the record you can hear a whizzing noise. That was a truck that went by and it stayed on the record."

When the single was released, it became apparent that the record company entrepreneurs knew little to nothing about the record business. Being familiar with a disc jockey in nearby Springfield, Massachusetts, they sent the record to him and he was the first to air the song. Within a week, as calls began to come in requesting copies of the record, a sense of panic broke out. "They didn't know anything about pressing records," Parris recalled. "The only thing they knew how to do was record it. That record went nowhere because of that."

The group's next recording session took place in another unconventional setting: the basement of a local church. "Marty was always looking for a deal," Parris said. "He knew about the basement in this church and said that if we could record there he thought that we could get a good sound. But how do you get permission to use the church to record in? He knew one of the parishioners, who was a sax player, and he had him speak to the priest and rented the basement of the church for almost nothing, but he let the sax player play on the record. That's who you hear on 'In the Still of the Nite.'"

Parris said that the group's entire album was recorded in the basement of the church. As for the origin of the classic song, it was in fact composed by Parris while he was on guard duty at a military base in Philadelphia, Pennsylvania. "In the Still of the Nite" was first released on the Standord Records label.

"Standord Records was owned by Marty Kugell and Tom Sokira," Parris said. "Later on they sold 'In the Still of the Nite' to Al Silver of Ember Records. When they sold it to Silver, they had a stockpile of their standard records of the song, which, of course, is worth more than the Ember label now. They took Ember's labels and put them over the Standord label to save money. So some of them out there today actually have the Standord label underneath."

The single soared almost immediately and climbed the charts to number three rhythm and blues and number twenty-four pop. But by the time that occurred, Parris was already reassigned to military duty in Japan.

"The song came out in March or April of 1956 and I left for Japan in April," he said. "The group used Bill Baker to replace me when they performed in support of the hit record. When he first came into the group, he wasn't the lead singer but sang first tenor. But the guy that they selected to sing lead and take my place was a little flakey and they could never get hold of him, so they made Bill the lead singer."

While many composers of that era were duped out of writer credit and, more important, royalties for many of the top songs that defined music of that time, Parris came through the experience unscathed.

"I slipped through the cracks," he said. "Unlike many of the other guys during that time, I still get my money for 'In the Still of the Nite.' I was fortunate enough to be with the attorney Lee Eastman, and he was good to me. You know that song has been recorded by about forty-five different people."

In Parris's absence, the Bill Baker-led Five Satins recorded the follow-up hit single, "To the Aisle," in August 1957. The release would also enter the Top 40 pop charts as well as climb into the Top 10 on the R&B chart. Upon Parris's discharge from the military, he returned home and eventually reorganized the group.

"It was just a stroke of luck the way that happened because you would think there would be a fight," he said. "What happened was, when I came home in 1957, I took a young lady down to the Apollo Theater just to see the show. I didn't even know who was on it. When we got there on the marquee was the Five Satins, Robert and Johnny, and Gladys Knight and the Pips, and we went in. The Five Satins did two songs and that's about the time that I decided that I wanted to put my group back together again. I went to put the group back and these guys just broke up. They didn't know what I was doing but they just couldn't get along or whatever and decided to call it quits."

In reality, the first song that Parris recorded after he was discharged from the service, "She's Gone with the Wind," was released as the Scarlets. But with Baker leaving to attempt a solo career and the other active members merely walking away, Parris encountered no opposition in his attempt to reorganize the Five Satins.

In 1959, the group scored a regional hit with "Shadows." A year later, in large part to the inclusion of "In the Still of the Nite" on the first of producer Art Laboe's *Oldies But Goodies* compilation albums, the song re-entered the pop charts, gaining additional exposure for the group. Off the resurgence of their sound and hit record, the Five Satins had a minor hit later in 1960 with its recording of the standard tune "I'll Be Seeing You."

While audience attention and tastes shifted to the incredibly popular groups of the British Invasion, Parris led various Five Satins lineups at performances in the United States and in Europe for the remainder of the decade. A renewed interest in the mellow and tight harmonic sounds of vocal groups in the early 1970s found the Five Satins headlining at a greatly increased schedule of oldies shows.

The group signed a recording deal with Kirshner Records in 1974 and released a single, "Two Different Worlds." In 1976, the Five Satins released a Top 50 hit single, "Everybody Stand Up and Clap Your Hands." under the name Black Satin. "We were trying to reinvent ourselves," Parris said. "We hadn't had a hit for a while and we wanted to get into the new game with everybody else, with disco and all of that stuff. I think Tavares was out with a couple of things and we liked that stuff."

Shortly after, they reverted back to the Five Satins name. In 1982 the group released its last single to enter the Top 100 chart with "Memories of Days Gone By." The song, released on Elektra Records, was a medley of former hit tunes that included, in addition to "In the Still of the Nite," "Tears On My Pillow," "Only You," and "Earth Angel."

Of the many concerts and venues that Parris and the Five Satins have performed at throughout a fifty-year career in music, it was hard for him to select one as a personal favorite. "That is so tough because I've been on so many of them and so many of them have been wonderful," he said. "As for a venue, I like Madison Square Garden in New York City and the Spectrum in Philadelphia.

"In looking at my body of work through the years, I am most proud of writing 'In the Still of the Nite.' There have been so many people that have recorded that song like Yusef Lateef, Lester Bowie, Johnny Mathis and Take Six, Boyz ll Men, and the Orlons. I'm just very proud of it."

In 2006, Fred Parris remains active on the oldies concert circuit, thrilling audiences with the enduring, classic song that he composed fifty years prior.

Billboard Top 40 Hits by the Five Satins

Date	Pos	Wks on Charts	Record Title	Label/ Number
09/29/56	24	06	In the Still of the Nite	Ember 1005
08/12/57	25	08	To the Aisle	Ember 1019

**Vito Picone
(The Elegants)**

Flushing, New York   **April 16, 2005**

The history of how the Elegants came to form and release a huge hit single in 1958, "Little Star," began when a group of teenagers started harmonizing on a boardwalk in Staten Island, one of the five boroughs of the City of New York.

In November 1956, Vito Picone composed a tune, "Darling Come Back," and recorded it with his vocal group, Pat Cordell and the Crescents. The group consisted of Picone, Patricia Croccitto, Ronnie Jones, and Carmen Romano. Off the local success of that song, the teenagers began to appear at shows with many of the top acts of the day, such as the Valentines, the Cadillacs, and the Five Satins.

"Listening to Alan Freed is the reason we all got interested in rock-and-roll at that time," Picone recalled. "From a singing standpoint, uniquely enough, I got myself in trouble in grammar school and as a punishment they put me in the glee club. They thought it was a punishment but I was actually the only guy in the club, so I had a ball. I loved it, and in the meantime, I learned a whole new technique because the teacher took all the baritones and taught us our parts, the tenors and their parts, and so on and so forth; and then we didn't see each other until we got into the assembly. At that point we couldn't make a mistake because all you knew was what she taught you. When you got together and heard this beautiful blend, I was hooked from that day on."

Picone recalled the attention that the young vocal group received when his composition "Darling Come Back" became a local favorite.

"That was a dream," he said. "We started that group with a young girl, Pat Croccitto, who changed her name to Pat Cordell, and she was the closest thing that we had to a Frankie Lymon-type singer. That's who we were trying to emulate, the Teenagers. I was the bass in that group and we wound up recording for Club Records, and that's when we went on what we thought was a tour. We went to Connecticut and stayed pretty much in the tri-state area."

But a promising future for the group was dashed when Croccitto's father objected to his fifteen-year-old daughter touring with the boys and halted their efforts. The decision caused the Crescents to disband, but the setback would not deter Picone's determination to forge forward in the music industry.

In late 1956, Picone formed another vocal group, this time an all-male aggregation. It included Romano, Arthur Venosa, James Moshella, and Frank Tardogna. Upon winning a local talent contest the group was signed to a recording deal with Aladdin Records. But the label, one that boasted a predominantly black artist clientele, failed to release a single recording made by the group.

"We won a contest and the winner got a recording deal," he said. "Needless to say, I think somebody did somebody a favor and it really had no merit to it at all. It was just a smoke screen and that was it."

Picone remembered how the new group's unique name was selected. "I was on my way to rehearsal one day, and as I turned a corner I saw a sign in the window of a local tavern that read 'Schenley, the whiskey of elegance.' When I got to rehearsal I transposed it to the Elegants and that was it."

Having penned a rock-and-roll song based on the Mozart-based nursery rhyme "Twinkle, Twinkle, Little Star," the frustrated but ever-determined group shopped their talents to other labels in the New York area.

Despite being only nineteen years old at the time, Kathy Watts was selected by the Elegants to serve as their manager. "She did what she could for the time," Picone said. "I don't really know if the part she played was instrumental because basically we auditioned live for some labels and that's how we received the contract to record 'Little Star.' She tried and worked diligently at it but it became a deterrent later on, because once the record became as big as it was, she was totally unprepared to do it on a professional level."

Eventually making contact with Bea Carlson of Hull Records, Picone pitched "Little Star," the song he composed with Venosa. "That was the first place we went to audition once Pat Cordell and the Crescents had broken up," he said. "The reason we went there is that we took the records that we were buying and took the addresses of the companies off the record labels. The Heartbeats were our favorite group, and because of the Heartbeats we looked at Hull Records and found the address on Broadway and we knocked on that door first. She flipped over the song and loved the harmony, and she asked us if we were interested in recording it and gave us a contract to take home to our parents to have our attorneys take a look at it. We just kept going from there."

While "Little Star" was based on and featured the wholesome storyline of the nursery rhyme "Twinkle, Twinkle, Little Star," the B-side of the single, "Getting Dizzy" gained a reputation for being somewhat raunchy and became the focus of controversy.

"I think they probably thought it was raunchy because they couldn't understand what I was singing," Picone said. "It was a very simple lyric stating that he had been jilted and was in a state of confusion and was just dizzy over the whole matter. There was nothing in there that was raunchy."

While the Elegants secured a recording contract with Hull Records, "Little Star" was released on the ABC Paramount label. "I think that was probably the genius at work," Picone said. "I really give Bea a lot of credit. She was also instrumental in adding one of the tags, 'Where are you little star?' in the beginning of the recording. We started it straight out singing the background and ended it with 'There you are little star.' She added the 'Where are you little star?' in the beginning of it.

"She realized that the song was bigger than she had anticipated and that she would not be able to have the distribution and the wherewithal to get it on a national level," he added. "She sublet us to ABC Paramount, who put us on their new record label Apt, and that was it."

The single climbed to number one in July 1958 and sold more than two million copies. At the time, the Elegants were only the second white doo-wop act to achieve that level of success. Off its popularity, the group began a schedule of appearances on a number of high-profile television and stage shows with many of the major recording artists of the day.

"We were never overwhelmed by the sudden attention mainly because we were young," Picone explained. "We just took it one day at a time and enjoyed ourselves. We now found ourselves working and traveling with people that just weeks before were our idols. We were also hanging out with guys our own age so it was like a bus trip from school. We just had a good time and let things fall where they may."

Legend has it that Laurie Records executive Gene Schwartz was so fascinated by the melody and success of "Little Star" that he urged songwriters Don Pomus and Mort Schuman to compose a similar-sounding tune for one of his acts. The resulting song, "Hushabye," became a hit recording for the Brooklyn vocal group, the Mystics.

"I was a little disappointed when I first heard it, not that I was jealous but I just thought that it would have been a prefect song for us to record," he said. "We did later on sign with Laurie Records and the story was that they went to the Colony Record store, bought the 45 recording of 'Little Star,' and broke it down into almost verse for verse and literally took the whole idea of 'Little Star.' They reversed the regular lead to a falsetto lead, obviously took the nursery rhyme, and the pattern of 'Hushabye' is exactly the same as 'Little Star.' I thought it would have been a great song for us to record and we would have been on our way after the second tune."

Following a brief stint with United Artists, the Elegants returned to ABC to record two powerful sides, "Tiny Cloud" and "I've Seen Everything." However, neither side appeared to benefit from a dedicated promotional effort from the label.

"We lost a lot of momentum once we were out on the road," Picone said. "We stayed on the road too long, and after we got back into the recording studio everybody wanted another 'Little Star.' We were constantly writing something similar to 'Little Star.' Just like the Mystics, there were five or six others groups that had already copied that style of singing and it was pretty much played out at that point. I think the distributors and basically the general public said enough is enough. We needed somebody to say, 'Guys, go back into the studio but come up with something interesting.'"

Both Warner Brothers and United Artists urged Picone to attempt a solo career and one even pitched him with an opportunity to record the song "Town Without Pity," one that went on to become a huge hit for Gene Pitney. Picone declined the offers, choosing to remain with the Elegants.

"Hindsight is always 20/20," Picone said with regard to his decision. "The biggest problem is that my cousin was vice president up there at Warner Brothers at the time and he didn't talk to me for seven years because he couldn't produce his cousin, who had the number-one record in the country. It was a very interesting deal there. They offered a five-year contract for a nice amount of dollars plus my royalties. But you have to remember that these weren't only guys that I sang with [the Elegants] on 'Little Star.' These are guys that we started kindergarten [with] together and we grew up together so there was never any intention of leaving them."

Eventually when the Elegants disbanded and Picone did attempt a solo career, he reformed a group, Vito and the Elegants. Following one release on the Laurie label, they backed an offbeat group, the Barbarians, on a recording titled "Moulty."

"Laurie had the song and Moulty was a young drummer who lost his hands in an accident and played very, very well despite his handicap," he said. "They needed background vocals and we were signed to the label, so it was just a transition that came naturally."

During the late 1960s, the Elegants remained inactive musically for the most part. "In the later 1960s we were pretty well lost for a while," Picone said. "I had an accident in the 1960s and lost sight in my left eye and was pretty well depressed for a while. That's when the group basically started to break up into different factions. But I formed a band similar to the Young Rascals and Paul Revere and the Raiders and those types of acts, and went out on the road with a group called Beau Jest and the Legions. I was Beau Jest with my Vandyke and my camel-colored jacket with epaulets and white pants like legionaries. We were a club band and we worked pretty much in the Midwest and down South throughout the 1960s. Then there was a revival in 1970 at the Academy of Music in Manhattan and it was supposed to be a one-night revival, but we haven't been out of work since that night."

In reflecting on a career that has included songwriting, performing, and being a personal manager for other recording artists, Picone summed up the pride that he has gained through his years in music.

"Nothing will ever compare to 'Little Star,'" he said. "Writing 'Little Star,' performing 'Little Star,' and having the ability by God to create a sound that has lasted more than forty-five years is definitely the highlight of my life. Dion had paid me a compliment on numerous occasions and in his liner notes in his box set that makes note that when he heard me singing at that point, it was very inspirational to him to go out and do 'Runaround Sue' and 'The Wanderer.' Coincidently, he was sitting next to me on the bus when I wrote 'Please Believe Me,' which was my second song, and that is most of the style of 'Runaround Sue' and 'The Wanderer.' He carried it five hundred miles further than I could have, and as a good friend of mine I'm very proud that he did."

Picone continues to lead a revised lineup of the Elegants at oldies shows into the twenty-first century.

Billboard Top 40 Hits by the Elegants

Date	Pos	Wks on Charts	Record Title	Label/ Number
07/28/58	01	16	Little Star	Apt 25005

Herb Reed
(The Platters)

Wildwood, New Jersey   **July 5, 2005**

One of the most popular and successful vocal groups in the history of music came together in Los Angeles, California, in 1953. Bass singer Herb Reed formed the group and was joined at the outset by Joe Jefferson, Cornell Gunter, and Alex Hodge. Early on, David Lynch replaced Jefferson and Tony Williams took Gunter's spot.

"I organized the Platters in 1953 and named the group after how the disc jockeys used to refer to records as being platters," Reed said.

The doo-wop group performed primarily at local talent contests. It was at one of those shows that music entrepreneur Ralph Bass heard the group and signed them to record for the Federal label, a subsidiary of King Records, located in Cincinnati, Ohio. The recordings made for Federal were for the most part nondescript and showed little to no flair or style any different from a number of other street-corner groups of the time.

The Platters actually recorded their first huge hit, "Only You," on two occasions, the first being on the Federal label. But the original recording

213

was never released. "On Federal, we didn't have a sound," Reed recalled. "We didn't know what we were doing and were just starting out. We didn't know anything about the studio and we were amateurs in there, and so all the stuff we were doing on Federal was amateurish."

The single most critical event in the Platters' brief history occurred when a songwriter from Chicago, Buck Ram, met the group. Ram had an established career in music, having arranged music for many of the major big bands such as Glenn Miller, Duke Ellington, Cab Calloway, Count Basie, and Tommy Dorsey. He also operated a talent agency in Los Angeles, wrote and arranged songs for Mills Music, and managed the pop group the Three Suns. When Ram came to meet the Platters he had already begun working with another Los Angeles vocal group, the Penguins. Reed reflected on his first meeting with Ram.

"I heard that a guy who was a songwriter from Chicago came out to Los Angeles to learn the business and to do some managing," he said. "We looked him up and found him and used to socialize with him at his office for a half a year or more. He kept hearing us sing at amateur shows. He liked us and we liked him so we decided to sign him up."

After assuming management of the Platters, Ram negotiated their release from the contract with Federal and signed the group with Mercury Records in 1955. He then began to assess the group, its sound, and its members' vocal contributions. His keen ear determined that the addition of a female vocalist into the group would enhance the Platters' sound and add a touch of sophistication to it. He selected Zola Taylor, a vocalist that was a member in another group that Ram managed, Shirley Gunter and the Queens. He then thrust tenor Tony Williams into the forefront and designated him the group's lead singer. The last personnel change that Ram made was to replace Hodge with Paul Robi. Having solidified the vocal arrangement of what would become the incredibly romantic Platters' trademark sound Ram was prepared to enter the recording studio.

With his revised lineup intact, Ram scheduled a recording session at Mercury to lay down one of his original compositions, "Only You." The Mercury release gained swift attention and entered the charts in October 1955. In addition to becoming a huge hit for the group (it reached number one on the rhythm and blues chart), their recording would reach historic proportions.

As was common practice at the time, a rhythm and blues record that became a hot property was quickly covered by a white group, the latter being assured of significant airplay and a subsequent rise up the pop charts. White vocal groups, such as the Diamonds, covered a huge amount of singles originally released by black artists and enjoyed great success from their recorded versions. As such, when "Only You" started to climb the charts, the Hilltoppers, a group of white vocalists from Western Kentucky College, covered the tune on the Dot record label. Their version eventually reached the number-eight slot on the pop chart.

However, after hitting the top of the rhythm and blues chart, the Platters' single of "Only You" crossed over to the pop chart as well and climbed to the number-five position. The unprecedented success gave it the distinction of becoming the first single by a black group to cross over and achieve a higher status than did its white competition's disc.

But despite the record's success, Reed said that it did not result in a surge of appearance requests for the group. "At that particular time a lot of the clubs wouldn't hire black entertainers," he said. "Having a hit with that song meant absolutely nothing toward getting us work."

The Platters' follow-up single, "The Great Pretender," became the group's first number-one pop recording. Off the two breakout hits, disc jockey Alan Freed included the Platters, performing both songs, in his rock-and-roll feature length film *Rock Around the Clock*. But the group never got to meet Freed during filming.

"I didn't see Alan Freed at all during that whole movie," Reed said. "The only time I saw him is when we performed at his shows at the Brooklyn Paramount and the Manhattan theaters. In the movie, we just did our scenes and singing before he even got there."

The motion picture would be the first of twenty-seven film projects the group participated in through the years.

When Ram brought in arranger Sammy Lowe to rework a tune that became popular for Vera Lynn and Sammy Kaye earlier, "My Prayer" proved to be a huge hit for the Platters. The sophisticated sound that the Platters had become known for motivated Ram to have them cover other earlier hits, done in the group's unique harmony. They included "If I Didn't Care" and "I'll Never Smile Again." In all, the Platters scored eleven two-sided hits and compiled more than thirty pop hit records by the early 1960s.

In 1958, the Platters introduced "Twilight Time" on Dick Clark's *American Bandstand* television show. An appearance on that show was revered by musical acts as having the ability to significantly affect the popularity and subsequent sales of a new single. But Reed said to attribute the success of any of the Platters' singles to a specific appearance was difficult to do.

"It's hard to understand what kind of an impact any of those things had on a record's success because in those days nobody called you and told you that you had a hit record," Reed said. "Nobody called to tell you that you were gaining on the charts or that you were even on the charts. You had no information at all about anything you were doing. Even the manager didn't tell you anything. You were just out there working and that's all you were doing. We didn't know that 'Only You' had been on the charts that long. In fact, nobody even called to tell us 'Only You' was even released or a hit recording."

"Twilight Time" went on to top the pop and rhythm and blues charts in April 1958. While the group toured France that October, they recorded the hugely popular hit song "Smoke Gets in Your Eyes."

Reed recalled performing in Europe and how the audiences overseas embraced the group. "The European audiences were so great that we decided and did spend 90 percent of our time performing to them," he said. "I loved it and they were fantastic. It was a whole other world and a beautiful world."

By 1961, the Platters began to experience changes in its personnel when Williams decided to embark on a solo career, and Zola Taylor and Paul Robi both left the group. While Sonny Turner was recruited to replace Williams, Sandra Dawn assumed the female vocal role and Nate Nelson, formerly of the Flamingos, took Robi's slot in the group. With Turner on lead vocals, the group enjoyed success with tunes like "I Love You 1,000 Times" and "With This Ring."

A number of biographical accounts on the Platters regarding Williams' departure are inaccurate in stating that another singer, Sonny Barnes, was hired to replace him in the group. Reed disputed the fact that Barnes performed with the group for a year, before being dismissed and replaced with Sonny Turner. "That's all wrong," he said. "Barnes was a guy that just came in to try out for the group. He couldn't sing at all and I believe his name was actually Johnny Barnes."

Despite an ingenious initiative developed by Ram in 1956 to protect the Platters' name, splintering among former group members and various aggregations and lineups began to perform as the Platters. In 1956, Ram had formed The Five Platters, Inc., and issued shares to each member in the group. But the agreement held a clause that prohibited any member that left the Platters from using the group's name in the future. The latter provision was ignored, resulting in litigation among the various lineups.

Reed recalled the legalities surrounding this practice and how it came to affect the group members. "We did form a group called the

Platters but found out that it was formed illegally, so the shares were null and void," Reed said. "They were told that it was done illegally, so it never meant anything."

As various members of the group splintered and began to form various lineups to perform as the Platters and those members splintered and formed other groups, the residual effect on Reed's ability to secure engagements was severely diminished due to pure economics. If a bogus lineup of Platters charged a minimal fee to perform at a specific show, in effect providing a promoter with the ability to advertise the world-famous Platters as being a part of his/her concert lineup, the Reed-led lineup of Platters would be hard-pressed to secure the gig at a higher price, despite the fact that he is a founding member and sole original still performing under the Platters name.

The same issue has plagued, among other classic acts of that era, the Drifters, the Coasters, and the Marvelettes, all of whom have boasted singers that in effect have duped audiences into paying to hear lineups without any original members or any credible ties whatsoever to the group performing. Reed shared his thoughts of the deceit and how it has burdened him through the years.

"In the beginning it made me angry and I stayed angry a long time," he said. "Then you realize that anger creates problems for you from within. It creates health problems, heart problems, and nerve problems if you stay angry all the time. And so you realize that the only way you can fight back is not through the courts, because they don't do a damn thing for you but; rather to travel, showcase yourself, stay clean, and do the best job you can and keep your name out there before the public. And you have to forget about that which you cannot do or help and get on with your life."

In 1997, a federal court in Nevada ruled that since Reed was the sole living member of the original Platters lineup, he assumed ownership of its name, along with the right to perform as such. Unfortunately, that has not been the case, as more than one hundred groups performing all around the world do so as the Platters. Reed and his contingent of Platters continue to perform in 2006 and, along with Sonny Turner, remain the only ones with legitimate ties to the Platters as heard on the original recordings.

Having recorded more than four hundred sides and selling in excess of eighty-nine million records, the Platters were inducted into the Rock and Roll Hall of Fame in Cleveland, Ohio, in 1990. But the induction ceremony proved to be distressing for Reed.

"It was the worst time of any award I ever had in my life," he said. "Phil Spector did the inductions and he didn't know that he was inducting us. He got up on the stage and started reading the names of the members on the board of the hall. A guy came out and said, 'Phil, the Platters,' and he said, 'Well, nobody told me.' That's just what he said."

Reed said that he is extremely proud that the lineup he performs with today represents the legendary sound of the Platters at a very high level. The group's classic stage presence and sweet, melodic harmonies remains a mainstay in elevating them to a class of sophistication and elegance.

Billboard Top 40 Hits by the Platters

Date	Pos	Wks on Charts	Record Title	Label/Number
10/01/55	05	20	Only You	Mercury 70633
12/24/55	01	19	The Great Pretender	Mercury 70753
			(You've Got)	
03/31/56	04	16	the Magic Touch	Mercury 70819
07/07/56	01	20	My Prayer/	
08/11/56	39	01	Heaven on Earth	Mercury 70893
10/06/56	11	12	You'll Never Never Know/	
10/13/56	23	09	It Isn't Right	Mercury 70948
01/12/57	20	06	On My Word of Honor/	
01/26/57	31	02	One in a Million	Mercury 71011
03/23/57	11	11	I'm Sorry/	
04/06/57	23	09	He's Mine	Mercury 71032
06/10/57	24	07	My Dream	Mercury 71093
04/07/58	01	14	Twilight Time	Mercury 71289
12/01/58	01	16	Smoke Gets in Your Eyes	Mercury 71383
04/06/59	12	11	Enchanted	Mercury 71427
02/15/60	08	11	Harbor Lights	Mercury 71563
08/22/60	36	01	Red Sails in the Sunset	Mercury 71656
10/24/60	21	08	To Each His Own	Mercury 71697
01/30/61	30	02	If I Didn't Care	Mercury 71749
08/21/61	25	04	I'll Never Smile Again	Mercury 71847
06/04/66	31	05	I Love You 1,000 Times	Musicor 1166
03/25/67	14	07	With This Ring	Musicor 1229

Martha Reeves
(The Vandellas)

Wildwood, New Jersey   **July 5, 2005**

The Supremes and Martha and the Vandellas defined the girl-group sound of the 1960s at Motown Records in Detroit, Michigan. Gaining major chart success with songs such as "Heat Wave," "Dancing in the Street," and "Nowhere to Run," the Vandellas consisted of Martha Reeves, Annette Sterling, and Rosiland Ashford.

Born in Eufaula, Alabama, on July 18, 1941, Reeves moved with her family to Detroit before her first birthday. Her early introduction to music came as a singer in her grandfather's church and at school. "That experience has also interested [me in] pursuing a career in politics because there are rumors that they might take music out of public schools," Reeves said. "I know that from the age of three years old, that music was my heart. With my mom teaching me how to retain lyrics, I had the knack and just loving lyrics, and performing interested me in a career in show business."

In 1959, Reeves first sang with the Fascinations before leaving to join the Del-Phis, a group that at the time included a fourth member,

Gloria Williams. While existing biographies credit Reeves with forming the latter group, she disputed that claim. "The Del-Phis already existed when I joined them," she said. "One of their singers, Beatrice, had moved out of the city and I was asked to replace her. We split up after the Del-Phis recorded 'I'll Let You Know' on the Checkmate label, an answer to a song we had done behind J. J. Barnes called 'Won't You Let Me Know.'"

Through Reeves's strong will and determination, and a couple of situations that found her and the group in the right place at the right time, the group soon topped the record charts as one of the finest acts of that era.

In 1961 Reeves won a talent contest as a solo artist and secured a nightclub engagement as a prize, performing as Martha LaVaille. It was at that engagement that she was noticed by Mickey Stevenson, an executive at Motown Records. "I haven't ever felt like I was a group because I had done solo and just had backups," she said. "I've always been a lead singer and one to step out front and sing all the lyrics and win the crowd. So I feel like I'm a single performer with backup singers."

During that early period, Reeves recalled focusing on rhythm and blues and performing renditions of songs such as "Gin House Blues," "Fly Me to the Moon," "Canadian Sunset," and other songs that were popular at that time.

Gaining Stevenson's attention got Reeves an invitation to Hitsville USA, Motown's headquarters in Detroit. "Mickey Stevenson approached me after I finished a performance at the nightclub," Reeves said. "I won an amateur contest and my reward was three nights at a nightclub. But my father, being the man that he was, would not let me in his house after twelve o'clock, so I had to do the happy hour. About eleven o'clock, on the last night of my engagement, on a Sunday, William Stevenson, better known as Mickey, approached me and said, 'You got talent. Come to Hitsville USA.' I did, the very next morning. Upon my arrival, I was asked to answer a telephone that threw me into a secretarial position, so I feel fortunate that I was a singer that could type."

While working as a secretary at Motown, a situation came up that found the label in need of background singers for one of its recording sessions. "I got a thirty-five-dollar-a-week salary in my secretarial job and I augmented that by singing background with other people, snapping my fingers and stomping my feet to whatever the rhythm was.

We didn't have synthesizers so we made up the rhythms on some of the records by clapping our hands."

In 1962, she and the Del-Phis got their first break when background vocalists were needed for one of the label's new artist's recording session. The artist was Marvin Gaye, and the Del-Phis laid down vocals on his first hit single, "Stubborn Kind of Fellow."

Reeves recalled that she was asked to recruit some girls to sing behind Gaye. "Stevenson asked me to get some girls to sing behind a guy named Marvin, who had been traveling with Smokey Robinson as his background drummer. I didn't know he was a singer but he had cut some records; but they weren't hits. Mickey asked me to get a specific group but they were in Chicago recording. I didn't want to bus my girls, so I called in some girls. I knew better than to go back to William Stevenson and tell him that I couldn't find any girls. I called Rosiland, Annette, and Gloria off their jobs and asked them if they would come in and sing behind this guy Marvin Gaye."

Reeves said that prior to that recording session Gaye had been just one more nondescript person at the studio. "He was so fine," she said. "He had been disguising himself with a pipe in his mouth, a hat on his head, and some glasses. When he took the glasses off his eyes, the hat off his head, and the pipe out of his mouth we stood behind him and just sang away. I think his good looks inspired us to do the background we did on 'Stubborn Kind of Fellow.' We went on to record 'Hitchhike' and 'Pride and Joy' with him."

While the background vocals on "Stubborn Kind of Fellow" were credited to the Vels, Stevenson's enthusiasm over the group's sound motivated him to record them on "You'll Never Cherish a Love So True" on Motown's subsidiary label, Mel-O-Dy. When the record failed to gain attention, Williams left the group and it remained a trio from that time on.

The quartet seized its next opportunity at a recording session scheduled for Motown artist Mary Wells, but accounts that documented the latter's failure to show up at the session were dispelled by Reeves. "It wasn't so much that Mary Wells failed to show up at the session but the union man showed up and they called me out of the A&R department to cover for a song that they were producing for Mary Wells," Reeves said. "The agreement with the union stipulated that no one could record unless the artist was there, so I was called to cover the mike. Berry was recording twenty-four hours a day and for some reason the union was making him adhere to rules that no one else had to."

It happened at the same time that Mary Wells planned to leave Motown. "I sang it the best I could, and when Berry Gordy heard it he told them to release it by me," she added. "So at the same time, we had recorded behind Marvin Gaye, and they said to put the same girls behind me, and that's how we got our first recording, 'I'll Have to Let Him Go.'"

The single became the first release for the newly named Martha and the Vandellas. A second release that year, "Come and Get These Memories," climbed to the number-five slot on the rhythm and blues chart.

Reeves named the group the Vandellas after her longtime idol Della Reese and a street in Detroit named Van Dyke. Following the release of "Come and Get These Memories," the girls came to the attention of the label's powerhouse songwriting and production team of Holland-Dozier-Holland. It would be a fruitful collaboration for both the artists and the creative team, with three consecutive Top 10 singles released over the next year. "Heat Wave," "Quicksand," and "Dancing in the Street" catapulted the group into the spotlight.

"It was a thrill working with Holland-Dozier-Holland because they had the knack of coming up with the sound that Berry was looking for," she said. "Lamont Dozier would play the piano, Eddie Holland would sing the lead to me, and Brian Holland would sing the background to the girls or with the girls. If you listen closely to 'A Love Like Yours Don't Come Knocking,' you'll hear Brian Holland singing louder than the two girls. He had the knack of the background vocals and they were very good to work with. They had their act together and it didn't take but one or two takes to record their songs."

Existing documents state that the group's biggest hit single, "Dancing in the Streets," came to Martha and the Vandellas when another artist, Kim Weston, turned it down. Again, Reeves found an opportunity to dispel a long-believed inaccuracy.

"Kim Weston was living with Mickey Stevenson at the time that he and Marvin Gaye wrote 'Dancing in the Streets' in their attic," Reeves said. "Marvin Gaye sang it first, and then Mickey for some reason thought that I could do a better job and introduced the song to me. Kim Weston never sang it. Please set the record straight."

As one hit single after another began to climb the charts and increase the group's popularity and demand for performances, Martha and the Vandellas embarked on multiple-city tours at a wide variety of venues.

"I don't have a favorite show or venue but my favorite thing is performing," she said. "I could name some places that I went to and would love to go again like the Copacabana, the Latin Casino, Leo's Casino, the Harrah, and the International Hilton. I love the Apollo Theater."

After the release of "Quicksand," Beard left the music business and was replaced by Betty Kelly, who had previously sung with the Velvelettes. Upon Kelly's eventual departure three years later, Reeves recruited her younger sister, Lois, and the group began to record as Martha Reeves and the Vandellas.

Following additional personnel changes in the group, along with Reeves' subsequent battle with a serious illness, the Vandellas decided to disband. They gave a farewell performance at Detroit's Cobo Hall in December 1972. Reeves reflected on that performance and the group's disbanding.

"We didn't have a decision to disband," she said. "It was a matter of records not selling, business petering out, and Motown making a move to Los Angeles. We had to make a decision to continue or not. I also became pregnant and had a son. So a lot of circumstances caused the group to disband. My sister Lois went on to sing with a group called Quiet Elegance and Sandra Tilly got married and moved to Texas, so it kind of ended that era."

Reports state that upon Motown's decision to relocate its operation to California, Reeves sued the company in an attempt to gain her release from the label. Once again, Reeves set the record straight. "That is all a misconception," she said. "I didn't sue to break my contract. Motown left Detroit in 1970 and they left me there too. My contract ran out. I sued for royalties in 1984 after not receiving them for eleven years. I never sued to leave Motown. Motown left me."

Reeves went on to record a self-titled solo album for MCA and then shifted musical styles to release two disco-oriented albums, *The Rest of My Life* on the Arista label in 1977 and *We Meet Again* the next year for Fantasy Records. The latter album contained songs composed by Reeves.

"I wrote the B-side for my very first song on Motown, one called 'My Baby Won't Come Back,'" she said. "I realized then that I wasn't ever going to get any publishing, and the writing was split 40-60 and I got 40 percent of my first composition on Motown, so I decided that I'd wait. Recently I recorded a CD, and I wrote all the songs except one. I've been writing songs all my life. In my book, *Dancing in the Streets*, I have original poems before every chapter."

In 1989, Reeves reunited with Sterling and Ashford (Holmes) to record a single, "Step into My Shoes," on the Motor City label. In 1995, Martha and the Vandellas were inducted into the Rock and Roll Hall of Fame.

Reeves currently performs with a new lineup of Vandellas at a number of oldies shows as well as at nightclubs nationwide.

Billboard Top 40 Hits by Martha and the Vandellas

Date	Pos	Wks on Charts	Record Title	Label/Number
05/18/63	29	08	Come and Get These Memories	Gordy 7014
08/17/63	04	11	Heat Wave	Gordy 7022
12/07/63	08	09	Quicksand	Gordy 7025
09/05/64	02	11	Dancing in the Street	Gordy 7033
12/26/64	34	04	Wild One	Gordy 7036
03/13/65	08	08	Nowhere to Run	Gordy 7039
09/11/65	36	02	You've Been in Love Too Long	Gordy 7045
02/19/66	22	07	My Baby Loves Me	Gordy 7048
11/12/66	09	07	I'm Ready for Love	Gordy 7056
03/18/67	10	10	Jimmy Mack	Gordy 7058
09/09/67	25	06	Love Bug Leave My Heart Alone	Gordy 7062
12/02/67	11	09	Honey Chile	Gordy 7067

Wally Roker
(The Heartbeats)

Islandia, New York   **November 13, 2005**

During the summer of 1956, five young men from Queens, New York, recorded a tune written by the group's lead singer, titled "A Thousand Miles Away." The group was the Heartbeats and its lead singer was one James Sheppard, who, after the Heartbeats disbanded, would score another hit record, "Daddy's Home," with his new group, Shep and the Limelites. Sadly, despite having a pleasing voice and writing talent, Sheppard also suffered from an attraction to alcohol, a fact that not only caused the Heartbeats to disband, but also eventually served as the contributing factor to his premature demise.

The story of the Heartbeats began in 1952 in a boy's restroom at Woodrow Wilson High School in South Ozone Park, New York. And while the location might seem unusual, the resonating sound that resulted from the restroom's tiled walls made it an attractive place for many teenage vocal groups to harmonize.

On the day in question, Albert Crump, a first tenor, and Vernon Sievers, a baritone (both members of a local group named the Hearts), were singing with a few friends in the restroom when bass singer Wally Roker walked in and began to harmonize with them. Having just lost a member of the group, Eddie Sievers, cousin of Vernon, Roker's chance vocalizing with the pair came at just the right time. Soon after, the Hearts added him to their lineup.

"I got the offer to join the Hearts in the bathroom at Woodrow Wilson High School," Roker recalled. "Vernon, Sievers, Albert Crump, and I all went to that school and that's when it all started. We started harmonizing in the bathroom and then finally got together at Robbie's [Tatum] house and finalized that I would be in the group."

Roker said that a few popular vocal groups of that era influenced the sound that the Hearts were trying to develop. "The Five Keys, the Clovers, the Drifters with Clyde McPhatter, the Dominos with Jackie Wilson, and Jimmy Ricks with the Ravens were the kinds of groups that we really liked," he said.

The Hearts began to hone their skills at regular rehearsals, with Crump handling the lead vocals. However, collectively its members sought a fifth voice. Roker explained why. "We were trying to get a real good harmony sound and we were looking for somebody that could also write songs and be a composer in the development of the group," he said. "We were, at that point, harmonizers of songs but didn't compose at all."

James Sheppard came to the group's attention through word of mouth. "We heard about him in St. Albans Park," he said. "We heard there was this guy that could really sing and would probably be good for the group. We looked him up, went by his house and talked to him, and got it together. We listened to him sing and felt it out."

Shortly after Sheppard joined the others, it was discovered that another vocal group had previously claimed the name Hearts and had in fact already released a single using it on the label. The group, Joyce West and the Hearts, had recorded "Lonely Nights," and the song was gaining steam on the airwaves. With little choice, the Hearts from Queens needed to come up with a new name.

"When we recorded 'Tormented' and were ready to put it out as the Hearts, the girl group known by the same name had a hit record in New York City that was doing very well," Roker said. "We couldn't use the name, so we had to figure out how to change the Hearts to whatever we were going to change it to. Beat just seemed natural: heartbeat. It was kind of a group decision."

A neighbor of Roker's, musician Illinois Jacquet, became the conduit between the Heartbeats and their first recording session, one that produced two original Sheppard compositions, "After Everybody's Gone" and "Tormented." Jacquet's brother, Russell, had just formed the Network Records label and the Heartbeats single became the company's first release.

"We auditioned for Illinois Jacquet in his basement in St. Albans [Queens]," Roker recalled. "I knew his wife, his daughter, and his friends, and I bugged him until he gave us an audition. After he finally gave the opportunity to sing for him, he called his brother [Russell] and told him to put us on record."

When the record was released, while Sheppard had solely composed "Tormented" and its B-side, "After Everybody's Gone," the writer credit on the label read Russell Jacquet and His Orchestra. Roker explained. "That was because it was a jazz orchestra that played behind us," he said. "They were famous, famous jazz musicians that played behind 'Tormented.' I believe it also read 'featuring the Five Heartbeats' but the people that were playing behind us were well-known jazz people."

Plagued by the label's severe lack of promotional ability, while the single did receive some airplay it failed to gain steam.

The group's future as a debut act on a record label followed when it traveled to Brooklyn, New York, in 1955 to lay down tracks with another budding label, Hull Records. Bea Carlson and Billy Dawn Smith, recently departed from the Herald label, had joined forces with William Henry Miller to form Hull. This time it was Sievers' neighbor Miller who served as the contact for the group.

"William Miller is the one that took us to Hull Records to meet Bea Caslon," Roker said. "Miller lived across the street from Vernon and he was the father of the Miller Sisters singing group and he felt that Caslon would record us. She used to be the executive secretary for Herald Records, a label that had many hits out at that time. She supposedly got tired of them taking advantage of the groups, not paying them properly or giving them right contracts, so she was going to start her own label. Miller took us down to meet her and we put 'Crazy for You' together at that time."

Released in September 1955, "Crazy for You" became a regional hit and the group was invited to appear on the weeklong bill of a Tommy (Dr. Jive) Smalls show at Harlem's Apollo Theater, one that included Bo Diddley, the Flamingos, Etta James, the Harptones, and Bill Doggett.

"I remember running around with the AGVA guy," Roker said. "He wanted twenty-five hundred dollars from all of us to join AGVA. We were making probably five hundred dollars for the week and he wanted twenty-five hundred dollars from us as a down payment to join AVGA because we couldn't sing in the Apollo unless we were AGVA members. Tommy Smalls was getting us at the lowest price because he wrote the record and he was doing us a favor by putting us on the show. We had all the odds against us in reference to having any power whatsoever. All we had was a hit record and we wanted to play the Apollo.

"Playing that first show was a tremendous experience in reference to learning how to be cool when they call you onstage at the Apollo Theater, because you never know what's going to happen," he added. "You never knew if they would be throwing something at you or kicking you in the butt in not appreciating you, booing you off stage. We were very concerned about being very professional and putting our best foot out. Before you went onstage you were totally nervous and worried about acceptance, sound, the microphone being on, and all that kind of stuff. In the end, it went very well, plus we had the first two or three rows of the Apollo filled with nothing but our fans. There was the Imperial Heartbeats, the Heartbeat this and Heartbeat that; we had like five or six fan clubs in the metropolitan area because we played a lot of small clubs and we went into a lot of little neighborhoods all around town."

Roker said that the strong following the Heartbeats had developed is the reason that "Crazy for You" became number one on the Dr. Jive radio show. "We had all the fan clubs calling the radio station promoting our record," he said.

The Apollo show was a huge success and the Heartbeats' momentum landed them onto another major New York City show, the Alan Freed Rock'n'Roll Holiday Jubilee. That bill included Lavern Baker, the Valentines, Teddy Randazzo and the Three Chuckles, the Cadillacs, Joe Williams and the Count Basie Orchestra, and the Wrens.

"Being on the Alan Freed show was outstanding because that was the biggest show in town," Roker said. "That was a very serious, serious situation for us."

Before leaving for a weeklong engagement at the Howard Theater in Washington, D.C., the Heartbeats returned to the studio to record four tunes, one of which, "Darling How Long," would become their second release for Hull.

The group began a continuous schedule of appearances, including being featured on the Hal Jackson six-show package at the Opera House in the Bronx, New York, as well as part of a mini-tour of New Jersey with the Ramon Bruce Rock and Roll Bandwagon show. Following another stint on a Dr. Jive show at the Apollo, Hull released the Heartbeats' third single, "Your Way," which was recorded at the same session as "Darling How Long." It too received favorable regional attention.

During the summer of 1956, the Heartbeats recorded "A Thousand Miles Away," a song written by Sheppard about his girlfriend who had moved from Brooklyn, New York, to Texas. The tune began to climb the charts immediately upon its release, but Roker feared that Hull did not have the ability to effectively promote the record. After failing to convince Carlson to lease the song to another label, Roker contacted George Goldner with the hope that it could be picked up by his Rama or Gee labels. Roker reflected on that decision and how it affected both the single and the group.

"That was my mistake," he said. "It affected the group['s] moving from a stable and strong position, [and] we were the most important act on the Hull label and going to a label where we were not the most important act on the label. It was also a label that we didn't know was controlled by Morris Levy and not George Goldner. So we went from the frying pan into the fire.

"I absolutely believe that the original label could not promote it, market it, and take it to number one, which is what I thought we deserved," he added. "But that wasn't as important as being with somebody who really cared for you and gave you anything you wanted. It didn't burn a bridge with Hull, and Bea understood and she was very agreeable to do whatever I wanted to do. But I look back on it as a very big mistake."

When a representative from Rama discussed the deal with Hull's executives, a deal was struck, and in November 1956, Rama released the single. While reaching number fifty-three on the pop charts, it soared to number five on the rhythm and blues charts.

In February 1957, Rama released "I Won't Be a Fool Anymore," and in March the Heartbeats recorded "Everybody's Somebody's Fool," which was released in May. By September, with the Heartbeats in the studio again, the Rama label was being phased out and the group was shifted to the Gee label. Gee released "After New Year's Eve" in late 1957 and the group continued a rigorous schedule of performances.

Of note to trivia buffs, Roker appeared on the Solitaires' Old Town recording of "Walkin' and Talkin'" in February 1958 when the group's regular bass, Fred Barksdale, missed the session. "I did the Solitaires a favor because their regular bass was in jail," Roker said. "Hemie Weiss, who owned the Old Town label, asked me to do him a favor and sit in for him on the record because they had a session and they were trying to get another record out. Plus, Buzzy Willis was a friend of mine and it was just a friendly kind of a thing to help them out."

At the same time, in an effort to motivate a crossover hit on the pop charts, the Heartbeats single "I Found a Job" was shifted to the Roulette label. The song was an answer tune to the Silhouettes' hit recording "Get a Job."

Despite the Heartbeats' popularity at appearances and the favorable reviews that their releases received, the group failed to make a dent on the charts. They subsequently found themselves recording on the Guyden label. But the lack of chart success was a mere ripple in the larger tumultuous waves that were causing internal strife within the group at the time. A growing tension between Sheppard and the other group members came to a head when the lead singer dozed off during a performance. Roker recounted the experience.

"The point of it is, we asked him to stop drinking, especially before we do shows," he said. "I gave him an ultimatum and told him that if he got drunk one more time I would kill the group. I told him that I cannot allow myself to be embarrassed by being onstage with someone that is wavering over the mike, can hardly stand up, and [can]not sing in key and do the songs the way we need the songs to be done. I told him that I'd rather not sing anymore."

Roker said that he didn't know if Sheppard's drinking dated to his early years or came after he joined the Heartbeats. "I don't know if he had the problem all the time but he always drank Gordon's gin," he said. "I think getting more popular drove him to be drunker than usual."

At the same time Sheppard's drinking got the best of him, the remaining members of the Heartbeats began to experiment with incredible four-part harmonies. Given that fact, it seemed feasible for the group to simply dismiss Sheppard and continue as a quartet. But Roker explained why that option did not exist.

"We had a feeling of loyalty to the five of us, establishing it and making it," Roker explained. "Basically we just never wanted to have anybody else and never looked on the outside for anything for us but what we had. We never thought of it as a business in a sense of firing Shep and hiring somebody else and we never looked at staying as a quartet."

After a failed attempt at a solo career, Sheppard formed another group, Shep and the Limelites. Some of its members originated from another local vocal group, the Videos. They enjoyed success with another Sheppard-penned tune "Daddy's Home" and performed together throughout the 1960s.

On January 24, 1970, Sheppard found himself in a familiar place, a local bar in Queens. Drunk and flashing a roll of cash that he'd earned for a Limelites appearance, he couldn't have known that some of the fellow bar patrons that he was willingly buying drinks for would end up taking his life. Followed from the bar and beaten unconscious, Sheppard froze to death by morning. The thugs had also stolen his clothes.

After the Heartbeats broke up, Roker continued to forge a successful career in the music industry. "I've sold millions of records," he said. "I've established many artists, starting with Wilbert Harrison and 'Kansas City,' to Gladys Knight and the Pips, the Shirelles, Chuck Jackson, the Isley Brothers, and Dionne Warwick. I developed all of these acts promotionally. I used my professional skills from the Heartbeats in talking to disc jockeys and giving them information about me and the Heartbeats and promoting new artists."

Roker's work through the years has resulted in the sales of hundreds of gold and platinum records, and in 1962, *Billboard Magazine* named him the hardest-working promoter in the industry given the fact that at the time he had up to ten records in the Top 100 charts for Septa Wand Records.

The remaining Heartbeats ventured into other professions, Sievers becoming an auto mechanic, Tatum entering the computer software field, and Crump developing different businesses including a stint as a nightclub owner in Brooklyn.

In 2003, to commemorate the fiftieth anniversary of the founding of the Heartbeats, its four original remaining members reunited in New Jersey to perform for the first time since the breakup at a United Group Harmony Association (UGHA) meeting. Walter Crump, brother of Albert assumed the role of lead singer that night and the group held the appreciative audience spellbound with its tight harmonies.

"We were motivated to reunite for that show due to a combination of the UGHA president, who gave us a group harmony recognition plaque some time ago and then his repeated calls asking us to perform," Roker said. "Vernon and I discussed it and figured we had nothing to lose, but we needed a lead singer. Crump said that his brother knew all our songs and sounded pretty much like Shep. We checked it out and it sounded pretty good so we took a shot."

But the group's firm oath of loyalty also played a huge part in their decision to reunite, Roker said. "It's in the family," he said. "It's a combination where it's Crump's brother, so it's Albert Crump, Walter Crump, Robert Tatum, Vernon Sievers, and Wally Roker, which still kept it like a family. It still wasn't like having an outsider come in to the family. It's probably a rare thing in this business for that kind of attitude to be taken about some little, silly singing group like the Heartbeats but that's our nature and the way we feel about it."

In reflecting on his lifetime of work in the music industry, Roker summed it up. "I'm proud of the Heartbeats in reference to who they are and what they represent and I'm proud of what I've accomplished as a promoter and a marketer in the industry," he said. "To me, the group has been like a number-one group and my promotion and marketing thing has been like number-one situation, so it's a combination of both of them. I've done the singing thing completely satisfied with the way we sing and the sound we have. And I've been very satisfied with having turned nothing people into famous people through my marketing and promotion."

The Heartbeats continue to perform at oldies shows nationwide.

Dominick "Randy" Safuto
(Randy and the Rainbows)

Patchogue, New York   **March 26, 2005**

In 1963, a male vocal group that formed in the Queens section of New York City recorded a tune that to this day has the ability to transform listeners back to a specific place and time in their life. "Denise," the feel-good tune, would become Randy and the Rainbows' sole Top 10 hit single, but its overall impact over time has ensured its inclusion in countless numbers of compilation albums representative of that era of music.

In 1959 brothers Dominick (Randy) and Frank Safuto, along with a cousin Eddie Scalla and a female vocalist from their Queens neighborhood, Rosalie Calindo, became the vocal group the Dialtones. "I have to thank my brother for motivating my interest in the music industry," Randy Safuto said. "He took me into his first group, Johnny and the Intrigues. We had about ten guys singing with us at the time but only four could actually carry a tune. Johnny Ciccone, my cousin Eddie, my brother Frank, and me went on to form the Dialtones. I was about eleven years old at the time."

When Ciccone went into the military, the group heard about Rosalie Calindo, a female vocalist who was the lead singer of a local all-girl group called the Medallions, one that had decided to disband. The Safutos went to meet Calindo at a local settlement house where the Medallions were performing at a dance.

"We spoke with Rosalie at the dance and told her that since the Medallions were breaking up, we'd like her to sing lead with our group," he said. "She agreed to give it a try. The first night we got together we must have done about five songs and the harmonies were great. We started rehearsing twice a week, and then Rosalie wrote a song called 'Johnny,' which we arranged with her."

At the same time the group's first manager, Tony DiAngelis, also wrote a song, "Till I Heard It from You." But feeling that he couldn't do much more to support the group, DiAngelis introduced them to Nick Rosado, someone who had connections in the music industry. With Rosado, the Dialtones paid a visit to George Goldner of the Gone and End record labels and sang the two original songs for him.

"After we sang we went outside, and a short time later Rosado came out and told us that Goldner was taking on the record," Safuto said. "We went back inside and Goldner told us that he loved the group, and then he pointed at me. He said that when he first met Frankie Lymon he was my age, and that was another reason he was taking us on. We recorded 'Till I Heard It from You' as the A-side and 'Johnny' as the B-side, but we told Goldner that we thought 'Johnny' should be the A-side. He put it out his way and it became a New York hit."

A few months later, when Kathy Young and the Innocents released "A Thousand Stars" and the song quickly climbed to number-three on the charts, Goldner called the Dialtones back into the studio. Admitting that he should have released "Johnny" as the A-side, Goldner instructed the label's arranger, Sammy Lowe, to play a number of songs for the group and asked them to select what they liked. One of the songs selected was "Twenty-Four Hours," a song they promptly recorded. But when the group prepared to record another side, their lead singer balked.

"Rosalie had just had it with all the baloney that was going on in the business," he said. "She felt that we were being screwed over by others and I tried to convince her that the president of a big record company was trying to work with us but she just had it. But what happened was, she fell in love with a guy in another band and got out of the business."

Within a couple of years, the Safuto brothers teamed up with another pair of siblings, Sal and Mike Zero, and Ken Arcipowski to form a quintet that would eventually become known as Randy and the Rainbows. In July 1963, backed by the same production team that handled the Tokens, Randy and the Rainbows released "Denise," a single that quickly climbed into the Top 10 record charts.

"We signed recording contracts as the Encores and went into the studio and recorded 'Denise,'" he said. "A few months later when the records were pressed we got a call to pick them up at the studio in the CBS building in Manhattan. We went in, looked at the labels, and we said, 'Beautiful, but who's Randy and the Rainbows?' And they said, 'That's the name of your group.' The next question we asked was, 'Who is Randy?' 'Well,' they said, 'you did the lead to it, so you're Randy.'"

As it turned out the executives at Laurie Records picked the name Randy and the Rainbows, and with little choice other than to agree, the group became known by that name from that day forward. In turn, Dominick Safuto became Randy.

After "Denise" entered the Top 10 pop charts, Randy and the Rainbows went on a cross-country concert tour with artists that included Dionne Warwick, the Chiffons, Darlene Love, and the Four Seasons. "It was great," Safuto said. "We toured throughout Pennsylvania and Canada, and we played arenas that were packed with sixty thousand people. On one part of the tour in Montreal the crowd was very rowdy. They walked us out to the stage and we had about six huge bouncers around us. There were fights breaking out everywhere. It was crazy.

"We got along beautiful with all the other groups," he continued. "What was great was that I loved the Four Seasons, and anything they released I went right out, bought it, and learned how to sing it. When we were on tour with them it was a great thing because we were singing some of their songs with them backstage. Frankie Valli liked me and I liked him."

The strong camaraderie and friendship that Safuto developed with Valli nearly resulted in what would have been a huge career move for him. "We had an engagement at East Meadow High School in Long Island and Frankie was there with Tom Jones, Pat Boone, and Murray the K," he said. "When we arrived Frankie said that he had to talk to me and he told me that Nicky [Massi] was leaving the group. Nicky and Frankie had a lot of arguments when we were out on tour with them. He told me that I was great, I knew his material, and they were getting ready to go into the studio to record some new stuff and he wanted me with him."

Safuto, wanting to digest the incredible offer and discuss it with his brother, told Valli that he'd call him in two weeks. But despite Frank Safuto's encouragement to make the move, Randy balked at the idea due to his loyalty to his brother and friends. Ironically, the move could have proved to be beneficial to both Safutos.

"Had I known that a month after I would have joined the group that Tommy DeVito would also be quitting the Seasons, they would have taken my brother right in," he said. "They knew that he knew their material. There's nobody to train. We know the stuff. We know how to sing. We know what we have to do. And that's it. It would have been beautiful. I would have left Randy and the Rainbows with the snap of my hand.

"I stayed with Randy and the Rainbows because I thought I had friends," he added. "Unfortunately, as you grow older you find out that the people you considered friends aren't what they seemed to be. When you catch them stealing thousands of dollars from you, they aren't your friends. As time went on, I was busy doing other things and couldn't take care of the business. Well, these friends took care of it okay."

If he had accepted Valli's offer to join the Four Seasons, Safuto would have been on the group's massive hit recordings that followed, including "Dawn," "Rag Doll," and "Ronnie."

Safuto reflected on another major show that the group appeared on, the hugely popular ten-day Murray the K Brooklyn Fox extravaganza. "You got so caught up in the excitement of doing the show that you don't even think about it," he said. "You get up and do your song and it's over that quick. All of a sudden there is a break and you're outside watching a movie with these other people who don't even know who you are. You sneak out, come in the back door, and wait for the crowd to simmer down a little bit. Then you'd sit down and it's so dark in there that they're not going to know who you are. That show was supposed to have been the biggest one Murray the K ever had."

The bill for the show was a stellar one, boasting acts such as Smokey Robinson, the Shirelles, Jay and the Americans, the Chiffons, Stevie Wonder, the Angels, and the Beach Boys. The wide array of talent made for interesting and impromptu harmonizing behind the scenes as well as on stage.

"It was party time backstage," Safuto said. "Singing among the acts was so great," Safuto said. "I wish a lot of that material could have been recorded but the record companies would not allow it. Today if that happened, they'd record it right away. It was different back then."

The follow-up single for the group, "Why Do Kids Grow Up?" had all the potential to score another hit. But one week after it was released the nation was stunned by the assassination of President John F. Kennedy in Dallas, Texas. Suddenly, the happy-go-lucky musical tunes that normally flowed across the airwaves were silenced during a period of national mourning for the slain leader. The single, along with others released during the tragic time, fell silently into oblivion.

"The assassination had a lot of effect on that single," Safuto said. "It had sold more than thirty-five thousand copies in the first three days after its release. The record company had already predicted that it would definitely be a much bigger hit than 'Denise.'"

The American recording industry barely started to rebound after the Kennedy tragedy when it was faced with the onslaught of the British Invasion. As groups such as the Beatles, the Rolling Stones, the Dave Clark Five, and other acts from England changed the face and style of musical tastes in the early to mid-1960s, American groups struggled to adapt to the shift.

"People didn't even want to bother with the American sound at that point," he said. "If you were from England and could hum record companies were recording you. It was a shame. We were going into the studio to record 'Listen People' because we were told that Herman's Hermits wasn't going to release it. I was given a copy of the tune and listened to it and the group got it down pat to record it the next day. The next morning I got up, showered, and started to get dressed when I hear on the radio, 'Here's a new one by Herman's Hermits,' and 'Listen People' came on."

In 1977 Crystal Ball Records released a Randy and the Rainbows a cappella rendition of the Dion and the Belmonts hit single "I Wonder Why." But the overall quality of the recording lacked a polished sound and subsequently faded, having gained little attention. "What happened was Eddie Engel of Crystal Ball Records copied that off of a WCBS-FM radio show that we did," Safuto said. "While we were on the Don K. Reed show, he asked us if we could do an a cappella number live on the air. Off the top of our heads we tried to figure what we were going to do and my brother suggested 'I Wonder Why.' We did it and Eddie recorded it off the radio and laid it down on record in the studio. That's why the quality wasn't there."

A year later, Blonde with Deborah Harry had success with a cover of "Denise." A few years later Harry met up with Randy and the Rainbows. "She acknowledged us in the early 1980s when we were performing at a show in New York City," he said. "She came down to see us at the venue and we went out to meet her after our set."

Through the years, the group has performed under a variety of other names including Madison Street and Them and Us. But Safuto seized this interview to set the record straight with regard to a group long credited with having included him and his brother Frank, one named Triangle. "Let's get that straight right now," he said. "Triangle has nothing to do with us. That is Vinny Carella trying to make it seem like he was Randy and the Rainbows. Please make this fact very clear. Vinny Carella was never a Randy and the Rainbows original, which he thinks he is. From what I understand today from people, Vinny Carella thinks he's Randy Safuto.

To clarify, Carella, a latter member of Randy and the Rainbows continues to perform with the Zero brothers under the group's name but apart from Randy and Frank Safuto.

"As for Madison Street and Them and Us, that was an attempt to get into different music styles during the disco era," Safuto said. "It was also due to the fact that a lot of people at the time would say that we had our time here, you're still good, but nobody's going to take anything by Randy and the Rainbows even though it's a new thing. They wanted a new name and a new tune."

At the close of the twentieth century, two aggregations of Randy and the Rainbows could be found performing at various oldies shows. But following his recovery from a serious illness, Randy Safuto and a new lineup of Rainbows that includes his brother and founding member Frank continues to maintain a strong schedule of performances at oldies shows.

As for the group's legacy as having charted a huge hit record with "Denise," Safuto feels good about the durability of the song through the years. "I hope that it ranks up there with some of the best records of that time," he said. "We sang it and did what we had to do, but it's the fans that made 'Denise' a hit. If they didn't buy it, it wouldn't have been a hit. I guess all the fans that bought it must love it. For me, it meant having fun in my time, traveling and meeting many, many people, and enjoying what I wanted to do my whole life."

Billboard Top 40 Hits by Randy and the Rainbows

Date	Pos	Wks on Charts	Record Title	Label/Number
07/27/63	10	10	Denise	Rust 5059

A family affair, from left, drummer Chris Safuto recently joined original Rainbows members Randy, his dad, and Frank, his uncle, at oldies show performances.

Peggy Santiglia
(The Angels)

Islandia, New York　　　　　　　　　　　　　**April 9, 2005**

The three members of the popular girl group the Angels came together in 1961 in Orange, New Jersey, the product of two different singing aggregations. While sisters Barbara and Phyllis Allbut were part of a female quartet called the Starlets, Peggy Santiglia sang with another group, the Delicates. Both groups made some headway in the music industry, the Starlets having recorded "P.S. I Love You" on the Astro Records label and the Delicates releasing "Black and White Thunderbird," among other tunes.

Delicates members Santiglia and Denise Ferri also wrote and sang "Submarine Race Watcher's Theme," a song that aired regularly on New York radio disc jockey Murray the K's wildly popular show.

"The first group I was in was called the Delicates because one of my closest friend's parents owned a delicatessen," Santiglia said. "We were all in elementary school and started singing and making up songs about our friends in the fifth grade and we were actually recording by the seventh grade. We played hooky from school and just thought in our youth or stupidity or something that this fellow Murray the K needed a theme song so, as fans listening to his show at night, we wrote 'The Submarine Race Watcher's Theme.'"

Santiglia came from a family that had a background in music; her dad played a number of instruments and her sister sang opera. That fact made it difficult for the young and budding vocalist to tell her parents that her interest was in rock-and-roll. In fact, Santiglia said that to listen to Murray the K's popular nighttime radio show on WINS in New York City, she had to sneak a transistor radio into her bedroom.

"The first thing that we did was to go to WINS and make believe that we had an appointment," she recalled. "Now, they knew it was a school day and we didn't have an appointment. I think we had more nerve than brains. We got on a number 55 bus on the corner in New Jersey and we went there with our songs written on notebooks and paper bags. They brought us right in and we sounded good and we rattled off all these songs that we made up about boys that we liked, cars, and we wrote 'Meusurray,' which he used for a theme song. We also wrote 'Submarine Race Watcher's' and another one named 'Grand Kook.' That very day, they brought us into a studio, recorded us, and when I got home that evening we were on the radio."

"That's the good part," she added. "The bad part is that we were so naïve about money or writing that we didn't know if it was logged a particular way at the radio station they weren't obligated to pay you. It wasn't just a freebie; the song was used for a few years plus we would go to the studio and record these answering things. Before the Ronettes, we were Murray the K's original dancing girls at those Brooklyn Fox and Paramount shows, before we had our own hit records. They probably owed us big bucks in royalties."

Since the girls were only in the seventh grade, they had chaperones assigned to look after them while performing at the hugely popular shows. And given school commitments, their performances were limited to spring and Christmas breaks, where they performed at eight or nine shows each day. Despite monetary issues, the exposure gained and support of Murray the K would be an intangible benefit in years to come.

"People heard us from those shows, and Billy Muir, who was a guitar player at the time, took us to a subsidiary of United Artists, and then from there Don Costa recorded us on our original songs," she said. "We were in the tail end of like a Steve and Edie session or something, so here our little songs that we originally brought in on our little notebooks were recorded with strings and forty-piece orchestras."

As members of both the Starlets and Delicates were underage and therefore unable to perform at nightclubs, they often appeared together at local record hops, and as a result became friends. When the sisters Allbut encountered problems with the lead singer of the Starlets, Linda Jankowski, she was replaced by Santaglia, whose contract with United Artists and then Roulette was soon expiring.

Santiglia recalled the first time she met the Allbut sisters. "We would meet at dance hops and places that we both performed at," she said. "The contrast between our styles was very interesting. They were very sweet and wore full dresses, had umbrellas, and would sing 'Pennies from Heaven,' and we thought we were hot stuff with our tight red dresses and we sang the Olympics' 'Western Movies.' We met backstage and just like our love of harmony and singing, we liked to talk together and sing backstage. And then, when they were looking for a lead singer, I was one of the people they thought about and my contract was running out at the time."

Linda Jankowski, who used the stage name Jansen, recorded the 1961 tune "'Til" with the quartet but was only with the group for eight or nine months. A second version of the song was recorded later on, which included Santiglia on lead vocals.

"She was with them initially but there were some personal problems that Linda reneged in something in her personal life pertaining to the contract," Santiglia said.

When Santiglia joined the group, it took on a different sound, sometimes described as a tougher edge. "The times were changing," she said. "It's not that I didn't enjoy singing beautiful ballads but I guess I kind of grew into that. The Delicates were more about kids singing about kids. The Angels initially were more sophisticated in a way. But as music was changing and kids were having their own music, it was a good mix."

The trio started to gain studio work as background singers for the likes of Jackie Wilson, Neil Diamond, and other major artists of that time. "I don't remember the first big background job we had but there were many, many that we backed like Trini Lopez, Jackie Wilson, and Frank Sinatra," she said. "We had more experience in the studio in a way than we did in personal appearances, which was unusual for young people at the time."

While Santiglia and the Angels were a popular choice for providing background vocals, she cited another group as being at the forefront of that form of work. "One of the most popular and fabulous background groups was led by Whitney Houston's mom, Cissy, who would put

245

together a group that had a certain sound," she said. "Sometimes they would actually have us work with them to blend the different sounds but it seems like we were doing backgrounds before we were even the Angels."

Despite the significant work done, one specific hit recording that has been long credited as having its background vocals accomplished by the Angels was in fact Santiglia and two other singers. "I did the background vocals on 'Lightnin' Strikes' with Lou Christie with one person from the Delicates and another singer who I was doing background vocals with at the time," she said. "It wasn't the Angels on that record."

In 1963, Bobby Feldman, a staff writer for April-Blackwood Music, was visiting a sweet shop in Brooklyn and overheard a verbal altercation between a young girl and a rather tough-looking teenage boy. The basis of the interaction was the girl's promise that her boyfriend was back in town and he would make the thug pay for spreading lies about her in school. That evening, together with writing partners Jerry Goldstein and Rich Gottehrer, the song "My Boyfriend's Back" was composed. The team presented the Angels with the song, one that would soon catapult them into stardom.

"Barbara and Jiggs [Phyllis] really knew it was going to be a hit," Santiglia said when she recalled first hearing the song. "They, in fact, had to be bought out of a contract that they were locked into before that time so they could record it. I don't have good memories about FGG [Freeman, Goldstein, Gottehrer]. In my opinion, they were totally unfair with us in terms of business. But, they did bring the song to us and there was quite a bit that we worked on and the part we ad-libbed in the studio. If I were less naïve I might have pushed for some little writing credit on some of the ad-libs."

That type of work during recording sessions was not unusual for the girls. "A lot of times that happened when we did background," she said. "I can remember Charlie Calello and the things we did with the Four Seasons or other people when they'd put us in a room and tell us to come up with a hook. I wasn't a great reader but Barbara was a trained musician and could play piano. That made a big difference early on in our travels as far as getting things musically beautiful."

Santiglia reflected on reports that state that the Angels originally recorded "My Boyfriend's Back" as a demo so that the music publisher could pitch the song to the Shirelles. "Well, maybe that was somebody else's idea to pitch it to another group but I think it was probably just a thought that wasn't necessarily shared with us," she said. "At that time you almost always did demos, even when you were the intended artist. You did it for the producers to show it to the big companies to get them interested."

Santiglia said that through the years, various accounts of the group's work, successes, and other career facts have been skewed and altered, the very reason this book was conceived. "In looking back I kind of chuckle now because they had us living in all kinds of different places, and a lot was public relations stuff that FGG put out about themselves," she said. "So maybe one of them said, 'Oh, we were thinking about the Shirelles.' It may be true and it may not."

Still high school students at the time, when the single began to climb the charts the Allbut sisters placed an urgent call to Santiglia, who was away on vacation with her parents, urging her to return quickly. With well over a million copies sold, the record climbed to the number-one slot and thrust the teenagers into a storm of stage and television appearances, including *American Bandstand*, Ed Sullivan, and multi-talent package concerts at the Brooklyn Fox and Paramount theaters.

"It was really exciting to do those television shows," she said. "The first time I was on Dick Clark it wasn't with the Angels; it was with the Delicates, and that was really exciting because this was the show that was about other kids. The first time I was on the show I was so afraid of the dancers because they were older than we were. We were thirteen and they were sixteen and we heard [that] if they don't like you they won't applaud. You're a kid and you get yourself worked up into this frenzy. To go from coming home from school and watching Dick Clark and dancing around to being on it was really exciting.

"Now, Ed Sullivan, because we were a little older and I was with the Angels, that was very big and exciting but our parents were more thrilled," she added. "We were going to be on with Kate Smith. To us, we heard about these famous people but it wasn't like Dick Clark, where it was teenagers."

Being thrust into the spotlight affected many young artists in different ways and had an impact on their personal lives. Santiglia said that having a hit record somewhat changed how people reacted toward her and the group. "To a degree things changed," she said. "But we all just came from nice, friendly families and I think in some ways people were maybe surprised that we were just regular kids but I never would have seen the things that I've seen. I came from a wonderful family with a wonderful background, that was very musical and all but we weren't a wealthy family. I lived with my parents and grandparents, was very spoiled with love and had a good life.

"But here I was working in Europe before I was out of my teens and traveling around the world," she continued. "I think I was probably on a plane before my parents were."

Having performed at many shows and venues around the world, Santiglia cited a few of her personal favorites throughout her career in music. "For different reasons, I have great memories," she said. "When we toured army and air force bases in Europe, that was thrilling for a lot of different reasons. First of all, we had all these poor men captive without their wives or their girlfriends. And of course playing the TV shows and the first time we played huge arenas like the Maple Leaf Gardens or Madison Square Garden in New York, it's just unbelievable."

Despite gaining fame off the success of "My Boyfriend's Back," the girls did not get their way with regard to choices of follow-up tunes. "I Adore Him" was not a song especially preferred by the Angels but given the producer's strong push to record it, they relented and it climbed to number twenty-five on the pop charts. The single's B-side, "Thank You and Good Nite," became the sign-off theme on the Murray the K radio show.

"We didn't like it ['I Adore Him'] then and I think that we were right and they made a mistake," Santiglia said. "We thought 'The Guy with the Black Eye' should have been the follow-up because it was a sequel and it was cute. And that was a time of sequels. They were trying at the time to copy a Phil Spector sound with 'I Adore Him,' plus they wrote the words in 'I Adore Him' and this was before the feminist movement, not that we are unfair feminists. But even to sing things like 'he's cheating on me but I don't care,' and 'I love him even though he's rotten,' it wasn't really something we wanted to do."

As the years passed by, Santiglia became a staff writer for April Blackwood Music, recorded and toured with the Serendipity Singers, and also recorded as Dusk, the female counterpart to the popular group Dawn. A founding member of the Tokens, Hank Medress produced the latter efforts, as well as those for Tony Orlando and Dawn.

"Those projects weren't meshed together," she said. "My work with April Blackwood Music was when Neil Diamond was a writer there and we did a lot of his demos and beginning backup stuff. I was still in high school at that time and Connie Francis' father used to drive me in sometimes because she went to the same school as me. I didn't realize it at the time because I was just a kid, but I had a room and a piano and I got to partner with some really famous and older partners because they used to rotate you. It was invaluable experience and wonderful."

248

In partnership with Bob Gaudio she wrote the Four Seasons hit "Beggin'," a composition that Santiglia said a lot of memories went into.

As for a personal preference toward composing, recording, and performing throughout her career, Santiglia was hard-pressed to define one over another. "They are so completely different, but to me it's hard to compare them," she said. "Writing comes from a part of your inside deepest thoughts. To put something out there that you feel from your heart has different sides. I have a commercial side of thinking with certain songs, but to communicate through song even if you're in a big crowd of people, you could tell when you're reaching somebody emotionally. Of course, that has to be with a certain kind of song. Over the years when we were traveling all over the world and did supper clubs and sang some gorgeous ballads with a full orchestra it's something that is a form of human communication. If someone said to me that I could have had millions of dollars that I was supposed to get but couldn't perform live I wouldn't take it. I know that sounds really silly but it's been such a big part of my life and I've met people from all over the world and it's a human opportunity that I can't explain."

In 1993, a made-for-TV movie, *My Boyfriend's Back*, was said to be loosely based on the Angels' career in music. Santiglia commented on the film.

"First of all, it wasn't even that loose," she said. "Shame on them, because whoever touted the project didn't go with an idea. It's similar to a book query but it's in person. We had heard through the grapevine— in fact had evidence of it at the time—that whoever it was actually used our photographs and us singing our songs in the background, and probably the reason why they changed the name of the group to the Bouffants was so that they didn't have to pay us.

"But whoever did it had to have known us very well up to a certain part in our lives because they had the lead singer involved with a cosmetic company, and that was the only other thing that I did when I was involved with cosmetic management," she continued. "And they had one person leave for a while to have a baby and that was Jiggs. The only part that was kind of sleazy and that we didn't like was that they had them bickering and while we were kids we sang everywhere, but they had them singing in a bowling alley and put a sleazy element to it. At the time we did try to go after it and tried to find out how come we weren't notified or paid anything. There were some sneaky things going on. Something was sent to a lawyer that was going to represent us, and then all of a sudden our proof was lost. There is that part still behind the scenes of the business that's really bad. At the time we were advised that they could keep us in litigation for years and years and we could end up owing them money at the end of it. So what's the point?"

Santiglia explained that even though the various members of the Angels explored other avenues in the music industry and in their personal lives, the group never split up. "That's because we are best friends," she said. "We love each other, knew each other's parents and grandparents, and we always put that first. Even though we live halfway across the country from each other we always call each other. We shared a part of our lives [that was] so unique that nobody else who is in our life now can come close to that. I don't mean in caring, but after all, when this phenomenon happened to us and we had a million-selling number-one record and were so young, our husbands weren't there then.

"In looking back it almost takes on more significance," she continued. "At the time we were singing, were doing, were concerned about what we were wearing and all, but we were there together. Early rock-and-roll was a part of Americana. I know we weren't there in the 1950s, but because we were already singing in the late 1950s, starting in grade school, we also feel very enmeshed in all that."

In 2005, Santiglia and Phyllis Allbut continue to perform at oldies shows as the Angels, while Barbara Allbut has revived her songwriting efforts in California. Of her entire body of work accomplished through the years, Santiglia reflected on the various segments of her career. "I love a song that I wrote with Bob Gaudio called 'September Rain' and it was recorded by Charlie Calello's orchestra and chorus," she said. "I guess I'm really most proud of the fact that here we are in middle age, at least, [and we] did not betray our friendship, still get to perform, and people still come out and we get to meet fans all over the country."

Billboard Top 40 **Hits by the Angels**

Date	Pos	Wks on Charts	Record Title	Label/Number
12/04/61	14	07	'Til	Caprice 107
04/07/62	38	01	Cry Baby Cry	Caprice 112
08/10/63	01	12	My Boyfriend's Back	Smash 1834
11/09/63	25	05	I Adore Him	Smash 1854

Ernie Sierra
(The Eternals)

Patchogue, New York   **September 24, 2005**

The all-Puerto Rican male vocal group that first began harmonizing in junior high school and on street corners of the South Bronx, New York, in 1955 as the Gleamers, and later the Orbits, would eventually release three outstanding singles that have enjoyed significant airplay for more than forty years. The quintet, lead singer Charlie Gerona, first tenor Fred Hodge, second tenor Ernie Sierra, baritone Arnie Torres, and bass Alex Miranda, began by performing covers of popular groups of that era such as the Flamingos and the Spaniels.

"I saw Frankie Lymon and the Teenagers at a theater in the Bronx when he was thirteen and that was the most thrilling, fantastic thing I'd ever seen," Sierra recalled. "Kids my age singing up there and they had a big record out at the time. I was about a year younger than Frankie and that's what started me off."

Around the time the Gleamers began to develop an original style, its lead singer started to compose songs in the vein of humorous stage acts like the Coasters and the Olympics. They decided to change the group name and came up with the Orbits. "We weren't trying to imitate anybody at that point," he said. "Charlie Gerona was good at drawing and he had sketched something with planets and all and with all our faces to see if we could put it on a record label. That's how we came up with the Orbits.

"As for the Eternals, Bill Martin came up with that name and we liked it better," he added. "He was a very religious man. He got that name out of the Bible and he was our manager. When he mentioned the Eternals, we liked it because when you're kids you know how it is; you think this is never going to end and we'd be together for the rest of our lives."

Martin was the manager of Sierra's older brother Richie's vocal group, the Trells. Watching that group rehearse at his house, Sierra felt that he could sing too.

"My parents did a lot of harmony in Spanish and I used to listen to it," he said. "Between them and listening to Richie's group I picked things up. The Trells sang a lot of blues and they had a bass singer that sounded a lot like the Spaniels' bass. The group's second tenor told Bill Martin about us and he came by the schoolyard where we rehearsed on different nights and introduced himself to us. He told us that he was interested in us and asked if we had any original songs and we sang 'Babalu' for him because we already had it. Some people thought that it was too Spanish, but we were all Puerto Ricans.

"When he asked if we really wrote that, we told him that we did and were working on another song, 'Christmas in the Jungle,'" he continued. "When he asked how that song went, we did a little for him. He asked if we would go to his house where he had a piano, and we went the next day. Bill was a good guy but the songs weren't copyrighted yet. He did put in music because we didn't know how to write music and all that, but you could get anybody to do that by paying them to do it. But then it's your song. He ended up putting his name on the song along with Charlie's."

Martin became the group's manager and subsequently introduced them to Morty Craft, the head of Melba Records. Upon meeting Craft the group faced its first dilemma. "We had the song 'Christmas in the Jungle,' but Christmas was already upon us," Sierra said. "They told us that by the time the record would get out Christmas would be over, and they wanted something fast. It was decided that we'd change the name from 'Christmas' to 'Rockin'' and that was [New York disc jockey] Bruce Morrow's idea. The rest of the lyrics stayed the same. It worked out good because if it stayed 'Christmas' it would only get played in December."

In spring 1959, the Eternals recorded their renamed song "Rockin' in the Jungle" at Beltone Studios. Released that summer on Craft's Hollywood Records label, the single climbed quickly in New York and subsequently cracked *Billboard*'s Top 100 national chart. By all accounts, the single had positioned the Eternals in perfect standing for their follow-up release, a song that should have gained even greater attention than the group's debut single.

"Babalu's Wedding Day," the group's follow-up effort, was another novelty tune that included the jungle sounds and tight harmonies that became the group's trademark with "Rockin' in the Jungle." The recording was enhanced with a musical background provided by sax great King Curtis and Mickey of Mickey and Sylvia fame. The single seemed poised to scale the national record charts. But when Martin decided to enact a lawsuit against some shady booking agents who were attempting to dupe, in the manager's eyes, the Eternals' profits and future dealings, the label ceased distribution of the new single. The beginnings of what appeared to be an up-and-coming recording career were stymied in its infancy.

"This will be the first time I talk about it, because all the groups got ripped off, but in the beginning we thought it was just us," Sierra said. "We even thought it might be a race issue because we were all Spanish. But as we got older and we did shows with other groups that were white, black, and whatever, we realized that we all got raped. We had a contract with a member of Bruce Morrow's family for one year and six sides. I guess he met these trashy guys who worked for *Variety* magazine. Bruce Morrow wanted them to be our agents but they never gave Bill Martin a copy of the contract.

"That was the biggest mistake Bill Martin ever made," he continued. "We were kids and whatever they said, we'd do. Morrow was never there after the early days, and these two guys came up to us and told us that they were agents and had connections at *Variety*. They told us that we were good and we could become stars, but the one-year contract troubled them because they said that when we make it big, after one year we could leave them. They said that it wasn't right. As kids, their explanation sounded logical to us."

The pair presented the group members with a new longer-term contract, but touting concern for their families, or so it appeared, they asked that their mothers look it over. "They said to see if our mothers are free because fathers are always busy working," he said. "I remember that. I brought my mother and we used to laugh because one of the group members, Arnie Torres, brought his grandmother and she couldn't even speak English. Anyway, the contract was signed. When Bill Martin found out about that 'Babalu' was already at number fourteen on the charts. He went to court and the record stopped. 'Babalu' would have been much bigger than 'Rockin' in the Jungle'. Martin won in court, although I don't know how much."

Years later, Sierra recalled, when he spoke with Martin, the former manager reminded him that the group always put him down because of the lawsuit and his eventual victory. "He still didn't tell me what he won but I really didn't care at that point," Sierra said. "I had a good job as a New York City police officer. But he told me that we stabbed him in the back. We didn't even know what stabbing in the back means. He should have gotten a copy of that first contract. We didn't even think about copies of contracts; we were just singing and having a good time."

Sierra said the group went back to Bill Martin under the terms of a two-year management agreement but every time they attempted to get a deal, the industry shut them out. "We had a lot of good stuff," Sierra said. "We had really good, funny novelty songs. WABC radio disc jockey Bob Lewis kept us on the air by recording some jingles for his show. There was one that I wrote that they told us we couldn't do. It was about the Lone Ranger with a 'Babalu' basic tune and they were concerned about copyrights."

In January 1961, the Eternals recorded what would become their last single, "Today," on Craft's Warwick label. Considered a likely hit record, legalities once again played a part in the single's demise. "Charlie Gerona wrote 'Today' by himself and Bill Martin put his name on it," Sierra said.

Despite the legal entanglements and lost opportunities, the Eternals still performed on the bills of many of the era's popular shows, hosted by, among others, Murray the K and Clay Cole. But a source of much dismay for Sierra is the fact that many biographies on the group state that they performed at a Brooklyn Paramount Rock and Roll Spectacular.

"That keeps coming up so let's get it straight," he said. "We never performed at the Brooklyn Paramount. I wish we had and I could tell you how good it was playing there. But I'm an honest guy and have to say we didn't perform there. But we did Clay Cole and Murray the K, who was a very funny guy. He used to play the drums behind us. At that time you put the record on and we'd lip-sync, so we told him it was okay to play, but not too loud. We had a ball with him."

"As for being on the same bill with many of the big names, people would think that we were nervous," he added. "We were kids and weren't nervous at all. I didn't care who was on the show. I didn't care if the president of the United States was watching us. We were having a good time."

The group disbanded in 1962, but Martin attempted to keep it going with revised lineups. "I was eighteen years old and started my family early," Sierra said. "I was working and they tried to keep the group going with different guys."

Sierra's motivation to return to the Eternals lineup for a reunion performance in 1972 at New York City's Academy of Music was pretty basic. "I came back for the six hundred bucks that I was paid," he laughed. "The show was great because we must have brought in, without exaggeration, about three hundred and fifty people from the old neighborhood in the Bronx. They were all in the balcony and when we went on they went crazy. That show got me a little nervous because we hadn't sung in such a long time. My brother Richie sang with us for that show."

While the Eternals still perform at area oldies gigs, the group finds itself in the same position as other acts of that era in that, as radio formats continue to abandon the music of the 1950s in favor of that of later decades, concerts and in turn engagements become rarer and rarer as the years pass.

"We didn't perform at as many shows in 2005 as we did last year, or the year before," he said. "With the demise of WCBS-FM radio [which formerly had oldies format programming] in New York City and great, longtime disc jockeys like Don K. Reed and Bobby Jay, who are now out of work, I listen to what they replaced the music with and it's not for us. By dropping formats like CBS, it's like we're all dead and never existed. I don't think these programmers know what they're doing. People that are my age have the money; I have a great pension and others have social security. The kids only buy the records like we did at their age. But we listen to the commercials and spend the money on advertisers' products."

A proud man who cherishes his involvement in the music industry, Sierra reflected on his career. "I am proud that I got the chance to write the flip side to 'Babalu's Wedding Day' called 'My Girl,' which was about a special lady named Terry, who was my girl at that time and was my wife for twenty-seven years," he said. "That's one of Don K. Reed's favorite songs. It's funny because once in a while people come up to me and ask if I wrote 'My Girl,' the one by the Temptations. I say, 'I wish; it's not the one you're thinking about.' But I am very proud of the one I wrote for Terry."

Dave Somerville
(The Diamonds)

Hollywood, California   **May 12, 2005**

Originating in Toronto, Canada, the all-male quartet the Diamonds came to fame in the mid-1950s by recording a series of hit singles that were covers of songs originally released by popular black recording artists of that time. Comprised of Phil Leavitt, Bill Reed, Ted Kowalski and Dave Somerville, the group was likened to other popular vocal aggregations such as the Crew Cuts and the Four Lads.

While doing research for this book, some biographical accounts were discovered that list two of the Diamonds members as being native to California. Somerville said that the confusion began with replacement members in the group, although their involvement came during the 1950s. "All the original Diamonds came from Toronto," he said. "In 1953, we met at the Canadian Broadcasting Corporation. In 1957, when our original baritone quit he was replaced by another Canadian, Mike Douglas. In 1959, when the bass and tenor left at the same time, I replaced them with Californians."

257

While vacationing at Crystal Beach in Lake Erie in the early 1950s, Leavitt and some friends began to harmonize, to the enjoyment of those around them. Upon entering the University of Toronto, he met Kowalski and soon the nucleus of the Diamonds singing group began to come together.

The group subsequently met Dave Somerville, a classically trained singer and engineer at the Canadian Broadcasting Corporation (CBC). He agreed to sneak the group into the studios to rehearse and also took over as their manager. But at their first gig, a minstrel show at a local church, the group's lead singer, Stan Fisher, couldn't make it and Somerville, knowing all the parts, filled in. After a rousing ovation from the appreciative audience, the group decided to turn professional. Fisher's decision to remain in college resulted in Somerville joining the group full-time, singing lead.

During the group's early days, the Diamonds experimented with several singing styles including four-part barber shop harmonies. They were also influenced by a black rhythm and blues group from Detroit, Michigan, who, despite working at their craft part-time started to teach the Diamonds their own unique style of singing every time they performed in Toronto.

"We were emulating groups that we liked at the time like the Mills Brothers, the Ames Brothers, and, in particular, the Golden Gate Quartet," he said. "There was also a group from Detroit named the Revelaires. We were essentially entertaining ourselves by making these chords great."

During the summer of 1955, the Diamonds landed a slot on the popular Arthur Godfrey television talent show, where they tied for first place in the competition. That accomplishment secured the group a week's engagement on Godfrey's radio show. Off that exposure, they were offered a recording contract with Coral Records. Their first record was "Black Denim Trousers and Motorcycle Boots," a song that soon became a hit single for another vocal group, the Cheers.

The Diamonds' version became a local hit in Toronto and they accepted an engagement, performing at the Alpine Village Club in Cleveland, Ohio. While there, they met local disc jockey Bill Randle, who had discovered other vocal groups at the time.

"We knew that he was influential and had discovered several people, notably among them the Crew Cuts, who were a Toronto group," Somerville recalled. "We thought, 'Why don't we get a job in Cleveland on the off chance that we can get to meet this guy?' In the beginning of the year in 1956, we had a job at the Alpine Village in Cleveland, and on the last night of our performances, we met the famous Bill Randle. We sang five songs for him a cappella at his twenty-to-twenty-eight dance at the Manger Hotel. He was impressed enough with those songs to present us to Mercury and he also played 'Why Do Fools Fall in Love' for us right away."

After signing a recording contract with Mercury Records, the Diamonds began to adapt rhythm and blues hit songs into their own style and started to gain airplay on white pop radio stations. It was common at that time for white recording artists to cover rhythm and blues songs that became hits for black artists.

But Somerville said that the Diamonds' practice of covering rhythm and blues hits for airplay on white radio stations was not their initial intention. "That was not our flash to do that," he said. "Bill Randle picked both sides of our first four releases and we had four hits in a row. So he, along with Mercury Records really directed our material because before that we'd been a swing group and singing spirituals and barber shop tunes. It actually disrupted the kind of democratic arrangement that had always existed in the group because now it was Dave singing lead and the other three guys felt less important."

The group's first success, a cover of the Frankie Lymon and the Teenagers hit "Why Do Fools Fall in Love," became a number-twelve hit for them in March 1956. Their follow-up single, the Willows' "Church Bells May Ring," also entered the Top 20 pop charts, and in March 1957, the group scored its biggest hit with a rendition of the Gladiolas' hit song "Little Darlin." In reality, the tune was intended as the flip side of a single that boasted an original tune, "Faithful and True."

"Little Darlin'" climbed to the number-two slot on the national pop charts, topped only by Elvis Presley's "All Shook Up."

"On the afternoon of March 5, 1957, we had already prepared four original songs to record at a session starting at midnight at Universal Studios with Bill Putnam, the engineer," Somerville said. "We'd gone back to our hotel after an afternoon rehearsal and were called back to Mercury Records and they played this song for us, 'Little Darlin' by the Gladiolas. We were essentially told that we were going to record it. We learned it in about a half hour and made some notes on it. That night at midnight, when the session started we recorded the four original songs, and it got to be 3:45 a.m. and the producer announced that that was it and said goodnight to everybody and the drummer left. Suddenly, somebody said, 'Oh, oh, that song from this afternoon, 'Little Darlin.' We re-learned the song and recorded it in one take in a fifteen-minute period."

In the fall of 1957, the Diamonds joined a rock-and-roll bus tour for two months of one-night shows with the likes of Fats Domino, Buddy Holly, the Everly Brothers, and Chuck Berry. "That was the very first major rock-and-roll tour," Somerville said. "It set the stage for big money-making concerts in the future. It was also the first major tour where black and white artists worked together and we had thirteen acts on the bus. Inevitably, when you travel with somebody for a couple of months your attitudes are affected. I was fortunate enough a lot of the time to sit next to Buddy Holly. Black people rode in the front and white people rode in the back. I think that was because on previous trips, that was just where they sat by choice, so when the white people joined the tour, the back of the bus was left for us.

"Another story that I heard about that [bus seating arrangement] was that because when you worked in the South to segregated audiences and had to stay at separate hotels, the bus driver would drive to the black hotel first and the front half of the bus would conveniently exit, and then the rest of us would go to the white hotel," he added.

In addition to logistical seating on the bus and lodging at different hotels, some venues in the Southern states presented challenges to the acts when the black and white audiences were physically separated by the stage. "Sometimes when we worked in one of those split-theater situations, where there is a stage in the middle and there's an audience on one side that you face and behind you there's another audience, some acts worked straight across so that everybody had a view of the side of you."

When the Diamonds' recording of "Little Darlin'" was released, it had the distinction of being the very first one issued in a 45 RPM format. "I don't remember there being too much hoopla about the new format," he said. "But while we rode the bus together, I was most impressed when Buddy Holly pulled out this battery-operated 45 RPM player from a bag at his feet. He put on a record by the Everly Brothers and it was kind of amazing to me seeing this little portable deal with a strange-looking record on it. Of course, all the hits of that transition period were on both 78's and 45's."

Somerville recalled another artist on the bus, Chuck Berry, borrowing his guitar and sticking the bus driver's microphone into it to play his tunes during rides from place to place. "He used to actually Scotch tape the driver's microphone in the on position and he'd stick it in the sound hole to make it louder," he said. "The Everly Brothers had their guitars in the storage bin under the bus and Buddy's was electric and I had my little acoustic classical guitar, which was the only one on the bus, so it got passed around."

It is well documented that one of the Diamonds' biggest fans was Elvis Presley. "Unfortunately, we did not have the opportunity to meet him," he said. "I certainly would have loved that. But I'm told by numerous people that hung out with him at his house that he loved to listen to our records. As a matter of fact, I have a home recording of Elvis learning to sing 'Little Darlin.' And then later he recorded it and did it in concert."

In late 1957, the Diamonds recorded a huge dance hit called "The Stroll." It received significant attention on Dick Clark's popular television dance show *American Bandstand*. "It happened as a result of a conversation that we had with Dick Clark during the early part of December 1957," Somerville recalled. "He said that the kids were doing a line dance called the Stroll to Chuck Willis's recording, 'C. C. Ryder,' but there was no song called 'The Stroll.' So we asked Clyde Otis, a fledgling songwriter at that time [who] had a hit with Nat 'King' Cole and later was responsible for all of Brook Benton's career songs, to create a song for us with that title. About a week after Dick made the suggestion, we had a record in his hands and the kids on *American Bandstand* then began to dance to our record.

"Fats Domino's band played on it, King Curtis played sax, and the Ray Charles Singers from the *Perry Como Show* were in the background," he added. "I can remember the great Cornelius Coleman, Fats's drummer, playing over in the corner. We did 'Walking Along' that same session and another song that, in my opinion, is the Diamonds' best recording, 'A Mother's Love,' which was another Clyde Otis song."

Somerville noted the fact that "The Stroll" being featured on *American Bandstand* had a huge impact on its overall success. "If you hadn't seen it being danced, you might not have been as impressed with it," he said.

By late 1957, Leavitt, having become weary of life on the road and wanting to start a family back home in Toronto, decided to leave the Diamonds. He was replaced by Mike Douglas, a friend of Reed and Kowalski.

In addition to performing on concert bills that included many of the country's hottest acts, the Diamonds also appeared in the musical motion picture *The Beat*.

Despite the continuing success, by 1959 Reed and Kowalski also decided to leave the Diamonds. The group scored its final hit in August

1961, reaching number twenty-two on the charts with "One Summer Night."

Having recorded sixteen hit records between 1956 and 1961, Somerville named his personal favorites. "I enjoy listening to 'A Mother's Love,' 'Walking Along,' 'High Sign,' 'Happy Years,' and I certainly like 'Little Darlin,'" he said. "And we had a song called 'The Crumble,' which is a pretty primitive recording. Those are my favorites."

In August 1961, Somerville left the Diamonds to sing folk music, a style of music that he sang as a child. He also wanted to embark on a solo career.

"I changed my name to my first name, which is hyphenated, David-Troy," he said. "I got married and didn't tell anybody that I'd been in the Diamonds. I disassociated myself from that completely and I worked folk clubs across the county and abroad and spent months in Japan singing in nightclubs. For the most part it was just me and a classical guitar, but I had band arrangements also so that I could do swing-type tunes like Bobby Darin. At that time I was managed by Buck Ram, who wrote 'Only You' and 'The Great Pretender,' and he managed the Platters."

While Ram kept Somerville working in folk clubs, he said that politics was never his field and so he never entertained with the hierarchy of the folk music movement of the time. "A lot of people couldn't understand that I didn't want to mix politics with my music, but I was never into that," he said.

On the road four months a year these days, Somerville estimated that he performs at about seventy-five shows annually, which includes three cruises for Holland America and Royal-Caribbean Lines, casino appearances, package oldies shows, and black-tie events. In recent years he has also teamed with two other group's lead singers for a revue titled "Three Tenors of Pop." At those shows, Somerville is joined by former Association lead Jim Yester and former Four Preps lead Bruce Belland.

"It originally started in 1988 when we updated the Four Preps with the original bass singer, the original lead singer, and we added the original lead singer of the Lettermen, Jim Pike, and me," he said. "Then, after seven or eight years, Jim Pike left and we brought in Jim Yester of the Association. Then our bass singer, Ed Cobb, passed away and so the new Four Preps was now a trio and we didn't think we wanted to add another member to replace him, so we went on as three golden groups in one."

Never one to slow down, Somerville said that he is very proud of current projects that he is involved with. "I've got a children's CD called

The Cosmic Adventures of Diamond Dave, and I have another called *On the 1957 Rock and Roll Greyhound Bus*, where I perform great songs from those pioneer jukebox giants that I used to travel with," he said. "And we are working on a song, 'What Would I Do Without My Music,' which is a tune Elvis was preparing to record when he passed away. I'm also getting ready to record a Christmas DVD in North Carolina with Maurice Williams. He's an absolute sweetheart and he wrote the song that is the main reason that I'm still in show business."

In 1984, the Diamonds were presented with the Canadian Juno Hall of Fame Award, and in 2004 they were voted into the Vocal Group Hall of Fame, based in Sharon, Pennsylvania.

The original Diamonds have reunited occasionally to perform at oldies shows through the years. In June 2004 they performed in Hawaii, minus Reed, who was attempting to recover from an operation. Suffering from cancer, he passed away in October of that year. At the July 2005 Vocal Group Hall of Fame induction ceremony, held in Wildwood, New Jersey, the Diamonds' remaining original members performed at the celebration concert.

Billboard Top 40 Hits by the Diamonds

Date	Pos	Wks on Charts	Record Title	Label/Number
03/17/56	12	11	Why Do Fools Fall in Love	Mercury 70790
05/12/56	14	11	The Church Bells May Ring	Mercury 70835
07/28/56	30	02	Love, Love, Love	Mercury 70889
09/29/56	34	01	Soft Summer Breeze/	
09/29/56	35	02	Ka-Ding-Dong	Mercury 70934
03/15/57	02	21	Little Darlin	Mercury 71060
07/15/57	13	02	Words of Love	Mercury 71128
09/30/57	16	01	Zip Zip	Mercury 71165
11/04/57	10	08	Silhouettes	Mercury 71197
01/06/58	04	14	The Stroll	Mercury 71242
05/19/58	37	01	High Sign	Mercury 71291
07/28/58	16	01	Kathy-O	Mercury 71330
11/17/58	29	06	Walking Along	Mercury 71366
02/09/59	18	10	She Say (Oom Dooby Doom)	Mercury 71404
08/07/61	22	04	One Summer Night	Mercury 71831

The original Diamonds, from left, Dave Somerville, Phil Leavitt, and Ted Kowalski hold their induction statues at the Vocal Group Hall of Fame induction ceremony and concert. At far right is Dave Jackson, who filled in at the show for departed Diamonds original member Bill Reed.

Gordon Stoker
(The Jordanaires)

While they are best known as the group that provided background vocals on all of Elvis Presley's recordings and at stage appearances from 1956 through 1970, that claim hardly defines the Jordanaires career in music. Consider the fact that in the more than fifty years that they have been together, the Jordanaires have sung on more Top 10 recordings than any group in history, and are represented on some 2.6 billion records sold through the years.

Forming in Springfield, Missouri, in the late 1940s, the original lineup consisted of Bob Hubbard, brothers Bill and Monty Matthews, and Culley Holt. The group sang barbershop tunes and gospel and when they moved to Nashville, Tennessee, in 1949, they quickly landed a spot on the Grand Ole Opry.

The early 1950s saw changes in personnel as Gordon Stoker and Hoyt Hawkins replaced Hubbard and Bill Matthews, and soon after Monty Matthews was replaced by Neal Matthews (no relation). "The piano player in the Jordanaires was drafted into the military in 1950 and they auditioned for a replacement, and that's how I joined the group," Stoker said. "I played piano on a lot of Elvis's records and a lot of other country acts' records. In 1952, the first tenor in the Jordanaires, Bill Matthews, had a nervous breakdown and I replaced him. I'd been singing second tenor and didn't even know I could sing first tenor. We were booked for a club date in Detroit and the baritone said that I had to sing that part because we had eight more days to appear there. I forced myself to sing it and I'm very thankful that he pushed me to do it."

Stoker reflected on the experience of being a regular act at the legendary Grand Ole Opry in Nashville, Tennessee. "It was exciting," he said. "Everyone more or less wants to be on the Grand Ole Opry. They try for it; even Elvis tried out for the Grand Ole Opry. They needed a male quartet and we auditioned and we ended up there from then on. We actually were on until we had to resign because we had so many recording sessions going on in Nashville we had to quit."

The Jordanaires was the first white group to sing spirituals. By 1954, they were providing background vocals for artists like Red Foley and Jimmy Wakely, and the following year, following an appearance in Memphis, Tennessee, with Eddy Arnold, a young singer and huge fan of the group approached them backstage. That encounter, while taken lightly at the time, became a defining moment in the Jordanaires' career.

"We loved the Golden Gate Quartet and we loved to copy that sound," Stoker said. "I'm so thankful that we did because that sound is what attracted Elvis. We would sing hand-clapping spirituals on the network portion of the Grand Ole Opry radio show on Saturday nights. Elvis heard us sing on that show and when we went to Memphis with Eddy Arnold in 1955, he came backstage not to meet Eddy Arnold, but to meet us. He'd been hearing us sing on the Opry.

"Elvis told us that night that if he ever got a major recording contract he wanted us to work with him," he added. "In 1956 when they signed him, he asked for us. That was a relationship we had with him for fifteen years."

On January 10, 1956, Presley entered a recording studio for his first RCA Records session and laid down tracks for "I Got a Woman," "Heartbreak Hotel," and "Money Honey." The next day, Stoker received a call from RCA producer Chet Atkins, who asked him to join two other session singers to back Presley on a couple of tunes.

Stoker recalled getting that call. "Chet said, 'We just signed this long-sideburned kid from Memphis; he's just a passing fad and won't be around long.' And he asked me to come in and use Ben and Brock

Speer," he said. "I told him I knew those guys but I've never used them before; but the label had just signed them and wanted to use them. I knew that Elvis wanted to use the Jordanaires. When I got to the session, Ben and Brock were already there and we did background for 'I Want You, I Need You, I Love You' and 'I Was the One.'

"Elvis asked me where the rest of the Jordanaires were and I told him that Chet didn't want to use them," Stoker continued. "He didn't like Chet Atkins 'til the day he died because of that. Chet didn't mean anything by it but Elvis thought that Chet was pulling something over on him."

The budding superstar told him that he wanted all the Jordanaires singing on his future records. From 1956 through 1969 they backed Elvis on nearly every recording he made. The five singers became close friends and professional allies, all having close ties to gospel music, Stoker said. "He [Elvis] really wanted to sing gospel songs," he said. "He had a real hard time with RCA because he wanted to do some religious records and they said, 'Look, we paid millions for your recording contract and we're not gonna let you do religious records.' Elvis told them that he was because he wanted to. He finally got his way and really the only Grammys that he ever won were for his religious songs, I'm sorry to say. He should have won many Grammy's but he didn't."

The mutual respect that Presley and the Jordanaires shared is obvious when you consider that at a time when background musicians, producers, and engineers never received credit on a record label, Presley insisted that the Jordanaires be listed. The unprecedented action resulted in unheard-of recognition for the background vocalists.

"It meant a lot," Stoker said. "In the early days the band members didn't get credit, the artists who designed album covers didn't get credit; but Elvis wanted everyone who played on the recording session as well as the vocal group to get credit. He had to fight RCA even on that. He asked them to put our name on the first records the four of us did with him, which was 'Don't Be Cruel' and 'Hound Dog,' and they said, 'We don't want to mix up Elvis Presley,' but he said he wanted it to read Elvis Presley with the Jordanaires and that's what he did for a long time. I'm very thankful for that."

Stoker recalled fond memories about making feature-length motion pictures with Presley. "Everything we did with Elvis was a lot of fun," he said. "He was just a ball of fire and had a lot of personality. He loved to joke and tell jokes."

The Jordanaires also accompanied Elvis on a number of concert appearances and television shows. His performance on the Sunday night WCBS Ed Sullivan television show was viewed by huge numbers of his growing fan base. "He always wanted us as close to him as we could be," Stoker said. "He also wanted to do 'Peace in the Valley' for his mother and they said, 'No, you're not going to do a religious song on this show.' They'd never had a religious song done on the *Ed Sullivan Show* and wouldn't let him do one. We did get to do it and I'll always treasure that.

"My favorite is when I played piano on 'Ready Teddy,'" he continued. "The three guys stood beside me but I was sitting at the piano."

In 1969, Elvis signed a contract for an extended run of performances at the Las Vegas Hilton Hotel in Nevada. The Jordanaires opted not to leave Nashville to join him. "We already had forty sessions booked in Nashville," he said. "That's all we do is background. And we had a commitment to sing on a Coca-Cola commercial too. That paid us more money than working a whole year with Elvis. Those jingles pay a lot. We'll always regret that we couldn't go to Vegas with him but we just couldn't go. His guitar player and drummer, Scotty and D. J., didn't go either because they were also doing sessions in Nashville.

"I've always thought that Vegas is what took his life," Stoker said. "He wasn't able to do two shows a night."

Among the 2,500 recording artists that the Jordanaires have provided background vocals for on some thirty thousand sides recorded through the years, they can be heard on Jimmy Dean's "Big Bad John," Jim Reeves's "Four Walls," Loretta Lynn's "Coal Miner's Daughter," Patsy Cline's "Crazy," and Ricky Nelson's "Travelin' Man."

Working sometimes six days a week in response to demand, Stoker explained how they first got into background work. "We always liked to be in the background because the background is what takes the pressure off," he said. "To cut hit records you've always got to be pushing and promoting and going out to promote your records. But to stay in the background, it's the easy life and there's no pressure. Elvis and a lot of other stars we worked with had a lot of pressure on them. It's a pleasure to go to a studio, listen to a demo, and go up and cut the song. There is no pressure at all."

In looking back at the countless recordings done with other artists, Stoker cited some as being personal favorites. "Almost everything we did with Patsy Cline I absolutely loved," he said. "I also loved many things that we did with Ricky Nelson, like 'Poor Little Fool' and 'Lonesome Town.' Those are just great recordings and we got the greatest background sound on Ricky Nelson stuff and he was such a dear friend."

Stoker explained what has become known in the recording industry as the numbers system, first developed in 1955 by the Jordanaires' Neal Matthews to expedite learning and singing background at studio sessions. "We used it for some five years before we could get any musicians in Nashville," he said. "That's where the tonic chord is one. If you're in the key of C, C is one. Four is F and five is G. That's the one, four, five chord, in the key of C. Whatever key you go to, the tonic is still one. It's what we call a shorthand version, because you've got to be able to do harmony quick to do sessions in Nashville. If you can't do it quick, they'll get rid of you."

The influence that the Jordanaires have had on all genres of music became apparent when they received accolades from former Beatle Paul McCartney. "We met him in one of the studios in Nashville," Stoker recalled. "He and Linda were there doing something for an album and I went into the control room to meet him. The producer had told him that one of the Jordanaires was there and Paul said that he wanted to meet me. He told me that the Beatles learned to sing harmony by listening to the Jordanaires. He said that when they got an Elvis record they wouldn't listen to Elvis, but would listen to us singing background. That's really one of the nicest compliments that has ever been paid us."

Honored with the CMA Masters Award for their lifetime contribution to music in 1984, the Jordanaires continue to maintain a heavy schedule of session work in Nashville as well as performing in a tribute to both Presley and Patsy Cline in Las Vegas. The group was inducted into the Vocal Group Hall of Fame in July 2005.

"I guess what I am really proud of is all the halls of fame that we've been put in," Stoker said. "We're in the Vocal Group Hall of Fame, the Country Music Hall of Fame, the Gospel Music Hall of Fame, the Rockabilly Hall of Fame, the North American Hall of Fame, and it's just wonderful. I tell the guys that the next one is the Eternal Hall of Fame."

The Jordanaires' Gordon Stoker laughs as group bass
singer Ray Walker recounts some humorous tales
during their induction into the Vocal Group Hall of Fame
in 2005. Walker joined the group in June 1958

Emil Stucchio
(The Classics)

East Meadow, New York   **May 14, 2005**

Originally formed as the Perennials, the vocal group from Brooklyn, New York, was made up of lead singer Emil Stucchio, first tenor Tony Victor, second tenor Johnny Gambale, and bass/baritone Jamie Troy. "In the fall of 1958 Tony Victor and I were going to St. Francis Prep, and the four of us were all attending high school when we came together," Stucchio said.

Despite the fact that some biographies written on the group claim otherwise, Stucchio confirmed that none of the quartet's members ever sang with another Brooklyn vocal group called the Del Rays. "The only one that came from the Del Rays is Lou Rotundo and he went on to sing with the Passions," he said.

The group renamed itself the Classics when a club's MC suffered from bad memory while introducing them. "We were doing a show in a place on New Utrecht Avenue called the Club Illusion," he said. "We were there with a group called the Neons. The host of the show, Sam Sardi, asked what the name of our group was and we told him the Perennials. He asked us again just before we were ready to go on what the group's name was, and as the Neons came off the stage, Sardi announced, 'Ladies and gentlemen, how about a nice round of applause for these kids from Brooklyn, New York, the ... the ... the Classics.' We all looked around and thought there was another group coming on. He waved us on and we did the show. After the show I asked him why he called us the Classics and he said, 'If I couldn't remember your name from here to there, who's going to remember your name when they leave here?' He was right." From that night on they were known as the Classics!

Cutting their teeth in the business by performing at neighborhood dances and clubs, they came to the attention of Jim Gribble in 1959, and subsequently recorded an original tune called "Cinderella."

"Louie [Rotundo] was with the Passions at that time, and of course the Mystics were with Gribble at the time," Stucchio said. "The Mystics recorded 'Hushabye' and then brought the Passions up and they recorded 'Just To Be With You.' Then Louie told us that they were having auditions at Gribble's office and said we should go down. We went down and there were about five groups there, every one of them better than us. But Gribble said that he was looking for pretty faces and he told us that he wanted to record us and asked if we had anything original. We came out with 'Cinderella' and recorded it a week later.

"When we recorded 'Cinderella' the first disc jockey to play it in New York was Jocko," he added. "I used to listen to his show regularly and all of a sudden I heard him say, 'Ooh papa della, that's 'Cinderella' by the Classics,' and he played our song. At that time, WMGM was a radio station and a guy named Peter Trip used to do a Top 40 survey every night. After a month or so, we made the Top 30 and then the Top 20."

The group went on to record "Angel Angela" and "Life Is but a Dream," which when picked up by Mercury Records climbed the rhythm and blues charts.

After backing singer Herb Lance on a recording of "Blue Moon," a single that climbed to number fifty on the *Billboard* charts the group moved to the Musicnote label in 1963. Their debut release with the new label, "Till Then," entered the Top 20 that July and became the group's signature song.

"Naturally, when you have a record that becomes a national hit you feel like this is going to be your life; you're gonna have music for the rest of your life. And it has been for all of us. Being a young kid—I was only nineteen at the time—I felt that this was a goal that as friends we had achieved."

The group began to appear on the bills of many concerts and bus tours, an experience that Stucchio found difficult to adequately describe. "I don't know if anybody could capture it and put into words what that was like," he said. "In hindsight, as you look back at some of the people that you were on the road with that eventually became major stars like Paul Anka, Ricky Nelson, and those type of people, it's unbelievable. I was on the bus with the Platters, the Drifters, and I can remember the first time I met the Flamingos. To me they were men. I can remember Zeke smoking an ivory pipe. I was a kid and he was like my father."

The Classics, like many of the vocal groups that originated in Brooklyn, enjoyed harmonizing to 1920s and 1930s standard tunes such as "P.S. I Love You" and "Wrap Up Your Troubles in Dreams." "When we switched from Mercury to Musicnote, Andy Leonetti told us that we were best suited for standards," he said. "The very first standard that we recorded was 'Till Then' and was a success. When we released 'P.S. I Love You' it was voted record of the week on WMCA and WABC radio in New York. *American Bandstand* used to feature voting for the top songs and we swept that. It also made the *Cashbox* with a bullet around 1964 for one or two weeks before it dropped right off when the English groups came in and changed the whole complexion of music."

The group began to move from one label to another including Dart and Stork Records. That fact has been cited as a primary reason that the Classics did not benefit from proper promotion when they released a new recording.

"I think that each time we chose to move from one label to another it was with the best intentions and it was to try to approach music with the changing times," Stucchio said. "When we recorded 'Till Then' and 'P.S. I Love You' with Musicnote, at that time the standards were going good. When we went to sign with Blue Horizon Records, which at the time had recorded the McCoys and War, the songwriting team of Feldman, Gotteher, and Goldstein told us they wrote some songs that they thought were perfect for us. We went in to record them and got these elaborate sessions and they actually released some songs of ours that didn't do as well. I thought the sessions were great and I thought the songs were great, but they didn't make it."

While groups like the Classics, the Mystics, and the Passions produced an elegant harmony on their recordings, new styles of music such as the West Coast surf sound and that of the British Invasion were shifting audience preference during the mid-1960s.

"I think the British Invasion more than anything else affected us," Stucchio said. "In 1964 when we released 'P.S. I Love You,' the Beatles were dominating the charts. Then right behind them came the Rolling Stones and Freddy and the Dreamers. When I'm asked how it affected me, I say to this day that there are so many more talented people than myself that never had the opportunity that I had, so I'm forever grateful for having had it.

"Did it change my life? Yes," he added. "The dynamics of my life changed because I then had a family and went out and got a job outside of music. As fate would have it, I was able to juggle two careers by singing on weekends and being a police officer with New York City. It worked out great because I was able to feed the family, get the benefits, and still juggle the music. When I retired, music just went through the roof, so it all worked out."

During the 1970s, Stucchio, Troy, and Rotundo formed the Profits, a group that recorded for Sire Records. "Sire/Blue Horizon had an idea," he said. "They wanted to do like a beach-type version of 'The Wind' by the Diablos, and it was beautiful the way they did it. We went to Media Sound Studios and they created an island sound."

The Classics, the Mystics, and the Passions have remained close friends through the years and have performed on the same bill a number of times as well as filled in for each other's lineup on occasion. "I was with the Mystics for about a year," Stucchio said. "While I was working with them, they used to do nice dance steps and they tortured me about the way I danced. Then I sang with Albie and Louie from the Passions and we went out as the Classics for about thirteen years."

When vocalist Michael Parquet decided to leave a more recent lineup of the Classics, Stucchio made the decision to replace him with Teresa McClean, the first female to have ever been in the group. Stucchio spoke about the altered sound that the group enjoyed with the addition of her vocal range.

"Michael was a tremendous addition to the group but he got busy with his business and had to leave," he said. "When he left, at this stage of our lives we had to get someone that had the vocal ability plus the time to do it, plus they have to blend in personality-wise with us as well. I went through the different rituals that you go through to find a replacement, and then I thought that I could be so bold to take a chance on someone that has a great talent and could certainly add to the dynamic of the group. This girl was with a group called the Chicklettes and I recruited her."

Stucchio stays extremely busy in 2006 performing one hundred shows a year not only with Classics but also in a joint conglomeration with the Mystics and the Passions, a performance called the Brooklyn Reunion, and in staging an Italian show.

Reflecting on a more-than-forty-year personal friendship among the members of the three Brooklyn vocal groups, Stucchio explained its lasting power. "Speaking for myself, I can say that if it wasn't for them I would have never had a shot," he said. "The Mystics went up there and opened the door for us and the Passions. If it wasn't for Lou [Rotundo] suggesting that I go up for the audition we wouldn't be here. I not only respect these guys as people but I have respect for them as artists too. They sing well and, to be honest, I love working with them. It's a lot of fun."

In looking back on his career in music, Stucchio viewed it as fulfilling. "The people that grew up in that era, the 1950s and 1960s—it was a fun time and if we were part of the fun and enjoyment that they had during that time, I would appreciate if they would remember us fondly with a smile of their face, saying that they remember the songs the Classics did and [that] we were great to see," he said. "That would be a nice tribute."

Billboard Top 40 Hits by the Classics

Date	Pos	Wks on Charts	Record Title	Label/Number
07/20/63	20	05	Till Then	Musicnote 1116

John Sylvia
(The Tune Weavers)

Islandia, New York   **November 12, 2005**

A classic example of how a label's ability to properly promote and distribute a record in relation to its popularity and success is the song "Happy, Happy Birthday Baby" by a Massachusetts group named the Tune Weavers. Originally released in 1957 by the small Casa Grande record label, the single fizzled with little attention.

Had it not been embraced and given airplay by two Philadelphia disc jockeys and subsequently picked up by the larger Chess Records of Chicago, Illinois, the single, which has become a perennial favorite, would have faded into obscurity.

The origin of the group was a brother-and-sister act, that being the duo of Gilbert and Margo Lopez. And the focus of the pair was not rhythm and blues but rather jazz and pop. In 1956 two additional members joined the pair, one being Margo's husband, John Sylvia, and the other her childhood friend and schoolmate Charlotte Davis. The quartet took the name the Tone Weavers and began to incorporate rhythm and blues into their repertoire, along with pop favorites by groups such as the Four Freshmen.

"We focused on various types of music ranging from jazz, rhythm and blues, and old standards," Sylvia said.

Where, when, and how the quartet evolved from the Tone Weavers to the Tune Weavers is a matter of debate but Sylvia shared his recollection. "What I remember is that an MC at a club that we were performing at introduced the group as the Tune Weavers instead of the Tone Weavers," he said. "But Charlotte said that that might not be accurate because she at the time had a fiancé and he gave us the name Tune Weavers. So [I've] always been skeptical as to how it really came about, but that's the two versions."

Sylvia recalled how the group secured its first recording opportunity. "We were doing some local shows, performing at various clubs, and Frank [Paul, owner of Casa Grande Records] happened to be at one of the shows. He got very interested once he heard us and saw us perform."

Upon auditioning the group and hearing Margo's original composition, "Happy, Happy Birthday Baby," a recording session was held in March 1957 and the single was quickly released. But given Casa Grande's limited resources to properly handle the disc, it stalled. Sylvia reflected on the initial failure of the song.

"There is no question that the record stalled because of Casa Grande's inability to promote it," he said. "The only means of promoting it that we were doing in the Massachusetts area was visiting some of the local radio stations and also doing record hops every Friday and Saturday night. We would do as many as four or six record hops in the same night. What we would do is go to where we knew the biggest records hops were being held and that's where we would go to try to promote the record. We would go there, spend maybe a half hour or whatever, leave there, and go to as many as we could to get the record known."

Sylvia said that the crowd reaction at each record hop visited was so favorable that it encouraged the group to forge ahead in the attempt to gain attention. "The teenagers of that era are a special breed," he said. "They were so attentive and appreciated music more so than the generation of today and they were very knowledgeable. They would just stand there and watch you perform and they were very, very grateful. The nicest thing about that time and record hops is that just about anybody that you can name at the time that we were promoting ourselves were doing the same thing. Frankie Avalon, Paul Anka, you name it; all of the performers of that era were doing the same thing. We would go to a record hop and there would be three or four other artists waiting to go on after us.

"The admission to record hops back then was ninety-nine cents," he continued. "For ninety-nine cents these kids were getting to see the top artists of that era."

By summer 1957, Joe Niagra and Hy Lit, two popular disc jockeys on WIBG radio in Philadelphia, Pennsylvania, came by the record and began to give it airplay. Through that airplay the song grabbed the attention of another music titan in the City of Brotherly Love, one Dick Clark. Preparing to expand his *American Bandstand* television dance show into the national spotlight, Clark became enamored with the tune.

"A disc jockey from the Philadelphia area played our song, and from what we know, he played it in error," Sylvia said. "It wasn't part of his format but somehow or other he played 'Happy, Happy Birthday Baby.' He immediately got swamped with calls about the song and listeners wanted to know who the group was. That's how it all came about."

The group benefited by the subsequent sale of the single's distribution rights from Casa Grande to the larger and more powerful Chess Record label. Chess's clout and national presence thrust the record into the mainstream, gaining the group and the song significant attention. But the Chess version and the Casa Grande version of "Happy, Happy Birthday Baby" have different endings. While the original Casa Grande recording features a four-note sax ending, the Chess version ends immediately following the last vocal note.

"We didn't record the song twice and have no idea at all why the sax notes were eliminated from the Chess release," he said. "We would naturally have preferred the original version."

Sylvia recalled how the Chess label also attempted to capitalize on the flip side of "Happy, Happy Birthday Baby," a rendition of "Old Man River." "A lot of people are not aware that 'Old Man River,' the B-side to 'Happy, Happy Birthday Baby,' did very, very well for us too," he said. "It did so well that Chess Records ended up splitting that record. What they did, and it was common for Chess to do things of this nature, was to take 'Old Man River,' put an instrumental on its B-side, and released it as a single of its own. Because it did so well, they wanted to see if they could promote 'Old Man River' away from being the B-side of 'Happy, Happy Birthday Baby.' My rough guess is that the instrumental that they put on its B-side was a tune called 'Yo Yo Walk.'"

Shortly after "Happy, Happy Birthday Baby" hit the charts, the Tune Weavers appeared with Little Richard, the Cleftones, Jimmie Rodgers, the Five Keys, and the Clovers on the bill of Alan Freed's Labor Day show at the Brooklyn Paramount.

"Little Richard was the headliner of that show," Sylvia recalled. "That was quite a show. Of all the shows that we did in the 1950s, I don't know if it was because it was our first show that was the most memorable one of that era that we performed at. Back then we were doing as much as four or five shows a day. You would start off with a matinee at eleven o'clock in the morning and back then there were fifteen groups on the show. You'd do a show, go grab a sandwich, and come back and do it again. It was for one whole week at the Paramount. Being teenagers we had the energy to do it and didn't feel it as much."

Following that show, the Tune Weavers left to tour the Southern states in a series of one-night concerts. "The Southern states were something very memorable, but not good memories, unfortunately," Sylvia said. "While we were in the North there was no problem performing and traveling. But as soon as we hit the Southern states, we had to immediately split the buses up. The white artists like the Every Brothers rode in one bus and the non-white artists rode in a separate bus and that was mandatory. That was the segregation of the South. That's one of the unpleasant memories that still stays with me. You don't forget things like that."

Sylvia said that performing to the Southern audiences was a challenge as well. "That too was very strange," he said. "Back then the black audience and the white audience couldn't intermingle. I remember someplace in North Carolina that we performed at and it was a very strange setup. On the main floor the white audience was able to dance and watch the show. The black audience would have to be in the balcony, the next level up, and there was no dancing area up there. They could just sit and watch the performance. To take it one step further, if you had an integrated group, the integrated group could not perform on stage at the same time with black and white performers. Back then the Del Vikings were one of the first groups to have black and white vocalists and they would not be able to perform down South as they were. In some cases the group would have to be altered, minus the person of color that was different from the others.

"One of the most memorable incidents I experienced that is just locked into my mind happened in one of the deep Southern states," he continued. "We could not perform singing to the white audience or the black audience. I'm out on stage and they had a dance area on the left of the stage and another area on the right. One side was black and the other was white. The stage divided the two audiences. The weirdest thing about it was that we could not perform facing the black audience or facing the white audience. We had to sing facing the wall, not facing either audience."

There were no black-owned hotels at that time, Sylvia recalled. "The only places that the black artists could stay at were at private homes," he said. "That's where we would go. We'd go to these nice big homes that were owned by black families that would put up the artists. They would have so many of us at this house and so many at another house down the street and we would get picked up by the bus after breakfast and head for the next town."

In November 1957 Herald Records bought the rights to Casa Grande's masters recorded by the Tune Weavers. "I think maybe the group would have been better off to some degree if we had stayed with Chess Records, because of the distribution and the strength that Chess had," he said. "Chess was very well known for promoting mostly black artists at that time and they had two labels, Chess and Checker."

Following the release of "I Remember Dear," the Tune Weavers performed on the bill of the sold out George "Hound Dog" Lorenz Eighth Anniversary Show of Stars in Hartford, Connecticut. Staged at the State Theater, the concert broke all box-office records for the venue.

In January 1958 they signed on to tour major cities with Paul Anka, Buddy Holly and the Crickets, and Danny and the Juniors. "That was a great, great lineup," he said. "It was a fun thing because I can remember that between shows some of the guys were shooting craps. I never got involved because I didn't gamble, but it was a real fun tour. The groups all got along so well and enjoyed each other's company."

The Tune Weavers continued to record tunes, including "Pamela Jean" and "Look Down That Lonesome Road." Margo Sylvia remained the primary composer of the group. "Margo was the heart and soul of the Tune Weavers, period," he said. "She was the original founder of the group and she was the one that put the group together and held the group together."

Similar to the fate of so many recording artists and composers of that era, while Margo Sylvia wrote the group's signature song, she never received monetary compensation for her effort. "She got writer's credit for writing 'Happy, Happy Birthday Baby,' but never got royalties for it," he said. "Shortly before she passed away, Margo went to some attorneys that handle music. Like so many other artists from the 1950s who were trying to recoup some of the monies that they should have gotten but didn't, she tried to do the same. It was a common thing back then that record company owners would try to make a deal with you and trade off strong promotion of your record in return for you allowing them to put their name as a co-writer."

Fortunately, Sylvia said the record label of the group's hit single credits Margo and her brother Gilbert as having composed the tune.

Charlotte Davis left the group toward the end of the decade and with replacement Bill Morris the Tune Weavers released two more singles in the early 1960s. Recordings of "My Congratulations Baby" and "Congratulations on Your Wedding" attempted to grab the same attention as "Birthday," but fell short. Morris was married to one of Margo's first cousins and had been singing with a number of local groups in the Boston area. With him, they continued to perform until around 1963.

A few years prior to her death in 1991, Margo Sylvia released a multitrack recording as the Tune Weavers, one that had her providing all the harmony parts as well as lead vocal. It was released on the Classic Artists label. Gil Lopez passed away in 1998.

In 2003, John Sylvia reunited with Davis to organize a new lineup of Tune Weavers, upon the group's induction into the Doo Wop Hall of Fame in Boston, Massachusetts. "Charlotte had gone to Symphony Hall in Boston to a doo-wop show because another group from the area that we were close with, the G-Clefs, was receiving a lifetime achievement award," Sylvia said. "After the show, Harvey Robbins, the producer of the show, asked the G-Clefs if they knew how to contact the Tune Weavers. Harvey then called Charlotte, who in turn contacted me, and he wanted us to accept a lifetime achievement award in 2003 at Symphony Hall. I said yes immediately but I did not want just Charlotte and me to go to Symphony Hall, get on stage to receive a plaque, and walk off. I felt that would be a good time to pay tribute to Margo and her brother Gilbert."

Sylvia told Davis that the only way he would consider doing it was to recruit additional singers and to perform the group's signature song on the stage of Symphony Hall. "I wanted to keep the same identity, that being two male and two female singers," he said. "A couple of years prior to that I was in partnership in a nightclub and restaurant where we hosted shows and featured karaoke every Saturday night. This couple used to come in every Saturday and they were good performers, singing individually and sometimes they'd do a duet. They happen to be the two people that I asked to join us and are with the Tune Weavers now."

When Sylvia and Davis rehearsed with the two singers, Alice Fernandes and Burt Pina, they had but one objective. That was to perfect "Happy, Happy Birthday Baby," to perform the song at Symphony Hall, and to accept the award. "That night we did our signature song, we got a standing ovation, and Harvey presented us with the plaques," he said. Two of Gilbert's sons were there and came on stage to accept for him, and one of Margo and my sons received for his mother. The nicest part of that was that when we were recording 'Happy, Happy Birthday Baby,' Margo was pregnant with him. That was a very, very touching moment and I got very emotional."

A significant fact regarding the Tune Weaver's signature song is one that results in much emotion for Sylvia as he reminisced about how and when it was written. "What many people are not aware of is that 'Happy, Happy Birthday Baby' was written on my behalf," he said. "The true story is that Margo and I were courting and we ran into some difficulty and went our separate ways for a very short time. That is when she wrote 'Happy, Happy Birthday Baby.' If you listen to the words of the song, especially when she identifies, 'I was your pretty, you were my baby,' those were not the original words of the song. Margo had a nickname for me and I had a nickname for her and those were the original words that she used in that song. For recording purposes, she ended up deleting her nickname and my nickname and adding the new words."

Today's lineup of Tune Weavers began to accept gigs at other oldies shows after the Symphony Hall tribute and started to rehearse many of the old standards that they transform into their own unique harmony. The group continues to perform to standing ovations. "We've been at shows all around the country now and the audience response to our return as well as all the groups is so wonderful," Sylvia said. "It's not often that a person gets a second chance around for something that they enjoy doing. If you had told me ten years ago that I would be back doing what I'm doing now I would have said that there was no way it could be possible. This is a second chance around for Charlotte and for me and it is fantastic."

Billboard Top 40 Hits by the Tune Weavers

Date	Pos	Wks on Charts	Record Title	Label/Number
09/23/57	05	14	Happy, Happy Birthday Baby	Checker 872

Nedra Talley
(The Ronettes)

Wildwood, New Jersey   **July 7, 2005**

Cited as having recorded one of the most romantic songs of the rock-and-roll era, "Be My Baby," and widely regarded as having defined the Phil Spector-produced Wall of Sound, the Ronettes have been described as vulnerable but tough and sexy but sweet. Their harmony, high energy, and slick stage presence left an indelible mark on the music industry and represents the classic mid-1960s girl-group persona.

Growing up in the Washington Heights section of New York City, sisters Veronica and Estelle Bennett and their cousin Nedra Talley gained early exposure to music in the form of hometown talent such as Frankie Lymon and the Teenagers and Little Anthony and the Imperials.

"My grandma pushed my mom to encourage us to succeed, to do something and go somewhere with our gift to sing," Talley said. "It was at my grandma's house that my mom would push us to sing but it actually started off with more than just the three of us. All the cousins would go into a room and we'd entertain ourselves."

After a while, Talley said, her mother made trips to downtown Manhattan to visit agencies in the hope of securing interest in the youngsters. "My mother was a singer but didn't quite go and do what she wanted to do," Talley said. "So she was always there behind me and the girls."

While existing biographies on the group state that the girls first performed at the Apollo Theatre as the Darling Sisters, Talley disputed that fact. "When we appeared at the Apollo for an amateur show, we were not the Darling Sisters," she said. "When we first went there it was with six cousins, one boy and five girls. We didn't even have a name at that show. By the next time we performed at the Apollo, we were already named the Ronettes."

Despite being nameless, the cousins took first place at the competition. Talley recalled that her male cousin sang in the fashion of Frankie Lymon, while the girls did their dance routines and backed him up. "Ronnie was always the shortest cousin and I was the youngest," she recalled.

Eventually the Bennett sisters and Talley came to the attention of Philip Halikus, who became their manager. "I believe that we met Philip Halikus when we were downtown going around the Brill Building practicing," she said. "I remember him setting up and paying for some rehearsal studios for us and bringing in a piano player. He was an older man and he sort of pushed his way into being around us and then was willing to invest and have us meet with some business people."

In 1961, when a New York City club manager mistook the three girls for an act he'd booked at the famous Peppermint Lounge in New York City rather than just fans waiting outside to enter the club, the trio seized the opportunity and performed a rousing rendition of a Ray Charles tune, "What I Say." Receiving thunderous applause for the effort, the trio was immediately booked for regular appearances, for which they were paid ten dollars a night.

"Back then when the three of us were going down to the Peppermint Lounge, we always dressed alike," Talley said. "We were dressed alike, standing in line, and suddenly the bouncer came over and said, 'Oh, they are here; come on in.' We said okay and went in and began dancing literally on the railing and they thought we were good. They asked if we wanted to come back. That's when Joey Dee was working there. When the guy saw us dressed alike he just assumed we were a group that they were waiting for to entertain."

Shortly after, the girls met popular New York disc jockey, Murray (the K) Kauffman, who recruited them to become dancing girls at his Brooklyn Fox shows. "Murray the K was with WINS radio and actually I ended up marrying the assistant music director of the station, Scott Ross," she said. "Murray the K was the really hot disc jockey at the time and we had signed with Colpix Records and went to the station to meet him. We had the look and that's when he did the 'swinging soiree' and the dancing girls and he asked us if we wanted to do one of his shows. He used the term 'his dancing girls,' but we were not. We were already the Ronettes."

In 1961, the group recorded their first single, "I Want a Boy," on the Colpix label as Ronnie and the Relatives. But subsequent singles, "I'm On the Wagon," "Silhouettes," and "Good Girls," were released as the Ronettes. Talley explained how the name change came about.

"My mother and my uncle were sitting together trying to come up with a name," she said. "There was really nothing to Ronnie and the Relatives. It was just everyone trying to come up with different names. But then we put R-O, which stands for Ronnie, N-E stands for Nedra, and E-S stands for Estelle. My mother and the group of relatives put all those combinations in different ways and came up with the Ronettes."

While the Ronettes were recording their own singles, the group also provided background vocals for a number of other artists, such as Bobby Rydell, Del Shannon, and Joey Dee. Talley recalled those recording sessions and working with the top acts of that era, but stressed the fact that they more than likely came about as casual encounters.

"There were times where we'd do a session with somebody but not as professional background singers, but more as friends helping each other," she said. "You ended up knowing somebody and going to one of their sessions, and they'd ask if we wanted to sing on the record."

One of the most conflicting sagas in the Ronettes history is how the group came to first meet legendary producer Phil Spector. One states that when Estelle Bennett dialed a wrong telephone number while attempting to learn about a recording date, she reached Spector by accident. Another tale credits a staff writer from *Sixteen Magazine* as having introduced the trio to him. Talley set the record straight.

"The story about Estelle's phone call is just stupid," Talley said. "Let's think about this. There are eight million people living in New York City. What are the chances that she would reach him by accident? What really happened is that he [Spector] came backstage when we were at the Brooklyn Fox. I cannot remember who brought him backstage but he was at our door. He saw us perform and wanted to meet us."

Spector had previously worked with the Crystals, as well as Darlene Love and the Blossoms, but saw something both unique and marketable in the Ronettes.

The first single released by the group on Spector's Phillies record label in July 1963 was a Jeff Barry, Ellie Greenwich, Spector composition, "Be My Baby." The combination of outstanding vocals and Spector's production turned out a record that has long been considered a classic of the era. By September, the single climbed to number two in the United States and number four in England.

Talley recalled first hearing the song played on the radio. "You just could not believe, when you were out in a city the size that we were, that there was your song playing over the radio," she said. "We were proud of the song anyway and we just wanted to cry when we heard it. It was just unbelievable."

Off the success of their debut single on the label, the Ronettes returned to the recording studio in November 1963 to lay down tracks for "Baby I Love You," a record that benefited from having the additional vocals of Darlene Love and the Blossoms and Cher. Spector, employing an innovative and creative production style, overdubbed again and again until some twenty-five voices filled the background. It would become known in the industry as the Wall of Sound. The recording also featured the driving piano playing of Leon Russell.

"That session was a lot of fun and it was one of those things where the camaraderie was working, you felt the genius of the music, and everyone pitched in," Talley said. "We worked on other people's recordings and they worked on ours, and we all always tried to make each other's record the best we could."

The Ronettes joined forces with other artists again to record Spector's holiday album *A Christmas Gift for You*. Talley recalled a particularly funny incident that ended one night's recording session for the album. "When we were making the album we were working late into the night," she said. "We were all sitting around and people would start telling all sorts of stories. If it's really, really late and you are really tired, everything gets hysterically funny. At one point we were all laughing and Darlene [Love] threw her head back and her wig went flying off of her head. We fell on the floor crying so hard that Phil had to end the session. We just had a ball."

When the album was released, its potential for success suffered due to the simultaneous assassination of President John F. Kennedy and a nation overwhelmed with grief for its fallen leader. Talley has vivid memories of that fateful day in Dallas, Texas, since the Ronettes happened to be in the city at the time.

"We were there on the day that he [JFK] was shot," she said. "We were scheduled to perform there at a show. We'd driven all night to Dallas and got there early. We knew he was coming and so everybody stayed up at our windows looking for him and the television was on in the room. All of a sudden a commotion broke out and they announced that the president was shot. It was hysteria even with the groups, and we were all crying and couldn't really function. The show was cancelled and we waited a few days to get our bearings. I remember sitting in the lobby waiting to check out of the hotel and saw Oswald getting shot on the television. It affected the spirit of what we were all feeling because we were so devastated, but by being there it was like even closer to home."

The Ronettes joined Dick Clark's Caravan of Stars tour and performed with many of the era's biggest names. "In the beginning I went in there and couldn't believe that there was Jimmy Clanton singing 'Just a Dream,' and we'd get halfway dressed and stand on the side of the stage to listen to everyone else perform," she said. "We were so tired by the end of that tour that I was dreaming every night that I was driving a bus that went out of control.

"Dick Clark was wonderful," she added. "He was the most gracious person. In the front of the bus they had removed a few seats and replaced it with a cot for Dick to sleep on. We would get so tired we'd sleep on the floor and he'd always give up his cot to the artists. I used to take a pillow and sleep in the luggage rack. I was that skinny then. But it was so much fun."

During long night drives, Talley said, there would always be a few artists that liked to tell jokes through the night and keep the others awake and entertained. She also recalled experiencing various forms of racism for the first time during the tour.

"They would tell us about problems in the hotels," she said. "I remember thinking to myself, 'What is going on?' Coming from New York we had never dealt with that."

By January 1964, "Baby I Love You" climbed to number twenty-four in the United States and number eleven in England. In February the Ronettes left for a tour of England, but Talley took this interview to correct a longstanding myth, one that claimed the Ronettes went overseas with the intent of touring with the Rolling Stones.

"When we went to tour over there, we were booked there as headliners," she said. "When we got there we met different groups on the show. We were sitting in our dressing room and the show was ready to start, so we wanted to get dressed. These guys told us they were already dressed and we looked at them. We looked at what they were wearing, which was just plain street clothes, and thought, 'Surely they jest.' That was our introduction to the Rolling Stones."

Another British group came to the Ronettes' attention through a show promoter. "The promoter told us that there was this group, the Beatles, that wanted to give us a party," she said. "We ended up going over to the Beatles' place and they had this big party laid out for us and we had a great time. We were running around the place playing games like kids."

When the Beatles stormed onto the music scene, the Ronettes association with the band proved to be a huge benefit to disc jockey Murray (the K) Kauffman, who would tout himself as the "Fifth Beatle." "Murray the K met the Beatles through us because we had been together earlier," Talley said. "When we came back to the States, both the Beatles and the Rolling Stones were planning to tour and the debate was which group we would tour with. They both wanted us to tour with them but the business decision ended up with our touring with the Beatles."

That tour would be a memorable one for the Ronettes. "The thing with the business is that you get a certain amount of days to get to work with other groups and you get closer and closer," she said. "But we did see certain sides of the Beatles when they came to America and the craziness that surrounded them. It was a different level than we'd ever known."

While the groups stayed at the same hotels while on tour, when they arrived in New York, Talley's mother became the supreme hostess to the ground-breaking superstars. "My mom was cooking for the Stones up at the house," Talley recalled. "I lived in a high-rise building on Riverside Drive and when the word got out that the Stones were in the building, chaos broke out."

One tour that the Ronettes participated in overseas was performing for American servicemen stationed there. But media reports of the shows soured Talley on the press. "It was wonderful performing for them," she said. "I felt like I really was that girl from home that was there with them. Unfortunately, some article said that the boys were on the floor looking up our dresses and it was so untrue. We were literally taking turns to kiss everybody on the cheek. It was like, 'I'm the closest thing to your sister; I'm here and I appreciate what you're doing for our country.'"

While overseas, the Ronettes recordings of "The Best Part of Breaking Up," and "Do I Love You?" were released on the Phillies label. But a change began to surface upon the group's return to the United States, that being Spector's growing attention toward Ronnie, both professionally and personally. While the Ronettes all sang on the next two releases, a Barry/Greenwich/Spector original tune called "Why Don't They Let Us Fall in Love" and "So Young," a cover of the Students' ballad, both were released under the name Veronica. Both recordings were withdrawn soon after release.

The Ronettes also provided background vocals for the Righteous Brothers on their memorable recording "You've Lost That Loving Feeling." "Everybody just sort of loved being a part of that session," she said. "With Phil, he could have done something and somebody would walk in and he'd say, 'I want you to snap your fingers,' or 'I want you to do this or that.' He was always thinking of some kind of mix or whatever. But we knew that the song was going to be a big hit."

The last Ronettes single to enter *Billboard*'s Top 40 in November 1964 was the Barry Mann/Cynthia Weil/Spector composition "Waking in the Rain." The song would earn Spector his only Grammy Award, for Best Sound Effects. The Ronettes disbanded in 1966, and two years later Spector and Ronnie Bennett married, a union that ended in 1974. Talley and Estelle Bennett also got married.

"In 1966 I had a personal awakening as far as the Lord was concerned," Talley said. "I had been out there since I was fourteen years old, had a recording contract by fifteen, a million seller by seventeen, done the travel and had the success, and I just decided that there was more to life. I just had an encounter where God said to me, 'I'm God.' For me, it was a defining moment, and looking back on a lot of the interviews I did you'd always hear me saying, 'I want to marry, I love cooking, I want a family, I want children.' I was always more family oriented.

"Some of the things that were going on on the road you hid," she added. "And Ronnie was dating Phil and he had a way of sort of trying to conquer and divide. We were a trio from our earliest days and we were family. His way of doing it was by saying, 'I need Ronnie to do this project,' but it would be at our expense. He had the best of both worlds and my personal feeling was that we were a trio. The day we were not a trio, I had already done it all and didn't need anymore.

"I appreciate the love of the people but I personally don't live for the applause; that's not what fulfills me," she said. "It is my family and my friends. It touches me in my heart because I know that people love those songs and it's a part of the tapestry of their life and my life. When I had the encounter with God, you can't have two Gods, and the music industry can be a God. That's when I walked away from the business."

After marrying Scott Ross, the couple moved to upstate New York and started a Christian community, which featured a theater group, and a record company that specialized in Christian music. Ross subsequently went on to win *Billboard* and Angel Awards and was nominated for two Ace Awards for his work on the *Straight Talk* television show on the Christian Broadcasting Network.

In 1973, Ronnie reformed the Ronettes, this time with newcomers Denise Edwards and Chip Fields. The trio performed that year at a Richard Nader Rock and Roll Revival concert at New York City's Madison Square Garden. A number of solo efforts by Ronnie followed and she continues to perform in 2006.

The Ronettes were elected into the Vocal Group Hall of Fall in 2004 and inducted at a three-day event in Wildwood, New Jersey, the following year. At the induction celebration, Talley performed the group's hit song "Be My Baby," backed by both her daughter and granddaughter, while her mother, who years earlier motivated three young cousins to perfect their singing act, observed proudly from the audience.

Billboard Top 40 Hits by the Ronettes

Date	Pos	Wks on Charts	Record Title	Label/Number
09/14/63	02	10	Be My Baby	Phillies 116
01/11/64	24	06	Baby, I Love You	Phillies 118
05/16/64	39	01	(The Best Part of) Breakin' Up	Phillies 120
07/18/64	34	04	Do I Love You?	Phillies 121
11/21/64	23	07	Walking In the Rain	Phillies 123

Nedra Talley, center is congratulated upon being inducted into the Vocal Group Hall of Fame as a founding member of the legendary Ronettes. With her are current members of the Vandellas, left, Mary Wilson of the Supremes, second from right, and Florence LaRue of the 5th Dimension, far right.

Joe Terranova (Terry)
(Danny and the Juniors)

Flushing, New York   **April 16, 2005**

In 1955, four students from John Bertram High School in Philadelphia, Pennsylvania, joined to form a vocal group called the Juvenaires. Made up of Dave White, Danny Rapp, Joe Terranova (Terry), and Frank Maffei, the teenagers were heard practicing one evening by a producer and neighbor, John Medora, who introduced them to Artie Singer, owner of Singular Records. Singer eventually became the group's manager.

During the group's audition with Singer, one particular tune, a White/Medora original called "Do the Bop," caught his attention. After the Juvenaires recorded that tune along with "Sometimes When I'm Alone," Singer took the single to Dick Clark. At Clark's suggestion, the song was reworked and named "At the Hop." The popular disc jockey felt that while the popularity of "the bop," the dance that the song was based on, was waning, dance hops were thriving. His opinion was correct and soon after its release and a chance appearance by the group on Clark's *American Bandstand* television show, "At the Hop" was released on the

ABC Paramount label. It climbed to the number-one spot on the charts and sold more than two million records worldwide.

Despite having gained significant fame during their heyday, a number of inaccuracies exist in biographies written about the group. Terry dispelled them during the interview and set the record straight.

"In our early days, Frankie Lymon and the Teenagers had an influence on the sound that we tried to develop," Terry said. "They were the sharpest act out there and came out just before we did. That period was the beginning of what I call pop-rock-and-roll because before that rock-and-roll was really underground. I would guess by 1955 it started to go pop. We were also influenced by the harmonies of the Four Lads and the Four Aces. When we put our stuff together, we sort of were a combination of both that pop culture and new pop culture, of course, turning into rock-and-roll."

Some accounts of the group claim that the Juvenaires used to harmonize in front of producer John Madara's house and speculate on whether the location was chosen as blind luck or careful planning on their part. Terry provided the answer.

"Actually we didn't know who John was," he said. "Dave (White) knew him but I wasn't introduced to him at that time. We would pick different corners to sing because we would get chased. After nine o'clock at night the neighbors would say, 'Hey listen, do you think you could move this someplace else?' This guy Eddie Williams had a garage, which was close to John's house, and sometimes we could get in the garage and sometimes we couldn't, so we would go see if we could. This one particular night we couldn't, so we sang outside and he heard us by chance."

Terry recalled Madara's introducing the group to Artie Singer and getting feedback from Dick Clark regarding one of Madara and White's original tunes, "Do the Bop." "Dick Clark liked the song but he mentioned the idea that 'the bop' would be a very quickly moving dance," he said. "Dances would come in and then they would go out of fashion and he said that by the time we got the record released, 'the bop' will be passé. He suggested that we change the name to 'At the Hop,' because record hops looked like they were going to be around for a while. In fact, actually as kids we didn't really know what record hops were. There was only a few of them. They were really just regular dances where kids would go. I guess the hop became popularized along with the record so we were just at the right place, with the right title, at the right time."

In November 1957 "At the Hop" was released and it was credited to Danny and the Juniors. Terry remembered how the name change came about. "We were called the Juvenaires and the record company very wisely in fact explained to us that usually a lead singer would emerge [from a group]. Before us there was the Hilltoppers, and then Jimmy Sacca emerged from that group. There was the Four Aces and Al Alberts emerged from that group. The reason that he knew that is because right when he [Singer] was recording us, Al Alberts was leaving the Four Aces and he was the vocal coach of Freddie Diodati, who replaced Al. That must have been fresh on his mind."

Singer suggested calling the group Danny and the Juniors, a name he considered catchy and one that put the lead singer's name out front. "It was a great idea," Terry said. "After that came Dion and the Belmonts, and one-name artists like Fabian."

Danny and the Juniors' first of nearly fifty appearances on *American Bandstand* occurred when another group couldn't make it. But the longtime belief and documented fact that the group that failed to show was Little Anthony and the Imperials was disproved by Terry.

"We did the local portion, which was most of the show," Terry said. "Dick only went a half-hour national at that time. I remember getting a phone call from our manager and he asked if I could get the guys to get over there for that portion, which I think was in the middle of the show. We got together, ran down and did it, and the phone lights lit up and suddenly we had a national record.

"As for what group didn't show, I thought it was Little Anthony too, but I talked to him about a month ago and he said that it couldn't have been them because they didn't start until after we did."

As a result of their appearance and success on *American Bandstand*, ABC Paramount released "At the Hop" and within a month it topped the charts. But Terry said that the sudden fame didn't faze the group members, primarily because of their age.

"You don't think of it as newfound fame; you don't even think of it as fame at the time," he said. "You're a kid and it was the first venture that we really ever did so it comes at you very fast and it's very hectic and suddenly you're traveling and going and you're caught up in it. There is no time to think about it. You just react."

Off the success of their debut single, the group began to perform on the bills of many shows that featured big-name acts such as Fats Domino, Chuck Berry, Buddy Holly, Jerry Lee Lewis, and the Platters. They gained significant exposure while appearing as part of the famous Alan Freed Big Beat show. But the new style of music did not endear itself to everyone, and when a radio station in St. Louis, Missouri, sponsored a rock-and-roll record-smashing event, Danny and the Juniors became enraged at the action. So much so that White composed what became that style of music's unofficial anthem.

"In actuality, 'Rock and Roll Is Here to Stay' was written sort of as a protest," Terry recalled. "We had just come off a tour and the newspapers didn't treat rock-and-roll artists very fairly back in those days. They'd sort of give you trashy write-ups. It was an Alan Freed tour with Chuck Berry and a ton of really good artists and they'd write it up as 'Rock Comes to Cincinnati and Smells Out the Arena' and things like that.

"We were mentioning that at dinner one night at my house," he continued. "We had some 45's playing in the background and somehow the B-side of one of Little Richard's 45's got on there and it had a line in it, 'Rock-and-roll is here to stay.' It wasn't called that but it just had that one line that he said it. In the middle of the conversation, my father said, 'Did you hear that line, rock-and-roll is here to stay? Why don't you guys write something about that and get your point across?' And that's how it was written."

"Rock and Roll Is Here to Stay" entered the Top 20 and became a staple of AM radio during spring 1958. In July 1958, the group scored another Top 40 hit with "Dottie."

Following a few other releases that failed to gain momentum, White left the group to pursue independent record production. "David was becoming very successful as a writer," Terry said. "He wrote 'One, Two, Three,' and he wrote stuff for the Sherrys, and 'You Don't Own Me' for Leslie Gore, so I presume that maybe the road wasn't for him and he felt that he was more a writer because he wrote most of our songs. He teamed up with John Madara and they put a production company together. The way it affected the group is we just had to change the structures of the harmonies. The way we did that was to keep the harmonies close because now we were three guys and you have a lead singer that was moving around. So wherever he goes, instead of singing a straight second-tenor part or a straight baritone part, one of the other two guys had to move to keep the triad together."

The group went on to sign a recording deal with Swan Records and charted with "Twistin' USA," but the great ability that they displayed singing ballads, especially on a cover of the Heartbeats' "A Thousand Miles Away," didn't seem to get the attention that it deserved. Terry agreed that the group's effort with that style of song was overlooked.

"In those days, in the beginning you could get a two-sided hit like we did with 'Sometimes,'" he said. "Then later on, as the business of rock-and-roll became more of a business, I think record companies saw the buying public different. There were more artists on the scene and they would put out more records and they really didn't have the time to work an artist and say, 'Well, hey look, this B-side is getting a little traction so let's push that a little while we're at it. I think it just became the nature of the business that two-sided hits ended."

In the summer of 1961, Danny and the Juniors recorded a sequel to their debut hit single titled "Back to the Hop." "Dave and I sat down and wrote that song," Terry said. "We were looking for material for our next session and an unfortunate thing happened to us. The record took off like a rocket in California, and Baltimore, Washington, Philadelphia, and about eight major markets. But the business of being in the record company, if you were an ASCAP writer and Dick Clark played your record once, you made three hundred and twenty dollars for that play. If you were a BMI writer, you got a nickel. The guys at Swan that wrote songs for us knew that and they didn't write 'Back to the Hop'; they wrote the other side. So, after two weeks of playing 'Back to the Hop,' even though it was climbing up the charts, they switched the record.

"They weren't sure whether 'Back to the Hop' would be a big hit or not so they just switched the side and made themselves two weeks of money," he added. "In the meantime, 'Back to the Hop' went straight into the toilet."

As was the case for many American recording artists, the British Invasion all but stifled follow-up releases by the group as tastes in music went through radical changes. Terry experienced brief work stints outside the music industry. "When the Beatles came in I worked with the company my dad worked for, for about a year," he said. "I also worked in the catering industry, singing at weddings and things, and did that until we got called to perform at the Academy of Music in New York."

The rock-and-roll revival show at the Academy of Music in 1970 has been cited by many groups that flourished during the late 1950s and early 1960s as having served to revitalize their music and public attention.

In the 1970s Terry and Danny Rapp had an oldies show on WCAM radio in New Jersey. Terry recalled how that project came about. "Jerry Blavat used to be our road manager," he said. "We were talking to him one day about the fact that radio in New York was hot. Even though we were working on Saturdays, the weeks we didn't work we did the show live and the weeks we were working, we taped it. We gave it a shot and it lasted almost a year. Then we got much too busy to do it."

A splintering of Danny and the Juniors occurred during the 1970s, with one lineup led by Rapp and another contingent that included Terry and Maffei continuing to tour the country. Terry explained what had occurred. "Groups are like marriages, and they have fights and when you're on the road like we were at that time with one hundred twenty-five dates a year, you get different ideas how things should be," Terry said. "Danny just decided that he wanted to leave and he went out as Danny first and we went out as the Juniors. We did very well as the Juniors, but he had a tough time being just Danny. He wanted to go on his own like most lead singers do. It was tough to sell that."

The group eventually joined forces after a brief stint apart, but soon parted ways again. "The second time we split he [Rapp] decided he needed to use the whole name," Terry said. "We said, 'If you do, we do too.' He was headstrong in that respect and he wanted to do his own thing. We also wanted to fly and do dates and his flying was nil. He wanted to do what was called a Holiday Inn circuit back then. He would go in a van and do all these local gigs and we would do most of the major shows in the big arenas and television."

Rapp suffered from a series of personal problems, including alcoholism, insecurity, a failed marriage, and a fear of flying, and tragically, he committed suicide in 1983. "Danny was a very quiet guy and kept his personal life really to himself," Terry said. "He would never really say anything, but he drank quiet a bit and the combination of that and he went through a divorce. I think in order to commit suicide like that you have to have a lot of things wrong."

Terry said that he had just spoken to Rapp prior to the tragedy, since they were suing their record company together despite working apart. "He just sounded tired but we all get tired on the road," he said. "I didn't suspect that anything like that would happen."

Another major inaccuracy listed in a few biographies written on Danny and the Juniors cites saxophone player Lenny Baker, a co-founder of the later rock-and-roll group Sha Na Na, as having played in the Juniors band prior to forming his own group.

"Lenny Baker was in a group called Danny and the Juniors out of Boston, Massachusetts," Terry said. "The Joyce Agency, who was booking that group, claimed that they had the rights to the name because that was the last agency that we were with before we decided to disband. He put that group together in Boston, we heard about it, and we sent cease and desist orders because we owned the trademark from 1957. They stopped and then we had to go to Boston and actually work up there a few times so that people would know who we were."

Despite the fact that Baker had no prior association with Danny and the Juniors, his later group, Sha Na Na, and their renditions of some of the Juniors' hit recordings caused resurgence in demand for appearances at oldies shows nationwide.

"It had a phenomenal effect on us," Terry said. "They were the hit of Woodstock and they sang 'At the Hop' and 'Rock and Roll Is Here to Stay.' The success of their show, the fact that they would sing those songs all the time, and they sold a great album called *Rock and Roll Is Here to Stay*, really gave a big resurgence for our group. They are terrific guys. One time a couple of years back we were working at an outdoor casino in a tent and we hired a band that never showed up. The guys in Sha Na Na said, 'Don't worry, we play instruments and we'll back you up.' We went on together and it was phenomenal. They are the nicest guys in the world and it was one of the biggest kicks of my life.

"On the other side, we always worked for Jon Bauman, who is Bowzer from Sha Na Na and is a very close friend of mine and one of my best buddies," Terry added.

In addition to maintaining a busy schedule of concert appearances in 2006, Terry and Maffei host a radio show, appropriately named "Rock and Roll Is Here to Stay," every Monday night on WVLT in New Jersey. Terry has also taken an active role in the awareness and promotion of a public law designed to weed out bogus lineups that represent themselves as original rock-and-roll acts. The legislation, titled Truth in Music, is strongly supported by, among others, Bauman, Mary Wilson of the Supremes, and Carl Gardiner of the Coasters.

Several states have already passed the bill and efforts continue to see it passed in all fifty states.

Billboard Top 40 Hits by Danny and the Juniors

Date	Pos	Wks on Charts	Record Title	Label/Number
12/09/57	01	18	At the Hop	ABC-Para 9871
03/10/58	19	07	Rock and Roll Is Here to Stay	ABC-Para 9888
07/21/58	39	01	Dottie	ABC-Para 9926
10/10/60	27	03	Twistin' USA	Swan 4060

Charlie Thomas
(The Crowns/The Drifters)

Harrison, New York   **March 19, 2005**

If ever a wish were granted to a group of young and locally popular singers from the streets of Harlem, New York, then that must have been the case with the Crowns. While revered in Harlem as a vocal group that boasted tight harmonies and a smooth sound, the success of their hit singles was limited to the New York area.

But during a 1958 engagement at the Apollo Theater, one brief but earth-shattering discussion between two managers, their own and one of another group appearing on that show's bill, resulted in the Crowns instantaneously transforming into the legendary Drifters.

Founded in the early 1950s and originally named the Five Crowns, the group was managed by Lover Patterson, who also handled the famous Cadillacs. Signed to a recording contract with Rainbow Records in 1952, the quintet, which was made up of Wilbur Paul, Dock Green, James Clarks, John Clark, and Claudie Clark, debuted a single, "You're My Inspiration," that became a number-nine *Cashbox* chart hit in New York.

The group followed with three releases on Rainbow, but each failed to generate attention. Despite that fact, "Why Don't You Believe Me" is still considered by die-hard doo-wop fans as representative of their finest work. Moving to the Old Town label, the group continued to struggle for recognition on the record charts.

In 1955, Green reformed the Five Crowns with a new lineup, but after releasing two failed singles, yet another aggregation was born, this one made up of Green, James Clark, and newcomers Elsbeary Hobbs, Charlie Thomas, and Benjamin Nelson, who would eventually record under the name Ben E. King.

Thomas explained how, in the mid-1950s, he came to join the revamped lineup of the Five Crowns. "We were all from the neighborhood and brought up together," he said. "The Harptones and the Five Crowns used to be very close back at the age of fifteen years old and we ran together at a little fish-and-chips joint. Benny [Nelson/King]'s father used to have a store and he sold hot dogs and that's how I met Benny, by going there."

Lover Patterson lived across the street from the elder Nelson's store. "He wanted to get the Five Crowns together and every weekend he'd take some guys out to do the Five Crowns songs," Thomas said. "We used to go with him and sing tunes like 'You Came to Me" and 'A Star.' I was so glad because I didn't have a job and the little seventy-five cents that Lover Patterson used to give us for being the Five Crowns was a joy to have."

In late 1958, during an appearance at Harlem's Apollo Theater, the Crowns were faced with an opportunity of such great proportion that it was almost inconceivable to them. George Treadwell had managed the legendary rhythm and blues vocal group the Drifters since 1954. Originally boasting the talented Clyde McPhatter as its lead singer, the group, despite achieving national hits and star status in the music industry, had fallen into disarray. Plagued by in-fighting and a huge dissatisfaction with Treadwell's ultimate control over both their fame and limited fortunes, the group began to challenge their manager for well-deserved pay hikes. When he wouldn't budge on the subject, dissention grew within the group.

Facing a major contractual obligation with the Drifters and weary of the constant and ever-growing protests of Drifters' members, on May 30, 1958, Treadwell visited the Crowns dressing room after hearing them perform and being impressed with their sound. First discussing his plight with Patterson and then with the group itself, he offered the youngsters what must have seemed like the opportunity of a lifetime;

that being the chance to immediately transform themselves from the Crowns to the legendary Drifters.

Thomas reflected back on that evening. "The Five Crowns were on the amateur show at the Apollo and we won," he said. "We sang 'Never Walk Alone' and it won the crowd. Who ever won the contest would stay there for two weeks and appear with the superstar that was coming in the next week. We were fortunate to be there with the Drifters, Ray Charles, Little Willie John, and the Duke Ellington Band.

"One night Mr. Shipman [owner of the Apollo] came into our room with George Treadwell and he said that he wanted us to become the Drifters," he continued. "I told him that we couldn't become the Drifters, they were right outside. But he [Treadwell] told us that he had to let them go because they were drinking a lot of whiskey and they had a lot of contracts and he didn't want to send them across the globe. They turned us into the Drifters right there."

Upon reaching an agreement, the existing Drifters were fired, and the members of the Crowns saw each of their individual contracts sold to Treadwell. Under terms of the agreement, the new Drifters lineup performed at a number of gigs, restricted to singing all the old hits that McPhatter and company had recorded earlier. A certain pall of awkwardness followed the group, with each audience being fully aware that the five singers before them were not the same artists that had recorded the songs being performed.

Following Atlantic Records' release of a Drifters album comprised entirely of material that was recorded by the original lineup between 1955 and 1958, the label decided to take a chance on the new group. On March 6, 1959, under the guidance of producers Jerry Leiber and Mike Stoller, the quintet entered the recording studio manned with an original Nelson tune, "There Goes My Baby," and laid down tracks for their first session as the Drifters.

While Thomas had handled singing lead beautifully up to that time, a case of microphone fright prompted the label's executives to enlist Nelson to handle lead vocals on the recording.

"I got shook up when we got in the studio and they put Benny in to sing lead on the song," Thomas said. "But they used my voice and Benny's voice, pieced it up and came up with 'There Goes My Baby.' Benny wrote that song and it was beautiful. I was looking to make a whole lot of money; I mean millions and trillions. I was broke and had no money. My mother gave me five hundred dollars to buy a cab and I was out there driving just to keep myself up. They gave Benny fifty dollars for that song.

"That was a whole lot of money to Benny too because we were young and didn't know the business," he said. "Lover Patterson knew the business. George Treadwell knew the business. That was the problem. They knew too much and we didn't know anything."

"There Goes My Baby," with its elaborate production that included overlaying Latin percussion and full string section, baffled some people at the label, as it was the first of its kind in the rhythm and blues genre. So mystified were the company executives that producer Jerry Wexler described the sound as being akin to picking up two different radio stations simultaneously.

Despite the concern, when the single was released it climbed quickly to the number-two slot and crossed over to the pop charts, capturing significant rave reviews from both black and white audiences. While Clyde McPhatter was a major force in the music industry, his work with the original Drifters, while popular with the rhythm and blues audience, failed to ever cross over into the mainstream music marketplace. The new Drifters changed that and through the years scored sixteen Top 40 hit recordings between 1959 and 1964.

Their debut single also became the first for any Drifters contingent to get airplay in Europe. "We broke the sound barrier and changed everything around with the violin strings," Thomas recalled.

The Drifters benefited by having the opportunity to work with Leiber and Stoller, the hottest songwriting and production team in the industry. Thomas recalled working with the dynamic pair.

"They were some weird dudes," Thomas laughed. "One used to come in the room wearing one sneaker and one sandal, but that was flower child days. Right now when I see them I just look at them and laugh. They still love me and I love them."

At the time, a casual observer would most certainly assume that life was good for the new Drifters. However, in reality the very same issues that resulted in turmoil and dissent with members of the original Drifters began to cause similar effects with the present version.

Upon the Drifters' formation, McPhatter organized the group under the auspices of his own business entity, called Drifters Incorporated. His motivation to form the business was to guarantee that he would reap a share of the group's earnings, something that eluded him when he was with his previous group, the Dominos. McPhatter split the business on an equal basis with the Drifters' manager, George Treadwell, but upon his departure to embark on a solo career his interest was sold to Treadwell and not to the other group members.

The new arrangement, in effect, resulted in Treadwell securing full ownership of the five-member lineup, whoever it might consist of. For the group members, original or otherwise, they became merely paid employees of the corporation, and reaped a weekly salary regardless of the amount of performances or appearances they engaged in. From all accounts, that salary was a paltry sum compared to the appearance fees that the corporation, or basically Treadwell, took in.

Since no member got a share of royalties gained from record sales, received no extra stipend from multi-show performance schedules, and retained no right whatsoever to use the Drifters name upon departure from the group, the recipe for disaster was obvious.

Thomas recalled the financial and corporate arrangement that the Drifters operated under, the same one that caused the demise of the original lineup, and in effect doomed the group to a revolving-door cast of members through the years.

"We were getting one hundred seventy-five dollars a week and she [Faye Treadwell] was pocketing all the money," he said. "All the scandal that came out of that hurt a wonderful name like the Drifters, but it's still puffing on and I'm going to see that it keeps on."

Nelson was the first to display disenchantment with the arrangement. Working countless shows over many miles, sometimes six days a week for months on end, he found it impossible to live on the salary that Treadwell paid each member. Eventually approaching Treadwell for a raise and being turned down, Nelson left the group.

A sticky situation came to light at that time when Patterson produced a separate contract that he had with Nelson as a solo artist, one that was sealed prior to Treadwell's offer to the Crowns. After fragile negotiations, a deal was struck that called for Nelson to record as a solo artist on Atlantic's subsidiary label, Atco, while also recording with the Drifters until a replacement could be found.

Ironically, the agreement resulted in Nelson's voice being featured on many of the group's classic hit records, such as "Dance With Me," "This Magic Moment," "I Count the Tears," and "Save the Last Dance For Me." By the time he was replaced in the group in spring 1960, Nelson had assumed a new stage name, Ben E. King, and began his solo career.

Following King's departure, and the subsequent quick exit of his replacement, Johnny Williams, the group recruited Rudy Lewis, who had sung with the Clara Ward Singers. Lewis would lead the Drifters on classic recordings like "Some Kind of Wonderful," "Up on the Roof," and "On Broadway."

By 1963, with Leiber and Stoller dedicating their energies into their newly formed Red Bird label, the Drifters began an association with producer Bert Berns. With him they recorded "Vaya Con Dios," a single that experienced moderate success. The following year the songwriting team of Art Resnick and Kenny Young presented the group with "Under the Boardwalk." But a May 1964 recording session for the tune experienced a crisis when Lewis was found dead in his apartment just hours before.

Second tenor Johnny Moore, who was in his second go-around with the Drifters at the time, was called into action and created magic as the single soared to number four on the charts.

When the British Invasion took over the airwaves and many American artists struggled to adapt to the changing sound, Thomas said that the Drifters remained true to their established sound and continued to prosper.

"When the Beatles came to the States, everybody thought that the Drifters would change their style," he said. "The Drifters were just as hot as the Beatles when they started, but somehow the Beatles got all the money and the Drifters got nothing. But it was their time in those days but we did not change at all. We just kept putting out what we did with Atlantic Records. Thanks to Leiber and Stoller, Carole King, Burt Bacharach, [and] Dionne Warwick and the Warwick Singers sticking with us, it made my career during that time worthwhile."

In later years, especially after Treadwell passed away in 1967, the Drifters became the center of much controversy as multiple lineups— many with no credible link to either the original or the later lineup— began to perform as the legitimate group. Lawsuits and allegations somewhat clouded the actual history of the Drifters during the 1970s. At the time, founding member Bill Pinkney toured with his Original Drifters, Thomas continued to lead a lineup, and Johnny Moore maintained ties to Treadwell's widow, Faye, the latter lineup eventually moving to England.

"When George Treadwell replaced Bill Pinkney in the Drifters, he couldn't replace him as a man," Thomas said. "He [Pinkney] did what he did with the Drifters. As for a lot of the others, you can't stop people from singing music. I don't think it's wrong for them to sing the music but to accept the money and say that they are truly the Drifters is wrong."

With the death of Moore in the 1990s, Thomas and Pinkney continue to lead their own lineups at shows nationwide. Aside from these two artists, both with direct and established ties to the Drifters legacy, and despite countless trademark lawsuits that continue to be filed, numerous bogus lineups find steady work performing as the Drifters right into 2006.

Now relocated in the nation's capital, Thomas continues to lead the Drifters at a number of oldies shows. "I have always been on the move, keeping my career alive even though many of the Drifters were starting to fade apart," he said. "Guys were passing on, like Barry Hobbs, Dock Green, and Rudy Lewis, and they were my friends. I was starting to feel lonely and had to take some time to collect myself and let me know that I was still here to keep it all going."

Thomas said that the Drifters bond is still strong as he continues to maintain regular contact with King and Pinkney, as well as with the families of Lewis, Hobbs, and Moore. A man with deep-rooted religious beliefs, Thomas is a proud man; proud of the legacy that he was fortunate to have been a part of.

"I am most proud of being a Drifter," he said. "I don't need too much. I just want to know that I did what I had to do and it was right. Sometimes in my church I feel guilt because I sing rock-and-roll. But my minister says, 'You gotta eat.' I would like to be remembered as being just one of the giants of rock-and-roll; just one of them!"

At a January 2006 oldies show in Uncasville, Connecticut, produced by Jon Bauman, former front man of Sha Na Na, Pinkney and Thomas made a rare joint appearance to perform together. The two artists represented the original and later versions of the Treadwell Drifters and were the recipients of a thunderous audience response upon performing their respective hit songs.

Billboard *Top 40* Hits by the Drifters

Date	Pos	Wks on Charts	Record Title	Label/Number
06/29/59	02	14	There Goes My Baby	Atlantic 2040
11/02/59	15	09	Dance With Me/	
11/23/59	33	05	True Love, True Love	Atlantic 2040
03/14/60	16	06	This Magic Moment	Atlantic 2050
09/19/60	01	14	Save the Last Dance for Me	Atlantic 2071
12/31/60	17	07	I Count the Tears	Atlantic 2087
04/10/61	32	06	Some Kind of Wonderful	Atlantic 2096
06/26/61	14	08	Please Stay	Atlantic 2105
09/25/61	16	09	Sweets for My Sweet	Atlantic 2117
03/24/62	28	04	When My Little Girl Is Smiling	Atlantic 2134
12/29/62	05	11	Up On the Roof	Atlantic 2162
04/06/63	09	08	On Broadway	Atlantic 2182
10/05/63	25	05	I'll Take You Home	Atlantic 2201
07/11/64	04	12	Under the Boardwalk	Atlantic 2237
10/10/64	33	05	I've Got Sand in My Shoes	Atlantic 2253
11/28/64	18	07	Saturday Night at the Movies	Atlantic 2260

Jay Traynor
(The Mystics—Jay and the Americans)

Albany, New York   **June 17, 2005**

Like many teenagers of the late 1950s, Jay Traynor was attracted to rock-and-roll record hops. While attending one such show at his high school in upstate New York, Traynor was so impressed with the acts that performed that he became motivated to seek a spot for himself in the music industry.

"Although I liked rock-and-roll, I didn't sing or perform prior to attending one particular show at Greenville High School," he said. "A group called the Fidelities came to our school with a disc jockey and performed a song, 'These Are the Things We Love,' and it inspired me to sing. I had moved up there from Brooklyn when I was three years old. It was that performance that motivated me to get into music."

His journey began when he visited popular WABY Albany, New York, disc jockey Pete Barry, who had accompanied one of the groups that performed at the school show. "I went up to his station and tried a few things, talked, and became friendly, but nothing really came of

313

it," he said. "I really don't think that he had the ability to make anything happen. It seemed like it did because I was a young kid."

While little came from the contact with Barry, Traynor's determination never waned. Moving to Mineola, Long Island, in 1959, Traynor began to sing with a friend's vocal group in Queens. The pair had met during a summer employment stint in upstate New York.

"I was working at a place called World Top Acres in Greenville, New York," Traynor recalled. "It was like a resort and people would come up during the summertime. I met this one young guy named Gene McMann and he had a group back in Queens. When I moved to Mineola I went to see them, they liked the way I sang and I started to sing with them."

The group, which was named the Ab Tones, used to practice at different members' homes and after a while ventured into the New York City subway system. Long known for its ability to project a pleasing acoustic sound, given the subway's tiled walls, it was a favorite rehearsal spot for many groups. Besides, Traynor recalled, when a train pulled into a station and deposited a significant number of passengers, the group had an instant audience.

After the group had performed at a few record hops, an acquaintance of theirs got an audition with Mickey and Sylvia, who, besides singing ("Love Is Strange"), owned a production company and recorded other acts. "We went to Manhattan to their apartment on the West Side and sang for them but nothing came out of that," he said. "I remember that we sounded pretty good too. We were definitely a subway doo-wop group and sang a cappella."

After parting ways with the Ab Tones, Traynor moved to Brooklyn to live with his grandparents in Brooklyn and one day made a trip to meet with Jim Gribble, manager of a number of other vocal groups.

"When I moved to Mineola I met a guy there who knew folks at Jim's office and he sent me there," he said. "I was a wide-eyed kid, not knowing anything. If you could sing a song, Jim took you into his stable. He had tons of singers in his stable and part of it was the groups the Passions and the Mystics. Paul Simon was in the office all the time and Artie Kornfeld too, guys who later on became famous for their work. I didn't have a deal or anything. I just kind of hung out there with other singers in the office."

After journeying up to Gribble's office time and time again and failing to generate any foreseeable prospects, Traynor began to get frustrated. But one day he learned that the Mystics were searching for a lead singer to replace Phil Cracolici, who was leaving the group. The Mystics had already scored a popular hit single with "Hushabye."

A quintet from Brooklyn originally named the Overons, the Mystics consisted of Bob Ferrante, Al Contrera, George Galfo, and the Cracolici brothers, Al and Phil. When he heard about an audition to find a replacement lead singer for the group, Traynor participated. Given that he lived in Bayridge, near the Mystics' Bensonhurst neighborhood, he somewhat resembled departing member Phil Cracolici, knew all of the group's songs, and possessed a strong vocal range; he was selected to join the group. He was the last of fifteen vocalists to audition.

"As a young kid I was very, very excited and the way it happened was very strange," Traynor said. "I had been going to Jim's office day after day and I was getting disgusted. I remember walking down Broadway one day and saying to myself that I wasn't going to visit the office anymore. Then I decided that I would go in one more time. I walked into the office and there were all these guys in there. Artie Kornfeld was sitting on the couch and he was the next to last guy going in and he told me that they were auditioning for the Mystics. After Artie went in, I got to audition.

"I knew all of the Mystics' songs because they were always there in the office," he continued. "Strangely enough I had just moved to the Bayridge section of Brooklyn, which is near to where they lived in Bensonhurst. I was the right height to fit into Phil's suits and sang well and it all worked out."

On May 11, 1960, the Mystics went to RCA Studios with Traynor on lead and recorded "White Cliffs of Dover", "Blue Star" and "Over the Rainbow." An Alan Freed tour followed with other featured artists on a bill that included Freddy Cannon, Teddy Randazo, and Bobby Freeman.

As a new member of the Mystics, Traynor described feeling elated about performing at a number of shows with the group. "The first show was in New Jersey and I was scared out of my mind driving there in the car," he said. "I was trying to remember all the lyrics and what to do. Actually they were all very good to me. I remember messing up the lyrics on one song out of five or six and I felt awful about that, but they said not to worry about it.

"I also remember doing the last thing that Alan Freed ever did: the East Coast Tour," he added. "That was a great bill, with the Orioles, Teddy Randazzo, and the Blue Bells. I really didn't get to know Alan Freed but he was always sitting in the front of the bus and standing off to the side of the stage while we performed."

Traynor's future with the Mystics looked promising, that is, until one fateful day when a misunderstanding terminated his tenure with the group. Excited about being a member of the Mystics, Traynor readily agreed to get a friend a signed photo of the group. In an effort to make good on the promise he visited Gribble's office to secure a photo but the manager wasn't there.

"A friend of mine wanted a picture of the Mystics and I went into the office to get one for him," he recalled. "Another guy was in there and told me that there was probably a picture in Jim's desk and to get one. I'm a kid from the country and not one to go stealing things. I went into Jim's desk drawer to try to find one and he walked in and kicked me out. I got really scared and the truth is I don't really know whether he told the other Mystics to get another singer, but I was done with them."

An enraged Gribble threw Traynor out of his office, and out of the Mystics. Shortly afterward, Traynor received a call from Sandy Yaguda, who together with another aspiring singer, Kenny Rosenberg (Vance), heard that he was no longer with the Mystics and asked if he wanted to form a group with them. The trio had met during one of Traynor's gigs with the Mystics. He jumped at the offer to join them.

"The Mystics did a Clay Cole show in downtown Manhattan and the Harbor Lites were on that show," he said. "We said hello and exchanged phone numbers. Somehow, they knew I wasn't in the Mystics anymore, contacted me, and we got together at Sandy's house."

A friend of Yaguda's, Howie Kirschenbaum (Kane), became the fourth vocalist in the group and when an acquaintance of Vance's, Terry Philips, who was a producer and writer, offered to help the new group, they recorded a demo of the Five Keys tune "Wisdom of a Fool." Philips arranged for the group to meet the songwriting and production team of Jerry Leiber and Mike Stoller.

"Kenny Vance had a friend named Terry Philips, who produced children's records," he said. "He was trying to cross over into more pop stuff and got himself associated with Leiber and Stoller. Kenny told Terry that we had a singing group and we auditioned for him and then Leiber and Stoller told him to make some demos of us. We did it and they liked what they heard."

While Traynor disputed various accounts that claim the group got into an argument with Leiber and Stoller during their initial meeting, he recalled that the duo did seem to cool on the idea of signing the group.

"There was never an argument but they somehow had a change of heart," Traynor said. "I think they listened back and figured that they'd had a lot of success with a lot of black artists like the Drifters and the Coasters and writing crazy songs, and they had second thoughts about us. Looking back, we weren't really a doo-wop group; we were more like the first boy band, something like the Backstreet Boys.

"God bless Kenny; he went back to them and I don't think he said anything in any harsh tones, but he appealed to them and they said okay," he added.

Since Leiber and Stoller were well known for working with acts such as the Coasters and, as such, were into spoof names and recordings, the pair suggested naming the new group Binky Jones and the Americans. If it weren't for significant pushback from the group's members, that name could have stuck.

"Terry came to Sandy's house one day, gave us the contracts and said that they were going to call us the Americans," Traynor recalled. "We liked that. We went back to the office and were rehearsing for our first recording, 'Tonight' from *West Side Story*, and they all of a sudden said that they were going to call us Binky Jones and the Americans. We were flabbergasted. I suggested that we use my nickname, Jay, and they agreed. I didn't want to be Binky Jones for the rest of my life. They used to come up with crazy things."

Many entertainers interviewed for this book cited one huge sore point of misinformation that has followed them throughout life. Traynor is no exception and readily sought to set the record straight.

"A number of years ago on *Entertainment Tonight*, John Tesh announced that there was a lawsuit between Jay Traynor and Jay Black," Traynor said. "He went on to say that it was a really funny thing that neither one of them is really named Jay; one is named David and the other one is John. Well, yes, my name is John legally but my grandfather nicknamed me Jay and I've been Jay all of my life. There was no other reason for the name in the group to be Jay, because that's my nickname."

Upon its release, "Tonight" became a popular single in New York and sold forty thousand copies. "We went into the office one day to work on that song," he said. "I was a country boy and hadn't even heard of *West Side Story* but Sandy and the guys had seen it. They played the song for me and I started singing it right off the top of my head, from what I was hearing from them. That's why I never really sang the song exactly like the Broadway show tune. I sang it a little bit different and from the way I did it they developed the rhythm that we used."

The group's follow-up single, a tune named "Dawning," stalled upon its release. But six months later, as a result of a disc jockey on the West Coast who flipped over the record and embraced the B-side, "She Cried" climbed the charts and became the groups' first hit single. Traynor recalled the experience.

"'Dawning' came out and Cousin Brucie in New York jumped on it and we thought it was going to take off," he said. "But it didn't do much in other cities and started to die in New York too. I heard that some disc jockey in San Francisco liked the song ['She Cried'] so much that he locked himself in the studio and just kept playing the song. It went number one in every city in the United States. But because it started in San Francisco and slowly came across the country, by the time it hit number one in New York City it was dying off the charts in California. It never got that big push but moved slowly throughout the country. So while it hit number one at every station in the country, it only went to number four in *Cashbox* and number five in *Billboard*."

When they cut "She Cried," Jay and the Americans guitarist Marty Sanders was asked to sing on the recording, and from that time on the group was a quintet.

With a hit on their hands, demands on the group to travel and perform mounted. Traynor reflected on that time period. "I was working at a bank to keep going and I had to quit the job because we were getting a lot of bookings at the time," he said. "We were working pretty good at first but because we didn't have a follow-up hit, things changed and I had to get out there and make a living."

As for accounts that state Traynor began to miss rehearsals and seriously contemplated going solo at the time, he said that was partly true. "One of the reasons that I remember leaving the group is the discouragement I felt over not having follow-up hits, and having to get a job and work at the same time.

"I do remember going up to Leiber and Stoller's office to talk about what was going on," he added. "I think at the time, because of the discouragement and having to work and earn a living, I said that I wanted to leave the group. I got into a little bit of a fight with Sandy and it almost became a little bit of fisticuffs. No one threw punches but Howie came in and stopped it."

Traynor secured a job as a mail boy at Warner Brothers Music, which published standards, Broadway show tunes, and folk music. "All during that time I worked with Bob Dylan and Peter, Paul, and Mary, and artists like that," he said.

"At the time, Jeff Barry and Ellie Greenwich were working at Leiber and Stoller's office, writing tunes and doing some production for them," he said. "They approached me after I left the group and said that Phil

Spector wanted to work with me. I was supposed to be the only white artist on the Christmas album. I rehearsed 'Little Drummer Boy' in a Phil Spector style, but at the time Phil was looking to move to Los Angeles. The draft was on my back and I had to enlist in the Marine Corps Reserves because I didn't want to get drafted. By the time I got out six months later, he was on the West Coast and it never came to be."

Traynor eventually signed with Coral Records as a solo artist. "I had a couple of records that came out as just Jay," he said. "I also had another stint recording wise with Don Costa Productions, but nothing big."

In need of a replacement for Traynor, Sanders told the group about a friend that had sung with him in high school, David Blatt (Jay Black). Following an audition in which he sang "Cara Mia," he joined as the new Jay, recorded "Only in America," and the rest is history.

Traynor subsequently traveled the country behind the scenes as a road tour manager for the rock band Mountain. Tiring of the road, he moved back to Albany, New York, and took a job at an NBC television affiliate doing lighting, studio camera assignments, and graphic arts. He maintained his work in music by forming a group called Friends, performing what he described as an Al Jarreau style of music. When he heard a local big band on the radio, he called its leader and, as luck would have it, he was looking for a singer. Traynor assumed that role in the Joey Thomas Big Band and secured a weekly radio show on public broadcasting.

As for having any regrets about leaving Jay and the Americans, Traynor explained his feelings. "I look back on it and I really don't know what would have happened if I would have stayed," he said. "Maybe those songs wouldn't have made it and maybe we wouldn't have done those songs. Part of me says whatever happened, let it be, and another part of me says, 'Gee, I wish I would have stayed.' And now I see from the other guys that they kind of wish I had stayed."

Traynor reunited to perform with the original lineup of Jay and the Americans when the group was inducted into the Vocal Group Hall of Fame in 2002. In early 2006 he joined Jay Siegel and the Tokens and is currently appearing at oldies shows as a member of that group.

Billboard Top 40 Hits by Jay and the Americans

Date	Pos	Wks on Charts	Record Title	Label/Number
04/07/62	05	11	She Cried	United Art. 415

Milt Trenier
(The Treniers)

Wildwood, New Jersey   **October 15, 2005**

Some accounts cite the Treniers as rock-and-roll's first self-contained group. Twin brothers Claude and Cliff Trenier had natural musical talent, a fact that took precedence over class studies when the pair attended Alabama State College.

Born in Mobile, Alabama, the twins connected with college classmates Don Hill, who played saxophone, and pianist Gene Gilbeaux to entertain, and when Claude took over leadership of the Alabama State Collegians Orchestra, Cliff assumed the role of romantic balladeer in the group. After leaving school and a subsequent stint in the military during World War II, Claude began to perform with the Jimmie Lunceford Orchestra, recruiting Cliff to sing on a recording of "Buzz Buzz Buzz."

Eventually, the Trenier brothers, Gilbeaux, and Hill formed a series of groups, performing as the Gene Gilbeaux Orchestra, the Trenier Twins, the Rockin' Rollin' Treniers, and finally the Treniers. The act became known for its stage antics as much as for its rich musical renditions. During the early 1950s, with the addition of older brother, Buddy, and younger brother, Milt, the Treniers signed a recording contract with the Okeh label and started to churn out a series of explosive and pioneering rock-and-roll sides.

Having recorded fan favorites that include "Hadacol, That's All," "Poon Tang," and "Day Old Bread and Canned Beans," 1951's "Go Go Go" climbed the charts and became a Top 10 hit for the group.

Milt Trenier was the tenth child born to the family and grew up in a household that relished music. "I had seven brothers and two sisters and all of the brothers that came before me were musically inclined," he said. "Also, my father played the French horn in the number-one marching band in Mobile, which started the Mardi Gras before New Orleans had it. My mother was a school teacher and also taught piano. But most of my brothers began to sing."

While Milt's eldest brother, Denny, was the first to delve into singing, first in Mobile and then in Milwaukee, Wisconsin, it was his twin brothers, Cliff and Claude, that really got the ball rolling in the family during the 1940s. By 1949, the brothers were known as the Rockin' Rollin' Treniers.

"I came along a little later on, but that started at a club in Chicago called the Blue Note," he said. "The guy there told my brothers that they played a different kind of music and he needed to put their names on the marquee. He asked them what style music they played and they told him 'a little bit of everything.' 'Well, it sounds like you guys are the rockin' and rollin' Treniers,' and he put that on the sign."

Most of the group's early work was a mix of blues and ballads. Trenier recalled how the group developed their music. "I joined the group in April 1953 and they had already been performing," he said. "They kind of got their rhythm from a combination of the Jimmy Lunceford Swing Band and Louie Jordan and put their own touch of swing. That's how they started the feel that they got."

With the addition of Buddy and Milt, the group turned out recordings such as "Rockin' Is Our Business" and "It Rocks, It Rolls, It Swings." The Treniers quickly attracted enthusiastic and appreciative audiences who were dazzled by the group's acrobatic and perfectly synchronized dance routines, burlesque comedy, and other stunts on stage. "Believe it or not, there were a lot of people that gave us basic ideas," Milt Trenier said. "The Clark Brothers and the Step Brothers and other guys that were dancers gave the group ideas. But a lot of it was just whatever came to us at the time. If it worked we'd leave it in."

The group also became known for performing several controversial songs that addressed topics ranging from overindulgence with drink to date rape, which in reality was how a genteel society viewed the new raucous style of music called rock-and-roll.

The Treniers soon began to make regular appearances on some of early television's most popular shows. In 1954, they performed on the *Colgate Comedy Hour* with Dean Martin and Jerry Lewis. "Jerry Lewis had seen us before on the *Ed Sullivan* and *Jackie Gleason* shows," Trenier recalled. "He saw one bit that we did called the Bug Dance where my brother Claude would throw the bug over to Cliff and Cliff would throw it to somebody else. Jerry said, 'I'd like to do that bit with you guys. Would you do it on my show?' We did 'Rockin's Our Business' and we threw the bug to him and he loved that because he could dance and do his antics with it."

The Treniers and Lewis developed a fast bond with each other during that show, one that saw Lewis join them as a drummer during their performance. "That was live in those days and they had a little more than a minute left at the end of the show," he said. "Dean Martin wanted to do another song and Jerry said that there wasn't enough time for another song. We started playing and the director was signaling that we needed to fill more time. All of a sudden, Jerry was looking at the clock and jumped onto the drums and started playing. The Treniers spontaneously started chanting 'Palmolive Soap' over and over and we just improvised. I remember after that show Jerry Lewis just fell out and they took him out on a stretcher. He was just exhausted."

Trenier reflected on what impact his group might have had on other groups that followed, specifically those that were defined by their tight dance routines and slick stage presence. "I think a number of them were influenced by what we did," he said. "We were moving. When you were on television you couldn't just stand there and sing. They wanted to see what was happening. That's why television picked up on the Treniers right away, and I think that every group that got together after that, regardless of how good they were singing, someone put some choreography together for them."

In addition to the *Colgate Comedy Hour*, the Treniers appeared on the *Red Skelton, Paul Whiteman*, and *Steve Allen* shows. The exposure from those shows, given the group's visual act, proved to greatly bolster their popularity.

"The first network television show that we did was the *Jackie Gleason Show*," he recalled. "We were in New York and it happened that Jackie Gleason wasn't happy about his show going a little flat. He wanted something exiting and began to call agents all over New York and got in touch with our manager. He told Gleason that he had two groups in town, Louie Jordan and the Treniers, and Jackie told him to get us. We were all spread out over New York and I had to go in and out of different places trying to find everybody.

"By the time for us to go on camera, my brother Claude didn't even know we were going to be on network television," he continued. "We left a note for him at his hotel room and we were just about to go on, with me taking Claude's place, and he walked on stage about two minutes before the curtain opened. For some reason everything fell into place, we broke up the joint, and Jackie Gleason said that he wanted to have us on again."

The Treniers appeared in the feature-length motion picture *Don't Knock the Rock*, which also starred Billy Haley and the Comets, Little Richard, and disc jockey Alan Freed, for whom the group recorded an original tune that became his theme song.

Haley marveled at the Treniers' performance in *Don't Knock the Rock*, one that featured a spirited, hand-clapping, finger-snapping version of their song "Rockin' On Saturday Night," but he first saw them perform at an appearance in Wildwood, New Jersey. While the Treniers performed at the Riptide Club, Haley and his country band, the Saddlemen, were appearing across the street. The budding superstar, later to be dubbed "the father of rock-and-roll," used to frequently attend the Treniers' performances.

"He [Haley] kind of combined what the Treniers were doing and put a little rock into it and developed what they called rockabilly," Trenier said. "He'd sit out there with his guys and watch the show. At that time he wrote a song for my brother Claude called 'Rock-a-Beatin' Boogie.'"

Haley was once quoted as saying that the Treniers' *Go Go Go: The Treniers on TV* album actually inspired Alan Freed to coin a new style of music: rock-and-roll. "When Alan Freed had a radio show in Cleveland, my brothers were over there working for him," Trenier said. "He eventually had us in his movie *Don't Knock the Rock* and when he introduced us he said, 'The greatest rock-and-roll singers, the Treniers.'"

Besides *Don't Knock the Rock*, the Treniers appeared in *The Girl Can't Help It* and *Calypso Heat Wave*. The group enjoyed performing with many of the top acts of the day in those films. "We were in one movie, *Jukebox Rhythm*, too, with Jack Jones," he said. "We didn't get too involved with the making of the movies but a few times we were flying from Las Vegas to Los Angeles to do them. We'd get off at four or five o'clock in the morning and fly over to do the movie. We were very happy to get that kind of exposure."

By the end of the decade, rock-and-roll was being portrayed as an evil force by conservatives throughout the country. As one scandal after another surfaced and was highly publicized by opponents of the style of music, artists found themselves in the middle of controversy. Even Freed, who had promoted rock-and-roll more than anyone had, succumbed to the scandal of payola, a charge that ultimately ended his career.

The Treniers found themselves in a whirlwind of turmoil during a concert tour of England with Jerry Lee Lewis. It was on that fateful tour that Lewis self-destructed upon going public with his marriage to his teenage cousin.

The Treniers shifted gears and began to perform extensively at Las Vegas venues, bringing the house down with their exciting stage presence. In 1959, Milt Trenier made a decision to leave the group and embark on a solo career. "It was a combination of things that motivated me to do that," he said. "One was the style and the other thing sounds hokey but it isn't. All my life, my brothers had been taking care of the family. The twins were making money and every week they were sending my mother and father money to help them out. I figured that if maybe I could get something going, when they get to the point where they can't do it anymore I could help Mama out."

When he received a call inquiring whether he'd like to attempt a solo act at Brown's Hotel in the Catskill Mountains of upstate New York, he was wary, having performed exclusively with his brothers to that point. But when the siblings assured him that his spot in the group would always be there for him, he decided to take a chance.

"After about two weeks up in the Catskills I was so depressed," he recalled. "I was used to being with a swinging group, and all of a sudden I was up there by myself with a house band. I was doing a lot of standards. There was a comic up there that encouraged me to stay with it, and before long people started applauding and standing and I felt so good. From there, I started getting one job after another."

In 1977, Trenier opened a nightclub in Chicago, Illinois, called Milt Trenier's Lounge. It featured many great jazz and rhythm and blues artists. "I'd been traveling around and just closed in Pompano Beach, Florida, when I met my wife," he said. "She came from Chicago and said that we should try to look for a place local so that I wouldn't have to spend a week here and a week there. That way we could have a home in one place. We found a nightclub on Lakeshore Drive and opened up in 1977."

After seven years, he moved the club to various other locations in the city. But running the business while simultaneously performing proved to be an unsettling challenge for him and he eventually gave it up.

Still wanting to perform, he secured an open run at Yvettes Club on State Street. At seventy-six, he continues to work in the industry that he considers a labor of love to this day.

The group continued to perform to rave reviews even after founding member Cliff passed away in 1983. Milt Trenier continues to reside in Chicago.

Kenny Vance
(Jay and the Americans/Kenny Vance and the Planotones)

Flushing, New York   **October 22, 2005**

In 1959, Kenny Rosenberg (Vance) joined a vocal group called the Harbor Lites. The group's original members consisted of Sandy Yaguda, Linda Kahn, sisters Sydell and Gayle Sherman, and Richie Graff. Its name was chosen after the community of Belle Harbor, New York, one that its members called home.

Around the time that Vance joined the group, Kahn, Graff, and Gayle Sherman departed, leaving the contingent a trio.

Music biographies state that by the age of fifteen Vance began to travel to the legendary Brill Building in New York City in hopes of breaking into the music industry. In reality, his motivation began years earlier after being captivated by the beautiful harmonies that he heard at an early rock-and-roll show.

"The truth is that I went to see the Alan Freed shows when I was really younger than that, and then there were a couple of people in my neighborhood, older than me, and we started a group called the Harbor

Lites," Vance said. "It was Sydell Sherman and Sandy Yaguda, we were a trio, and they wrote the songs; she played the piano."

Following a period of rehearsals, the Harbor Lites approached a neighbor who was involved in the music industry, in hopes of securing an audition.

"A guy by the name of Stan Feldman was a neighbor in Rockaway, Queens, where we grew up," Vance said. "He had a record company called Ivy at 1697 Broadway, which is the Ed Sullivan Theater Building. The producer up at Ivy was George Weiss, who wrote 'What a Wonderful World' for Louie Armstrong. He had a lot of hits but at that time he was trying to make a go of making rhythm and blues records with kids. The label had 'Lullabye of the Bells' by the Deltaires and they also produced a lot of records like 'Darling Can't You Tell' by the Clusters."

The group's hard work paid off, as Feldman signed them to a recording contract. "We went to the studio and made a record for them called 'Is That Too Much to Ask' and 'What Would I Do without You,'" Vance recalled. "They sold it to Jaro International and it came out on the Jaro label."

Upon its release, due in large part to the support it received from popular New York disc jockey (Cousin) Brucie Morrow, the single became a regional hit for the group.

"After that, we needed a manager because we had a record out and wanted to get booked with these other groups," Vance said. "We wound up meeting a guy that had an office in the same building (as Feldman) and his name was Jim Gribble. He managed the Mystics and the Passions and the Mello-Kings and I met Paul Simon and Al Kooper up there. They were also young guys writing songs. We hung out and started to do backgrounds for a lot of people."

The Harbor Lites began to perform at shows and sock hops, one of which also featured the Mystics, a group that had recently scored a hit single, "Hushabye." While Phil Cracolici sang lead on the recording of "Hushabye," another vocalist, Jay Traynor had just stepped in as lead singer for the Mystics following Cracolici's departure. Vance, Yaguda, and Traynor met backstage and exchanged telephone numbers.

Traynor's involvement with the Mystics came to a sudden halt when a misunderstanding with Gribble resulted in his dismissal. At the same time, Vance and Yaguda had decided to form an all-male vocal group and learning of Traynor's recent departure from the Mystics they called to see if he might be interested in joining them. Yaguda also recruited a friend, Howie Kirschenbaum (Kane) to round out the quartet.

The unnamed group began to hone its skills and soon connected with another local resident, one Terry Philips. Phillips owned Perception Records. Following an audition and being impressed with their sound, Philips contacted Danny Kessler, who was partners in a publishing company with Jerry Leiber and Mike Stoller. Leiber and Stoller were at the top of their game at the time, writing and producing some of the industry's most successful music.

"A guy by the name of Terry Philips, who was working with Dion and Jerry Leiber and Mike Stoller, actually got me to sing on a couple of songs that Phil Spector produced," Vance recalled. "Spector also worked up there with Jerry and Mike, Tony Powers, Mark Barkin, Van McCoy, Jeff Barry, Ellie Greenwich, and Burt Bacharach."

Spector had produced Johnny Nash right around the same time he produced "Every Little Breath I Take" by Gene Pitney. He also produced a song called "It's a World of Tears" and "Some of Your Lovin'" on ABC Paramount. "He [Philips] introduced us to Jerry Leiber and Mike Stoller and we auditioned for them, singing an a cappella song called 'Wisdom of a Fool,'" Vance said. "It was Jay Traynor, Sandy Yaguda, Howie Kane, and me. After we sang they decided that they were going to make a record with us.

"At the time they were very successful with the Coasters and the Drifters and they got an independent record deal with United Artists and they needed product," he continued. "They made a record with us, called 'Tonight' from *West Side Story*, which was a movie that United Artists had coming out." But Vance recalled how the group nearly lost their golden opportunity with the songwriting/production team and how a heart-to-heart conversation with his mother played a huge role in averting a near catastrophe.

"It's true," he said. "We were getting ready to record 'Tonight' from *West Side Story* and Jerry Leiber said, 'You know, guys, it's just not working out. I'm going to have to terminate the thing.' I remember we walked out of there dejected and wound up going to a bar and getting drunk. I went home and my mother looked at me and she said, 'What?' I told her we'd been in the business a long time and things didn't go well with the Harbor Lites and now he told us he doesn't want to record us anymore. She said, 'You know what? Go back there tomorrow and tell him that you've been in the business a long time and that he can't do this to you. It's not fair; you finally thought you were with professional people.' I wound up going back there the next day, waiting in the office. They came in and I went back and I said to Jerry and Mike, 'You can't do this to us. We're shattered. We're destroyed.' I remember Jerry said to tell the guys to come back tomorrow. We wound up coming back and making the record. I owe it to my mother."

As a result of their production arrangement with United Artists, Leiber and Stoller got the group signed to a contract with the label. But a slight issue needed to be resolved: the group was still nameless. Given the success that Leiber and Stoller had with spoof material, they decided to name the group Binky Jones and the Americans, a moniker that was unanimously rejected by its members. After some discussion they settled on Jay and the Americans.

Since their recording label, United Artists, also produced the motion picture *West Side Story*, Jay and the Americans was offered the opportunity to record one of the musical's numbers, "Tonight." Upon its release the single sold more than fifty thousand copies in New York. Enthusiastic about the attention generated by their debut single, the group returned to the studio to record "Dawning" as their follow-up record. Another tune, "She Cried," served as the single's B-side.

"We cut this other song, like a throwaway on the flip side, called 'She Cried,'" Vance recalled. "They promoted 'Dawning,' and then a guy on the West Coast locked himself in a room as the story goes and played 'She Cried' and played it and played it, and 'She Cried' became a Top 5 record in 1962. Then we had to go on the road and I remember the first job we got was in New Haven, Connecticut, playing in a firehouse. Then we actually wound up going to Wildwood, New Jersey, playing with the Isley Brothers, who had 'Twist and Shout,' and Steve Gibson and the Modern Red Caps, which was an old group like the Treniers. We did three shows a night, at ten, twelve, and two, at a place called the Beachcomber and we met Lenny Bruce and the Kingston Trio and developed lifelong friendships. When we went out to California to be on Shindig in 1964, we went up to Lenny Bruce's house and hung around with him because we kept the friendship going."

Off the success of "She Cried," Jay and the Americans soon released an album of the same name. In support of their new album, Jay and the Americans maintained a heavy schedule of performances. But despite the flurry of activity and fame, when the group's next two singles failed to generate significant attention, Traynor and the group parted ways.

"Jerry and Mike loved Jay Traynor," Vance said. "He was a soulful guy, a rhythm and blues singer. After we made 'She Cried' we recorded a song called 'This Is It,' which is a great record. Then we recorded 'Tomorrow.' After 'Tomorrow' came out as a single and it bombed that was basically it. In those days no one would have dreamt that here we would be, forty years later still doing this. In those days, Frankie Lymon had a bunch of hits and then he was done. All those groups; it was the same thing. It was the same with us. That was it; we had a hit and it was over.

"I went back to school for about six months and I tried to figure it all out," he said. "We got together and called Jay Traynor and he was actually on his own. I think he made a record or was about to do one on the Coral label, and felt he didn't need us. At that point we had hired a guitar player (Marty Sanders) that was making more money than we were because in those days, even with a number-one record, if you made three hundred dollars a night that was a lot. And you had to buy suits, pay commission, and get to the job. Nowadays, you have a hit record and you're set for life. But in those days, even if you were on Ed Sullivan, he'd pay you twenty-five hundred bucks."

In need of a new lead singer, Sanders told the group about a high school friend, David Blatt, who he had sung with and formed a duo. Together they had recorded one single that was purchased by Atlantic Records but failed to gain momentum. Encouraged to bring him in for an audition, Blatt sang an a cappella rendition of "Cara Mia" at Yaguda's house the following day and soon became a member of the group. He changed his name to Jay Black to maintain the group's identity.

Vance recalled their first meeting with Black. "He [Sanders] made a record with Jay Black [David Blatt] for Atlantic Records right around the same time the Harbor Lites were making a record," he said. "They called themselves the Two Chaps and they had a record called 'Forgive Me.' Marty said that he knew this guy who was a shoe salesman. We were waiting at Sandy's house and this 1956 Chevy pulls up with a rope holding the hood down and this 'hitter' gets out of the car. He came in and he had that voice and he actually had 'Cara Mia' at the time."

Black's debut single with the Americans came largely as a result of Atlantic Records' decision to pull a recording intended to be released by the Drifters, "Only in America." The label's executives felt that having a black group record a song with lyrics that touted their ability to actually become president at a time that preceded the civil rights movement was absurd. Haunted by Jay and the Americans to provide the group with better-quality material, the song was offered to them.

"We brought him [Black] up to Jerry and Mike and they had just cut a track with the Drifters called 'Only in America.' When they played it for me I said, 'Wouldn't that be great if you could give it to us?' I guess it made sense to them and they took us into the studio, and they took the Drifters off and put us on and it became a hit."

Soon after, Leiber and Stoller began to cool on the prospect of producing records for Jay and the Americans, seeming to have an aversion toward Black. "They said he sounded like Alan Jones," Vance said. "It wasn't their style. It wasn't like they were putting him down." The group began hanging out at Kama Sutra Productions with Artie Riff and he produced 'Come a Little Bit Closer," "Let's Lock the Door," and "Think of the Good Times." United Artists subsequently bought the group's contract from Leiber and Stoller.

Jay and the Americans' growing popularity and success resulted in their selection as the opening act for the Beatles' first performance in the United States in 1964. A year later, they would repeat the feat for the Rolling Stones' first American performance.

Ever since he auditioned for the group, Black was determined to record "Cara Mia." But he experienced resistance from the label's executives, who felt the song would never generate attention. As such, Jay and the Americans restricted the song to live performances. Upon their shift to United Artists in 1965, Gerry Granahan, of Dicky Doo and the Don'ts and "No Chemise Please" fame and then a producer at the label, assumed control of the group's recordings.

"That is when we finally got to record 'Cara Mia,'" Vance said. "Actually, that's when the whole other phase came in and we did 'Some Enchanted Evening' and 'Sunday and Me,' which was Neil Diamond's first hit song."

Despite years of opposition and predictions of failure, upon its release "Cara Mia" climbed to the top of the charts and has remained one of the group's most beloved tunes.

In 1969, the group formed JATA (Jay and the Americans) Enterprises and recorded an album of oldies titled *Sands of Time*. The group began to record self-written material, of which Vance co-wrote "Livin' Above Your Head," "Learning How to Fly," and "Capture the Moment." The production, business end, and creative side of the industry appealed to Vance and that exposure would serve to prepare him for a whole new direction in his career.

"The guys who played on those records are Donald Fagen and Walter Becker [Steely Dan]," he said. "They knocked on our door one day and I started producing records with them and we wanted to give them money so we had them play on our records. I think when we met the Beatles and the Stones and we hung around with them since we were their opening act, for me it seemed like there was something else going on there. We always modeled ourselves after the doo-wop groups. But I watched Jerry and Mike make records. I watched Burt

Bacarach make records. I watched Phil Spector make records. I kind of knew how to do it and then we started writing songs and it kind of got me into writing and producing. When Donald and Walter came around I started producing records with them, and the first film that I did was with them, called *You Gotta Walk It Like You Talk It.*"

In 1978, a feature-length motion picture that depicted the life of Alan Freed, *American Hot Wax*, was released. Vance composed the theme for the score and produced the soundtrack. "Because I had done that one prior movie, I did an album for Atlantic called *Vance 32*, which had the original 'Looking for an Echo' on it," he said. "Then a guy out in California, Don Philips, heard the record and turned the producers of a movie, *American Hot Wax,* onto the song. They heard 'Looking for an Echo' and wanted to meet me. They flew me out and I ended up doing all the music for the film, putting all the groups together, putting my friends in the movie, with me and the original Planotones and it was a thrill. And then I was hot for a minute in Hollywood, and so I wound up doing *Animal House* and producing the soundtrack album. From there I did *The Warriors* in 1979, became the musical director of *Saturday Night Live* in 1980, and in 1984 I found John Cafferty and did *Eddie and the Cruisers*. Actually, it is my voice that comes through Sal's mouth at the Holiday Inn scene in the movie. I also played the record producer, Lew Isen, in the film."

That wasn't the only acting role that Vance has tackled through the years. "When I worked on *Saturday Night Live* the producer of the show, Jean Doumanian, was a good friend of Woody Allen," Vance said. "He'd [Allen] come over to the show and said that he could use me. I ended up in about five or six of his films."

In 1992, Vance reformed the previously fictional group used in *American Hot Wax*, the Planotones. Seven years later, "Looking for an Echo" was the subject of a motion picture starring Armand Assante.

"I don't know what it is that makes our group popular but it's like a cult thing," he said. "Our audience seems to be transformed into teenagers and we are transformed into these teen idols. The other groups that we perform with at the shows are great but there is something wild that goes on with us."

Looking back on a phenomenal career in entertainment, one that includes musical milestones with Jay and the Americans and with the Planotones, songwriting, producing, composing soundtracks and movie scores, and acting, Vance cited his greatest sense of pride.

"I think when I look at *American Hot Wax* and I see the work that I did on that, and I know what I did in putting all the groups together, I put the whole tapestry of it and it totally captures the spirit of that time; it's a document for all times," he said. "I think the most important thing is keeping my humanity, and I'm happy to still do it. I don't have any airs about it. It's about sharing it with everybody and I'm the vehicle. I just feel blessed that I've been able to do it."

As for the future, Vance said that he has a couple of projects in the works, possibly Broadway and films. His excitement and energy level is apparent; his commitment to quality and excellence unwavering; and his appreciation for his fans endless.

"Basically, we were from the neighborhood, very provincial guys just singing doo-wop on the corner, and then Jerry and Mike made a hit with us and the next thing you know we are on the road and in show business," Vance said. "It wasn't premeditated, where I thought, 'Oh, I've got to get into show business.' I was a doo-wop singer and we had a hit. So the next thing you have to do is go on the road and all of a sudden we're on a bus and traveling around with Dick Clark."

In 2006, Kane and Yaguda both work outside the music industry, while Sanders co-wrote "Bad Reputation," a Joan Jett song featured in the animated movie *Shrek*. Black continues to perform the Jay and the American hit songs at shows with his backup band. Traynor recently joined Jay Siegel and the Tokens to perform at oldies concerts. And Vance continues to lead the Planotones, a group that in 2006 unquestionably holds the distinction of being in the highest demand at concerts nationwide.

Jay and the Americans were inducted into the Vocal Group Hall of Fame in 2002.

Billboard Top 40 Hits by Jay and the Americans

Date	Pos	Wks on Charts	Record Title	Label/Number
04/07/62	05	11	She Cried	United Art. 415
09/21/63	25	04	Only in America	United Art. 626
10/03/64	03	11	Come a little Bit Closer	United Art. 759
01/16/65	11	07	Let's Lock the Door (And Throw away the Key)	United Art. 805
06/19/65	04	11	Cara Mia	United Art. 881
09/25/65	13	06	Some Enchanted Evening	United Art. 919
12/04/65	18	06	Sunday and Me	United Art. 948
06/11/66	25	04	Crying	United Art. 50016
01/25/69	06	10	This Magic Moment	United Art. 50475
01/17/70	19	07	Walkin' in the Rain	United Art. 50605

Mary Wilson
(The Supremes)

Wildwood, New Jersey   **July 7, 2005**

While the Supremes were not the first girl group to chart a hit record for the new Motown record label, they went on to become one of the most successful female vocal groups of all time. The group originated when Florence Ballad formed an ensemble called the Primettes. The other members, all from Detroit, Michigan's Brewster projects, were Diane Ross, Mary Wilson, and Betty McGlown.

While some biographies written about the group state that the Primettes formed while the girls were still in high school, Wilson disputed that fact. "First of all, to set the record straight we started singing in 1959 and we were still in elementary school," Wilson said. "Florence was thirteen and Diane and I were twelve and a half years old. The fourth member, Betty McGlown, was sixteen years old. We were the Primettes and six months later we continued to sing throughout high school."

Wilson said that a few popular recording artists at that time influenced the sound that the Primettes attempted to develop. "I would say that the Chantels were the premier girl group that everybody wanted to emulate," she said. "However, the Shirelles I believe inspired us the most. They were more our type of group and a lot of the songs that we sang were the Shirelles' songs. The Drifters obviously influenced us but they were a male group, so we were more interested in the female singers.

"I really liked jazz artists because in Detroit we had a lot of great jazz singers," she added. "Detroit is a jazz town so I grew up listening to the likes of Sarah Vaughn, Nancy Wilson, and folks like that."

The girls met Milton Jenkins, who managed other vocal groups in the area. "When we started singing in elementary school it was with a group of guys called the Primes," Wilson said. "They were three guys and their manager was Milton Jenkins. He wanted the Primes to put together a kind of package so that when he sold them he could sell a package to a club or whatever. That package consisted of the Primes and some of the guys recruited Florence. She brought me in and Paul Williams brought in Diane."

While the Primes and Primettes rehearsed together, conflicting reports exist that differ on whether or not the male and female contingents ever performed on the same stage together. "That's a good point because in the movie *The Temptations*, they had it that we performed together and we did not," she said. "We never performed with the Primes, even though that was the intention, so people assumed that. This is one of the first times I've ever cleared the record because I always wanted the record to stay unclear until it was set straight by me.

"Throughout the years I've seen a lot of people take what I've said and through them, with a source here and a source there, they tried to make the story," she added. "But I know that story is not correct. And I know when it is corrected." And here it is corrected and the record is set straight!

Another account that Wilson explained as being skewed is how the group came to secure an audition with Motown. A longstanding story states that following an initial audition with Smokey Robinson of the Miracles, one that was arranged by his sister and a friend of Ross, the Primettes got the opportunity to do likewise for Motown founder Berry Gordy. Wilson disputed that claim.

"That's another area we have to clear up," she said. "It wasn't just Smokey who got us the audition. We actually won a contest in Canada and a couple of people from Motown saw us. They gave the idea to Berry that we wanted an audition and Smokey was one of those people. It is true that Smokey and his group, the Miracles were partly responsible for setting up the meeting, but we put the word out and there were others involved."

Following the audition with Berry, one that did not prove fruitful, the Primettes made the acquaintance of songwriter Richard Morris, who introduced the group to Bob West of Lupine Records.

"When we had the audition at Motown it didn't go well," Wilson recalled. "Berry Gordy, at the end of the audition, didn't say that he didn't like us or we didn't sing well but that we were very young. He was a new company, with a lot of guys hanging around, and here comes four young girls and I'm sure he saw trouble. I'm sure he didn't want to deal with that. It was more that attitude, but of course, we didn't know that. I remember Florence saying that Berry must not know real talent if he didn't like us.

"When we had the audition, Richard Morris was one of the writers that were there with Berry and he heard how good we were," she continued. "When Berry turned us down he said, 'Listen, I work with another record company called Lupine and maybe I can take you over there.' He did, and during our time there we did our first professional recording, 'Pretty Baby' and 'Tears of Sorrow.'"

At the time, the girls shared singing lead vocal. As such, when the group recorded their debut single, Wilson sang lead on "Pretty Baby," while Ross did likewise on the B-side, "Tears of Sorrow." When McGlown decided to leave the group, Barbara Martin replaced her and remained with them until 1963, but was never credited on their early Motown material.

The Primettes became background vocalists for Lupine, working with other artists on the label that included Don Revel, Wilson Pickett, and Eddie Floyd. "I think our time at Lupine totally helped us because that was our first introduction to doing recording sessions," she said. "If nothing else it let us know that we really wanted to do it. We were bitten by it and we said, 'Okay, let's go back to Motown and really record.'"

In 1961 their persistence and hard work paid off as they finally signed a recording deal with Motown. But Gordy was not fond of the group's name and asked them to come up with a new one. Ballad suggested the Supremes, and everyone agreed.

"We went back to Motown and just hung around there as the Primettes, hoping that Berry would eventually sign us," she said. "They had artists that were really doing well like the Miracles, Mary Wells, and Marv Johnson. In early 1961, he said, 'Okay, I'm going to sign you girls since you're not going to go away.' He was about to sign us but said that he didn't like our name and told us to come up with another one.

"We would go all over the neighborhood, the churches, wherever we went, and asked everybody for ideas," she continued. "We collected all kinds of names but when we got to sign the actual contract, both Diane and I hadn't come up with anything we liked and still hoped that Berry would forget and we could keep the Primettes. But he didn't and he asked us for the new name. Florence said, 'I have one.' She looked at the list and said, 'Here's one here: the Supremes. I like that one.' So we had to take it. In retrospect, it was a great name."

Having the attributes to learn quickly and develop distinct harmonies, the group backed up other Motown artists including Marvin Gaye, Stevie Wonder, and Mary Wells. Just landing with the Motown label was gratification beyond their dreams.

"There was no doubt in my mind, or Diane's, or Florence's, that that is where we belonged," Wilson said. "They were going places and you could see it. They had a good sound and we liked the energy. Nobody was doing what they were doing. When you walked in there you could see that they were serious about making music. And it was all young people, not like today with all the big corporate people at the head and all the underlings working. Everybody was working together and working toward the common goal of creating music. I knew that is where I wanted to be. It was like landing right in the middle of Disneyland."

Subsequent to the Supremes signing with Motown, two members of their male counterparts, the Primes, merged with another local group, the Distants, and also signed with Motown, as the Temptations. The two groups recorded "Not Now I'll Tell You Later" early on. "We always felt that we were brother-and-sister groups and so it was like coming together with our brothers," she said. "We both realized, without talking to each other, that we had landed at Motown."

When Martin left the Supremes after the group's first few singles failed to gain attention, Ross, Ballad, and Wilson continued as a trio. Gordy remained convinced that the Supremes' talent and good looks was a winning combination, and in late 1963, they charted their first Top 40 hit with "When the Lovelight Starts Shining Through His Eyes."

While all three members of the Supremes continued to share the lead vocal role at that point, Wilson explained how that shifted as time passed.

"We all did sing lead and people always bring that up and I'm really happy that they do," she said. "But in a way it puts me in an awkward

340

situation because it always looks like I'm saying that Diane wasn't always the one, but it's the truth. We were a versatile group, like the Pointer Sisters, where everyone had a style and a voice. What Berry did was to favor one particular style, which was Diane. So that meant that since he wanted that style, the other two were not used out front. It put us in a lesser role and that's how it happened."

One year later, with the release of "Where Did Our Love Go," the Supremes began a string of five consecutive number-one hits that included "Baby Love," "Stop! In the Name of Love," "Come See About Me," and "Back in My Arms Again."

The huge hit singles that the Supremes recorded were all composed by Motown's super talents Holland-Dozier-Holland. "We had a lot of records that we recorded that were good but didn't quite put us over the top," Wilson said. "So when Berry said that we were so serious and focused, he put us with his top writing team and we got that first hit and we were on our way."

The songwriting team composed every Supremes release through 1967.

Despite the huge success and high visibility that the Supremes generated in concerts, on television, and on record, underlying tensions began to spout as other female Motown artists, and Ballad and Wilson felt somewhat overshadowed by what seemed to be an inordinate amount of attention showed by Gordy toward Ross. In 1967, Ballad was replaced in the Supremes by Cindy Birdsong for what was described as increasingly unprofessional behavior. Birdsong was recruited from another popular group, Patti LaBelle and the Bluebelles.

Wilson recalled that period. "That's very unfair that they had to put it out that way," she said. "What people really didn't know was that Florence had a very horrific experience happen to her when she was fourteen years old. She had been raped. And that was never a resolved situation. It was a time period when black folks didn't go to psychiatrists, and first of all you kept it quiet and dealt with it as best you could.

"I say all of that to give the benefit of the doubt to Florence and [to explain] why her behavior became worse and worse," she continued. "She was dealing with something that even money, even what we had become, famous, didn't take care of. There was an inner turmoil that was going on. If there was something in the business that irritated me, or Diane, we would accept it or work through it in a certain way. But with her personal problems it was difficult for her to be rational, so eventually those kinds of things started eating away at her; she started acting badly. But it was her own inner battles and no one addressed those issues. Eventually she became so distraught with the drinking and trying to hide her pain. I loved Florence; Diane too. But you're at a point in your life where you're on top of the world and someone's behavior is abnormal, and no one has the time; the machinery is moving on. It's not to say they didn't care about Florence, but they didn't understand why she was acting that way when she was on top of the world."

Wilson recalled a professionally challenging period of time at Motown, with the departure of their exclusive songwriting team. "When Holland-Dozier-Holland left, that really was a time that the company was floundering, and we were floundering because we were used to having those hit records coming out one after another," she said. "Berry and the A&R department were very conscientious in trying to get a top record for us. They came up with a group of writers that composed 'Love Child.' But before that happened they put out a lot of things that just weren't top quality. With 'Love Child' they found a new life."

Wilson spoke about the tensions that had begun to develop within the group and confirmed that neither she nor Birdsong even participated in recording 'Love Child' or another of the group's hit singles, 'Someday We'll Be Together.' "With the company in turmoil and the departure of Holland-Dozier-Holland, producers would submit songs and maybe get Diane to record them to see how it sounded and we were kind of left out," she said. "Then of course it was because Diane would be leaving soon."

From the time of Ballad's departure, the group became known as Diana Ross and the Supremes amid growing speculation that Gordy intended to eventually break her away from the group in favor of a solo career. That speculation came to fruition in November 1969, when Ross left the Supremes.

With Jean Terrell brought in to replace Ross, and the group experiencing other personnel changes throughout the next few years, the Supremes released several fine recordings, such as "Stoned Love" and "Nathan Jones." They also recorded a duet, "River Deep—Mountain High" with the Four Tops. Through it all, Wilson remained the one constant, original member of the Supremes.

Ross has remained a solo artist through the years. Wilson, who cut one solo album for Motown in 1979, *Red Hot,* co-wrote the book *Dreamgirl: My Life as a Supreme,* which documented her perceptions of widespread abuses that artists at Motown endured during the label's glory years.

"Everyone thinks that I was motivated to write the book but I had been keeping a diary ever since we were seventeen years old with the intention of writing a book," she said. "I didn't conjure up things and didn't go back to find things; that's just what I had written all along."

In 1987, Wilson released a single, "Don't Get Mad, Get Even," on the Motor City Records label and a follow-up, "Oooh Child," in 1989. She remains a popular solo artist into 2006. Sadly, Florence Ballad ended up on welfare and died in 1976.

Despite the amazing career that she continues to enjoy in music today, Wilson readily cites her children and grandchildren as the thing she has the most pride in. "That's me as a human being," she said. "In terms of my professional career, I am most proud of the body of work that the Supremes have had; the career; the path that we chose in terms of the kind of group that we were. I'm not putting Motown down but trying to show where the credit should lie, and that is with me and Florence and Diane for daring to dream, for pursuing Berry Gordy and staying there and keeping ourselves at such a high quality. We were able to make our dreams come true. Then, of course, it came with the help and direction of Motown and Berry Gordy. But I really believe that the initial credit has got to go to those three little black girls who dared to dream, and I don't want anyone to take that away from us."

Not one to shy away from new challenges, Wilson was appointed by Colin Powell and the State Department as a cultural ambassador for the United States. In that position, she travels around the world as a goodwill ambassador. She graduated from New York University in 2001 with a degree in liberal arts. And she was recently awarded an honorary doctorate from Payne College in Augusta, Georgia.

The Supremes were inducted into the Rock and Roll Hall of Fame in 1988 and the Vocal Group Hall of Fame in 1998.

Billboard Top 40 Hits by the Supremes

Date	Pos	Wks on Charts	Record Title	Label/Number
12/28/63	23	07	When the Lovelight Starts Shining Through His Eyes	Motown 1051
07/18/64	01	13	Where Did Our Love Go	Motown 1060
10/10/64	01	12	Baby Love	Motown 1066
11/21/64	01	13	Come See About Me	Motown 1068
03/06/65	01	10	Stop! In the Name of Love	Motown 1074
05/08/65	01	10	Back in My Arms Again	Motown 1075
08/14/65	11	07	Nothing But Heartaches	Motown 1080
10/30/65	01	10	I Hear A Symphony	Motown 1083
01/29/66	05	08	My World Is Empty Without You	Motown 1089
05/07/66	09	07	Love Is Like An Itching In My Heart	Motown 1094
08/20/66	01	11	You Can't Hurry Love	Motown 1097
11/05/66	01	10	You Keep Me Hangin' On	Motown 1101
02/04/67	01	10	Love Is Here and Now You're Gone	Motown 1103
04/15/67	01	10	The Happening	Motown 1107
08/19/67	02	10	Reflections	Motown 1111
11/25/67	09	06	In and Out of Love	Motown 1116
04/06/68	28	05	Forever Came Today	Motown 1122
07/06/68	30	03	Some Things You Never Get Used To	Motown 1126
10/26/68	01	15	Love Child	Motown 1135
02/01/69	10	07	I'm Livin' in Shame	Motown 1139
04/26/69	27	05	The Composer	Motown 1146
06/14/69	31	04	No Matter What Sign You Are	Motown 1148
11/15/69	01	15	Someday We'll Be Together	Motown 1156
03/14/70	10	10	Up the Ladder to the Roof	Motown 1162
08/01/70	21	08	Everybody's Got The Right To Love	Motown 1167
11/21/70	07	12	Stoned Love	Motown 1172
05/22/71	16	08	Nathan Jones	Motown 1182
01/29/72	16	09	Floy Joy	Motown 1195
06/03/72	37	03	Automatically Sunshine	Motown 1200
08/07/76	40	01	I'm Gonna Let My Heart Do The Walking	Motown 1391

Billboard Top 40 Hits by the Supremes & Four Tops

Date	Pos	Wks on Charts	Record Title	Label/ Number
12/12/70	14	08	River Deep—Mountain High	Motown 1173

Billboard Top 40 Hits by the Supremes & Temptations

Date	Pos	Wks on Charts	Record Title	Label/ Number
12/14/68	02	12	I'm Gonna Make You Love Me	Motown 1137
03/22/69	25	06	I'll Try Something New	Motown 1142

Founding members of the Harptones, from left, Willie Winfield, Raoul Cita, and William Dempsey James continue to vocalize their unique harmonies at countless concerts.

Willie Winfield, William Dempsey James (The Harptones)

Harrison, New York   **March 19, 2005**

Despite failing to chart a national hit record during their heyday, the Harptones are among the most revered and respected vocal groups to have come from Harlem, New York, during the 1950s. Known for their smooth and tight harmonies, the distinctive lead vocals of their lead singer, Willie Winfield, and the moving lyrics of pianist Raoul Cita, the group continues to have a loyal following well into the twenty-first century.

In reality, the Harptones was a combination of members that originated in two separate vocal groups, the Winfield Brothers and the Skylarks. In 1951, the latter contingent, made up of William Dempsey James, Curtis Cherebin, and Freddie Taylor made a practice of harmonizing in the schoolyard of Wadleigh Junior High School in Harlem. After another member, Eugene Cooke, joined the group they

347

journeyed to the famed Apollo Theatre and entered an amateur talent contest. After they had performed their rendition of "My Dear Dearest Darling," the Apollo audience, long known for brutal honesty and criticism, booed them off the stage.

Another vocal group, which has been long documented as being called the Harps but in reality was the Winfield Brothers, was comprised of siblings Willie, Clyde, brother-in-law Jimmy Winfield, Johnny Bronson, and William Galloway. They held regular rehearsals beneath either the Manhattan or Brooklyn bridges. When Galloway sought out a pianist for the group, he met Raoul Cita and soon some members of the Skylarks merged with them to form the Harps. The new group was made up of Willie Winfield on lead, Bill Dempsey James on first tenor, Clyde Winfield on second tenor, William Galloway on baritone, Curtis Cherebin on bass, and Raoul Cita serving as the pianist and musical arranger.

"My brothers [Clyde and Jimmy] originally used to sing as the Windfield Brothers," Willie Winfield said. "We went uptown and met the members of the Skylarks.

"We started singing together, like a group within a group," James added. "We were out there on the corners, ten guys all singing together. As time went by, some guys started dropping out and didn't want to sing anymore and that's how it came down to the final five that became the Harps."

In November 1953, after rehearsing their new blend of harmonies for a while, the Harps took a stab at the Apollo's amateur night and walked off with its first prize for having performed a Louie Prima tune, "A Sunday Kind of Love." As fate would have it, a representative from MGM Records was at the show, and on his invitation the Harps visited its offices at 1650 Broadway to audition for the company.

Unfortunately for MGM, while the group waited in the hallway for more than one hour and began to harmonize to kill time, Morty Craft and Leo Rogers, both aspiring music entrepreneurs, took them across the street to meet with their associate, Monte Bruce. Upon hearing the group the three partners decided on the spot to form a new record label, Bruce Records, and sign the Harps as its first act.

"We went up to 1650 Broadway to meet with this fellow and started singing in the hallway," James recalled. "Leo heard us, came over and took us across the street, and he auditioned us at his office."

With a recording session arranged, the Harps experienced some personnel changes when Cherebin bowed to his parents' insistence that he give up singing in favor of a formal education and Clyde Winfield was drafted into military service.

"One of the guy's [Cherebin] mothers wanted him to be an engineer at the time," Winfield said. "He was our bass singer and he had to leave the group. We picked up Billy Brown to take his place on bass.

"As for the Five Crowns, we picked up Nick Clark, who was a tenor with that group," James added. "He took the place of the tenor that also left."

Off the huge ovation received at the Apollo, the group recorded "Sunday Kind of Love" on the Bruce label but just prior to its release Cita changed the group's name to the Harptones in order to avoid confusion with a gospel group called the Harps of Music.

Upon its release, the first disc jockey to give the Harptones airplay was the legendary Hal Jackson. James reflected on the impact Jackson had on the new group. "He was kind of a mentor to us," he said. "He was someone that knew a little bit about the business and gave us advice on what to do and not do. And he carried us along with him when he promoted shows.

"We used to do a lot of his shows down in Washington, D.C., while he was there and he broke our record, 'A Sunday Kind of Love' on his radio show," Winfield added.

The group also became a fast favorite of disc jockey Alan Freed and appeared on the bill of his first live show in New York. "It was tremendous because he had a big following," James said. "We had never seen that many people at one time and the theater was packed."

As the single continued to bring attention to the Harptones, the group secured engagements at theaters along the East Coast that attracted a predominantly black audience. Referred to as the chitlin circuit, they included the Howard Theatre in Washington, D.C., The Royal in Baltimore, and, of course, the Apollo in Harlem.

After recording two follow-up sides, a Cita original titled "My Memories of You" and "I Depend on You," the latter featuring Clark on lead, the Harptones became victims of creative theft. It was not uncommon for one act to basically lift another's work and record it unbeknownst to the original artist, upon which it became a race to see who could release it first. That was the case with a Harptones tune, "Why Should I Love."

During the process of taking the Harptones twenty-two attempts to record the song, another vocal group working down the hall, the Four Aces, heard it, liked it, recorded it note for note, and won the race to the airwaves. It was used as the B-side to the Four Aces release "Skokkian."

When "Skokkian" became a hit single, jukebox owners refused to put the Harptones' single "Why Should I Love You" in its equipment since a version of the song already existed there. It basically stifled any hope of exposure for the Harptones' version when it was released.

"They were working right next door to us and could hear us," James recalled. "But they couldn't take it unless our record company gave them permission first. That was Leo Rogers and Morty Craft; just a bunch of crooks," Winfield added. "They [the Four Aces] paid them money and that was it."

By fall of 1954, despite a number of outstanding recordings and positive local airplay given to Harptones' releases, it became apparent that the Bruce label was inept in promoting and distributing the records at a level that would gain the group national attention. A year later, Bruce Records declared bankruptcy and Rogers took the Harptones to meet Hy Weiss of Old Town Records. Ready to unveil a subsidiary label, Paradise, Weiss signed the group.

During spring 1955, the Harptones recorded another Cita masterpiece for Paradise, "Life Is But a Dream." Oddly, the greater clout of a Weiss-promoted single fell short for the Harptones' gem and despite climbing to number four in New York City, the record failed to gain national attention.

The Harptones soon joined Freed again to appear at a week-long Labor Day First Anniversary Show at the Brooklyn Paramount. The schedule called for five performances every day, and six on weekends. "That was very hard work," Winfield said. "They brought Tony Bennett in to perform on that show and he actually got laryngitis singing 'Rags to Riches' so many times. He couldn't take that many shows. But it worked out and he made it."

"We were kind of used to working that way, though, because at the Apollo Theatre you worked that way too," James added. "We did many shows a day there."

James recalled having an opportunity to spend time and share harmonies backstage between the Freed shows with many of the top artists of that period. "We went into each other's dressing rooms, singing spirituals and other tunes all the time," he said. "We got to know each other and laughed and joked and had a great time. The money wasn't good, but we had a good time."

That November, Paradise released a follow-up Harptones single, "My Success (It All Depends on You)." The group also provided background vocals for Ruth McFadden while at Paradise, singing on her recording of "Loving a Boy Like You."

Growing with frustration, the Harptones left Weiss in December 1955 for Andrea Records, a company that was formed by Rogers and a partner, Sid Arky. But their sole effort on the label failed to gain attention. Due to Cita's prior work with Rama and Gee Records president George Goldner, the Harptones recorded "That's the Way It Goes" on Rama, a song that became a fan favorite.

In 1956, the Harptones appeared in the motion picture *Rockin' the Blues*. "It was a new experience for us," James said. "It was something like doing a television show. You'd come in to do the spot at a certain hour to do the filming, but first you had to go to the sound studio to make the recording. We [other acts] were never all there at the same time. Until you actually get to see the finished picture you realize that this group was there and that group was also there."

Winfield expressed a sense of pride in the fact that while other groups of the era relied on expert assistance in developing elaborate choreography for their performance, and in this specific case, for the filming of *Rockin' the Blues*, the Harptones developed their own moves. "All groups that fancied around on stage went to Cholly Atkins to get their routines, but we made up our own," he said. "We were just a dancing group but we never had a professional person to help us. We did have one, and he wasn't coming around right so we didn't bother to go to him anymore."

After recording "The Shrine of St. Cecilia," the group was shattered by the untimely death of their bass singer, Billy Brown. Cita decided to leave the group shortly thereafter.

A familiar face, Cherebin replaced Brown in the group. While working with Goldner, the Harptones sang background for other artists under the name the Royale Cita Chorus, a contingent that sometimes included members of the Joytones and the Lyrics. They backed up Mabel King on her recording of "Second-Hand Love." Around this time King and Cita collaborated on songs and formed a publishing company together. King later acted on Broadway, and television, and in motion pictures.

When Galloway decided to leave the group he was replaced by Milton Love, who sang lead with the Solitaires. But the new lineup was short lived as the Harptones dissolved soon after.

When Craft formed Warwick Records in 1959, he sought out the former Harptones and convinced them to reform and record for his new label. With Winfield, James, Clark, Cherebin, and Cita all aboard, they recorded three singles over the next two years. A few other label changes followed, including Coed, Companion, Cub, and KT, and in

1964, as the Soothers, they waxed one single on the Port label. Shortly after their attempt at reinventing themselves, the Soothers/Harptones disbanded.

Winfield and James spoke about the struggle the group experienced in breaking onto the national charts despite achieving a huge following and success in the New York market. "The promoting of our labels was not good," James said. "You could be on a small label and get national coverage but if they don't promote it, it's not going to do well. They just didn't have good promotions. And while some small labels would get a bigger company to help them promote a record, they [Bruce Records] didn't do that. They tried to do it themselves and they were too green."

The members of the Harptones suffered similar financial pitfalls, as did many other famous vocal groups of that period, one that saw slick managers and promoters pocketing the bulk of the funds generated and leaving the actual artists struggling to pay bills. "They [managers] were taking all the money and we didn't feel like living from week to week," Winfield said. "It also got bad after we caught on and they started bootlegging our records. I didn't even know what bootlegging was. I thought bootlegging was running liquor."

"When you are having families, it gets very tough," James said.

"Rudy West [of the Five Keys] worked in the same Post Office that I passed the test to work at in Norfolk, Virginia, but during that time my mother passed away and I moved back to New York," Winfield said.

"I was in the business of delivery and thought I'd get into funeral directing but I turned that away," he added. "I went to the New York City Transit Authority," James said. "I was a conductor and then got promoted to motorman."

It wasn't until Cita received an invitation for the Harptones to appear at a 1970 rock-and-roll revival show, held at the New York Academy of Music, that the vocalists reformed and performed to a rousing ovation. Sponsored by *Rock Magazine*, that show and subsequent revival shows during the period motivated the Harptones to continue to perform. In 2006, the group still generates standing ovations at various oldies shows. The Harptones were inducted into the Vocal Group Hall of Fame in 2002.

Kathy Young
(Kathy Young and the Innocents)

Islandia, New York   **November 12, 2005**

During the process of researching various sources to compile the questions used in interviews for this book, it became obvious rather quickly that a number of erroneous and/or conflicting biographical facts regarding many recording artists existed. In Kathy Young's case, the discrepancies began with her entry into the music industry and continued through her swift and meteoric rise into the Top 5 record charts.

Young's story begins at a young age, and while the youngster was shy her musical ability and self-assurance was firm.

"I just grew up with music," Young said. "My mom and dad both played guitar and sang, and my dad was from the South and Sunday afternoon was spent sitting around, eating fried chicken and singing gospel songs with a couple of other families. Everybody played and everybody sang and that's how I grew up."

Getting her first guitar at five years old and teaching herself how to play and read music, Young said that within a year she had written her first song.

Although being stage shy, when a friend entered her in a junior high school talent show she not only persevered but also won the contest. "I knew when I was five years old that I was going to be a singer but I never thought about standing on a stage," she said. "My thought was being in a studio, having all that great music, and turning the lights down and hearing my voice coming out of the speakers. But at that school, if your name was entered into the talent show you had to audition. The principal came and got me out of class. I had no idea and it just happened. I wasn't nervous and I always thought I would be because I'm a quite shy person. But once the music began I was okay."

The first inaccuracy that is featured in biographies on Young starts by misrepresenting her initial contact with the Innocents, an all-male vocal group that came to record and score a Top 5 hit single with her. While Young did in fact attend a Wink Martindale television show called *Dance Party* with her mom, she was not discovered while sitting in its audience, as many references state. And, despite countless reports to the contrary, she did not go to the show to see the Innocents perform, but rather another guest and one that was her favorite recording artist at the time.

"It was Frankie Avalon," Young confirmed. "I was crazy about Frankie Avalon. I knew the Innocents song 'Honest I Do,' but they weren't at the show.

"I belonged to a girl's club and we liked to have slumber parties, hang out, and do girl stuff," she said. "We would also try to do something good at least once a week like help an elderly person rake their leaves or wash their windows or car. I had written to all the record companies in Hollywood that I was a great singer and wanted an audition, and I got all the 'don't call us, we'll call you' letters. But I found out that I could rent a studio and a band and cut a demo for two hundred and twenty-five dollars. The girls believed in me so much that they were going to loan me the money. We had one-hundred and seventy-five dollars saved from car washes and dinner events that we held."

When Young and her friends learned that Frankie Avalon was scheduled to appear on *Dance Party*, all thirty girls journeyed to Pacific Ocean Park, the site of the show. "My mom happened to be one of the drivers that took some of us there," Young recalled.

Given the fact that the Innocents were not a part of that show, the story that cites Young as being so impressed with them that she

354

was motivated to introduce herself to the vocal group after the show while they signed autographs, is clearly inaccurate. In reality, Young never even met one member of the Innocents until their impromptu and completely unplanned harmonizing behind her as she sang "A Thousand Stars" in a recording studio. Young explained what really occurred at the show.

"Where I happened to be sitting, I could look down into the green room and see the artists walking around before the show," she said. "I saw this one gentleman walking around but he wasn't really with an artist; he was just talking to everybody.

"After the show, we were out in the amusement park and he was there and I thought, 'Oh my gosh, this man knows people,'" she said. "I didn't know anyone in Hollywood; I lived in Long Beach. I had nothing to do with anybody in show business. I just made a bee-line for him and said, 'How do you make a record if you don't know anybody in show business?' I just rambled on and on. All the girls surrounded him and he couldn't get away. They started telling him that I was great and I sang all the time and wrote songs and was really, really good. He stood there listening to everybody and then my mom walked over and asked him if I was bothering him. He said, 'No, is she serious?' All the girls said, 'Yes, she is.'"

The gentleman turned out to be Jim Lee, who would go on to manage the Innocents, although at that time he wasn't associated with Indigo Records. Lee told Young that enthusiasm went a long way and she in turn assured him that she did sing and had full intentions of getting into the business one day. Having friends that owned a record company, Lee gave her their card and promised to call them and tell them that he heard her sing, thought she was good, and felt that they should audition her. "That's your break," Lee told her. "You better be good."

Young did not call the record company for three weeks, opting to practice endlessly to prepare for her big chance. "I knew that you don't get a second chance to make a first impression so I had to be the very best I could be," she said. "This was like a lifetime dream. By the time I did call them, he [Lee] was working for them [Indigo Records] as their audition manager. When he answered the phone and asked me where I had been I told him that I had to be really, really good and had to practice a lot. He told me to come in the next day."

Excited over the prospect of having secured an audition, Young went to her best friend's house for a sleepover. "I'm fourteen years old, know nobody in Hollywood, and I have a record audition the next day," she said. "It's like a movie. I'm beside myself. But inside I knew since I was five years old that I would do this. I never had a doubt."

Young described herself and her best friend as extremely sports minded and competitive. They ventured to the backyard and her friend's swimming pool. "She was going to dive in at one end of the pool and I was going to dive in the other end," Young said. "We were going to see who could swim underwater and get to the other end first. We were being very risqué for fourteen years old and had only a long beach towel wrapped around us, with no bathing suits underneath. As I began to dive in the shallow end, the towel started to come undone and I grabbed for it. I went straight to the bottom of the pool, knocked myself out cold, and had a concussion. She swam to the other end and got out looking for me. I was down there drowning and she had to pull me out and give me CPR. I probably should have gone to the hospital but didn't."

Heartbroken over the lost opportunity, the following day Young's mom called Lee to explain what had happened. He assured them that when she recovered he would be sure to audition her. It took another three weeks for Young to feel well enough to audition.

The next source of bad information that exists involves Young's eventual audition with Lee. While stating that Young initially sang one of her favorite songs at the time, "A Thousand Stars," in reality, she sang some tunes that she had composed. It was at that point that Lee handed her a copy of sheet music and asked her to practice it and come back the next day, which she did. That song, heard for the first time by Young, was "A Thousand Stars."

"I sat down, played my guitar and sang some songs that I had written, and Jim asked me if I could read music," Young said. "When I told him yes, he pulled out that song ['A Thousand Stars'] and I read it and he asked me to come back the next night."

During the three-week period in which Young was recovering from her accident, a disc jockey in Bakersfield, California, sent in "A Thousand Stars" with the hope that the Innocents would record it. But the record company rejected the tune, citing the fact that another male group, the Rivileers, had already recorded it. They also preferred that a female record it but didn't have one under contract. Young showed up at the studio two days later.

A recording session was planned exclusively for Young and did not come on the tail end of an Innocents session, as has been long documented. The Innocents did, however, finish a day-long session for their own album and were simply in the studio as Young took to the microphone.

"I went back and did a test, and then two nights later after an Innocents' album session, that's how Kathy and the Innocents came to be. They were finished, just hanging around because they'd been recording all day. This little fourteen-year-old girl comes in to cut a record and just as all of us do when there's music playing, they started singing and harmonizing behind me, and it just blended so well. We all knew that night that it was a hit."

When "A Thousand Stars" climbed the charts to become a number-three pop and a number-six rhythm and blues hit record, Young began a series of appearances in support of it. "My life changed tremendously," she said. "I was never on the in-crowd. I wasn't a geek but I was just kind of a sports kid. All of a sudden I was Miss Popular. Unfortunately, but fortunately in a lot of ways, I was instantly on the road. It hit in Los Angeles the week of my fifteenth birthday. I remember driving down the street the very first time I heard it on the radio and I just started crying. I can remember exactly where I was and my mom was with me."

Ironically, Young's first professional appearance after "A Thousand Stars" was released was on Wink Martindale's *Dance Party* television show, the same one on which she first saw Jim Lee. "That appearance was only two months after I was sitting in the audience of the same show," she said. "Honestly, I just felt like that is where I was supposed to be and wasn't nervous at all."

The Innocents continued to record their own songs and released "Kathy" in tribute to Young. "I knew about it before they recorded it and I thought it was great," she said. "They were older than me but we became close. We weren't related but we acted like typical brothers and a sister."

That Christmas season, Young and the Innocents flew to New York for a television appearance and to perform on the bill of a twelve-day Rock and Roll Spectacular at the Brooklyn Fox Theater. "I was everybody's little sister during that show," she said. "The Shirelles, Bobby Vee, Brenda Lee, Connie Francis, and Bo Diddley were on that show and they were all great. Bo Diddley broke his leg during a show. I always stood in the wings during the shows because I love to watch everybody perform and especially him. One day my mom made me do homework and I didn't get to stand there and he fell and broke his leg. He came back and found me and said, 'Don't you ever not be in the wings if you and I are in a show together, because you are my good luck charm.'"

Young went on to record four more singles on the Indigo label before Lee and Joel Scott founded Monogram Records. In 1964, she recorded two duets with Chris Montez. "I loved those singles," she said. "For one thing, I never saw myself as a single artist because I always loved to sing harmony. I had a great time working with Chris."

Young appeared on Dick Clark's *American Bandstand* several times. She reflected on that time period and the experience. "Back then, it was one of those things that everything just somehow happened," she said. "I think because I was so young I wasn't aware of the impact of doing the show. I was on *American Bandstand* right away and Dick Clark gave me my gold record on the show in February."

In 1964, the Innocents disbanded and Young was backed up during an engagement at the Pandora's Box by the Walker Brothers. She eventually married one of its members, John Maus, but the marriage was kept a secret for six months. "That was because in England, the kids truly believed that they could marry a singer," she said. "Being only three guys in the group and they were just hitting, the management truly felt that if the fans found out that one of them was married it would really hurt their popularity, so we kept it quiet. A reporter found out that we were married, called us, and told us that he'd give us twenty-four hours to announce it."

When the couple married, they relocated to England and suddenly called musicians like the Beatles and the Rolling Stones personal friends. "It was unreal," Young said. "Just to live that lifestyle was one of the reasons why the marriage broke up. We would have one hundred and fifty kids outside our door every single day. They would follow me through the grocery store. He and I couldn't go anyplace together. We would try to go to the movies, sneak in the back door in the alley, and two minutes after we'd go into the theater the kids would know. We would have to leave because it was disruptive to the other people there. We had to move time after time after time because they'd create havoc. But without the fans, you're nobody. Our life was just exactly like what you see about the Beatles."

In 1969, Young returned to California and in the early 1990s she sued Indigo Records to gain control of her recorded material. "I now own all the rights to my music," she said. "The company dissolved and went bankrupt and at the time I was awarded 10 percent of the company, which was worthless. But it turned out to be a blessing, since because of that I was able to now own all the rights and everything comes to me.

"I didn't go into singing to make money, so the fact that they didn't pay me didn't matter," she said. "And I was a kid so I wasn't trying to raise a family like someone that this is their livelihood."

In October 1993, Young performed at the Greek Theatre in Los Angeles, the first time in years that she took the stage. "All those years, during all that time, it was hard not to be singing," she said. "Every time I was around a band, I wanted to be up there singing but I was raising a family. A career is one thing and family is another, and I couldn't be on the road and be raising my kids. My kids still always come first."

Young reflected on what motivated her to return to the stage. "I had a choice when my second husband and I divorced," she said. "I was either going to go back to school and get a degree in child psychology or return to my passion. That wasn't a question; I'm returning to my passion. I love singing."

Young continues to perform at a number of shows throughout the country.

Billboard Top 40 Hits by Kathy Young and the Innocents

Date	Pos	Wks on Charts	Record Title	Label/ Number
10/31/60	03	15	A Thousand Stars	Indigo 108
03/06/61	30	06	Happy Birthday Blues	Indigo 115

Flip Side

Aside from the excitement and the fame gained from being in the limelight, the vast majority of recording artists that broke into the music scene during the 1950s and early 1960s failed to reap the same financial benefits as did their managers, record company executives, promoters, and industry leaders. While some explain the situation as having been the result of a general perception at the time that the new style of music, rock-and-roll, was a passing fad, a number of savvy people became extremely wealthy while many artists that became household names were left searching for employment outside the industry just to support themselves.

Given the fact that many of the vocal groups that gained fame during the 1950s consisted of youngsters who were discovered singing on neighborhood street corners and in subway stations, it's no surprise that they were unaware of business practices that took place. In fact, the goings-on in the business side of the music industry were as foreign to them as were the cities and worldwide locations in which many of them performed. In short, while the unsuspecting youth displayed creative talent, their thrill and excitement over the ability to hear their voices on the radio masked the underhanded dealings that in effect misdirected monetary compensation due to them for their efforts.

One of the most glaring injustices that existed during the period was a practice so commonplace that it is discussed today in matter-of-fact terms. It involved the misrepresentation of writer credit for some of the most popular and biggest hit songs of the era. While a young and aspiring artist might have actually penned a tune that was heard regularly on radio broadcasts, a quick glance at the record label clearly indicates another person's name as having composed it. Many times that person would be the artist's manager, a disc jockey, or the record company owner.

Simply put, if an artist wanted his or her composition heard and promoted, the accepted practice of the day was to release or at the least share the creative writing credit, along with the lucrative royalty payments that would follow.

Many people are aware of the fact that Alan Freed, a popular disc jockey that actually coined the phrase "rock-and-roll," was brought down on very public charges of payola, that is, the practice of accepting a form of compensation in return for radio airplay of a specific record. In reality, the deception that existed went well beyond Freed.

Herman Santiago, an original member of the extremely popular Harlem, New York, vocal contingent the Teenagers, one that boasted a young Frankie Lymon as its lead singer, recalled developing the lyrics and music for the group's signature song, "Why Do Fools Fall in Love." When a neighbor presented Santiago with some poems that his girlfriend wrote to him, one appealed to him more than the others did. It was titled, "Why Do Birds Sing So Gay?" While Santiago wrote the tune based on the poem he was handed, the first pressing of the single gave writing credit to (George) Goldner, (Frankie) Lymon, and (Herman) Santiago. All pressings released after the initial one limited writer credit to Goldner and Lymon. In reality neither had anything to do with its composition.

"They just took me out of it and kept everything," Santiago said. "When we recorded 'Why Do Fools Fall in Love,' Goldner asked what names we wanted on the record. I said, 'Well, you can put Herman Santiago,' and I could have said anybody but the word Frankie came out of my mouth. And that would've been the last person I would name since we had the song before he even joined the group. So they put our two names, and then those people always put their own names on your material and Goldner was added. We were there for the taking because we didn't even have anything copywrited or anything.

"In 1993 we took that case to court because I never gave up fighting for the rights to that song," he continued. "We got a lawyer at the time and we managed to win the case. But a few years later the judges got together and decided to turn it around on the appeal." The appeal decision was based on statute of limitations, the same ruling that has prevented many composers of that time to collect their earned payments.

When the Teenagers followed their debut success with another Santiago-penned song, "I Want You to Be My Girl," he was once again denied writer credit, the record label featuring the names Goldner and (Richard) Barrett. "The same thing happened and that was because we were little kids in a pond full of sharks," Santiago said.

Apparently the expansiveness of one's overall popularity and public adoration in music had no effect whatsoever on their susceptibility to being duped out of their just rewards for that success. Consider one Ellas McDaniel, a guitar player who served as one of the pioneering architects of the style of music called rock-and-roll. As Bo Diddley, he regularly performed on the top shows of the day to standing ovations and rousing applause, generating significant record sales and concerts receipts in the process. He is also cited as having been the motivating influence on countless artists that followed him, including the Beatles, the Rolling Stones, and Aerosmith. But in 2005 and at seventy-four years old, while still passionate about his music and ever enjoying the enthusiasm of audiences worldwide, due to lost royalties during the heyday of his career he is forced to maintain a continual schedule of performances to survive.

"The reason these guys have gotten away with not paying royalties owed to me is that in America we have this thing called statute of limitations," Diddley said. "If you don't catch them in a certain period of time, you might as well leave them alone because you're not going to get anything. Going to get a lawyer is just a waste of your time and money. They tell you that it's been fifty years but I don't care who it is, if you owe the government for fifty years, they are going to get their money. Why is it any different for me?

"These people cannot show any check that I cashed, so they can't say they paid me," he said. "I got stuff all over the world; where's my money? A lot of us got taken advantage of because we were entertainers and we were interested in performing for the people and the record company took care of the business."

Unlike Santiago, Diddley did not have a manager or company executive claim writer's credit on the record labels of his songs. But he did encounter significant deceit.

"They used to put Ellas McDaniel on the records, and then they quit and started putting E. McDaniel. Then I found some stuff that was listed Eddie McDaniel. E. McDaniel could be Eddie McDaniel or [it] could be Edward McDaniel. This is how they got away with a lot of stuff. A lot of stuff went around behind and passed right by me. I could squawk, but I had no papers to squawk with because I didn't handle the bill of ladings on how many records were pressed. I understand that the Chess brothers had a pressing plant in one of the buildings in downtown Chicago that none of us artists knew anything about. So they were pressing up stuff that we had no idea about.

"I resent the idea that they actually did this," Diddley said. "Everything I have ever owned, I owned from working on the road. But what happened to my royalties? I should be a multimillionaire today but I have to continue to work. It's a good old American rip-off. We got people like Red Dog Records, which was in New Orleans, [that] released a lot of material in Germany with little books to go with the records. I've got some of them [at] home and I've never seen any money from it.

"MCA tried to sue them and I can never figure what ever happened with that," he said. "They were going to try to distribute the money to the people but I don't think they got anything from it. I think the Red Dog owner transferred money into his wife's account and stuff like that. The government should be able to question how his wife came into that money. It's something that really needs to be tackled."

Diddley opined that years after the original deception took place, the children of the now-deceased savvy and less-than-honest businessmen that took advantage of unsuspecting artists don't have a clue as to how their family fortune was amassed.

"A lot of those guys are dead now and their kids are getting the money [royalties] and they don't know what their parents did," he said. "A lot of their parents were plain old thugs."

If having your creative work torn away from you for all time weren't enough of a tragedy, consider another issue that continues to plague a number of vocal groups to this day, that being the practice of having four of five singers with no ties whatsoever to one of the classic acts of the 1950s and 1960s, representing themselves and actually earning a living by performing as them at venues around the world. Groups such as the Drifters, the Coasters, the Platters, the Marvelettes, and even the Supremes have suffered significantly through the years as bogus contingents of singers contracted with concert promoters to appear on the bills of various oldie shows as the original artists.

The scenario, in some cases, can be mind-boggling. Joe Q. Public shells out hard-earned cash to purchase tickets to a concert, one that features a number of famous and legendary groups. As the first extremely popular group with numerous hit recordings to their credit is introduced and takes the stage, something should seem wrong. As the lead singer approaches the microphone to sing the first tune, he eloquently announces, "Back in 1958 we had the extreme pleasure to record this song, one that, thanks to you, climbed to number one on the charts."

The problem is that the lead singer, along with his entourage of background vocalists, are all in their early thirties and weren't even a glimmer in their mother's eye when the original group recorded the song.

That is not to say that all bogus groups are that obvious. But regardless, they not only deceive an unsuspecting public but also significantly diminish the original artists' ability to secure work and to command the fees that, through their hard work and legendary careers, they are entitled to. The reason for the latter issue is pretty clear.

If an unknowing or uncaring promoter has the option to offer a group like the Platters or the Drifters, whose name recognition would result in high interest and greater ticket sales for a specific show, and has the opportunity to contract a variation of the group at a greatly reduced price, many times it will occur, whether the group is authentic or not. In some cases, the promoter is unaware of the discrepancy.

In recent years, original artists that include Joe Terry of Danny and the Juniors, Carl Gardner of the Coasters, Mary Wilson of the Supremes, Tony Butala of the Letterman, and Jon Bauman, "Bowzer" from Sha Na Na, have combined their resources to promote a campaign as well as legislation designed to prohibit vocalists from billing themselves and performing as a famous group, in absence of at least one original member. Bauman, who produces "Rock and Roll Party" concerts, shows that feature several legendary and original artists, has been a strong proponent of the issue, both at his shows and at official hearings. Named the Truth in Music Bill, it has been passed in many states, and their initiative continues to ensure that it will be enacted in all fifty.

It is important to note that trademarks play a big role in the existing problem. In the 1950s it was rare that any group or its members secured a trademark on the group name. In subsequent years, unscrupulous people have seized the opportunity to gain a trademark on a specific group's name. Then, having secured the trademark, they feel free to perform as that group. Various legal battles have ensued when an original group member and the assuming artist tangle over the rights to use the name. And while it might seem absurd that someone having no association or genuine tie to the original outfit should even question the original artist's claim, it has occurred time and time again.

Even in cases where the original artist holds a trademark on the group name, initiating legal action against bogus contingents that might perform in other states and/or abroad is cost prohibitive, prompting most to wallow in their frustration and disgust.

"Trademark is a very narrow law that is very easy to learn about," said Joe Terry, original member of Danny and the Juniors. "Since we have a trademark and [have been] as protected as can be since 1957, it was easy for Frank [Maffei] and I to learn what it was all about. As these groups that are franchised, like the thirty-five-year-old singers that go out and perform as the Drifters and the Coasters, became more prevalent, we decided to go to Washington and try to straighten out this problem.

"At any one point you can now find twenty sets of Platters working in this country on a Saturday night," he continued. "That takes away from the rest of the original acts. When there are twenty sets of Platters available and that group has the most hit records of all groups by far, they will be the first choice of a buyer [promoter]. Once those twenty Platters groups are booked, the other acts start getting booked and so on. They are stealing the work that we started in the beginning."

In Pennsylvania, legislation that recently passed in support of the original recording artists is a consumer fraud law. "When a trademark law is violated and results in confusion, then it becomes consumer fraud," Terry said. "When the public is confused and they go to a show and the show doesn't give them at least the continuing entity of the featured group performing, that is fraud and the public should be able to complain and go to the attorney general of the state. There should be fines levied, if not imprisonment. It is no different than taking a Botany 500 label and putting it into a Wal-Mart suit, and that is the analogy that everyone should think of with it. When people see it happening they should question it."

Terry said that there are cases where a group of individuals have legally purchased a trademark name of an original act that no longer performs. "The Diamonds name was purchased by four guys on the West Coast from a manager in Canada," he said. "There's nothing wrong with that because you are selling a business and there is only that one entity that is out there. They now are the Diamonds, similar to the Vogues and a few other cases."

"The problem exists when someone claims to be licensed by an original member's cousin, and that's what we've got to stop because that is not a continuing entity," he said. "A continuing entity is like Frank and me, being here all these years."

Barbara Hawkins, the lead singer of the Dixie Cups, said that her group experienced other vocalists' attempts at portraying themselves as the original singers.

"Some time ago in New York, a friend of ours called and said that he heard we were going to be performing at a local club on such and such a date," Hawkins said. "I said, 'How is that even possible when I don't even have a contract for that appearance?' He told me that the show was being advertised and he gave me the name of the club, the owner's name and telephone number, and I called him up. I told the owner that I couldn't find my contract and asked what date it was. He told me the date and how many shows we were doing and asked if I wanted him to mail me the contract. I told him that I was in the process of moving, called my lawyer, and explained what was going on. He called the club owner and asked the names of the Dixie Cups that were going to be performing. The guy gave him three names and my lawyer explained to him who he was and why he was calling. He told him if the names did not include Barbara Hawkins and Rosa Hawkins, you don't have the Dixie Cups."

Hawkins's lawyer warned the club owner that whoever he had contracted to appear had better not perform as the Dixie Cups. "I had some friends up there and they went to the show that night and the guy said that he was sorry that the Dixie Cups couldn't make it, but the other group did not perform," Hawkins said.

"It's really wrong with these bogus groups performing because the public thinks that they are getting the real deal and they are not," she said.

One would think that one of the most successful female vocal groups in the history of music would be immune to being victimized by phony lineups performing under their name, but sadly that is not the case. Mary Wilson, founding member of the Motown super group the Supremes, has been a longtime advocate of the Truth in Music legislation. She cited several groups that have appeared as perhaps the most recognizable of all girl groups of the 1960s.

"There are five or six Supremes and nine or ten Marvelettes groups performing all over the world and taking over our legacy," Wilson said. "We want everyone to go to their congressional representative and senator and try to get the Truth in Music Bill passed where we, the original artists, have rights. We need to have laws that will stop people from taking over our famous names, and that is just what they are doing.

"People say, 'Oh, we just want to hear the music,' and they go to a show with fake groups in it," she said. "Don't go to a show with fake groups. If you know there is not one original member in a group that you see perform out there, don't go in. If you really want to hear the music and you really love the music, then do right by the people who made that music."

Printed in the United States
205608BV00001B/280-327/A